DAWN OF DESTINY

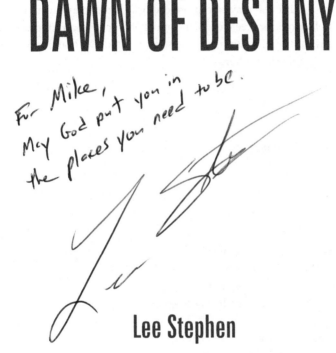

For Mike,
May God put you in the places you need to be.

Lee Stephen

stone aside
publishing

Stone Aside Publishing, L.L.C.

ISBN: 978-0-9979390-2-6

Original Edit by Arlene Prunkl
New Edition Edit Assisted by Grammarly
Original Book Design by Fiona Raven
New Edition Book Design by Lee Stephen

Original Publication November 14, 2006
New Edition Publication November 14, 2023
Printed in USA
V1

Published by
Stone Aside Publishing, L.L.C.

Dedicated to

GOD

Always, forever.

0

IT WAS A TRAIN WRECK. A total train wreck. Those were the thoughts of Captain Brent Lilan, commanding officer of Falcon Squad. His unit was dispatched to Cleveland, where the alien species known as the *Bakma* had descended and attacked. The Earth Defense Network—EDEN—had sent the veteran unit into the city to defend it. It was a situation similar to many Falcon Squad had been in, except in this case, everything that could have gone wrong had. Communications equipment had failed. Streets that were supposed to exist didn't. Even the concrete beneath Lilan's boots was against him, as a freezing rain had transformed the ground into a veritable ice rink. But worst of all, Intelligence had been wrong about everything—the number of Bakma craft, the number of Bakma on the ground. Everything. The result was a Falcon Squad bloodbath.

Lilan epitomized an EDEN veteran—a crew cut of steel gray hair, a body tattooed with scars, and a penetrating glare that reflected a pessimistic wisdom about the reality of the Alien War. Though unrecognized on the streets of the common man, the command staff at *Richmond* base knew him well. He was their closer. He was the one they didn't have to worry about. He was the one that always got the job done.

Except for today.

A white, streaking plasma bolt whizzed past Lilan's head, narrowly missing him as he slipped on the slick city street. After scampering around the corner of an alleyway, he flung himself against one of its brick walls to regain his balance. He muttered a string of obscenities. It was time to pull out. It was time to salvage whatever was left of Falcon Squad and return to base. The fate of Cleveland would rest in the hands of whoever else *Richmond* could muster up on a whim.

Lilan loathed the Bakma—more than any other species. They fought dirty. They fought like cowards. With their purple, leathery skin, dark bulging eyes, and mouthful of sharp, serrated teeth, he loathed the sight of them almost as much as he loathed their stench.

Reloading his E-35 assault rifle, Lilan barked into his comm. "Tacker, sniper at the bank! Corner of Ontario and Rockwell. Flush him from behind if you can, but don't force it!"

Confirmation came, and Lilan regripped his weapon. Easing his head around the corner of the alleyway, he wiped his helmet visor and caught sight of two soldiers hunkering down behind a car across the street. Alan Henrick and Ben Yalen. Tacker aside, they were the only other soldiers he had left. It was time to make their retreat official. Adjusting his comm, he was greeted by pops of ear-splitting static. Wincing, he slapped the side of his helmet as if the effort would help. It didn't. "Vecking piece of…" Cutting off the comm, he cupped his hands around his mouth and just yelled, *"Hey!"* When the soldiers looked his way, he signaled to fall back. Acknowledging, they abandoned the car to scamper to new cover.

Lilan ducked back, and his focus returned to his comm. He had to overcome the gremlins in the communication systems and reestablish contact with Tacker. The thought of losing his best soldier in a tactical debacle like this was too much. After several seconds of professional "fiddling," the static in the line disappeared just in time.

"Sniper down!" Tacker said over the channel.

Lilan sighed in relief. "Listen, I just gave Henrick and Yalen the order to fall back. We're getting out of this hellhole."

"This is an abject catastrophe, captain," said Tacker.

"Tell me about it. Make your way to the LZ. I'll meet you there." After Tacker affirmed, Lilan looked skyward. *"Seven,* where are you?"

Choppy static returned to the channel—just for a moment, thankfully. *"Seven* in orbit, captain."

"We're falling back to the LZ. Meet us there."

"On my way, sir."

The Vulture transport broke its low orbit over the city and pointed its nose north. Lilan's focus returned to the street. "Tacker, do you have a clear path to the LZ, or do you need *Seven* to pick you up?"

Tacker's voice crackled again. "Sir, I—" and that was it. There was a *pop,* and silence flooded the line. Tacker's voice was gone.

Lilan froze. "Tacker? Tacker! *Seven,* what was the—" He paused as a plasma bolt tore through Yalen's back. A spray of red emerged from the soldier's chest; he collapsed to the ground. Lilan continued. "*Seven*, what was the last known position of Lieutenant Tacker?"

"Last comm was approximately four hundred yards southwest of your location, sir."

"Can you swing by that location on your way to the LZ?" Lilan waited for an answer from the pilot, but none came. "*Seven*?" The choppy, static pops of communication failure reemerged. The captain snarled. "Vecking junk."

Four hundred yards southwest. With the twists and turns of an unfamiliar city, that was much too far to travel on foot. Judging by what Lilan had heard on the comm, either Tacker was fighting for his life or already dead. That *pop* that'd cut them off hadn't been static interference. Scanning for a faster mode of transportation than his feet, Lilan found one in a sedan parked just off the side of the alley. He returned his gaze to the rainy street, where three Bakma warriors crept toward Yalen's body.

Lilan stalked silently toward the sedan, his body crouched as he tried to keep the vehicle between his line of sight and the Bakmas'. For several seconds, however, he had an unobstructed view of the aliens. He was able to watch them as they knelt to look at Yalen's body. One of the Bakma reached down to nudge the corpse. When Yalen didn't move, the alien angled his head and leaned closer. It was not often that Bakma could get that close to a human body without trepidation. Lilan would make sure it was their last opportunity. Leaning over the sedan's hood, Lilan aimed his E-35 at the three clustered aliens. "Take *this* to your leader," he whispered. His finger slowly squeezed the trigger.

"*Tcha-kassal'ar!*"

From farther down the street, a fourth Bakma emerged to shout at his brethren. Lilan's finger released the trigger without firing, and he pressed his body down against the hood. The three Bakma turned to meet the new arrival as Bakmanese—the name humans had given the Bakma language—was spewed back and forth. The Bakma by Yalen trotted toward their comrade, who himself then turned to move out of view. Lilan lifted his head to watch them disappear. Some quick pick-offs he'd had time for. But a firefight against an unknown number of adversaries? No. He needed to get to Tacker.

Hurrying toward Yalen once the coast was clear, he hoisted the fallen soldier over his shoulder and returned to the sedan. Lowering Yalen to the ground, Lilan shattered the driver's side window with the butt of his assault rifle. After a quick hotwire of the engine, Lilan stowed Yalen's body in the back seat. That Henrick had left Yalen behind wasn't cowardice—it was standard procedure if hostiles were present. Rescues were priorities. Recoveries could wait. Pressing the accelerator, Lilan turned the sedan around in the middle of the street and began the drive to Tacker's last known position.

Though an occasional plasma bolt flashed across the hood, Lilan reached Tacker's position with minimal resistance. As soon as he spotted Tacker, he understood why their connection had been interrupted. The sniper's helmet was attached to his belt, its visor shattered, and its blue and silver finish charred black. Blood dripped from the sniper's forehead and ear.

"What happened?" Lilan asked as Tacker leapt inside.

After briefly looking at Yalen's body, Tacker buckled up and answered, "They had *two* snipers." He wiped his hand down his bloodied, wet face. "They just weren't very good."

Vulture-7 was waiting for the two men at the landing zone. Only Henrick waited with it, the buckled-over, heaving soldier a symbol of the mission's colossal failure. As Tacker abandoned the car and climbed aboard the blunt-nosed transport, Lilan offered the battle-torn streets of Cleveland one more gaze. One more long, purposeful look to take it all in. After nine years with EDEN, missions had a way of blending together. Of one being indistinguishable from the next. But this one…this one would leave a mark. A devastated city and a decimated unit—the lovechildren of bad luck and underestimation. A train wreck, to be sure.

One the captain now owned.

PART I

1

THE DOOR TO Room 419 slid open. Scott Remington stood in the doorway, staring inside. So this was it. This was home. This was where *they* had decided home was, anyway. His hazel eyes swept the room as he took it in. It was smaller than his room at the Academy. It was more cramped. There were metal bunks pushed up against the right wall. These were smaller, too.

He sighed and rubbed the back of his neck. This was all wrong. When he'd enlisted for EDEN, his recruiters asked him if he'd had a geographic preference. He'd told them *Detroit Station*. He had gone to school at Michigan. That's where *she* was. When they'd handed him his post-graduation duty assignment and he saw it was *Richmond*, he couldn't believe it. He scratched his head, fingertips disappearing under his short brown hair.

Scott was five feet and eleven inches tall, with a body as toned as one would expect from a soldier fresh out of *Philadelphia* Academy. He was a handsome young man, or at least she thought so. Her opinion was the only one that mattered. After a final breath of preparation, he stepped inside the room. It was done. He was officially there.

He slipped the duffle bag from his shoulder and plopped it on the floor. Turning around, he stepped back to the door and eased it shut with a quiet click. He scrutinized the room again.

A sink was built into the wall in the far corner, complemented by a small, cracked mirror. Moving to the faucet, Scott turned its rusty knob. Ice-cold water poured out. He slid his hands beneath the stream, massaged his face, rubbed his sleeve against his eyes, and then turned the water off. What a dump this room was. Besides the large monitor built into the wall—a standard for just about every room in every base—everything looked old and decrepit. Somehow, he felt he shouldn't have been surprised.

Returning to his duffle bag, Scott crouched and tugged the metal zipper open. Inside was a collection of folded clothes, on top of which sat a black leather-backed Scripture, the name "Scott James Remington" inscribed in gold at the bottom right-hand corner. He passed his hand along the book's glossy surface. *God, what am I doing here?* He took hold of the book and rose to his feet, placing it atop the nightstand next to the bottom bunk.

The next item from the bag was a worn-out football, stained with grass and dirt from recent use. He could still smell the leather despite the ball's wear and tear. After gripping it for a moment, he rolled it beneath the bunk.

His gaze returned to the bag, where it lingered. *Her.* As much of her as there could be, anyway. It was the picture of a brown-eyed, beautiful brunette. Her smile caused two dimples to appear just beyond her lips; her snow-white teeth sparkled from within the gold boundaries of the frame. Everything about her, from the lustrous layers of her textured bob to the kiss of Chinese ancestry in her eyes, enthralled him. In the lower right corner, the words *I love you!* were scripted in black marker. Beneath it was her name—Nicole. His focus returned to her face, and he breathed in softly. He hated *Richmond* even more. Rising, he set the picture atop his nightstand, her face angled to the bed.

Scott spent the next half hour unpacking. There was no hurry in the task, only the sluggish lethargy that came after the stress of a move. As soon as he had finished, he turned off the lights and dropped down on the bottom bunk, sliding his hands behind his head. For the first time that day, his eyes fell shut.

Within minutes, he was asleep.

The door swung open. A shaft of light cut in from the hall. Scott winced, his eyes squinting as he stared at the doorway, where he saw the silhouette of a broad-shouldered man with a duffle bag similar to Scott's slung over his shoulder. Before Scott could gather his senses, the light was flicked on, and the stranger stepped inside. He blinked as he saw Scott in bed. "Hey, sorry about that. I didn't expect anyone else to be here yet."

Scott propped himself up on his elbows. He mumbled incoherently as the stranger tossed his duffle bag onto the floor and extended a hand. "Hey. Name's David Jurgen."

David's features came into detail as Scott groggily accepted the handshake. He wore a buzz fade of black hair, complemented by green eyes, bronze skin, and a five o'clock shadow. Faint streaks of gray filtered past his sideburns. He offered Scott a genuine smile. "Guessing we're roommates, then. Our convoy just got in from *Philadelphia*—guess yours came in earlier. Sorry about waking you up, man." His thick Brooklyn accent glinted with Hispanic flair.

Peering at the clock on his nightstand, Scott said, "No, it's all right... what time is it?"

"Four past midnight."

"Oh, wow."

David knelt next to his duffle bag and unzipped it. He smiled. "Yeah, the night's young." He reached into the bag, where he produced several pictures. He began to set them atop a shelf on the wall. "I'm guessing if you wanted this shelf, you'd have claimed it by now. Mind?"

"No, not at all." Only one picture of Scott's mattered, and it was already in place.

"What's your name, compadre?"

Scott blinked. "Hmm? Oh, I'm sorry. I'm still a little, you know..."

"Out of it? Yeah, you look it."

"Scott Remington."

"Scott Remington, huh? Well, nice to meet you."

Scott's gaze fell on the pictures. There were several family pictures, but the ones that stood out showed David in police uniform. Other uniformed men stood around him. "You did police work?"

"Nineteen years, NYPD."

"Oh wow...*nineteen*...?"

David laughed as he adjusted the photos. "I already know the next question you're gonna ask. Come on, out with it."

"I'm sorry, my next question?"

"How old am I?" He cast a sidelong look at Scott and smirked. "You were thinkin' it."

It was true—he was. And his sheepish chuckle gave it away. "Nah, man."

"Forty-one. That's four, with a one after it."

"Yeah," Scott laughed, "I know what forty-one is."

"*Cuarenta y uno. Quarantuno* in Italian. Old as dirt, my friend! One foot in the grave."

Gesturing to the hall, Scott said, "They might have some walkers in the lobby if you want me to go check for you."

David's smile widened, and he released a single but emphatic, "Ha!" Satisfied with his work on the shelf, he stepped back and looked at Scott. "So what about you, pal? What's your story? Where you come from?"

Scott leaned against the lower bunk wall. "Lincoln, but I went to school at Michigan. I went to *Philadelphia* straight from there. Well, I didn't finish Michigan. Left in my last year."

"Lincoln...?"

"Nebraska."

"Why'd you leave school for *this*?"

Scott hated that question. The answer always sounded contrived. He hesitated for a moment before responding. "I don't know, I mean...Earth is under attack, right? Everybody's got to do their part." It was an obvious and acceptable answer—it also wasn't the real one. Not for him, anyway. "And I guess I like, kind of felt led here."

"*Led* here?"

David was going to make him explain it. "I dunno. You ever feel like God's trying to tell you to do something?"

"Ahhh." Illumination came to David's face. He nodded his head. "You're one of *them* guys."

Not sure whether he should laugh or sigh, Scott settled on both. "Yeah, I guess I am."

David slapped Scott on his propped knee. "Hey, that's all good. No atheists in the foxhole, right?" Scott smiled faintly as David said, "Well look, I'm gonna take a walk around for a bit, get the lay of the land. Wanna come?"

Thankful the conversation deviated from religion, Scott nodded with eagerness. "Yeah, absolutely." He was awake now, anyway. "Where to, first?"

"The hall."

"Okay," Scott said with mirthful resignation. "So *you're* one of *them* guys."

At the throwback of his own words in his face, David laughed. "I think I'm gonna like you. I think I will."

The light to Room 419 was flicked off, and the two men stepped into the hallway.

Richmond was the smallest of the major EDEN bases on Earth. It was the only one classified as a Class-1. There were five classes, each representing the number of enlisted soldiers. Eleven bases were considered major: EDEN Command, *Atlanta*, *Nagoya*, *Novosibirsk*, *Philadelphia*, *Richmond*, *Berlin*, *Dublin*, *London*, *Leningrad*, and *Cairo*. There were hundreds of smaller EDEN sites—such as *Detroit Station*—across the planet, but they were more comparable to police or fire stations than sprawling military compounds.

The juxtaposition of massive EDEN bases to smaller city stations was as telling an indicator as existed of EDEN's multifaceted, occasionally clunky structural composition. The world at large considered EDEN a global military. In the tactile sense, it operated more like an international response agency. It was like nothing before it, for until now, no need for such a monstrosity had existed. Even its ranking structure was a conglomerate of traditional and "future forward" terminology. Privates were classified as alphas, betas, or gammas based on experience and ability. Delta troopers—also called the delta corps—were soldiers who had proven their mettle enough to be considered experts in their respective fields. For most soldiers, the journey ended there. Some deltas went on to become epsilons, EDEN's designation for officers-in-training. If an epsilon proved their worth, they were placed in a squad's officer core. The officer core was the first place where traditional military ranks made an appearance in EDEN, with two lieutenants always sharing tertiary duties. The rank of executor came next, designating a unit's XO, with captains sitting at the top of a squad's proverbial food chain.

The ranks continued upward, with various degrees of majors, colonels, and generals making up the multiheaded monster that was EDEN's infantry and air force. But for most soldiers, life existed on the squad level, and there was little need to consider anything above that. For a military that operated like a response agency and was managed like a corporation, the "not my lane" mentality of the enlisted was understandable when it came to EDEN's affairs at large. Few could even name any of the twelve "judges" that made up the Council portion of EDEN's High Command, located at an undisclosed place somewhere on Earth and lorded over by a singular president. Since EDEN's inception at the start of the Alien War, its president had been a man named Carl Pauling—likely the only person in the High Command that every soldier could identify in a lineup. But those were global affairs. One could scarcely be concerned with such things when plasma bolts were flying overhead.

As Scott and David ventured through *Richmond*'s corridors, they found sparse activity despite the late-night arrival of recruits from *Philadelphia*. There were occasional clusters of soldiers in places such as the training center, but for the most part, the base felt dormant. This was to be expected with the traditional early hours of EDEN training regimens. The base layout was simple and effective, and in virtually no time, they managed to venture through just about every allowable area.

All the while the two men walked, they also talked. David unfolded his story to Scott—about how he was married to his wife of seventeen years, Sharon, and how they had two boys, both in grade school in New York City. David's stint with the NYPD was proud, and he left with honorable notice to enroll with EDEN. Sharon and their kids still lived in the city, though they were mulling a transplant to Richmond to be closer to him.

In turn, Scott told him about Nicole.

The clocks peaked at 0100 when they finally returned to their wing of the living quarters. The hallways were vacant, and a stark silence reverberated from the walls. The only sign of life anywhere was from far down the hall, in the form of a silhouetted man leaning against a doorframe—the room it led into was the only source of light in the whole place. As they drew nearer, they realized that the room in question was beside theirs—Room 421. The silhouetted man tilted his head in their direction.

He was slender, his height compensating for a lack of bulk. His arms were folded across his chest as he leaned against the doorframe and watched them beneath a tuft of dusty brown hair.

"Time to meet the neighbors," said David quietly to Scott. Seconds later, he raised his hand to wave. "Hey there."

The stranger flinched as he was addressed, then shifted bodily to face them. Everything about the motion was uncomfortable, from the tensing of his shoulders to the awkward way he averted eye contact by gazing off to the side at the floor. He mumbled a response. "Howdy."

He had to be from Texas.

The insignia on his uniform identified him as an alpha private. David extended his hand. "David Jurgen. I live next door."

Scott offered his hand immediately after. "Scott Remington, good to meet you. We're in 419."

The stranger shook Scott's hand tentatively. His discomfort was impossible to ignore. He looked young, barely in his twenties, if at all. Averting his eyes, he again shied toward the doorway. "I'm Jayden. Timmons."

"Jayden Timmons?" David asked.

"Yessir."

David smiled warmly. "Hey man, we're new on the scene, too. Away with the 'sir.'"

A new voice emerged from 421—one in the thickest Irish accent Scott had ever heard. "Hey! Who's tha' yeh blatherin' with?"

"Our neighbors," Jayden answered.

Scott walked past Jayden to look into the room. A young man with an impish grin sat at the edge of the lower bunk. His viridian gaze surveyed Scott beneath a scattered mess of brown hair. As he kicked to his feet, one word came to Scott's mind. *Energy.*

"Hi. Scott Remington. I live next door."

The newcomer slapped out a handshake. "Howyeh! Becan McCrae, likewise it's a pleasure! Yeh go by Remmy?"

Scott laughed a bit. "Yeah, Remmy works." Remmy actually worked well. A lot of his friends at Michigan called him that. It felt good to hear again.

"Class! Who yeh got with you?"

David leaned inside and offered his hand. "David Jurgen. Good to meet you."

Becan swatted David's palm. "Yis muckers, eh?"

"Uhh, we're roommates," Scott said uncertainly. He could only assume that a mucker was a roommate. Or a friend. Or something along those lines. Even though *Philadelphia* was a melting pot for nationalities—the only EDEN Academy on the planet—Scott had never met anyone from Ireland there.

"Righ', righ', roommates. Tha's wha' I meant."

David grinned. "Where are you from?"

"Broadford, Ireland. Yeh really have to ask, do yeh?"

"Are you guys just in from *Philadelphia*, too?" Scott asked.

"We are. Guessin' we're all alphas then, righ'?"

Scott nodded as Jayden slipped back into the room. As soon as Becan saw him, he said, "Tha's me boyo Jay, he's a bit o' a quiet one. He's one o' them cowboys."

Jayden made for his bunk bed and snagged a brown cowboy hat from the bed stand. He placed it firmly on his head.

"Jay's a sniper, he is," Becan said.

"You're a sniper?" Scott asked with an inspired stare. That was impressive. He knew a few snipers in *Philadelphia*, and their training was to be envied.

"Yeah…"

"Congratulations, man."

"Thanks…"

Becan's gaze shifted to David, where it lingered for several moments. "How old are yeh?"

"Why?" David's eyes narrowed.

"Yeh look…older."

"I'm forty-one."

"*Tha's* why yeh look older…"

"How old are you, wise guy?"

"A lot less old than *you* are!"

A question was lingering in Scott's head, and he had to ask. "Why didn't you get stationed at *Dublin*?"

"*Tha's* a grand question. I've no bloody clue."

Scott laughed and shook his head. *Richmond* didn't seem so far from home anymore. "And I thought being stationed outside of Michigan was bad. How does your family feel about this? They've got to be missing you like crazy."

"I've got no family," Becan said. "Me ma an' me da died years ago. I've got no brothers or sisters."

Scott was oddly relieved by Becan's answer. Scott had lost his parents, too, back when he was in high school. They died in a car accident. Finding someone else who knew what it was like to lose parents at a young age was always comforting. He felt an unspoken connection with them.

"Wha' abou' you now?" Becan asked. "Leave annyone back in the great state o' Michigan?"

"A fiancée and a brother," Scott answered. Mark. He hadn't seen Mark in months. Scott was like a brother *and* a father to him. Mark was still in his teens but almost finished with high school. He planned to follow Scott's footsteps into EDEN, no matter how hard Scott tried to talk him out of it. "Mark lives in Nebraska, though."

"So wha' abou' this girl?"

"Her name is Nicole. We've been together for six years, she came to Michigan with me. We dated in high school, went to college together."

"So yeh been with this girl for six years an' you're not married yet?"

"We're engaged. Haven't been able to set a date, though. I thought we'd be able to after the Academy, but I didn't think they'd send me here. Believe me, nobody wants it to happen sooner than I do."

Becan nodded. "A lot o' people I knew in *Philadelphia* got married. Never understood tha', I didn't. Gettin' married in the middle o' the Academy. Tha' place is hectic enough as it is."

"Yeah," Jayden said. "It's pretty crazy. I don't know how people had time to get hitched, training kept me busy around the clock."

It was an odd mix, *Philadelphia*. On one hand, it was combat training. On the other, it was no different from college. Amid workouts, drills, and weapons training, there were classroom courses with names that sounded like they came straight out of a university booklet. Geography 101, Urban Tactics, Environmental Combat 300. You didn't only graduate from the Academy with a sense of accomplishment, you felt like you earned a fast-tracked college degree.

Arms folded as he listened, David smiled. "I understand why people get married there. It's the whole, 'I might be about to go out and die,' thing. A last-ditch attempt to find true love before hitting the trenches."

"Do you guys feel like *Philadelphia* prepared you for this?" Scott asked the group at large.

"I think it did," Becan answered. "I know a lot o' people find it weird with the classes an' everything, but everybody seems to come ou' all righ'."

At that, David chuckled. "I hate to break it to you boys, but you'll get more training in the first ten minutes of actual combat than you did in all of *Philadelphia*. When that first bullet flies—plasma bolt, whatever—man...it's education time. It's the same way with police work. It's all fun and games till you gotta make that first arrest. That's when you really learn something." Stifling a yawn, he said, "I know what they're trying to do, though. They're trying to create smarter soldiers, and they think the best way to do that is through coursework combined with combat training. It's a different approach, but I think it works. We'll certainly see, right?"

"I bloody *loved* Xenobiology," said Becan.

Scott concurred. Xenobiology alone made the Academy worth it. There were few things more fascinating than the in-depth study of extraterrestrials. "I totally agree," he said. "What was your favorite species to learn about?"

There were three alien species in all that had made contact with Earth: the Bakma, Ceratopians, and Ithini. Utilized by them were two animal units: canrassis and necrilids. It was startling how little EDEN knew about each one outside general biology. Their cultures, relationships, and most notably, their motives for attacking Earth remained a mystery.

"*Favorite* species?" Becan asked. "I'd like to say necrilids, but really tha' class jus' scared the hell out o' me. I liked learnin' abou' the Ceratopians, though."

Ceratopians. The brutes of the Alien War, like a page out of the prehistoric. Five-horned, bone-frilled warriors. Lumbering terrors whose heads bore a striking resemblance to a pentaceratops, minus the beak. "Ceratopian class was good," Scott said. "You're right about the necrilids, though, they're pretty freaky. I think that's why people aren't as high on that class as you'd think, because as cool as they are, in the back of your mind you're thinking, '*Veck*, I might have to *fight* that thing one day.'"

"Yeah, exactly. Those things are scary as all hell."

There was so much about the Alien War that didn't make sense. Three distinct species appeared at almost the same time: the grotesque Bakma, the reptilian Ceratopians, and the quintessentially gray Ithinis—a long-suspected-to-exist species that the Alien War actually confirmed, as alien encounters and abductions by beings that looked like them had been reported for ages. The Ithini were the only connection that the Bakma and Ceratopians shared, as both species worked with the Ithini but were never seen with each other. It wasn't clear whether the Ithini were supervisors, servants, or something else.

Then, there were canrassis and necrilids. Canrassis—bearlike, spider-eyed war beasts with vestigial arms—were used by both the Bakma and the Ceratopians as mounted rides or animal labor. Necrilids were only ever seen with Ceratopians. That was just as well, as necrilids were generally regarded as the worst creatures imaginable. Dark-skinned, sharp-clawed, long-fanged predators. Eaters of the dead.

Why were the Ithini and canrassi the only shared link between the Bakma and Ceratopians? Why weren't the Bakma and Ceratopians connected with one another, and why did only the Ceratopians utilize necrilids? They were all pertinent questions. But one question lingered above them. Why were they all after Earth? They appeared and attacked simultaneously, within months of each other, without offering a clue as to their motives. It was a simple question without a single answer.

David pushed up from his chair. The other men looked at him. "What's up?" Scott asked.

"Nothing," answered David. "I think I'm just about to turn in." He stifled a second yawn. "I'm feeling that move from *Philadelphia* now."

Becan smirked. "So early? It's only two in the mornin'." David gave him a withering look, but the Irishman just laughed. "Fair enough, then. It was grand meetin' yeh."

A moment later, Scott stood up from his prop against the wall. "Yeah, I think that's probably a good idea for all of us. Daylight's gonna come quick."

"Yeah. Righ', well I'm sure we'll see yis both tomorrow, then." Becan plopped back down on his bunk and flung up a wave. "Night, Remmy. Night, Dave."

"Good night, guys," Jayden said.

Scott and David bid farewell, stepped into the hall, and closed the door to Room 421.

"Nice guys," Scott said. They seemed a rather odd couple, but he'd found them both friendly—in their own ways.

"Yeah," David agreed. "Interesting little job of pairing EDEN did there."

"Yeah, really." Scott opened Room 419's door and stepped in.

For the next several minutes, the two men prepared for the night. They took turns brushing their teeth at the sink, then slipped out of their uniforms and into nightwear. David climbed to the upper bunk as Scott flicked the light off from below. "You know, we're liable to all be in the same unit," David said. "It would make sense, with our rooms side by side and all."

"I hope so," Scott said as he climbed into the bottom bunk. "That'd be fun." He closed his eyes.

Silence hung in the room for several seconds before David spoke. "Right, because you know, EDEN stands for Earth's Daily Entertainment Network."

Scott made a face in the dark. "Ha ha. Whatever, good night." David chuckled, and Scott shook his head. "Earth's Daily Entertainment Network. I don't even know what that means."

"Aw, come on."

"That might be the worst non-joke I've ever heard."

"I was grasping at straws."

"Clearly."

After a final chuckle, David said, "All right, all right. Good night."

"Good night, man."

Scott pulled the covers to his chin and turned over on his side. The initial uneasiness he'd felt upon his arrival at *Richmond* had simmered down. It helped to have other people to share such feelings with now. He looked forward to seeing Becan and Jayden again. He looked forward to learning more about them and learning more about David. Considering the uncertainty of purpose he'd felt when he'd first set foot in his room, it was great to look forward to anything. His mouth stretched open in a yawn, and he shut his eyes again.

For a second time, sleep found him quickly.

2

THE DOOR TO General James Hutchin's room slid open as Lilan stepped inside and paused at attention. Even though it was barely morning, Lilan's uniform and crew cut were models of perfection. He gave the impression of a man who had been awake for hours. The door closed behind him, and Hutchin removed his reading glasses from his face. "At ease, captain." The general was a well-structured man, younger than Lilan, though his hair was streaked with dashes of gray.

Lilan's muscles relaxed. "Sir."

Hutchin motioned to the chair in front of his desk. "Have a seat, Brent." Lilan rested a hand on the back of the indicated chair and slid down into it. "I know I've already expressed it, but I'll do so again. I'm sorry about your squad. Those were great men we lost."

Lilan nodded. "Yes, sir, they were."

"As I said on Wednesday, this is war, and these things are unavoidable. That's why we don't make too many friends in this business."

"Yes, sir."

"I have no doubts that you will take this newly assigned crew and turn them into a squad as functional as your last. Am I correct?"

Lilan's posture straightened. "Yes, sir."

"I expect no less." Hutchin pushed back his chair and opened the topmost drawer of his desk. He produced a single manila folder and handed it across the desktop. "Here is your new crew, captain."

Lilan accepted the folder, though his eyes remained on Hutchin. "Did you take my recommendation to promote John Tacker to executor?"

"I did. Tacker's had a good career with us, I think he'll fit the role well. He was a good recommendation."

"Thank you, sir." Lilan opened the manila folder and examined its contents. Hutchin focused on Lilan's expression as it shifted from stoic to confused and finally to disbelieving. "Sir, this has to be a mistake."

"There's no mistake, captain," Hutchin answered. "That's your new roster."

Lilan's eyes flashed across the desk. "General, sir, this shows every single soldier other than Tacker, Henrick, and myself as an alpha."

Hutchin's reply was blunt. "You are being assigned a rookie squad."

"Sir, Alan Henrick was an exception," said Lilan, "but even he was a beta when he entered Falcon. These are *all* alphas."

"I understand, captain, but there is no mistake. That is your new squad."

Pointing to the bottom of the paper, the captain said, "You took away my *pilot*? What the hell are we gonna fly out on, the wings of angels?"

Despite Lilan's emphatic tone, Hutchin's remained tempered. "A new pilot is forthcoming. And yes, before you ask, it'll also be a rookie."

Lilan looked away. After fidgeting uncomfortably in his chair, he returned his focus to the general. "Permission to speak freely, sir?"

"My assumption was that you would."

"Falcon has a reputation to protect. We worked hard to earn it. It does the entire squad a great injustice to replace those polished veterans with rookies straight out of the Academy."

Hutchin leaned against the armrest of his chair. "First of all, the *we* you're referring to consists of three people. The old squad is gone."

"Sir, I understand that, but—"

"Do you think rookies can benefit and learn from your example?"

"Sir, yes, sir, but I—"

"Then I expect you to do your job as a captain and lead this crew as you led the previous crew. I don't care about reputation. I care about results. I don't care if you were Klaus Faerber and this was Vector Squad, you'd still get a team full of rookies if that's all we had to choose from. We're undermanned. You know that. This is all we can afford to give you, and if we break up any other squad further, we'll be jeopardizing *their* capabilities. That never has been acceptable, and it won't start being acceptable now."

"I understand that, sir—"

Hutchin cut him off again. "This is how it's going to be. When I make a decision, that decision is final. Now, you will take this team, and you will lead them as you led the Falcon of yesterday. Take the assignment that's been handed to you, and turn it into something to be proud of. Do what I've come to expect of you. Make a bad situation good."

Lilan opened his mouth to reply, but no words came out. The decision had already been made, and the word *trainer* hovered in his mind. The room fell quiet, and he sighed in surrender. "Yes, sir."

"Is there anything else?"

Lilan bit his tongue. "No, sir."

"Excellent. Your soldiers have been notified and will meet in the hangar for your formal introduction at ten hundred. I'm sure you'll have no trouble breaking them in."

"No, sir." Lilan closed the manila folder and stood up. "If there's nothing else?"

"Nothing else. You're dismissed."

"Thank you, sir." Lilan nodded to the general, turned around, and left the room.

*　　*　　*

IT WASN'T UNTIL 0830 hours that Scott, David, Becan, and Jayden awoke from their slumbers—a luxury they knew they wouldn't experience again for some time. Like the Academy with its break-of-dawn musters, EDEN bases thrived on early morning schedules. Being awake and alert for morning muster had been one of Scott's greatest challenges to overcome in *Philadelphia.* If he could sleep for just a single day until what felt like a natural hour for him, he was going to do it. As soon as he, David, and their new friends next door were fully awake, they made their way to the cafeteria to grab a late breakfast.

Upon returning to their rooms, all four men received messages on their personal communicators—or *comms,* as they were commonly called. Part phone, part enhanced multiway radio, comms replaced all soldiers' personal phones, which they were required to leave at home when they arrived at *Philadelphia.* Comms were carried by soldiers at all times and, in combat, could be both wirelessly and hard linked to one's helmet while the comm sat affixed to a dedicated slot in the armor.

Soldiers were allowed to add personal contacts to their comms once they received them. For Scott, that consisted only of Nicole and his younger brother, Mark—both of whom he needed to call now that he was on base. He would, in time.

The message on Scott and his comrades' comm displays bore simple instructions: *Report to the hangar at 1000 for unit assignment.* With little time to spare, they dismissed further conversation and made their way to the hangar.

Though the *Richmond* main hangar was spacious, it paled in comparison to the massive hangars found at larger bases. Nonetheless, the four soldiers found themselves transfixed on the ceiling—if for nothing more than to feel the tremendous depth of the room. Vulture transports and Vindicator fighters covered the ground space in neat rows, and mammoth Grizzly APCs—Armored Personnel Carriers—sat parked in preparation for a mission. The mere sight of it all broke goosebumps across their arms and sent forth a powerful, overwhelming sensation—the extraterrestrials had picked the wrong planet to fight.

It was no challenge locating the meeting area, as two short rows of steel chairs lined the center of the hangar—roughly a dozen of them, it seemed. They were almost all full, occupied by various men and women, all of whom chattered in hushed tones with one another as their gazes occasionally roamed the room. At the front of the rows stood an empty, olive-colored podium.

Scott, David, Becan, and Jayden claimed the few chairs that remained, all of which were on the front row. Glancing back, Scott made eye contact with the man behind him—a stocky black soldier with a pencil-thin mustache. Scott offered the man his hand. "Hey, Scott Remington."

"Mike Carter," the man said, his voice rich and gravelly.

Scott looked at the man's insignia, which identified him as a combat medic—and an alpha private. "You're new too, huh?"

Michael chuckled in a single, hushed breath. "Look around, man."

As requested, Scott surveyed the rest of the men and women in the chairs. From one to the other, all the way down the line, their insignias were the lone common theme. "Oh, wow."

Next to him, David asked, "What you 'oh wow-ing' about?"

"Everyone's an alpha, here."

Looking back, David also caught eyes with Michael. After a brief handshake and introduction, David followed Scott's gaze around the room. "Well, how about that?"

"We can't all be in the same unit, right?" asked Scott.

Smiling quasi-sardonically, Michael shook his head and leaned back. "You want to be dropped in the middle of a warzone with a squad full of rookies?"

No. No, he didn't. "Yeah, we've got to be in different units. This must just be some...I don't know. Orientation thing."

"You gonna reserve a hangar to have an orientation for eleven soldiers?" Michael asked.

Sure enough, there were eleven of them. Twelve chairs, eleven present. An uneasy feeling swelled in Scott's stomach. "Nah. No way."

"Well, we're gonna see, aren't we?"

A set of synchronized footsteps emerged from across the hangar, prompting the soldiers to collectively turn and look, where they saw three men making their approach. The man in the front was older, his crew cut as gray as the concrete beneath them. The man behind and to his right—one taller and steel-faced—walked with perfect posture and a small gym bag in hand. The last man, smaller and with short, curly hair, brought up the rear. With these three men clearly officers, every soldier in the seating area rose and snapped to attention.

The older man continued his march until he came to the podium in front of the alphas. When he placed his palms at its edges, it wobbled back and forth. He grimaced, shot the briefest of glares to his two counterparts, and then stepped from behind the podium to face the alphas directly. Clearing his throat, he spoke. "At ease, soldiers. I am Captain Brent Lilan. To my right is Executor John Tacker, and to his right is Lieutenant Alan Henrick." The two identified men—Tacker and Henrick—surveyed the alphas impassively. "The three of us make up the officer core of Falcon Squad. If you haven't put it together yet, we are your new commanding officers." He fell silent for several seconds, almost as if trying to determine how to proceed. "As you may have noticed already, you are all alpha privates. You're all fresh out of *Philadelphia*. That's not typical for a unit of this caliber. To elucidate on that, I must first briefly explain a bit of the history behind this squad.

"Falcon is one of the oldest squads at *Richmond*. It's been here since the base's establishment, and I have been her commanding officer for just as long. We've had a long and outstanding tradition of experience and leadership, and we're one of the most respected units at this base.

"Unfortunately, change has been thrust upon us. Several days ago, Falcon was decimated by the Bakma in Cleveland, Ohio. Though all losses present learning opportunities, a squad wipe of this magnitude, in which only the command staff survives, is almost unprecedented—and can only be accomplished by a special blend of unforeseen circumstances and bad luck. Lady Luck is a bitter mistress, and when she turns on you...well, you're looking at the result of that now."

Of all the things Scott wanted to hear about on his first day out of the Academy, squad wipes were at the bottom of the list. An uneasy feeling swelled in the pit of his stomach.

"*Richmond* is the smallest EDEN base on Earth," Lilan said. "We don't receive nearly the number of new recruits as other bases do. In short, this facility is undermanned, and you are all we have to fill the shoes of those lost in battle."

They were all *Richmond* had. They weren't selected, placed with intent, or eagerly anticipated to any degree. They were just *it*. Warm bodies. Whatever cloud of excitement and optimism might have existed among the alphas before, it'd all but evaporated now.

The captain went on. "That's why you're here now. That's not what you want to hear. It's not what I want to see. But that's how it is." He opened his mouth again, then hesitated, seeming to teeter on the edge of adding something to his prior statement. All the while, his eyes shifted from one alpha to the next, to the next. Whatever thought of his was on the cusp of being entertained, he allowed it to go unspoken—perhaps, for the better. Exhaling a breath that seemed demoralizingly close to a sigh, he finally continued.

"This isn't a traditional war we've been faced with. This is a war unlike any we've ever seen. It's a war in which we can't choose the battlegrounds we fight on. It's a war in which we don't have the luxury of going on the offensive. An attack can happen anywhere on the planet at any time. It's almost impossible to form coherent battle plans since we rarely know what the battlefield will look like until we step off the transport. You can go from asleep in your beds to the middle of a firefight in minutes.

"Deaths are inevitable. My job as your commanding officer is to make sure your chance of dying by your own mistakes is diminished, and it's your job as my soldiers to help me reach that goal by paying attention, following orders, and working as a team. With that said, I'm going to allow you to get better acquainted with another member of the team, in Executor Tacker. As executors often do, he will serve as the conduit between myself and you all. Speaking to him is like speaking to me."

Executor—an EDEN-unique position that was part second-in-command, part liaison. Scott had heard in *Philadelphia* that executors often played a more critical role in squad command structures than captains despite being a rung lower on the ladder. Customarily, captains didn't mingle with the enlisted, leaving all things interpersonal to their executors. If anyone seemed the type to adhere to custom, it was Lilan. And if he was already pawning them off to Tacker? Well, that spoke volumes about a great many things.

"Executor," Lilan said, looking at Tacker and nodding, "I give them to you. Lieutenant Henrick, if you'll come with me, please."

"Yes, sir," Henrick said, following Lilan as he exited.

There were no bones about it. Scott was feeling Captain Lilan about as much as Captain Lilan seemed to be feeling them. *A squad wipe. We're the replacements for a squad wipe. This guy's veteran squad was obliterated, and now he's leading a bunch of rookies.* Spiritual faith had played such an integral part in Scott's decision to enlist. He was having a hard time summoning up any now.

All attention shifted to Tacker as he took Lilan's place. He offered the alphas a faint smile as he cleared his throat.

"Good afternoon, Falcons. As the captain stated, my name is John Tacker, and I am the executor of this squad. That means you'll all be directly under my supervision." He fell silent momentarily before the faintest smirk crept up from his lips. He nodded his head sideways in the direction Lilan had disappeared off to. "That means you won't be directly under *his*. That's reason to smile, right?" It took a moment, but a chorus of nervous chuckles escaped the alphas—as if they weren't sure they were allowed to do so. Tone staying casual, Tacker said, "All right, circle up. Big circle, about twenty feet across. Go. I'm in it, too." Gym bag still in hand, he took his place in the circle as it slowly developed.

It took the alphas a moment, but they finally managed to space themselves at the right distance to proportion the circle properly. Scott found himself with David on one side and Michael on the other—and with a great view of some of the other members of the squad. Almost directly across from him was Becan, who'd "somehow" managed to find himself next to a comely young woman with a bright red ponytail. Next to the ginger was a petite black woman with her braids in a bun, followed by a rail-thin, platinum-blond soldier with an oblong face that screamed more *dorky wizard* than *Earth defender*. On the other side of Becan stood Executor Tacker, followed by an athletic, almost preppy-looking soldier with brown, side-swept hair—and a cocky smirk to match it. Before Scott could take a good look at the others, all of whom were on his side of the circle, Tacker reached down and unzipped the gym bag he'd carried into the hangar. What Scott saw next made him smile.

Rising with a polished, new pigskin, Tacker asked, "Who likes football?"

So this was clearly not a formal affair—and it was one Scott had no hesitation speaking up about. "Oh, man—right here, sir." Absolutely right there. A second later, Tacker sent Scott a nice, clean toss. Reaching up to snatch it, Scott rotated the ball in his hands until he'd put the laces in the proper position.

"The rules are as follows," Tacker said. "You throw the ball to someone, you get to ask them a question. Answer honestly, then toss it to someone else. Before you answer your first question, give your name, age, and position."

Now, it made sense. This was a get-to-know-you session. Scott had done these in college, though a football had never been used as the instrument of inquiry. Oddly enough, they'd never done anything remotely this informal in the Academy. He'd expected things to get more rigid, not less.

"I made the first toss," Tacker said, "so I get the first question." His sharp gaze swiveled to Scott. "Why'd you want the football so bad?"

Cracking a grin, Scott answered, "I played at Michigan, sir."

"Mm," Tacker said, pressing his lips together and shaking his head in apparent disappointment. "Wrong."

The grin left Scott's face. Wrong? "Umm. Sir, I played at Michigan." As if putting *sir* at the beginning instead of the end might somehow accomplish something.

Next to Scott, David cleared his throat. "Name," he murmured through closed lips.

Scott looked at him. "What?"

"*Name.*"

Oh, veck. Sighing, he patted the football a single time and shook his own head. "Scott Remington. Twenty-three. Infantry, sir." *Way to be an idiot.* Around the circle, several of the alphas chuckled and smirked—not exactly the reaction he'd been going for. "And yes, I played quarterback for the Michigan Bobcats."

David looked at him and raised an eyebrow. Across the circle, the ginger's eyes narrowed skeptically.

Scott caught the gesture and smirked. "Backup."

"Scott Remington," Tacker said, "twenty-three-year-old former quarterback for the Michigan Bobcats, now serving his planet as an infantryman in Falcon Squad. That's about as all-American hero as you can get, so good luck following that, whoever's next. Ball's in your hands, Private Remington."

As much as he wanted to let one fly, he didn't want to follow messing up his introduction with knocking a teammate's lights out. Gaze settling on the ginger, the natural choice as she was directly across from him, he tossed a beautifully arcing spiral right into the palm of her hands. As soon as she caught it, he asked, "Where are you from?" It was about as basic a question as he could ask, but he had nothing else to work with for the moment.

Her stare settled on him before the edge of her mouth curved with wryness. "Natasha Valer. Twenty-three. Infantry." The words were laced with intent—meant to make a point.

"Yeah, you can follow instructions, well done," Scott said.

"Philadelphia," she said.

"We all came from *Philadelphia*. I meant where are you *actually* from?"

That wry smirk remained. "Philadelphia."

"You mean like, you were born there?"

"I'm sorry," she said, "that was your one question."

From his place next to her, Becan grinned from ear to ear. Tacker laughed under his breath. "You're having a rough start, QB."

Natasha sought out her target, hurling the ball toward a giant of a black man next to Michael, two down from Scott. The throw was awkward, but the man caught it with surprising deftness for someone his size. Despite his hulking frame, the black man's expression was genuinely jolly.

"What are you most *passionate* about?" Natasha asked, eyes flickering to Scott one more time as if to hammer home the point that her question was far superior to, "where are you from?"

Point taken.

"Donald Bell," the black man said in a voice as baritone as it was backwoods. "Twenty-four. Demolitionist. And I'm most *passionate* about protecting my quarterback." When Natasha tilted her head in confusion, he looked at Scott. "O-Line, baby. I got your back."

This guy played offensive line? "Come on, really?" That was awesome.

"I ain't gonna let her hurt ya."

Biting her lower lip, Natasha crossed her arms and playfully eyed them.

"That's good," Scott said, "because she's kind of freaking me out."

Several of the others laughed, Tacker included.

"Y'all don't be foolin'," Donald said, pointing Scott's way. "I actually played this dude. I went to Central Illinois. He started against us. Boy can ball."

Scott remembered that game. It was his junior year—Michigan's starter pulled a hamstring the week before. Central had no film on him; he lit them up like the Fourth of July. It was by far the best game of his collegiate career. Followed, of course, by two sloppy losses. But he still had that moment.

After gripping the ball, which looked like a toy in his massive hand, Donald slung it across the way to Becan. The Irishman's attempt to catch it was an abject failure, resulting in him having to chase it about fifteen feet as it bounced across the concrete. "Bleedin' hell!" Becan exclaimed as he finally caught up to it. When his accent was unleashed, wide-eyed grins broke out among the crowd—none bigger than Donald's.

"The hell?" Donald said as he started to laugh nearly uncontrollably. "Are you a leprechaun?"

And at that, the rest of them lost it.

"*Tha's* your veckin' question?" Becan asked incredulously, continuing before Tacker could chastise him for breaking form. "Becan McCrae, twenty-two, infantry, *not* a bloody leprechaun."

"No," Donald said, laughing at himself to the point where he could barely speak. "Man, that wasn't…that wasn't…" The more he laughed as he struggled to speak, the more everyone else around him laughed as they witnessed it.

As for Becan, he wasn't having it. "Yeah, tha' was your question. Movin' on." Trying to hold the football, which he was handling like some kind of alien device, he cocked his arm awkwardly back before shifting gears, dropping it over his foot, and kicking it like he was trying to play soccer. He succeeded only in sending it streaking toward Natasha's head right next to him.

Flinching in pure reaction, she reached up and snagged it mere inches from smacking her square in the face. Eyes wide, she stared at the ball, then at him. "Were you *trying* to give it to me?"

Clearing his throat, he shifted on his feet. "Of course, I was."

Scott and David swapped knowing smirks. There was zero chance he was aiming for her.

Before anyone could comment, Becan asked her, "Wha's your favorite color?"

"What's my favorite *color*?"

"Yeah, tha's wha' I asked."

She stared at him stupidly. "Burnt rust."

"…wait, wha'? Tha's a thing?"

Rearing back, Natasha hurled the ball across the circle, where David caught it. Eyes narrowing, she asked, "Are you really an alpha private?"

After catching the ball, David looked down at it as his fingers played with their grip. Looking up again, he answered, "David Jurgen, forty-one, infantry, and yes, I am really an alpha private."

This time, it was Tacker who cut in. "You were with the NYPD, right?"

"Yes, sir. Nineteen years. Got tired of bringing in bad men, thought I'd take down some Ithini instead."

"How is it that you bring nineteen years of experience to the table and you still come in as an alpha? You should be a gamma. Beta at the least."

Half shaking his head, David said, "Apples and oranges, sir. That's what I was told, as it pertains to police work and fighting aliens."

"Apples and oranges," Tacker said, repeating the phrase in resignation. "So says the brain trust."

"So they say, sir."

Tacker offered David a smile—the most sincere he'd offered anyone to that point. "You're up, Jurgen."

There was no hesitation. His green eyes locked on the executor, David threw Tacker the ball. Tacker caught it as if he'd half expected it all along. Tucking the ball at his side, he nodded in David's direction. "Question's yours, private."

"Why are we really throwing a football around, sir?"

And now, in a single bold gesture by the oldest among them, everyone in the circle was captivated. Even Natasha's smirk, practically trademarked by that point, was absent in the presence of apprehension and curiosity.

Tacker stared at David for almost ten seconds before turning his eyes to the rest of them—as if they, not David, needed to hear what he was about to say. "You can probably see the bruise on my forehead and the cut in the middle of it." He pointed to the indicated spot on his temple, discolored but half hidden by the front of his hairline, as short as it was. "That's where a plasma bolt hit the side of my helmet, where it rocked my head and probably came a half inch away from shattering my skull right where I stood. That was in Cleveland, where we lost everyone except the captain, Lieutenant Henrick, and myself. That was my closest call."

After looking down momentarily, he offered a single breath of humorless laughter. "You know, we call these things *plasma* bolts, but the truth is, we really don't know what the hell they are. There's some sort of plasma discharge mechanism built into the weapon itself, or so I've heard the techies say, that gives these energy bolts their high rate of speed and temperature. I've heard them say if we'd ever get hit by a bolt of *actual* plasma, there really wouldn't be much of anything left to look at." He shook his head slowly. "I don't know, man. I guess I believe them."

Scott glanced about the circle as Tacker spoke, just to capture the group's aura. Every eye was wholly fixed. Save Scott's own glancing, no one moved a muscle. He looked at Tacker again.

"I also don't know how a spacecraft can completely dematerialize then materialize from view, but there we have the Bakma Noboat. One second, you think the skies are clear, the next, you've got three enemy spacecraft bearing down on you. Or how something as frail and delicate looking as an Ithini can suddenly tap into your mind and inject you with so much fear that you can't even move. Again, I just don't know."

He looked at David. "You wanted to know why we're standing here in the middle of a hangar, throwing a football around and asking each other questions. It's because of all those *I don't knows*. It's because those *I don't knows* are going to leap out and grab you, time and time again, whether you're ready for them or not—and usually, you're not. We've been fighting these things for nine years, and we still don't know what they are. We don't know where they come from. We still don't know the full extent of what weapons they have in their arsenal—and every now and then, they'll pull a new one on you.

"When you get hit with those *I don't knows* in your worst possible moment, when your ammunition is almost out, and your transport can't reach the hot zone, and the forecast said dry, but it's pouring down raining, and you can feel death breathing down the back of your collar...your training's not going to save you. What you went through in *Philadelphia*'s not going to save you. It'll have helped. It'll have gotten you that far. But that's where that road stops.

"What'll save you," he said, looking at Scott and gesturing to Natasha, "is knowing that she's got fight in her and can stand her ground for one more minute while you rescue your comrade who's dying in the street." His gaze swiveled to Becan, and he pointed at David. "It's knowing that he won't do the stupid thing. Knowing he'll give his life to protect someone because he did it for two decades when he wore a badge." Pointing at Donald, he surveyed the group at large. "It's knowing that this big guy is worth saving. Is worth dashing out of cover for...and probably bringing a friend along with you because he's pretty vecking huge. Knowing each other, *feeling* each other, is what's going to get you over that hump when all the chips are down and it truly is do or die. Now I can stand here and yell at you, and bark orders, and rant and rave about training, and discipline, and the chain of command, but if at the end of the day, I don't know who you are...I might just be tempted to give ninety-nine percent instead of the one hundred percent required to save your life. I don't want to be just a ninety-nine-percent guy. I hope none of you want to just be that, either." Putting the football back in his hand, he patted it once, then held it up for all to see. "This is the one percent that'll make the difference."

Silence fell. The Falcons' collective gazes remained steadfast on their new executor, their laughs and wry looks replaced by wide eyes and tense shoulders. Their innocence—for as fleeting as it might have been—gave way to stoic realization. To a sudden comprehension of what mattered the most. Scott felt it. He knew the others felt it, too.

This is my team. These are the men and women I'm going to ride with. That I'm going to war with. Tacker's right. It's the moments like this—and the ones that will follow—that will make the difference.

Cocking the ball back, Tacker sent it sailing across the circle to a short soldier with spiky black hair. The soldier snatched it and looked across at the executor, who nodded. "Your turn, private. Why are you here?"

The private's name, as it turned out, was David Zigler. He was there because he was a self-proclaimed "military enthusiast." When he finished answering, he threw the ball to the next soldier—the preppy with side-swept hair. His name was John Donner, an infantryman with an affinity for fast cars. Next was Henry Mathis, the lanky, blond-haired soldier with the oblong face Scott had seen earlier, who'd made the career switch into EDEN from life as a *talk-seller*—a throwback occupation where one literally went door to door selling everything from "self-cleaning" utensils to life insurance. Next was combat technician Shekeia Rhodes, the young black woman with the braided bun, who had one of the raspiest but warmest voices Scott had ever heard. Michael Carter—the only one in the group whose roommate had not yet arrived—then got his turn to speak, as did Jayden after him. Twelve distinct stories and personalities, Tacker included. Twelve roles to fill.

As the question-and-answer session came to a close, Tacker instructed the soldiers to go to their assigned transport—*Vulture-7*—and link their comms to their new armor sets. He then informed them of Falcon Squad's five-minute rule. Whenever their comms beeped to signify a mission tone out, they had five minutes to get from wherever they were to *Vulture-7*. With the lightning-quick strike capabilities of the alien invaders, fast and efficient response times were critical to saving lives.

This was also when it was revealed that Michael's roommate, the last member of Falcon Squad they were waiting on to arrive, would be their pilot. Tacker had no information on him—only that they could not partake in a mission until his arrival, for obvious reasons. And so—for the time being, at least—it seemed that Falcon Squad was off the response hook.

After linking their comms, the new Falcons took some time to familiarize themselves with their gear inside *Vulture-7.* All Vulture interiors were the same, with two rows of twelve seats a piece, all mounted along the side walls and facing the center of the troop bay. Lockers were built into the walls between each seat, each displaying the names of the soldiers whose gear was within. Upon opening those lockers, the soldiers saw their EDEN combat armor for the first time.

Simply put, there was nothing like it. Constructed from synthetic nacre, the lightweight body armor was strong enough to stop most bullets. It was colored in urban blue and silver—only the EDEN logo retained the sparkling, mother-of-pearl hues of the abalone shell source material. Capping it all off was the helmet, which featured a v-shaped, auto-tinting visor that protected everything from the nose upward, leaving only the mouth exposed.

Scott ran his fingers over the letters of his last name on the engraved tag beneath his insignia. *Remington.* There was something about seeing it there—seeing it in that context—that caused him to catch his breath a little.

He remembered the day he'd told Nicole he felt led to join EDEN. In more ways than one, telling her was more difficult than making the decision itself. It would have been easy for her to interpret such a sudden change in trajectory as him wanting to hit the reset button on life—a restart that potentially wouldn't involve her. He'd had to hit that button before when his parents died. But Nicole was the one to get him through that. That was when, at least in his mind, she transitioned from the girl he was dating to a potential life partner.

She went to his house daily, where he stayed with relatives who'd moved in to support him and Mark. The two brothers were just teenagers. They had no idea how to live life on their own. Thankfully for Scott, with Nicole steadfastly at his side, he didn't have to. He wasn't about to go on without her now. That was what he emphasized to her, over and over again, when he told her about that burning fire within him to join the effort. That she understood so compassionately only confirmed what he already knew: they were equally yoked in every way. They were meant to be. She embraced him, they kissed, then they prayed. He could vividly recall the day he brought her that paper accepting his enlistment and identifying his garrison as *Detroit Station*. He remembered that deep feeling of spiritual confirmation. He remembered that joy.

Then he got sent to *Richmond*.

Scott withdrew his fingers. He stared at his reflection in his new helmet's visor. At that fool staring back at him. That fool that thought he knew how all this would play out. But his was not to understand. It was just to obey.

Next to him, Shekeia Rhodes examined her new technician's kit. Scott watched her for a moment, then he smiled. "As long as *you* know how to work that thing."

She grinned. It stretched halfway across her face. "Oh, you know it. So I guess you're my seat buddy?"

"Yeah, looks like it." Of the two rows leading from the cockpit to the troop bay ramp, he was in the very first seat of the starboard row. It seemed they were in alphabetical order, with him next to Shekeia and directly across from Donald and Michael. Glancing past Shekeia, Scott saw that the seat on the other side of her was unclaimed. "Who's that?"

After looking at the name on the locker, Shekeia answered, "Robinson. Must be the pilot, maybe?"

"I don't want to sound like an idiot, but shouldn't the pilot be sitting up *there*?"

Shekeia laughed, her raspy voice turning into a loud cackle. "Hey, that's all right, I'm not complainin'! I get my own little private seat next to the star quarterback." She hummed a playful *mm-mm-mm*. "No one else to butt in, got you all to m'self."

Scott laughed self-deprecatingly. "Star quarterback, right."

"Just promise me one thing. Don't you grow some *ugly mustache* like our medic!"

Across from them, Michael looked their way. "What you talking about?" he asked.

Scott laughed, as did Donald, who was inspecting his minigun from his locker next to Michael's.

"I'm talkin' about that *mustache*," Shekeia said. "You got some little penciled-in thing. If you gonna grow a mustache, grow a *mustache*."

"Man, she say yo 'stache penciled in!" said Donald, guffawing even as the words came out.

"Yeah, I know who I'm *not* saving first," Michael said.

Shekeia scoffed. "You better save me first. You ever heard of *ladies* first?"

"That only applies to *ladies*."

"That's all right," said Shekeia, locking her arm with Scott's. "Star quarterback's gonna save me. Maybe we'll save each other."

Looking up from inspecting his medical kit, Michael said, "Or maybe you'll die in each other's arms, since your medic didn't help you, since you threw shade on his mustache."

"Mustache better take all the shade it can get," she fired back. "It certainly ain't *givin'* any."

Donald hooted with his fist over his mouth. "Hoo! Man, she on you!"

Laughing, Scott shook his head. Shekeia was a kick.

Shekeia gripped his arm tighter. "Now, why don't y'all just do y'all little thing over there," she said, gesturing to Donald and Michael with a pseudo-dismissive wave, "and I'm gonna sit here and get to know my future husband."

"Future husband," Michael said. "You *need* a husband."

"*So,*" Shekeia said as she faced Scott, "I think we first need to talk about settin' a date. And don't say in winter, because I don't do that cold thing."

Time to break it to her gently. Smirking, he said, "Well, *unfortunately,* my *fiancée* might take issue with that."

"Your *fiancée?*"

"That's right."

And just like that, she yanked her arm away and looked the other direction. "Well, we just don't need to talk no more. And you can even grow a mustache, I don't even care."

From the troop bay ramp, Tacker's voice emerged over the alphas' banter. "All right, team! Listen up."

Scott shifted his focus from Shekeia's picking to the executor. All chatter died down—all eyes went to Tacker.

"You've all done gear-up drills in *Philly,* but there's nothing like putting on your actual armor. Take some time to get to know it, to wear it. If there's a problem, you want to know now, not when we're flying into a hot zone." He gestured to the lockers. "Familiarize yourself with your weapons. Your tools, everything. They're your responsibility. When you're done, take some time to learn the base. It's going to be your home for a very long time."

A chorus of *yes, sirs* emerged from the Falcons.

After pausing for a moment, Tacker continued. "I expect great things from you. I demand great things. You're alphas, and there's a learning curve—I get that. But the Bakma don't, and the Ceratopians don't. Not even the Ithini. They don't care if you've been with EDEN for ten years or ten minutes, they won't hesitate to shoot you in the back of the head if they get the chance. Don't mistake the value I place in communication and familiarity with leniency when it comes to getting the job done then getting home alive.

"With that said, for the time being, you're on your own. Learn the base, then get ready for action. We're a pilot away from a green light to roll. You're dismissed."

Acknowledgments came, and then Tacker turned to make his way out of the transport.

At the entrance to the hangar, Lilan watched as Tacker returned to him—the veteran captain's eyes hidden behind dark sunglasses. His jaw tight, he ground on a toothpick until his executor was in earshot. Spitting the toothpick out onto the hangar floor, he asked simply, "What do you think of them?"

"I don't know what I *can* think at this point," Tacker answered. "I just hope they know what this is about. Where's Henrick?"

"Who cares?" Unfolding his arms, Lilan set his hands on his hips. "I saw that football thing."

Standing at Lilan's side, he watched the soldiers mull about near the troop bay, far away. "Yeah, I figured you'd love that."

"I hated it."

Tacker exhaled a single breath of laughter. "I know." He sighed. "It's just so important that they bond quickly. That might be the only thing that saves them when the fighting starts. I mean, they sent us a *talk-seller*, for crying out loud."

"Who do you think has potential?" Lilan asked.

Tacker's gaze narrowed. "I think Jurgen will do well. He should have come in as a beta at the lowest. Remington, Donner, Zigler maybe...I'm anxious to see what Timmons can do. There are a few that have potential, I think."

"Any foreseen problems?"

"Aside from the talk-seller—that's Mathis—I don't know. Nothing is glaring. It's just inexperience." After a moment of quiet, he looked Lilan's way. "You want me to have Henrick meet with them?"

Lilan harrumphed. "I want Henrick as far away from responsibility as I can keep him, but unfortunately, that's not an option. But for the time being, no, I don't." Tacker restrained a laugh, and Lilan continued. "You know what I want you to do, right?"

Tacker met Lilan's eyes, and he nodded. "Yes, sir. I do."

"The chaff will show," Lilan said, "given time. And an opportunity." After offering a cordial nod of departure, Lilan turned to make his way out of the hangar. Tacker remained behind only a minute more before he, too, departed. The alphas were left on their own.

3

THIRD TIME'S THE charm.

Or at least, Scott sure hoped so. Dialing up Nicole for a third time on his comm, he watched as three little dots flashed on the display beneath her name, the gentle, pulsing tones repeating as the signal reached out from Virginia to Michigan. He'd barely spoken to her the day before, with the move to *Richmond* in full swing. But now—for the moment—he had peace. He had his perfect opportunity to tell her everything about everything. To tell her how much he missed her. The only thing missing...was her.

"Hey, it's Nikki! I'm sorry I can't come to the phone, but if you leave a message, I'll call you back as soon as I can. Thanks!"

Releasing an *ugh*, Scott pressed the disconnect button on the display before her voicemail could begin recording.

"No luck, eh?" David asked from the top bunk, where he'd been lying back, flipping through the pages of a magazine.

"No, no luck," Scott answered.

Another page flipped. "Don't sweat it. She'll call you back."

He knew she would. He just would have preferred it if they could talk while he was alone—relatively speaking. Though David was physically present in the room, he was about as unintrusive a roommate as Scott could have wished for. The only Falcon who had more solitude was Michael, whose roommate was yet to arrive.

Sighing, Scott placed his comm on his nightstand and leaned back in his chair. "I just want her to pick up. You know that thing where you start to wonder if you did something wrong and she's not answering on purpose?"

Eyes still on the magazine, David chuckled. "Yeah, I know all about that." Pointing at the page in front of him, he looked at Scott and asked, "Did you see there's a recipe in here for enchiladas?"

"No, I honestly didn't."

"It's EDEN *Quarterly*. It's the standard mailout. Why would they include a recipe for enchiladas?"

Scott didn't want to break David's heart, but he really didn't care. "I don't know, man."

"But I mean think about it. What are we supposed to do with this? Where are we supposed to cook this?" He angled the page so Scott could see. "Look at this. *Cracking the Code on Alien Propulsion*, then right beneath it, *Nate's Yummy Enchiladas*. Who the hell is Nate? Why put this here? It's so out of place."

"I guess he makes good enchiladas."

David shook his head and said, "I can tell you one thing, compadre, I'm not eating enchiladas from a guy named Nate."

Why wasn't she answering? Staring at the blank display on his comm as if to will a call from her into existence, Scott exhaled a deflated breath.

"'In the mood for something Mexican?'" David read aloud. "'Wait till you try this yummy treat.'"

Scott's comm chirped; Nicole's name popped up on the screen. Sitting upright, he pressed the button to answer.

"Disaster averted," said David.

At long last, Nicole's face appeared on his display. Those dark, angular eyes—that gorgeous, white smile. That face he never got tired of seeing. He couldn't restrain his grin. "Hey—*finally!*"

"I'm sorry!" she said, wincing then beaming from her side of the display. "All your missed calls and your voicemail just popped up at the same time. I didn't even know you called till ten seconds ago!"

"Hey, as long as I get to talk to you now, I'm happy," he said.

Her smile held steadfast. "Well, I'm all yours! *How are things*? Did you get moved in all right?"

"Yeah, we got in *so* late last night."

"I figured you must've been tired and went to bed right away," she said.

From his top bunk, David chuckled knowingly, which prompted the briefest of looks from Scott. Just enough for her to notice.

"Who was that? Is that your roommate?"

"Yeah, that—"

"I want to meet him!" she said.

Rolling onto his side from the top bunk, David said loudly, "I want to meet *you!*"

Come on, really? Restraining a good-natured eye roll, Scott angled the screen so both he and David could be seen in the camera.

"Toss her up on the monitor!" David said, hopping down from the bunk and walking in front of Room 419's wall display.

With a good-natured sigh, Scott activated his comm's mirror feed. Any screen from a comm could be mirrored on any EDEN display—entire files could even be uploaded. It was an intentional design meant to make sharing group information more convenient. Or, in this case, introducing a roommate to one's fiancée. Despite the obvious temptation of casting tomfoolery on a screen during a serious briefing, it was a rarely attempted prank that never went unpunished.

Seconds later, Nicole's face appeared, enlarged on the wall display. Waving exuberantly, she said, "Hi! I'm Nikki!"

David's grin fell somewhere between mocking enthusiasm and genuine amusement. "Hi, Nikki! I'm David!"

"Hi, David!"

"Good grief, you're adorable."

"Aww, thank you!" she said, cocking her head in a way that made the strands of her textured bob fall to the wayside. It was—Scott had to admit—pretty adorable. Nicole had inherited her spunky, cute looks from her maternal grandmother, who had migrated to Nebraska with Nicole's grandfather from Hangzhou, China. Though Nicole's father was Caucasian, she herself heavily favored her grandmother at that age. Scott wasn't complaining. Judging by the photos, her grandmother was a knockout in her prime. "Okay," Nicole said chirpily, "I'm gonna talk to my fiancé now!"

Holding his hands up placatingly, David said, "He's all yours. Nice to have met you."

"Nice to have met you, too!"

Cutting off the mirrored feed and looking back at the comm display, Scott was about to say something before she beat him to the punch.

"So *tell me* about it! What's it like? Is it like *Philly*? Is it warmer there than here? How's the food?"

Scott was used to her rapid-fire delivery by this point in their relationship. She got like that whenever she got excited, especially if she was excited for someone else. Especially if that someone else was him. "The weather's nice, the food's *eh*."

"What'd you have for lunch? I had a chicken wrap."

"Salisbury steak with mashed potatoes. I don't know what's for dinner, yet."

David said, "We're making enchiladas!"

Scott shot him a look before looking back at Nicole. "We're not making enchiladas."

"*Pfft*," said David. "*You're* not, maybe."

"To answer your other question," Scott said to Nicole, "this place is definitely realer than *Philadelphia*. You walk around here and you're in the middle of Vultures, and Grizzlies, and everything. It's kind of cool, actually."

"Did you find out what unit you're in?"

"Yeah, it's called Falcon Squad. It's uhh…" How was he going to explain this one? "It's a unit made up entirely of rookies."

She stared at him briefly before blinking as if she'd misunderstood. "What?"

It's about the same kind of reaction he'd had—at least on the inside. "Every single person in the unit literally just got here from *Philadelphia*. Besides the officer core, I mean. There's a captain, an executor, one lieutenant, then all of us."

"Is it a brand new unit?"

This part, she was not going to like. "No, umm." He pressed his lips together as he tried to figure out how to maneuver through this. "So you know that attack they just had in Cleveland?"

"…yeah."

And here he went. "Falcon was there. They actually…had pretty much a squad wipe. Except for those three officers. So."

Confusion crossed her face before she shook herself out of it. "Wait, you mean everyone who was just in that unit is *dead*?"

"Yes." There was no other way he could answer. He held his hands up defensively. "But listen—"

"Well, that's just *swell*, Scott!"

His brow furrowing, David looked in Scott's direction.

"Listen," Scott said. "Just because Cleveland happened, it doesn't mean something like that'll happen again."

"And it doesn't mean it won't," she said.

Scott half-frowned. "You're right." It was already time to ease her. "But you also know what led me here."

What little energy remained in her voice melted away. "Yeah," she said—a flatness in her voice that Scott didn't find encouraging. "I know."

"…what's that supposed to mean?"

Seeming to catch herself, she brushed some strands from her forehead and sighed. "I'm sorry. That came out bad. We both know why you're there."

"Because I mean, if *you* don't, we can talk about it."

"I pray about it every night, okay? I know it's exciting, you're doing what you were called to do, I should just trust, et cetera, et cetera. I'm trying to trust." Closing her eyes, she drew a deep breath and released it. "Mustering trust, as we speak."

Clearing his throat, David raised a finger. "Can I butt in real quick, here? I don't mean to eavesdrop, but I mean, I can't *not* hear you guys."

Scott paused as if deliberating, but there was nothing to deliberate. If David wanted to say something, he'd let him say it. "Sure," Scott said.

David gestured to the comm. "Can I...?"

Looking back at Nicole, Scott said, "David wants to tell you something." He angled the screen in David's direction.

As soon as Nicole's arched brow came into view, David said, "I spent nineteen years as a beat cop in New York City. I'm a married man, got a pair of kids, the works. I know all about the *loved-ones* stuff, believe you me." He looked straight into Nicole's eyes. "I'm gonna take care of your future husband. To the best of my ability." Gesturing at Scott, he said, "I can tell that you guys are all about the faith thing. So with that in mind, consider that maybe, just *maybe*, there was a reason the Man upstairs paired your fiancé up with a guy who spent nineteen years protecting people, y'know?"

What an interesting way to have thought about it. What a perfect thing to say to Nicole to ease her mind. Scott listened more intently.

"That's actually a really good way to think about it," Nicole said, echoing Scott's mental sentiment.

David smiled. "I'll tell you what else I could do. I could take down your number and pass it on to my wife—her name's Sharon. All that time I was a cop, she lived that life that you're about to step into...worrying about her husband, his safety, all of it. You think you might want to talk to her?"

Nodding eagerly, Nicole answered, "I think I'd like that, yeah."

"You got it. I'll get your contact info from Scott and pass it on to her."

"Thank you so much, David."

"No problem."

Scott turned the screen back toward himself. While not wholly absent from Nicole's face, her worried expression was considerably more muted. He had his new roommate to thank for that.

Holding then releasing a purposeful breath again, Nicole locked eyes with Scott and offered a smile. "Okay. Sorry about all that, I just had a little moment."

"I know. It's okay."

"Let's rewind to the part where you were telling me all the *good* things! I want to hear about the good things. About the base, your new teammates, everything. Lay it all on me."

If she said so. The corner of his lips curved upward. "All right, then."

"Skip the part about the squad wipe."

Oh, he planned to. "So, you met David Jurgen. Let me tell you about *Becan McCrae.*"

Nicole raised one of her eyebrows and pointed off-screen as if that would have indicated something. "Wait, his last name is *Jurgen?*"

From his bunk, David's eyes narrowed.

Cracking the faintest of smirks, Scott said, "I hate to break it to you, babe, but you don't look like much of a Dupree."

She leered before matching his mischievous expression. "Okay. I probably deserved that."

"Mm-hmm."

"Moving on," she said, angling her head down to peer into his eyes. "I believe you were going to tell me about someone?"

Scott laughed. "Yeah. Becan. He's probably one of the most unique people I've ever met."

"Describe him in one word!"

Raising an eyebrow, Scott asked, "*One* word? I don't know if he *can* be described in one word."

She grinned. "Elaborate after! But I want one word for each new teammate—something I can attach to them in my head. Just for fun!"

"Well, if you insist."

"I insist!"

He leaned back against the wall, the comm's camera still on him as he looked down in thought. "One word for Becan McCrae. Mm!" Snapping his fingers, he smiled and looked at her. "I have the perfect one."

*   *   *

"Psychotomimetic," said Becan.

Blinking as she walked alongside him, Natasha looked at him sidelong and said, "*What?*"

"Psychotomimetic. Tha' means it makes yeh go crazy. Like, hallucinatin' an' stuff."

Setting her eyes forward again, she said, "I have never heard of necrilids having *musk glands* that make you go…psycho…luna—whatever."

"No, it's totally real. I heard it from someone in *Philly*. And it's *psychotomim*—"

"I don't care what it is. And I don't believe that's true. Don't you think if necrilids had musk glands that released pheromones that made you go crazy, they would tell us about it?"

The wild-haired Irishman stopped in the hallway and looked straight at her. "No, see, tha's the thing. We don't hear abou' it because they don't *want* us to hear abou' it."

She stared with incredulity. "Why would they not want us to know something like that?"

"Because we'd all quit. We'd all just leave, to hell with the consequences. I mean think abou' it. One second you're in a fight to the death with this thing, an' the next second you're sittin' on a magic rocket with your dead grandma, who's a water hydrant. Who in their righ' mind would sign up for *tha'*?"

Mouth hanging open, Natasha stared at him dumbfounded before finally saying, "You are the weirdest person I've ever met."

He stared right back, his green gaze hinting more at bewilderment than offense. "I guess tha's somethin'."

"And I *don't* believe that necrilids have hallucinogenic musk glands.'

"Well, I mean…is it really debatable by this point?"

"Your intelligence sure is."

He pressed his lips together in a duck face. "Touch."

"*Touché?*"

"Tha' too, yeah."

After the Falcons had dispersed from their hangar meeting with Lilan and Tacker, many had found themselves grouping up with some of their new comrades to hang out or explore the yet-undiscovered nooks and crannies that *Richmond* had to offer. Becan and Natasha were among the latter, the Irishman having latched onto the fiery-haired girl from Philadelphia like a lovestruck puppy. Seeming all too willing to play the object of affection, Natasha had humored Becan's scatterbrained quips for almost forty solid minutes.

"Can I ask yeh a personal question?" Becan asked as they passed a room that held a swimming pool.

As Natasha's gaze lingered on the pool for a moment, she half-cocked her head. "I find it hard to believe you'd pass on the opportunity."

"Yeh seemed a little flirty with Remmy."

Walking onward, she said, "Still waiting for your question."

"Uhh. Were yeh bein' a little flirty with Remmy?"

"What's it to you?"

Sliding his hands into his uniform pockets, he shrugged his shoulders. "It's nothin'. I was jus' wonderin'." After a moment, he said, "He's doin' a line, yeh know."

"I don't know what that means."

"It means he's spoken for."

Natasha's stare remained purposefully on the hallway ahead. "His fiancée, yes. I'm aware. Shekeia told me."

"Sooo…maybe tha' just doesn't seem like such a good idea, yeh know?"

"What doesn't, exactly?"

"Givin' the lusty eye to a guy who's already in a relationship."

At the remark, she smirked. "The lusty eye, huh? I wasn't aware I'd given him any eye at all—and most certainly not one I'd call *lusty*." Before Becan could reply, she stopped and looked at him. "Did it ever strike you that maybe I'm not all that interested in being serious? About anything? That maybe I just like to play? I just want to have some fun while I'm here."

Hands still in his pockets, Becan raised his eyebrows and nodded. "Well I mean, obviously. I know tha's why *I* signed up. To have fun."

She stared at him for several seconds before one side of her lips curled up. Her eyes narrowed faintly. "Cute."

"Wha's cute?"

"Your sarcasm," she said as she resumed her walk. "It's cute."

Catching up with her, he said, "I wasn't bein' sarcastic." The comment prompted her to stop and regard him, and he continued. "I'm just here to do whatever there is for me to do before I eat plasma. I know a lot o' people signed up to fight for the planet an' whatnot, but I'm not one o' them. I don't really care abou' the planet. I mean, who would I be leavin' it to? Me kids? Me family? I got none o' tha'. I'm an orphan in the world. If aliens take over, wha's tha' mean to me? All it takes is the righ' plasma bolt an' *poof*. Existence over." He shrugged again. "Kind o' hard to care when yeh don't exist."

She shook her head slowly. "I don't know if that's poetic or pitiful."

"Yeh know wha' I think it is?" he said. "Liberatin'. Means it's open season on havin' a good time. Maybe I'll have a gargle, maybe I'll kill some Bakma. In the end, we're all dust, annyway."

Very subtly, her eyebrows lowered. Barely a twitch. "How interesting a perspective."

"Yeah. Yeh know wha' else I think?" When she said nothing, he smirked with impishness. "I think I'm way more fun than you." Winking and with his hands still in his pockets, he strolled ahead, leaving her speechless. "I mean seriously!" he proclaimed boisterously as he walked on without her. "Which one o' us would *you* want to have a drink with?"

Her gaze stayed fixed as the distance grew between them, her expression teetering between uncertainty and something different. Something unexpected. But not displeased. At long last, and only after Becan had gone a considerable way ahead, she reacted. The corners of her lips curved up devilishly. Setting off ahead again, she quickened her pace to catch up.

*   *   *

"I think we need to read this together," Nicole said from the screen. "Let me go grab my Scripture." Scott watched as she propped her phone against something and then slipped out of view, leaving her dorm room the only thing on the screen.

Scott reached over to his nightstand and grabbed his own black, leather-bound Scripture. Leaning against the wall of his lower bunk, he waited for her to reappear.

To say that spirituality and faith were something Scott and Nicole shared was an understatement. It was their glue. It was the thing that held them together—that *had* held them together through whatever life had dealt them. Right now, life was dealing them distance. Scott knew that in the grand scheme of things, EDEN soldiers could be sent to any base on any part of the planet. There was nothing inherently unfair about that—it came with the territory. What stung was that all the way through *Philadelphia* up until a few days ago, he'd been led to believe he was staying in Detroit, close to her. What hurt was the sudden pulling of the rug from beneath his feet. Being stationed in *Richmond* wasn't unfair. It was just a surprise.

Scott glanced at Michael, who was leaning against Room 419's open doorway. The medic's arms were folded across his chest as he conversed quietly with David. Scott wasn't sure what they were discussing, but it, too, seemed an earnest conversation.

When Nicole finally reappeared, she had her Scripture in hand. She began to turn its pages until she stopped on a page and read. "But in all your ways trust God, for it is He who charts the pathways of men, not for the suffering of those who love Him, but for their good and for His glory."

It was a verse Scott knew well. He'd heard it countless times at church.

"Scott," Nicole said with a sigh, "I want to confess something. I was angry with you when you told me you were going to *Richmond*."

"I know you were," he said. That was one of the roughest phone calls he'd ever had to make.

She pressed her lips together. "I was a little angry with God, too. I know that's ridiculous, but—"

"—that's not ridiculous."

"—I just kind of thought things were going to go a certain way, then at the last minute, everything changed and it was like I didn't have anything to hold onto." She hesitated. "I haven't always felt what you've felt about this. I've shared that with you before. But," she said, holding her hands up, "that doesn't mean I don't believe it, and that doesn't mean I don't trust you or God about it. And I think that's why that verse stands out to me so much right now." She pressed her hand to her chest. "I need to work on my trust. You're like, way better at that than me. I can admit that."

"No, I'm not," Scott said with a semi-scoffing laugh.

"No, you are. To leave what you left, I'm still kind of floored by it. That's next-level trust. I'm not there, yet."

He smiled sadly. "Nikki…"

"I'm sorry that I got mad at you. I'm sorry I responded the way I did when you told me about *Richmond*—you didn't deserve it. That was my lack of trust speaking and not something you did wrong. Just…" She bit her lower lip. "Just know that there are days every now and then when I struggle with all of this. I am trying to be as positive as I can. Some days are harder than others. I feel like I did a pretty good job at the *beginning* of our call today!" She laughed softly.

He thought so, too. "You did great, considering the circumstances."

"I just want you to know that I'm with you on this. I just wanted you to hear me say it."

"I appreciate that, but I don't want you to just be with *me* on this." She'd know what he meant.

Closing her eyes, she nodded her head. "Yes, I know. I'm working on it."

Scott's attention averted from the comm camera as Michael abruptly stood upright from the doorframe, he and David shifting their bodies to face what was clearly someone in the hallway. Angling his head a bit,

Scott watched as a woman came into view. She looked about their age, with large, youthful eyes and a brown shag haircut. Scott attuned his ears.

"Do you guys happen to know who's in 424?" she asked. From where he was, Scott thought he could make out some sort of accent.

"I'm in 424," Michael answered. When she stared at him bug-eyed, he asked, "Why? What's up?"

Scott's focus returned to the comm when Nicole spoke. "Something up?"

"Nah," he answered. "Just someone…new?" He looked up again. Honestly, he wasn't sure what was going on over there, but judging by the sudden stunned look on Michael's face, the new girl had just told him something of significance.

From the screen, Nicole smiled. "Go. Go be with your new teammates."

"No, babe, it's okay—"

"Scott, these are the guys keeping you alive over there. I'm not asking you, I'm telling you. Go get to know them."

His eyes returned to the screen, and his heart melted a bit.

"I love you," she said.

A smile crept out. "I love you, too. More than you'll ever know."

She winked. "I think I have a pretty good idea. Now *go*. Make friends, mister. I'll talk to you later."

"I'll call you tonight."

"I'll be waiting." After blowing him a kiss, she reached forward to tap the screen. A second later, the connection closed.

It took all of one second for the emptiness to hit. All of one second to wish he'd never seen that young woman in the hall. To have Nicole's smiling face on that comm display again.

God, I hope You're right about all this.

It was a stupid thought—a foolish prayer if the half-second it took to think it could be considered a prayer at all. But it was a moment of all-too-human honesty. He hoped that God understood. Setting his comm down on his nightstand, Scott rose from his chair to approach David and Michael.

"Yeah but I mean, if it was open barracks or something I would understand, but they're two-person rooms," said Michael.

Walking up, Scott looked at David and Michael, then at the woman in the hall. At her feet was a filled duffle bag. "Hey. What's going on?"

David looked at Scott, raising his eyebrows indicatively. "Mike just met his roommate."

"*Really?*" Scott asked, attention returning to the woman, then to her nametag. Robinson. *Oh, veck.* This was their pilot. Clearing his throat to make the situation less awkward, he extended his hand to her. "Hey, I'm Scott Remington."

She accepted the gesture. "Lexie Robinson, nice to meet you," she said with a thick Australian accent. Lexie's focus returned immediately to Michael. "There must be someone we can talk to. This has got to just be a mistake."

"Yeah," said Michael, whose voice shook with what sounded like genuine nervousness. "No way they did this on purpose, it must be a mistake."

Chuckling sardonically to himself, David turned and stepped away. "Welcome to EDEN," Scott heard him mumble.

Michael apparently heard it, too. "I get that and all, but how they gonna put a guy and a girl in the same room?"

What a nightmare scenario that would have been, Scott thought. He could only imagine Nicole's reaction to finding out he was bunked with another woman. That would certainly not have helped their situation.

"I'm just saying," said David, turning around to face them again, "it's not going to be a mistake. She makes three women on the team. There's no even pairing there."

"So they just expect us to be cool with it like this?"

David slowly smirked. "I think they expect you to be grownups."

Still standing in the hall with a sheepish look, Lexie asked, "Do you at least want to take a walk with me to the billeting office? To see if there's maybe something they can do?"

"Yeah," answered Michael. "Maybe there's another unused room or something they can give you."

Scott understood their shared sense of urgency. Though David was right about EDEN expecting them to act like adults, there was still the potential for extreme awkwardness.

From up the hall, the voice of David Zigler emerged as he called to them. "Hey, guys!" Walking with him were John Donner, Henry Mathis, and Shekeia Rhodes. "Hope you didn't make plans for this evening, because I got you covered."

Scott didn't know much about Zigler—or John or Henry, for that matter. As the four approached, they cast their eyes briefly onto Lexie, who stepped back to allow them through, her eyes flickering with apprehension. Seizing the opportunity to take some pressure off her, Scott gestured to her as he looked at the newcomers. "Guys, this is Lexie, she's our pilot. She just got here to base." Looking at her, he raised an eyebrow. "Right?"

"Right," she answered quickly. "I was supposed to be sent to the new base in *Sydney*, but there was some sort of garrison screw-up."

"Lexie," Scott said, "this is Zigler, John, Henry, and Shekeia."

Casting a sharp look Scott's way, Zigler said, "You got a problem with my name or something?"

Scott blinked. "Umm, what?"

"I got a first name, you know," Zigler said.

"Yeah, and it's the same first name as him." Scott pointed at David. "I didn't want to confuse her."

From the doorframe, David smirked. "That's right—and I had my name first."

Rolling his eyes with what appeared to be genuine disgust, Zigler turned his focus back to the group at large. "I found out there's a bar just a little ways off base called *The Black Cherry*. I reserved us two excursion vehicles to go hit it up."

For a second time, Scott looked at him incredulously. "A *bar*?"

"Yeah," Zigler answered flatly. "A bar. You ever heard of those?" The spiky-haired soldier continued. "We're all going to go there together."

"We are?" asked David with skepticism and amusement.

"Yeah, we are, *Jurgen*."

Looking down at the floor, Scott shook his head and laughed. What an obnoxious little punk.

"Tacker wanted us to bond, so we're going to go there and bond," Zigler said. "I want you guys ready to go in ten minutes."

From the opposite direction of the hallway, another voice emerged. "Where are we goin' in ten minutes?" Becan. Walking alongside him was Natasha.

"I'm taking us to a bar," Zigler answered.

"Bleedin' ace!"

Raising his hand, Scott said, "Time out."

Zigler shot him a look. "No 'time out.' You'll do what you're told."

"Dude, check the ego for a minute and listen."

Before Scott could say anything else, Shekeia stepped toward him and snatched him by the arm. "I think it's a great idea." Her eyes stayed locked on Scott the whole time she spoke—the defusing intention behind her words loud and clear. "Spending time with our new teammates. Getting to know each other. Becoming a *team*."

Scott admired her attempt to quell a confrontation before it arose, but he still wasn't sold on going to a bar on day one. Eyes on her with equal deliberateness, he said, "I understand that, but do you really think going to a bar is a good idea on our very first day?"

"I think it's a grand idea!" said Becan.

Of course, he would.

"Tacker said we wouldn't get called out," said Zigler.

"Without a pilot," said Scott, gesturing to Lexie. "This is our pilot."

Zigler scoffed. "She literally just got here. She's not even unpacked. And I'm pretty sure she doesn't want to be responsible for ruining a good time for her new teammates by checking in with Tacker."

"Okay." That was enough. Scott shifted bodily to face Zigler, opening his mouth to say something—though Shekeia's hand gripping his arm halted him.

Looking at Lexie quizzically, Shekeia asked, "Did they assign you a roommate?"

Lexie smiled painfully, then pointed to Michael.

Shekeia's eyes widened. "*Mustache?*"

"Aw, come on," said Michael.

"They got you bunked up with *Mustache?* Oh, no, no, *no,* you can stay with us."

Clapping his hands and rubbing them together, Becan said, "Righ', so ten minutes, yeh said? I'll call up Jay, I think he's at the range." The Irishman turned away to call Jayden on his comm.

"What a *fun* time we're going to have!" Shekeia said, again turning her eyes to Scott with that same deliberate look. "Won't it be *fun?*"

"*I* think it'll be fun," said Natasha from beside them. She cast Scott a coy smirk.

David folded his arms and leaned against Room 419's doorframe. "I think it's a terrible idea. But someone's got to chaperone, so I guess I'm in."

Natasha looked at Lexie. "You coming, new girl?"

Brow furrowing with hesitation, Lexie answered, "I don't know...I haven't even unpacked yet."

"Do it later. The more, the merrier. And like Shekeia said, you can sleep with us if you're more comfortable. We'll make room."

"Yeah, you're coming," said Shekeia. "Not debatable."

Looking around, Natasha said, "I don't see Donald. Does he know?"

"He's Ziggy's roommate," Shekeia said, "I'm sure he knows about it."

By the sound of it, every other person was gung-ho about the bar run. Setting his hands on his hips, Scott sighed. Going would be a peer pressure move, no doubt, but these were indeed his new peers. Peers that could, as Nicole alluded to, save his life on the battlefield. "All right, what the heck," Scott said. "Let's do it."

"That's my quarterback!" said Shekeia, slapping him on the back with a grin. "He's my future husband, you know."

Natasha raised a wry brow. "Does his fiancée know that?"

"Not yet, but she'll get the message." She wrapped her arm around Scott's waist and pulled in against him. "Maybe we'll send some cute pictures together."

Shaking his head and laughing under his breath, Scott said to Shekeia and Natasha, "You two are ridiculous." He turned from them to retrieve his comm from his room.

David was already in there, tightening the straps on his boots. "I'm excited," David said. "Are you excited?" Before Scott could answer, David slapped him on the shoulder. "Hey, what's the worst that could happen?" All it took was a single look from Scott to send David into laughter. Seconds later, the older man was out the door.

Casting a look at Nicole's picture, Scott's eyes slowly narrowed. "Hey, don't look at me," he said as if she were standing right there before him. "I'm just doing what you said." He could see her eyes rolling in his head. Offering her picture a smirk, he slipped out the door behind David.

4

SCOTT WAS NOT a bar person. Truth be told, he could count on one hand the number of bars he'd set foot in. But none of those looked like *The Black Cherry*. Flashing lights. Pulsing music. Waitresses in short skirts sashaying around with finely balanced trays of cocktail glasses. This was far from the seedy, sad-country-on-the-jukebox dives he'd seen before. This was half a step away from a discothèque.

Which, of course, few people in Falcon Squad seemed to mind. Kicked back and relaxed around a black, graphite table, they bobbed their heads to the music as they laughed and chatted about everything from favorite back-home pastimes to shared experiences at *Philadelphia* Academy.

The group had checked out a pair of excursion vehicles intended for free soldier use in public transit. Though *The Black Cherry* wasn't exactly in walking distance, it wasn't terribly far from the base—and it carried the bonus of free admission for card-carrying members of EDEN. Zigler had heard about the place from a soldier in another unit upon inquiring about "someplace where soldiers can let off steam." Scott wasn't quite sure how Zigler had accumulated any amount of "steam" in less than twenty-four hours but to each their own. He had convinced himself that going out wasn't the worst decision in the world, and he was determined to stick to that conclusion until proven otherwise—and he prayed to God he wasn't proven otherwise.

"Do you guys think it's weird that we never heard from that other guy?" Henry asked, the blond-haired soldier and former talk-seller leaning against the table with both elbows. "The lieutenant, I can't even remember his name."

"Henrick," said John, the too-cool-for-school car jockey cracking a sly smirk. "That's literally a stone's throw from your name, and you can't remember it?"

Scott chuckled, as did a few others. There had been plenty of picking banter back and forth in the thirty-some minutes they'd been there thus far. It felt good to hear—even if he was one of the few for which alcohol wasn't a factor.

Kicked back in his chair with a beer, Zigler said, "I can tell you what that means. It means he doesn't need to speak because his actions speak for themselves. It means he's a bad man."

"Or he's an idiot," said David, "and they want to keep him as far away from public speaking as possible."

"Yeah, I'm pretty sure that's not it," said Zigler.

David shrugged. "Eh, what do I know? You're probably right." The wry look he shot Scott's way confirmed his sarcasm. Scott had to look in the other direction not to laugh.

"And what about that speech from Captain Lilan?" Henry asked. "Could he have seemed any less interested in us?"

"Well, I mean look at it from his perspective," said David. "The guy just had a squad wipe. We all heard him say that Falcon Squad was a squad with a great reputation. He just went from that to us."

Henry snapped his fingers. "Tacker, though. He was great. He was *so* personable; he made everyone feel special."

"He's an executor," said Scott. "They're the good cop in the whole good, bad routine."

"I know, but I mean, don't you think it would have been better if Lilan had been a part of that, too? That's just good customer service."

Raising an eyebrow, Natasha held back a mirthful grin. "*Customer* service?"

Seeming to realize the inherent silliness of the concept, Henry quickly shook his head. "No, no, I mean, *obviously* we're soldiers and not customers."

She shot Shekeia lascivious, wide eyes. "I'd be Tacker's customer."

"Ooh." Shekeia winked. "Tell it."

A frustrated Henry said, "Okay, replace customer service with like, bedside manner or something."

"I don't know," Natasha mused, "my mind kinda likes the idea of Tacker being my personal customer service rep."

Staring in Natasha's direction, Zigler said, "Guys, focus."

Scott, who'd been among those chuckling at the absurdity of it all, looked Zigler's way. "Dude, they're just having fun." *Focus? Really?*

Leaning past Scott, David looked down the table at Lexie. The Aussie pilot, who looked as tuckered and out of sorts as anyone could, was staring blankly into a mixed drink that Natasha and Shekeia had ordered for her but that she'd yet to touch. "Hey, Robinson," David said. Lexie nearly flinched, as if hearing someone say her name was the last thing she'd expected. She looked over at David. "Tell us about life on the other side of the planet."

Smiling a bit shyly, Lexie shrugged. "It's the same as life here, I suppose."

"Do the toilets really flush backward?"

She laughed. "No, I'm afraid that's a myth."

"Didn't you say you were supposed to get stationed there?" Scott asked. "At that new base in Sydney?"

"I was, yeah. Actually, they flew me all the way out there to be garrisoned, but there was some sort of mistake, so they flew me all the way back."

They flew her all the way out there? Eyes narrowing, Scott asked, "You mean before you got placed in Falcon?"

She nodded. "I went from *Philly*, to *Sydney*, back to *Philly*, then to *Richmond*, all in the span of about twenty-two hours."

Wide eyes abounded from one side of the table to the other.

"And you're not jetlagged?" David asked.

"Oh, no, I'm quite jetlagged," she laughed. "Actually, I don't know if I was there long enough to *get* jetlagged, so I'm really not sure what I am. But yeah, it's been kind of a whirlwind."

Staring at her quizzically, Becan asked, "Why didn't yeh say somethin' earlier when we said we were goin' ou'?"

Scott knew why. *Because she wasn't going to ruin an evening out for everyone, even if it wrecked her.* Of course, Zigler's guilt-tripping had a hand in that.

Lexie offered a sort of awkward, placating smile Becan's way—indicative of a search for an answer coming up short. "I mean, I'm fine and all." Her eyes flickered around the table at the many gazes upon her until, in an act of masterful deflection, she looked at Natasha and mustered up a smirk. "So this executor bloke's a real looker, is he?"

Smiling, Scott leaned back in his chair and listened to the conversation unfold. Lexie didn't care one way or the other about the executor or his looks. She just wanted the focus off her. Well played.

As Natasha and Shekeia elucidated on all things Tacker-related, Scott found his eyes wandering *The Black Cherry* again. They weren't the only ones in EDEN uniform—he could make out a soldier here and there among the other patrons. At the very least, it gave credence to Zigler's claim that soldiers from *Richmond* frequented the place, which made him feel the tiniest bit better about leaving the base grounds so quickly. This was nice. Getting to know his new comrades was nice. Getting to hear them laugh, and talk, and pick. Watching a little day-one meshing unfold.

"How old do you guys think the captain is?" John asked, leaning back as he ran a hand through his side-swept hair. "Fifties? Sixties? Retirement age?"

Zigler set down his mug of beer. "Looks like somewhere in his upper fifties, for sure. And men like that never retire."

Donald, the giant demolitionist, shook his head. "All's I know is he's for real. I can tell it. I don't wanna make him mad, man."

Scott smiled. "Old coaches were the *worst*. They would tell it like it is, every single time. Rip you to shreds."

Laughing, Donald pointed to him. "Yeah, you right!"

"But I guess in that way, they're also the best. You never have to worry if they're just telling you what you want to hear. They're not, so you can trust them."

"Still, man," said John again, "I feel like this guy's gotta be on his way out—there's only so much you can do when you hit that age, right?"

Zigler wagged his finger. "Don't forget that Klaus Faerber is forty-eight."

"Klaus Faerber is also the greatest unit leader to ever set foot on a battlefield," John answered, "so I don't think we can compare him to Lilan."

Scott was pretty sure that Klaus Faerber would have his rivals throughout the annals of history. But in the modern era? The statement may have well been true.

Klaus was the leader of Vector Squad, the most renowned and elite EDEN unit on the planet. Every member of Vector was the absolute best of the best—and Captain Faerber led them all. Clad in their famous purple and white battle armor, when they showed up, things got ugly for the aliens.

Vector Squad was based out of *Berlin* base, hence, they almost exclusively operated on that side of the planet. But they were known everywhere. Klaus Faerber was known everywhere. John was absolutely correct. Even with what Scott was sure was an impressive record, a captain like Lilan couldn't be compared to a living legend like Klaus.

"Anyone seen his son at *Philly*?" Michael asked.

Strom Faerber, Klaus's son, was a cadet at the Academy—and he was likely to be the most hyped soldier of the century upon graduating. Scott had never seen him, but he knew a handful who had. Word was he was a beast, just like his father.

Quiet up until then, Jayden raised his hand. "I saw him once." The group's collective focus turned to him. "He was liftin' weights in one of the training rooms with a bunch of guys around him. Like he had an entourage or somethin'."

That tracked about right.

"Guy looks just like his dad," Jayden said. "Blond hair, blue eyes. Maybe not as tall, but man, he's got the same face."

Zigler took a swig of beer. "If he takes his father's footsteps, he'll climb the chain of command like it's nothing."

Once again, Natasha leered lustily in Shekeia's direction. "Think Strom needs a customer service rep?"

"Oh, yeah," Shekeia answered, nodding exaggeratedly. "I think you ought to apply."

Natasha winked.

And Zigler lost it. "Would you knock it off?" he asked Natasha.

Perplexed looks swept the table as Natasha looked at Zigler dumbfoundedly. "Excuse me?"

"I'm trying to have conversations that actually matter, and you keep chiming in with your stupid hookup talk. Are you a soldier or a slut?"

The group collectively gasped. Eyes wide, Becan stood up. "Excuse me?"

"Strom will climb the chain of command just like his father!" proclaimed David loudly. "That's a very astute observation!"

"No, no, no, I want to hear wha' this guy jus' said!" said Becan.

David's volume remained high. "Maybe Strom will take the mantle of Vector one day! Wouldn't that be something? Hoo-boy!"

"I said I'm here to make a difference," said Zigler back to Becan. "Not to hit every piece of meat I come across."

David leaned back calmly and said, "Ah well, I tried."

Natasha shot to a stand herself. "Hit every piece of vecking *meat*?"

"Someone here better shut down this bucket o' snots before I knock his bleedin' lights ou'," Becan said.

"Bonding," Scott said flatly, looking at David. "This is bonding."

Zigler snarled at Becan, "I can't wait till I'm in charge of you, leprechaun."

"I can't wait till you die first," shot back Becan. The situation was devolving at breakneck speed.

Slamming his palms hard on the table, Michael glared at Zigler from farther down. "All right, this is what we're gonna do. You're both gonna stop bickering, you're gonna get back to drinking, and we're all gonna change the subject. Got it?"

"Who put you in charge?" Zigler asked.

"Boy, I'm 'bout to break you."

John motioned Michael's way and said to Zigler, "You do know he was a bouncer before this, right?"

"You have no *idea* who you're messing with," said Zigler to Michael.

This time, it was Shekeia who erupted. Slapping her own palms on the table, she glared daggers at Zigler. "No, *you* have no idea who you're messing with. I don't appreciate what you said about my friend, and I don't appreciate the way you're talking to my new teammates. We came to this bar because you insisted it was a great way to bond, but I swear to God, if you don't shut that punk mouth, I'mma take you out back and beat your face in. That's what it is, that's how it's gonna be. Understand?"

He waved her off. "Whatever."

"Oh, mm-mm, we 'bout to go."

And they *were* about to go. Scott could sense the aggression hovering around them like a black cloud. He knew that feeling well—that precursor to physical violence. He'd felt it many times in locker rooms and on the football field. This was on the precipice of changing from a shouting match to a one-sided brawl—and if someone didn't interject, Zigler would be rendered a bloodied heap on the floor of *The Black Cherry* by his own devices.

And so Scott interjected. Pointing straight at Zigler from his seat and raising his voice, not to shout, but to simply be heard, he said, "I'm going to make a prediction about you." He paused. "You're going to be one of the best members of this team."

From his seat, David raised an eyebrow. The others around Scott looked his way confoundedly. But at least the shouting had stopped.

Seeming to be momentarily taken aback, Zigler blinked and said, "I already know that—"

"Not for the reason you might think," Scott said, tactfully cutting him off. "It's because you care. You care about all of this. I mean, you heard Tacker's words and you took the initiative." He gestured to the table at large. "You arranged for everyone to get out here. You led the toast when we arrived, you're talking about things that matter to the war effort. You've got passion." He allowed himself to take a beat. "I had some guys on my college team with passion like yours. But you've got to learn to channel it. Keep the enemies out there." He pointed outside as if Bakma soldiers might be lurking about. "I know that deep down inside, you're afraid you don't belong here. That's okay. I am, too."

Almost immediately, David spoke up. "Me too."

Scott glanced over at him and then nodded. His roommate had his back in this. A few others, seeming to realize what Scott was actually doing, echoed the sentiment. Scott's gaze returned to Zigler. "But you do belong here. We all do. And it's just a matter of time until Tacker sees that. So prove it to him. Prove it to us. Channel that passion in the right way, and you're gonna fly up the ranks like you're a Faerber yourself."

The table fell quiet—or as quiet as it could fall, considering the revelry going on all around them. But in their case, and mercifully, the shouting had ceased—and a sheepish expression rested solely on Zigler's face as if he'd suddenly realized what he'd done. His voice far lower and more uncertain than it'd been at any time, he said to Scott simply, "Thanks..."

Scott smiled. "No problem, man."

Face tinging red, Zigler looked at Natasha. "Yeah, umm. I didn't mean all that. I was just—"

"It's fine," Natasha said abruptly, her voice sounding like she just wanted to move on.

Clearing his throat, David said to the group, "So for future reference, everyone, next time we get in a bar fight, it's supposed to be with *other* people."

Several in the group chuckled, Scott included.

David leaned over toward him. "Nice work," he quietly said.

At the same time, Scott caught sight of Shekeia, who was looking at him with a knowing smile of her own. Winking as if to say, "I see what you did, there," she raised her glass to him. Dipping his head in her direction, Scott took a drink of water.

Several seats down, Becan looked at Natasha and said, "Jus' so yeh know for whenever I'm pickin' on yeh, I don't think you're a piece o' meat. I just think you're kinda groovy."

Eyeing him for a moment, she slowly smiled. "Kinda groovy, huh?"

"Yeah, yeh know...cat's meow an' bee's knees an' all."

She laughed—with genuine warmth. "You're a dork. But you're kinda groovy, too."

The room began to beep. Scott blinked, the sound seeming to emanate from every direction. He and the soldiers around him glanced about the table. The beeps were loud; they were sequenced. The soldiers' collective focus shifted from the room down to their belts. Right to their comms.

A mission tone out.

The soldiers' jaws dropped, and for almost five full seconds, they stared dumbfounded. Then all hell broke loose. Everyone leapt backward from the table, their drinks and chairs toppling to the floor. The other patrons of the bar turned to the sudden chaos.

Falcon Squad bolted out the door—Scott glanced at the soldiers following him. "How much time did Tacker say we had?"

"Five minutes!" David answered.

"Like hell we're gettin' back in five minutes!" Becan said.

As everyone else piled in, Scott threw himself into the driver's seat of one of the vehicles and engaged the ignition. "We can make it!" The vehicle next to him, driven by John, roared and peeled out of *The Black Cherry*'s parking lot.

The drag race back to *Richmond* was pure chaos. Amid the screech of tires and the blasts of horns, the EDEN vehicles tore through the city streets. The military highway that led to *Richmond* base was on the city's outskirts, and traffic was dense. By the time they got there, it was 1817. They had received the call at 1809. *Richmond* loomed far in the distance, and the accelerators were slammed to the floorboards.

Scott radioed the EDEN checkpoints as they approached the airstrip, and they were given clearance to bypass the gates and go directly to the field. The vehicles skidded to halts on the tarmac as the clock read 1825. Eleven minutes late...and counting.

The soldiers reached the hangar eighteen minutes after the initial tone out—and thirteen minutes past the response time threshold. As the Falcons gasped for breath, their eyes scanned the hangar for any signs of life. They found only Executor Tacker. He wasn't difficult to spot—he was the only man in the hangar. There weren't even technicians about. The Vulture transports were there, though none were prepped for flight.

As the pace of the soldiers slowed, a wave of confusion washed over them. Something was not right. At that moment, Scott made the realization. He groaned, bent forward, and propped his hands against his knees.

It had been a test. It had been a vecking test.

Tacker's wicked glare scrutinized them. The soldiers knew they were in trouble as soon as he spoke. "I regret to inform the city of Cincinnati that, due to the inability of Falcon to reach its transport in time, a dozen citizens met untimely deaths while waiting for help to arrive." The soldiers buckled over in exhaustion, and the executor spoke into his comm. "Thank you, Command," he said. "It's over."

"Our pleasure, executor," the comm crackled. The beeping stopped. The hangar fell silent.

Tacker's scowl found Shekeia. "Ms. Rhodes, how long did I tell you that you had to reach the hangar for a tone out?"

Shekeia lowered her head, loose braids falling over her face. "Five minutes, sir."

Tacker shifted to Michael. "Can you vouch for that?"

The medic's shoulders sunk. "Yes, sir."

"Anyone want to guess how late you are?" Tacker asked. None of the soldiers spoke. "Oh, come on now, no one wants to venture a guess?" Once again, no one replied. Tacker's glare narrowed further. "Thirteen minutes late. *Thirteen* minutes. That, my fellow soldiers, is not pathetic. It goes *far* beyond pathetic. This is absolutely pitiful. This is worthless."

The soldiers bent forward as they caught their breaths.

"Stand up straight!"

Falcon Squad snapped upright. Their hands shot to their sides.

"You have brought shame and humiliation to this squad, and you haven't even been in it for a day! If this would have been a real call, people would have died because of you." Still surveying the Falcons, he stopped when he caught sight of Lexie. "Private Robinson, I presume?"

The Australian stammered, "Yes, sir."

"Hell of a first impression, private. I noticed your gear is sitting untouched in the transport. Any particular reason why you didn't link your comm up like everyone is supposed to upon first assignment?"

"I..." She swallowed. "I don't know, sir."

Hands on his hips, he stared her down. "You don't know?"

"No, sir." Her voice was shaking—the two words were barely discernable.

Tacker scanned the group at large. "Where in the world were all of you that it took *eighteen minutes* to get to the hangar?"

After a short span of silence, it was David who answered. "At a bar, sir."

"At a *bar?*" Tacker's eyes narrowed. "Let me guess. *The Black Cherry.*"

Pressing his lips together, David nodded a single time. "Yes, sir."

"Unbelievable."

Scott's stomach twisted. How could they have been so stupid? He was infuriated at himself for succumbing to the peer pressure. He should have stayed behind, even if it'd been by himself, instead of letting Zigler, in all his wisdom, lead them to a bar. Right into a trap.

Inhaling a long, hard breath through his nostrils, Tacker said, "Although I hoped tonight would turn out differently, I came prepared for the possibility that this would be the result. Everyone, walk with me." Turning away, Tacker marched out of the hangar toward the training grounds. As the group followed behind him, he spoke on. "On the training grounds, we have a course called Mud Lake. As the name implies, it creates quite a mess. I instructed some of the staff to spray it down this evening. To make it 'memorable' in the event my soldiers would have to run it. If you look ahead, you can see they're still wetting it."

Sure enough, Scott could see numerous individuals with water hoses spraying the ground. His body shivered. He knew what was coming.

"Mud Lake is not an obstacle course. There are no rope ladders to climb, no bars to crawl under. It's just seventy-five yards of knee-deep muck. It's a slog."

Behind Scott, he could hear Natasha whisper, "I'm gonna *kill* you, Zigler."

Oblivious to her words, Tacker went on. "At the start position, you'll find twelve backstraps. Attached to each backstrap are four sandbags—approximately a hundred and twenty pounds of dead weight, comparable to carrying a small civilian out of a hot zone. My thought tonight was that each of you would have to run Mud Lake once for every minute you were late, all while carrying a sandbag citizen on your back. I'll be honest: I thought you *might* be running one or two laps if you were late at all. Never did I imagine you'd be *thirteen* minutes late." Stopping at the precipice of the run, Tacker set his hands on his hips. "But that's your fault, not mine."

Scott surveyed the muddy field before them. In his head, he did the math. *This thing is seventy-five yards. A run to one end, then back again, is one fifty. We run that six times plus change, and it's...*

His shoulders sunk.

...ten football fields.

Ten football fields. Carrying sandbags. His hazel eyes turned to the men with the hoses who were watering it down. This was going to be miserable.

"Who's going to volunteer to demonstrate?" Tacker asked, his back still to the soldiers as he stared at Mud Lake.

Someone answered without hesitation. "I will, sir." Scott looked to his left, where he saw David step forward. The other Falcons watched him, as well.

Tacker turned to look back at David. For the faintest of moments, Scott thought he saw admiration on the executor's face. But the moment was short-lived. "As you wish. Jurgen," Tacker said, pointing to the collection of backstraps and sandbags, "suit up and start."

Ever so faintly, Scott heard David sigh. Stepping into the knee-deep mud, the former NYPD officer trudged toward the backstraps. When he drew within feet of them, Tacker subtly nodded to some of the nearby men with hoses. A second later, each hose was trained on David's head. David let loose an utterance of disgust as he was pelted. He was saturated instantly.

The act of putting on the backstrap, something that should have been simple, was made considerably more challenging by the mud and water jets. Even with his head down to force the water to hit his scalp, David was grimacing. Finally maneuvering the backstrap into place, he set off on the first leg of the journey—heavy step by agonizingly heavy step.

Tacker spoke as David marched. "There is no stopping. There is no 'not finishing.' After and only after everyone has completed the course is anyone allowed to leave."

Scott frowned as he watched David deflect jets of water with the top of his head. With no one else out there, he was an open target for everyone with a hose. It was time to change that. Without a prompt from Tacker, Scott marched into the mud to retrieve his own backstrap. He could sense Tacker looking at him from behind, though he didn't turn his head back to see him. Scott just waited for the water. It didn't take long. David's torment was momentarily staved as the water found Scott—and just like David, Scott had to lower his head just to be able to see. Lowering himself into the mud, he maneuvered his backstrap into place. It wasn't until he'd finished that he realized someone else had come with him. Jayden. The now-sopping-wet Texan was right there with Scott.

"Let this show you the price of being careless," Tacker said as the rest of Falcon Squad entered the mire. "It will be worse if you fail a second time."

There would be no second time. Even as water pelted him, even as he strained to move forward through the muck, Scott's determination was steadfast. This punishment he would not earn again.

Throughout the entirety of the run, none of the Falcons spoke. They barely even looked at one another. The sole moment of attempted cama-raderie came courtesy of Becan, who once trudged over to Natasha to help her from where she'd nearly faceplanted after a fall. The effort was short-lived, however, as the men with the hoses ordered Becan to move on without her. She had to get up on her own. Scott heard Becan utter a single word—*bollocks*—before he left Natasha to pick herself up out of the mud.

By the time the run was through, everyone had taken their share of wrong steps in the uneven field. Ironically, the only time the soldiers' heads weren't targeted by hoses was when their faces were utterly caked over—a subtle but stinging act of cruelty. By the time the last of them finished—Lexie Robinson—every single one of them was covered from head to toe. No one was there to offer any words of encouragement or consolation upon the run's completion. The men with the hoses simply left. As for Tacker, he'd left long ago.

At the very least, the hoses remained, enabling the Falcons to take turns hosing each other off. The men looked like they'd just left a war zone—the women, like drowned rats. Everyone looked disgusted by what'd transpired. As for Zigler, the organizer of this travesty, he got special treatment when his turn came to clean off. Every hose a Falcon claimed was targeted at his head—even long after the mud had washed off.

As they'd been the first to initiate the run, so too were Scott, David, and Jayden the last to leave the hangar after the hosing off was finished. Though they hadn't been instructed to by Tacker, the three men collected the hoses and put them away in hangar storage. They wanted to leave on that personal high note, even if it went unnoticed by anyone else. They needed their own moral win.

Scott never saw anyone else from Falcon that night, with one touching but sad exception. As he walked past Michael's room after taking a shower, he heard the hushed chokes of a young woman sobbing. A look through the cracked door revealed Lexie with her head buried in Michael's chest, the pilot releasing what little she must have had left. Scott watched secretly for a moment as Michael held her like a bodyguard, *shhh*-ing and whispering in his rich voice, "It's okay." It both warmed Scott's heart and broke it. Unseen to them, Scott moved on quietly to Room 419.

And thus, he and his comrades' first full day at EDEN was complete. To say it hadn't gone as Scott had hoped was an understatement to the extreme. But he knew enough to know that sometimes, the most important lessons were the ones learned the hardest. This one was learned hard.

Sleep came quickly for him and his counterparts that night. After their run through Mud Lake, none of them wanted the day to last any longer than it had to. Day one had come to a close.

What day two had in store, they were eager to find out.

5

SCOTT'S EYES CRACKED open, and he squinted through the darkness of his room. It was morning. Late morning. His body felt like dead weight, and an effort to lift his head resulted in an almost frightening level of limpness.

The Falcons' run of Mud Lake felt like a dream. He knew that several people had vomited over the course of the exercise, but he couldn't remember who. Everyone ended the run in a cold, mud-caked mess. And completely demoralized.

He looked at the clock and groaned. It was 0830. He had overslept for church. Despite the hit that the alien incursions had taken on organized religion, EDEN bases were still required to provide early morning services for a variety of faiths. In *Philadelphia*, he'd never missed a service. Now, here in *Richmond*, he was 0-for-1.

Closing his eyes, he drew a deep breath and then sighed. What a failure yesterday had been. What a totally predictable failure. It was easy to make Zigler the scapegoat for the whole ordeal, but the truth was, he had no one to blame but himself for succumbing to peer pressure. For letting himself down.

Mustering the strength and willpower to move his numb body, he slipped out of bed and stumbled to the sink, wetting his face with cold water. He padded to the closet and glanced at the upper bunk. David was still asleep.

Tugging up the zipper of his uniform, Scott gave a silent glance around the room. He crept to the door, opened it, and stepped into the hall.

Scott was not one known to make poor decisions. Good decision-making was a hallmark of the quarterback position. It was also utterly necessary when trying to live a life of faith. Going to *The Black Cherry* had been an uncharacteristic error. He'd known better—and the worst part was that he'd tried to justify it by thinking of Nicole's words about establishing camaraderie with his teammates. He should have passed on the bar and just called her again.

All these thoughts led to a frightening possibility: What if he wasn't as good at making decisions as he thought? What if his decision to join EDEN had been a mistake? What if he'd misinterpreted what he'd felt God was telling him—where God was leading him? What if Nicole's initial skepticism had been warranted?

Scott knew enough to know that on the heels of such an emotionally deflating personal failure as *The Black Cherry*, he was bound to have thoughts such as the ones he was having now. Such was the nature of feelings. All he could do was hope and pray that he truly was where he was meant to be.

The hallways were empty, which felt normal for a Sunday. After approaching a hall directory, Scott searched for Tacker's office. He found it and began walking in that direction.

Scott remembered vividly when the first thoughts of joining EDEN had entered his head. It'd happened in his sophomore year at Michigan's Fall Festival— a day-long Saturday event held every year on campus. Game booths, gathering tables, and food abounded. It was like an old-fashioned American fair.

Every year, a dunk tank was part of the festivities. On that particular year, the ones in the hot seat were football players. Scott, however, was not among them. Instead of being plunged into cold water, his job was to walk around the area picking up trash, collecting tickets, and occasionally making a run for dry towels. That evening, the task of draining and breaking down the tank had been left to him alone.

Nicole, who'd been assisting with a food stand on the other side of the pavilion, sought him out after her own tasks were finished. After she feigned disappointment in seeing him dry, he told her the honest truth: he just wasn't important enough to get dunked. Her rebuttal was a single word accompanied by a smile and a wink. "Yet."

Correlating one's importance to the world with something as frivolous as their level of participation in a dunk tank was ridiculous, Scott knew. But it spoke to a higher point. What was he doing? What was his plan? As a collegiate backup quarterback, how was he making any contribution to a world under attack? That day marked the first time he honestly asked himself, "Am I really where God wants me to be?" Through much time, thought, and prayer, the answer ultimately became *no*. And the more he thought upon it, the more another answer became clearer and clearer. He needed to sign up with EDEN. He couldn't explain why. There was no history of military service in his family. But that draw was there. That urging on his heart, that unsettling discomfort that came with knowing what one had to do but not yet having done it. That discomfort left him the day he enlisted.

And for Nicole, her discomfort began.

Still, that day at the festival never left them. It was still something they referenced, often accompanied by a wink, a smile, and her assurance that someday, he'd be big enough to dunk. He'd settle for just fulfilling his purpose.

Before he knew it, he stood before Tacker's door. The golden letters—Executor John Tacker—glared imposingly at him from the woodwork. What was he doing? Seeking out Tacker to apologize? This wasn't like football. An apology and a victory next week wouldn't erase a mistake of this caliber. This was EDEN. This was Earth. An errant throw could be rectified. The loss of lives could not.

His fist reached for the door, where it hovered against the wood. What would he say? That he was sorry? That it wouldn't happen again? That it was a rookie mistake? It was only a drill, but it was a telling one. Had it been real, citizens would have died. Graves would have been dug. They would have failed.

His hand returned to his side. The hallway remained silent as he continued to stare at the door. Finally, he pivoted his feet away from the door and walked slowly back down the hall. An apology would be useless. Tacker wouldn't want to hear it anyway. He probably wasn't even there.

David was still asleep when Scott returned to his room. It was easier to slide out of uniform than to climb in it, so Scott stripped to his boxers and hung his uniform with little disturbance. He brushed back the sheets of his bed and slipped under the covers. His eyes closed, and he fell back asleep.

* * *

WHEN SCOTT OPENED his eyes again, the lights were still off. The upper bunk was still silent. The room was still idle. He glanced at the clock. Almost 1000.

He wrenched himself out of bed, stretched, and looked into David's bunk, though David wasn't there. The room had been abandoned. With little else to do, Scott donned his uniform and stepped out into the hall.

He regretted not knocking on Tacker's door to apologize earlier but decided not to rectify the issue by doing it now. Instead, he wanted to remember the guilt of not following through. Of not owning up when he knew he should have. He wanted to remember it so that there would be no hesitation when the next opportunity to step up presented itself.

For now, he would search for his roommate.

The search did not take long. The nearest point of interest was the soldiers' lounge, and it was there that Scott found David, along with Becan, Henry, and Natasha. About a dozen people were in the room, and the four from Falcon Squad sat together at a table in the back corner. Scott weaved through the tables toward them.

David saw him first. "What's up, compadre?"

Scott stifled a yawn. He still felt tired despite his second round of sleep. "Not much...what are you guys up to?"

"Just talking about last night."

"Oh." He looked at Becan. "Where's Jay?"

"At the range," Becan answered. "Left there early this mornin'. Been there ever since, he has."

"He went by himself?"

"He did. Never said much o' nothin', jus' went."

That seemed to track for someone like Jayden. Pulling a chair up to the table and sitting down, Scott asked, "How long you guys been here?"

"About an hour," Natasha answered. "We probably spent most of that time talking about food." She laughed.

"Food?"

"Yeah, we ate together earlier. It was *bad*."

"What'd they have?"

"It's still up for debate."

"Wow," Scott said. "That's bad."

Henry blew out a breath, wincing as he did so. "You hurting as much as we are?"

Scott nodded. "If you think you hurt now, wait till tomorrow when the soreness sets in. That's gonna be killer."

Natasha smiled. "I don't know, this feels pretty killer. I'm tired, too. I woke up completely out of it; I haven't felt this bad since the first month of *Philadelphia*."

Scott laughed.

"What?"

"I loved my first month in *Philadelphia*."

Natasha *ugh*-ed. "Not me. The morning musters killed me. I am *not* an early bird."

"We got up real early in the force," David said. "*Real* early. When I was new it was hard to get used to, but after the first week or so, I loved it. Even on my off days, I'd get up before sunrise. It's just better in the morning."

Natasha leered. "I guess the Academy was a cakewalk for you then, right?"

"It wasn't a problem for me at all. I was used to it before I got there. As long as there's a pot of coffee in walking distance, I'm good to go."

Scott smiled. "I love coffee." There was nothing like the aroma of fresh brew to perk the nostrils. It alone could lure him out of bed on even the worst of mornings. "Speaking of which," he said as he stood up to fix himself a cup.

"I don't like it," Becan said. "Breakfast tea, now tha's grand."

"So what do you guys think about last night?" Scott asked.

"I think Zigler deserves a beating for convincing us all to go out," David said.

Natasha eyed him. "He deserves a beating for more than just that."

"The truth of the matter is, though," David said, "we all should have known better. Props to you, Scott, for trying to talk us out of it. We should've listened."

Sitting down with his coffee, Scott half-smirked. "Well, I was right there with you guys in the end, so don't give me too much credit."

David leaned back and folded his arms. "What makes this really bad is that they preach to us from day one about responsibility. I hate that I just went along with it. Going to bars isn't even my lifestyle. I dropped the ball."

With a harrumph, Becan said, "I think it was bollocks tha' he gave a test at all. I mean, tha' was day-bloody-one. Let us live a little bit, righ'?"

"I have no problem with him doing it," David said. "We got careless, and we got what we deserved. What if it were real? Those civilian deaths would've been on *us*."

"I think they should let people have the first nigh' to themselves," Becan answered. "Go ou', get steamed, get it out o' your system."

"As a soldier, you can't do that, though. We're on call twenty-four, seven—"

"Righ', righ', I know tha'. I know yeh got a point, I know it was a mistake. I just…veck, I wish we wouldn't have fallen for it. Tha's so clichéd, drillin' us on our first nigh'."

David looked across the table. "What do you think, Henry? You're quiet over there."

Scott followed David's gaze Henry's way. Henry was one of the soldiers he felt he knew the least, so he was eager to hear his thoughts on the matter.

Henry's mouth fell open. "Uhh…I don't know. I just…for me, I guess it was kind of a reality check."

"What do you mean?" Scott asked.

"It's just, when the comms started going off, it hit me. When it was all over, I wasn't even worried about what Tacker was saying. That didn't matter to me much. It's just when the comms started going off, that's what I remember. I remember thinking, oh veck, I really have to do it now."

"You mean fight?" asked David.

"Well…yeah. The first thing that popped into my head was that I could die tonight."

Becan said kindly enough, "Henry, tha's a *baaad* way to go abou' lookin' at it. Yeh can't be thinkin' like tha'…I mean, yeh start thinkin' like tha' in the middle of a war, an'—"

"Yeah, I know that. That's what made me start to really think about this."

David shook his head. "Think about what? EDEN?"

"Yeah. I hope this was the right thing for me to do."

"Henry, bud, you shouldn't be thinking about that *now*. That's something you think about before you sign the papers."

"I know, I know."

"Wha' made yeh decide to sign on, then?" Becan asked.

Henry reflected. "It's like…I just wanted to do it. I don't want to just do nothing. Everyone has their thing. I guess I didn't want mine to be talk-selling."

"That's a hell of a change of pace for the sake of changing pace," said David.

Hesitating a bit before going on, Henry said, "I guess a part of it was also just the respect factor, you know? I mean…I literally knocked on total strangers' doors trying to sell stuff. That doesn't exactly scream 'hero material.' But here, I can actually do something that makes a difference."

"But wha' if yeh die or get blown to bits?" Becan asked. "Is tha' better than talk-sellin'?"

"Yeah," Henry answered. "I thought it was, anyway. That's why I don't know now. It's like…that's how I came into it. I thought I wouldn't care about dying and stuff. Then last night came and it was like *bam*, this is real."

David leaned forward against the table. "It's a little late to be asking this, but are you ready for what you signed up for?"

"I want to be ready," he answered. "I'm trying."

Silence fell over the table. David leaned back again. "All right. I guess that's the best you can do."

The best he could do. That was really the story of what everyone was doing—the best that they could. It was admirable that Henry was trying to make a difference, even if he did seem to be questioning that decision now. He'd still stepped away from a relatively normal life to take up arms against the alien threat. Scott could relate to that.

It was strange the way the Alien War had redefined normalcy. The fact that quarterbacks, talk-sellers, and police officers could still exist spoke to the blurring of the lines between existential species crisis and life-as-it'd-always-been. But it hadn't started that way.

When the aliens appeared and attacked for the first time in 0002 NE, everything across the planet ground to a halt. Schools closed. Planes stopped flying. People hunkered down in their homes. The entire population of Earth braced for the impact of whatever was coming. The first year of the alien invasion had been dubbed *The Lost Year* simply because, during that time, it was as if the world had locked up. For all anyone knew, this was an extinction-level event. What was the point in loading kids onto school buses if the planet could count its remaining years on one hand?

It took the passing of that year for the realization to sink in that full-scale invasion didn't seem to be part of whatever the aliens were doing. Quite the contrary, their attacks always seemed to be followed up by periods of inactivity—as if humanity was being granted time to recover. By the time the first anniversary of the Alien War came, society was ready to move on—or at the very least, stop the alien attacks from dictating how life on Earth would be lived.

Schools resumed. Athletic events returned. Department stores reopened their doors. Everyday life went back to being everyday life, plus aliens.

Of course, EDEN had a massive part in that. One of its chief original goals was to allow humanity to return to being humanity. To allow life to continue. Yes, some things would be different—they had to be. But kids still needed to play baseball. People still needed to fall in love and get married. They still needed jobs to help pay the bills. Just as much as EDEN's mission was to defeat the alien threat, it was also to safeguard against the redefinition of life and living as a human being.

As the years passed and EDEN established itself, people grew tired of hearing about extraterrestrials all the time. And *with* EDEN there to protect humanity, the impact of the alien incursions dropped dramatically. Sometimes, aliens wouldn't attack for months, making it possible to even forget they were there. And that was what everyone wanted: to forget they were there. It was easier said than done, but at times, it actually seemed possible.

For Scott, going to college had done the most for his sense of life returning to some kind of normal. He'd barely recovered from the shock of his parents dying when first contact occurred. He'd spent years trying to figure out what his "new normal" was. Going to Michigan helped—even if he was a twenty-year-old freshman at the time. That was indeed one of the oddities of the Alien War. An entire year's worth of public education had been placed on hold for everyone. Though long-distance learning became a staple for many, nothing could replace being there with actual human beings in actual classrooms. Every country handled the reopening of schools differently. In the United States, all students simply picked up where they left off, just one year older. Even so, Scott waited an entire extra year after graduating high school before he enrolled in Michigan, as did many who were still trying to figure things out. The time off was good. It helped him focus…and shake the rust off his throwing arm.

Scott's thoughts, which had been wandering, returned to the conversation at the table.

"So wha' are yis theories abou' the war?" Becan asked. "Anny thoughts as to why we migh' even be in it?"

Natasha wrinkled her forehead. "You know what's funny? They never once mentioned that in *Philadelphia*. Theories."

"That's probably on purpose," David said. "They want to control the dissemination of information and don't want theories running rampant until they know something themselves."

"So when are they going to know something? I mean...how long has it been now? Ten years?"

"Nine. They came two years into the New Era."

"That's right," Henry said. "It was that January. It happened a week before the Second Annual World Peace Celebration."

David smiled sardonically. "Ironic, huh?"

Even though it was nearly a decade ago, Scott remembered that day like yesterday. Everyone did. Friday, January 11TH, 0002 NE. The world was anticipating the World Peace Celebration: the WPC. It was the day that honored mankind's transition from Old Era to New Era, an era of global harmony.

At 3:14 in the afternoon, local time, humanity made first contact with extraterrestrials in Hong Kong. It was the Bakma. Four of their Noboats—alien attack ships that could completely dematerialize from view—appeared over the city. There wasn't even time for humanity to hope for peaceful contact. The aliens engaged the moment they arrived. Thousands of citizens were killed before the Noboats vanished as mysteriously as they appeared, their ships disappearing into the sky. In fact, it was their sudden disappearance that gave birth to their names. When the ships vanished, the commander of Hong Kong's defense force asked his radar operator how many enemy 'boats' were still in the air. The radar operator's answer was obvious.

The world panicked, and EDEN was formed. The Earth Defense Network. Earth's unified attempt to defend itself from the very beings they sought to find for so long. For millennia, people wondered if they were alone in the galaxy. They finally had their answer.

By the time the Ceratopians and Ithini arrived in late May of that same year, there were three fully functional EDEN facilities on Earth: *Atlanta*, *Novosibirsk*, and *Berlin*. It was amazing how quickly EDEN was organized with a global community at the helm. It couldn't have been formed faster, as 0003 marked the year when the Alien War truly erupted. Incursions were no longer rare occurrences. They were commonplace. There were over one hundred and fifty alien attacks in 0003, as opposed to the five that took place in 0002. The increased attacks became the norm year after year. But they rarely consisted of more than a few skirmishes. For some reason, the aliens never seemed to bring the full load. It was still a mystery why.

Natasha leaned in toward David. "So nine years later, and we still don't know anything. Doesn't that strike anybody as a little weird?"

Scott nodded. Weird didn't begin to cover it.

"The news loves to talk about the Ithini Control Theory," said David.

"Well, it makes the most sense," said Scott. "The grays are the only ones that have been seen with both the Bakma and the Ceratopians."

"Then why don't the Bakma and the Ceratopians work together?"

"I don't know. I never said it was the right theory."

"So what do you think is going on?" Natasha pursed her lips.

David looked at her. "All I know is, I'm not sold on the Ithini being in control of anything. If you had the Bakma and the Ceratopians at your fingertips, why wouldn't you send them in together? Why wouldn't you put them in your own ships instead of sending them in theirs? We've never even seen an Ithini vessel. Imagine the Bakma and Ceratopians working side by side. Seems too good to pass up."

"Why don't we hear anything about interrogations?" asked Natasha. "They must've learned *something* by now."

"After *this* long? I'm sure they have," David answered. "It's just not something EDEN wants out in the public. That's all on a need-to-know basis and none of us need to know. The only thing we need to know how to do is shoot. We know the aliens are hostile—that's all that matters."

Henry looked at him. "How do we know they're *all* hostile?"

"Maybe shooting people is their customary way of saying hello," said Natasha.

"Sorry. Forget it."

Natasha giggled. "I'm just pickin'."

The table fell silent. Once again, Scott found himself lost in thought. It was a generally accepted fact by then that whatever the alien intruders were up to, invasion mustn't have been a part of it—at least, not yet. Their technology was vastly superior in almost all regards. With the number of spacecraft that'd attacked since the war began, it was clear they could amass invasion-sized forces. What was it they were after? *Was* it an invasion, just on their own timetable and in their own way? Was it some resource? No signs pointed to that as the answer. Science fiction had crafted a thousand narratives about what a war against hostile extraterrestrials might be like. None of those involved living an otherwise normal life, just occasionally with your eyes on the sky to make sure aliens didn't mess up your dinner plans, or your vacation, or your prom date. None of them predicted a war that was barely a war.

Yet, there they were.

Stretching his arms, Becan said, "Well, I think I'm gonna go an' check ou' the pool. Been itchin' to since we arrived."

Natasha eyed him for a moment before a slight grin emerged. "I could take a dip."

"Well, it'd be a pleasure to have yeh." He turned his gaze to the others. "Annyone else up for it?"

Scott waved them off politely. "No thanks, I'm still working on waking up. I don't want to drown in the pool."

Eyeing him coyly, Natasha asked, "What's the matter, Remington?" She licked her lips. "Afraid of a little mouth-to-mouth?"

"Man, you are *not* subtle," he said, laughing.

Placing her hand on his shoulder, she leaned into his ear and whispered, "But I *am* fun." Squeezing his shoulder a single time, she winked when he looked at her. Lifting a hand to wave, she said, "Ta, ta," and sashayed toward the door.

Rolling his eyes dramatically, Becan followed in her wake.

Several seconds after they'd left the room, Scott and David looked at one another. Amid sighs and chuckles, they shook their heads.

"That is a lost soul, right there," Scott said, half-smirking.

"That is *danger* flashing *danger*."

Eyes narrowed in confusion, Henry looked at Scott and asked, "Dude, did she just hit on you?"

Laughing, Scott shook his head. "So let me tell you what that is. That is a girl who likes trouble. I don't even think she cares where the trouble is. All that you just saw might have all been for Becan."

"Or," David said, "going for a swim with Becan might have been for *you*."

"That's the thing. You'll never know. It's playful till it's serious, but if you get serious, she'll tell you it's all play."

Tapping the edge of his coffee mug, David laughed and nodded.

"But like, she was being *open*," Henry said.

"Henry," Scott said, looking up at the ceiling before looking back at him, "she's playing the role she wants to play, which is disruptive flirt. She's said things to me. At *The Black Cherry*, she was all about Tacker. I guarantee, when they get in that pool, she's going to give Becan some eye candy."

Henry slumped back. "I want some eye candy."

"No, you do not," David said.

"Valer knows she's trouble, and she gets a kick out of it," Scott said.

"But at the *very* least," David said, lifting his mug as if in salute, "she's with someone right now who'll exercise sound judgment, not be led by his emotions, and handle things professionally."

At that, Scott laughed a little louder. "Right."

Natasha may have been a flirt, but if she ever wanted to pursue an *actual* relationship with someone, EDEN wouldn't stand in her way. One of the most striking differences between EDEN and Old Era militaries was in the realm of personal relationships. Though relationships between officers and enlisted were prohibited, the enlisted were free to pursue romantic endeavors with any other enlisted provided it didn't interfere with job performance or unit morale. Of course, the bar for what constituted an interference was low. Essentially, all a commanding officer had to say was, "Knock it off," and all extracurricular activities were expected to cease.

But by and large, EDEN was worlds more lenient than most militaries that preceded it. The general notion was that, with humanity facing an existential threat from the stars, soldiers would be allowed to hold onto as much of what made them human as they could get away with. Pursuing relationships with other humans definitely qualified.

Silence fell over the table; this time, Henry broke it. "I think I'm gonna head back to my room."

"You all right?" David asked.

"Yeah, I'm just tired."

"I think we're all pretty whipped up today," Scott said.

Henry stood up. "I'll talk to you guys later on."

"Later, bud."

"Take it easy, man."

The two men watched as Henry slipped out of the room. As soon as he was gone, David sighed. "I feel bad for him. He shouldn't be here."

Scott chuckled as he stared into his now-empty coffee cup. "You know who I feel bad for? Every person who leaves the table, because as soon as they're gone, we start talking about them."

"Yeah. That's why I'm leaving with *you*. I'm afraid you'll talk about me once I'm gone."

"Right, 'cause you know, I love to have conversations with myself."

"Right," David answered.

"I know what you mean, though. I thought about death before I signed up—I think everyone does. That's when you've got to come to grips with reality, not after you've gone through *Philadelphia*."

"Yeah," David said. "Just the same, I think I'll keep an extra eye on him."

Scott looked at the door where Henry had exited. "Yeah, I will, too."

After a second more, he rose from his chair. "I'm starving, man. I'm going to go grab a bite to eat."

"All right, man. I'll check you later."

The two men nodded to each other, stepped out of the soldiers' lounge, and went their separate ways.

What's my purpose for being here?

As Scott strolled through the hallways towards the cafeteria, thoughts of his own decision to enlist swirled in his head. Though he pitied Henry for what may have been a rash decision to join EDEN, part of Scott understood it well. It was the natural response to a quest for purpose. Scott had experienced the same thing when he'd signed on with EDEN.

As he strolled past the pool room with his hands in his pockets, Scott paused to look through the glass door. Sure enough, Becan and Natasha were in the pool—the former shirtless, the latter in full uniform as if Becan had just thrown her in. Splashing, wrestling, and laughing, the two looked like they were having a blast. He would never fall for the wiles of some other woman—especially one like Natasha—but he'd have been lying to himself if he said he wasn't a little bit envious of the fun frivolity.

I wish my girl was here.

Looking ahead, he strolled onward toward the cafeteria.

He had a purpose there. He was sure of it. The faith Nicole had put in him when he enlisted wouldn't be in vain. And Henry had a purpose there, too. So did David. So did Becan and Natasha. So did all of them. It was just a matter of trusting God and waiting to find out what those purposes were. And if his new comrades weren't people of faith, he'd have faith on their behalf.

Walking into the cafeteria, Scott grabbed himself a plate and sat down to eat.

The rest of the day was spent in routine. That evening, the members of Falcon Squad met in the hallway outside their rooms and discussed the day's events, from bad food to Tacker's discipline. When night came, they filed into their beds and slept.

This was the standard for the next few days, as group workouts and combat sessions took their place among morning activities. Life at *Richmond* took shape. Tacker never again mentioned the event that came to be known as the "Cincinnati Failure," nor were the soldiers late for any unit meetings. That lesson was learned.

The Falcon was ready for flight.

6

THE COMMS SOUNDED at a quarter to two, their piercing reverberations slicing through the silence of Room 419. Scott squinted in the darkness and sat upright in his bunk. *What in the world?* From the upper bunk, David stirred beneath the covers.

Beep! Beep! Beep!

It repeated for several seconds before Scott's eyes shot open wide. The comms! He leapt out of bed and scrambled toward the closet.

David blinked and propped up. His mouth hung open. "Wha—"

"The comms! The comms are going off!"

David repeated dazedly, "The comms are going off!" He dove to the floor and lunged for the closet. "We've got five minutes!"

Contorting his legs into his uniform, Scott said, "More like four!" He ripped his hands through his sleeves, tugged up the zipper, and grabbed his comm. "Let's go!"

They collided with Becan and Jayden as soon as they left the room. "This is it, boyos!" the Irishman exclaimed as they bolted down the hall, the other members of Falcon quickly joining them.

Technicians hurried back and forth across the hangar as soldiers piled into their Vulture transports. Right in the middle of it all was *Vulture-7*. Lilan, Tacker, and Henrick waited next to it.

"Everyone in the transport!" Tacker said. "Armor up. Robinson, prep for takeoff!"

The soldiers acknowledged with a unified *yes, sir* and dashed up the Vulture's ramp. They opened their lockers, where their combat armor awaited. As they strapped into their gear, Tacker ordered Lexie to lift. She acknowledged, and *Vulture-7* ascended over the airstrip.

Scott fastened his helmet and stared through the visor that covered his eyes. The illuminated heads-up display tapped into his weapon systems and health readout. He looked at Shekeia beside him. "You ready?" The moment the sensor in his visor registered her in his view, her name and vitals appeared on the HUD.

"I'm ready," she said, her voice shaking. "Are you ready?"

"I'm ready!"

Lilan stepped out from the cockpit, where he'd been sitting in the copilot's seat. "Executor, I have a call."

Tacker, loading his s-27 sniper rifle, nodded Lilan's way. "I've got them." His focus returned to the Falcons as Lilan returned to the cockpit beside Lexie. "Listen up, everyone! This is a hot drop. Approximately one hour ago, two Bakma Carriers entered Earth's atmosphere over Chicago with a full fighter escort! They dropped in the middle of the city, and all citizens have been instructed to shelter in place.

"The initial units that got dispatched got hit hard! We've been called in to provide additional support. Be prepared for extensive casualties!"

Across from Scott in the troop bay, Michael blew out a breath.

Tacker continued. "Noboats have *not* been reported, but that doesn't mean they aren't there! If anyone has reason to suspect they're above, alert someone immediately. If any materialize, take cover and hunker down! The city is out of power, so make sure your TCVS are on."

The soldiers acknowledged and activated the True-Color Vision in their visors. The world took on an ethereal hue.

Once again, Lilan emerged from the cockpit. After a brief word with Tacker, none of which Scott could decipher, the captain turned his attention to his soldiers. "Everyone, check your gear and get your minds right! This is what you all trained for. Let's save some lives!" He looked past the soldiers at Henrick, who was farther down in the troop bay. "Lieutenant." Henrick acknowledged and maneuvered through the troop bay, where he, Lilan, and Tacker began quietly conversing.

Scott looked down the troop bay at the rest of the Falcons. Though he couldn't see their whole faces through the visors, he could make out their body language. They were scared. They were nervous. Some fidgeted, while others sat rigid with their heads back. A palpable sense of danger hung in the air. This wasn't just some crashed spacecraft they were assaulting. This was a massive Bakma attack on an entire city—a rarity in this skirmish-filled war. This was being thrown into the fire. And so Scott, after his gear was checked over again, and again, and again, did the only thing he knew to do in the travel time he had.

He prayed. He prayed fervently. For himself, for his teammates. For the citizens of Chicago and the EDEN soldiers who were on the ground already. He prayed for everyone. About halfway through, he felt Shekeia's hand grip his firmly, the combat technician apparently having seen his head bowed and eyes closed. When he cracked his eyes to look at her, her head was bowed, too.

In what felt like no time, Tacker emerged from the cockpit to announce their descent. "Three minutes out, people!"

Hope for a smooth descent vanished as soon as *Vulture-7* entered Chicago. Ground plasma fire blasted against its metal hull. The pounding, though loud, would scarcely make a dent in the transport's armor.

"Touchdown in thirty!" Tacker said. "We're landing behind a barricade on South Michigan, so we should be able to exit without resistance. Nav data's going to your HUDS now!"

Sure enough, within seconds, the inside of Scott's visor illuminated with an overhead map of the landing zone.

"Stick together, and let's get to the barricade!"

The stomach-turning rush of a rapid descent kicked in, and landing thrusters roared. Seconds later, the Vulture clunked to a hard landing. The rear bay door lowered.

"Everyone out!" Tacker said. "Let's go!"

The remnants of a building lay strewed across South Michigan Avenue—the barricade. Weapons fire erupted on the other side. Burnt asphalt polluted the air. Injured soldiers littered the landing zone as their counterparts fired from atop the rubble. Above, a squadron of EDEN's Vindicator fighters streaked by.

Tacker pointed at Michael as the soldiers ran for the barricade. "Carter, start tending to these wounded!"

Michael disappeared into the throng of injured.

Tacker continued up the mound. "There's a company of Bakma en route to the barricade as we speak! Get to the summit and provide ground support. Be prepared for heavy resistance!"

Scott and Becan reached the summit of the barricade first, and their eyes immediately widened. Fire illuminated the cratered streets of South Michigan. Lightning-white plasma bolts streaked across the ground. Human shrieks were mixed with the weapons fire. It was a war zone. Bakma foot soldiers amassed in the streets. Even from a distance, their unmistakable black and brown armor identified them. Mingled with them were the brutish beasts themselves. Canrassis—the war beasts of the Bakma. They tromped ahead like miniature, fur-covered tyrannosaurs as Bakma riders sat firmly atop them and blasted the barricade with their mounted plasma cannons. The canrassis' soulless, round eyes—like the primary eyes of a spider—roamed the battlefield above their grotesquely oversized jaws.

Scott dropped to a knee and raised his E-35 assault rifle, but he held his fire for a moment. It was surreal. "Oh my God," he breathed.

Becan ducked to avoid plasma fire, and then he, too, raised his weapon. "There's no way in hell we're goin' to hold this off!"

David and Henry hit the summit next. Donald, harnessed with a minigun, followed.

Beside them, Jayden took cover behind a large piece of concrete and aimed around it with his sniper scope. *Pop!* He cracked the bolt-action. *Pop!*

David looked toward the Texan and then at Henry. "You okay over there?"

"Yeah!" Henry answered, voice cracking as he stumbled to avoid plasma fire. "I'm—I'm good!"

A white flash erupted several yards past Scott, and he felt the impact wave wash over him. Someone had been hit. He whipped around to see Zigler tumble backward down the barricade. Zigler's helmet smoldered, and he hollered.

Scott shouldered his E-35 and rushed toward the fallen soldier. "Hold still, I got you!"

Zigler struggled as he removed his helmet. A bloodied bruise bulged in the center of the soldier's forehead.

Grimacing, Scott asked, "You okay?"

"Yeah, watch out!" Zigler brushed past Scott, picked up his assault rifle, and charged back up the hill. Scott observed the soldier momentarily, then returned to Becan's side.

"He all righ'?"

"No."

Becan said nothing and continued to fire.

"EXECUTOR," LILAN said as he approached Tacker behind the barricade. "They've confirmed. Bakma reinforcements *are* coming in from farther down the road. We've gotta keep holding them."

Tacker nodded.

"We've got something else to worry about, though. There's a team from Cougar pinned down a couple blocks southwest of here near the Van Buren, South Wabash intersection. According to comm chatter, they're under direct assault from at least a dozen hostiles, and they're too wounded to put up any real resistance."

The executor crossed his arms. "And we're getting them out."

"Not you," Lilan said. "You're staying here. I'm sending Henrick after them. I want to give him a small team, just an in-and-out operation. They should be able to follow the shuttle rail that runs over the streets."

Tacker drew a breath. "With all due respect, sir, I wouldn't trust Henrick to walk my dog, let alone lead a rescue party."

"It's what we've got to work with," said Lilan. "You've spent more time with the alphas than I have. You got an idea of who you want to send?"

Rubbing the back of his neck, Tacker looked at the Falcons on the barricade. After a moment, he had his answer. A quick nod to Lilan confirmed it, and the captain patted him on the shoulder.

"It's all yours, executor."

Tacker queued up Falcon Squad on the comm. "Attention all Falcons, I want the following soldiers to meet me at the base of the mound: Lieutenant Henrick, Privates Jurgen, Remington, McCrae, Timmons, Valer, Donner, Carter."

Stopping briefly to turn around, Lilan said, "Too many, cut one loose!"

"Veck," Tacker whispered before he queued up the comm again. "Nix that, Jurgen, you stay put. Everyone else, meet with me." A minute later, the soldiers arrived. Tacker dropped to a knee to address them.

"Here's the deal, people. We've got some guys from Cougar Squad pinned down by Bakma several blocks southwest, by the intersection of South Wabash and Van Buren. Some are wounded. I want you to track their signal, get those Bakma off them, then get them back here. Search and rescue, not rocket science. There should be a shuttle rail going that direction—you should be able to just follow it from the ground." His focus shifted to Henrick. "Lieutenant, did the captain talk to you about this already?"

The lieutenant nodded. "Briefly, sir, but I get the gist."

Of Falcon's entire officer core, Scott knew Lieutenant Henrick the least. While the alpha privates primarily trained with Tacker, Henrick seemed to spend most of his time working with Lilan. The rumor was that Henrick, a new officer himself, was getting brought up to speed in the fine art of leadership. Scott certainly hoped that wasn't the case.

Tacker's eyes surveyed the privates, one after the other, until he finally sighed. After a brief shake of his head, he looked at Scott. "You ever start any games at Michigan, QB?"

"Uhh. Yes, sir."

"How'd you do?"

The truth hurt. "I went 1-2, sir."

"God help us." His focus shifted to the others. "Should Lieutenant Henrick fall, Remington is your designated second-in-command." Looking back at Scott, he asked, "That acceptable to you, private?"

Scott was taken aback. He was the XO for this op? It wasn't exactly like Tacker had a lot of options. He was clearly going with the only one among them who had been a leader of any sort. Nodding his head, Scott answered, "Yes, sir."

"Good. All right, gentlemen. Godspeed and bring those guys home."

The small band of soldiers moved immediately. Henrick led them to the far right of the mound, where he signaled them to gather around him. "We're going to use some side streets and alleyways. Check the nav points in your HUD."

Scott had no nav points on his HUD at all. A glance at Becan indicated that neither did the Irishman. Clearing his throat, Scott raised his hand to inform the lieutenant when he was abruptly cut off.

"Before you ask a question, let me explain the situation."

"Yes, sir, but—"

"*Before* you ask a question, let me explain the situation."

Raising both hands in defense, Scott went silent.

"As you can see, we're going to have to cross the barricade to get to the first alleyway. We'll all cross at once so we don't end up giving the Bakma a sequence to shoot at. Everyone got it?"

Scott opened his mouth again to tell Henrick that the nav points weren't there, but for a second time, Henrick spoke before Scott could get a word out.

"All right, good! Let's move on three. One, two, *three!*"

Henrick launched over the barricade and scampered toward the nearest alleyway. The others did the same. No plasma bolts followed them, and they soon found themselves alone and out of the Bakmas' collective sight.

This time, it was John who spoke up. "Am I the only one who doesn't have nav points here?"

"I don't have nav points," said Natasha quickly, as if trying to get the word in before Henrick could cut her off.

Henrick stopped his march down the alleyway and looked at him. "You don't have nav points?"

"No, sir."

"Who else doesn't have them?"

Every soldier on the team raised their hand.

Henrick spat. "Well, *veck*. The data network must be down."

Risking the repercussions of such an obvious suggestion, Scott asked, "Sir, did you send the points to us?"

"What?" Henrick asked, looking squarely at him.

"The nav points. Did you send them to us, sir?"

Lowering his weapon, Henrick approached him. "Everyone should have gotten them. I got mine right after I talked to the captain."

"Right," Scott said, "but at that time, we weren't even officially on the team yet. So I think you have to send them to us."

Natasha cleared her throat. "There should be an, umm, *send* icon."

Henrick looked down at his wrist, where a digital pad displayed what he was seeing on his HUD. After staring at it for a few moments, he tapped on the icon once, then several more times as he selected the targets to send to.

As soon as Scott's name was tapped, the nav points appeared in his HUD. "Got it!"

"Me, too!" said Becan. The other Falcons on the team acknowledged the same shortly after.

Natasha pointed to Henrick's wrist pad. "Sir, you might want to just assign us all to the same team to make things go faster. Just hit *custom*—"

"I know what I'm vecking doing, private," Henrick shot back.

At that moment, Scott realized it. *Oh God, he has no idea what he's doing.*

Henrick tapped on each team member's name as Natasha had prompted. As each person was added, their vitals appeared on everyone's HUDS.

Looking down at his own wrist pad, Scott cycled through them to ensure all were present.

"Okay," Henrick said, "according to what the captain told me earlier, there's a collapsed building about a hundred yards that way." He pointed to the end of the alleyway, where a rusty ladder was attached to a brick partition. "Let's get over that wall and make our way to it." Signaling them to follow, he trotted toward the ladder.

Becan, who'd lingered back with Scott, leaned over to him as soon as Henrick was out of earshot. "Wha's your confidence level?"

"Zero," Scott said.

It didn't take long for everyone to cross the wall, at which point they found themselves bunched together on the other side of the alleyway. It was perfectly symmetrical from the side whence they'd come, though it exited directly onto South Wabash—the main avenue they sought.

For the next several blocks, the rescue team was able to travel unhindered. Though exchanges of EDEN and Bakma weapons fire were constant, they seemed to be almost entirely on the other side of South Michigan. It wasn't until they'd trekked halfway to Cougar Squad's location that their first obstacle presented itself.

A pile of rubble walled off South Wabash, just as it did on South Michigan by the barricade. Unlike South Michigan, however, this rubble seemed impassable. A segment of the shuttle rail had collapsed, as had several buildings on the adjacent street, effectively sealing them in.

"Van Buren should be a little south of this rubble. We've got to find a way to cross it! Come on."

That Henrick's voice seemed to rise with his sense of urgency troubled Scott. Apparently, it troubled Becan, too.

"Great idea, jus' announce our presence to the world," he murmured.

All Scott could do was shake his head. "Maybe there's no Bakma here."

"If there are anny, they sure as bloody hell know where *we* are."

Jayden trotted up to them. "This guy's a moron," he whispered.

Moron or not, he was in charge. "Just follow his orders," Scott said.

Alternating between standing with his hands on his hips and being crouched in thought, Henrick stared at the mound of rubble with firm dedication. "We've got to find a way over this," he said.

John and Michael carefully tested several routes up the mound, only to have mini-avalanches force them hurriedly back down.

Meanwhile, Scott, Becan, Jayden, and Natasha were planning. "Look,"

Scott said, his eyes focused on the map on his HUD. "If we can go through that building that's right next to this mound of rubble, we can emerge pretty close to where we want to go."

"Yeah, I see it," said Jayden. "That might work."

Their discussion was interrupted when Henrick shouted their way. "Privates! What are you doing? Start testing routes up the mound!"

There he went again with that yelling. Walking briskly Henrick's way, Scott said, "Sir, we might have found an easier alternative route."

"I found a route, too," Henrick said, pointing at the mound. "It's over that mound!"

"I know, sir, but—"

The lieutenant walked directly up to Scott. "We're doing what we're doing! The longer you argue about it, the longer it'll take to find a way to get across. Now *move!*"

HUMAN AND BAKMA bodies littered South Michigan as Falcon Squad continued to engage. Numerous other squads fought alongside them, and the opposing forces stalemated.

Above the battle, a dogfight between EDEN Vindicators and Bakma Couriers—small, nimble Bakma fighters—broke loose.

BACK ON SOUTH WABASH, the search for a path up the rubble continued—as did the atmosphere of frustration and impatience.

Scott placed his boot on a chunk of concrete to test its weight. The moment he applied pressure to it, it rolled to the side, and several pieces of debris slid down on top of it. After backing away to avoid getting caught in a landslide, Scott faced Henrick again. "Sir, I *really* think you need to look at the alternative route we found."

In that instant, two sounds simultaneously erupted. The first was Henrick as he whipped around and shouted, *"Private Remington!"*

The second was plasma fire. Flashes of white streaked toward them, and Henrick, Scott, and John were jolted by the sheer force of the passing energy. A bolt struck Henrick in the chest, blood spatter from the impact splashing across Scott's armor as Scott stepped forward to catch Henrick before he fell. The gig was up. As the other soldiers on the team fell behind cover, Scott and John each took to one side of Henrick and ran for all they were worth to the building next to the mound—the very one Scott had tried to tell the lieutenant they could pass through.

From the other side of South Wabash, Becan howled in anger. "I'm up to ninety!"

Henrick moaned as John secured him against the wall. Pressed against the wall himself, Scott asked through the comm, "Can anyone over there see where that came from?"

Becan poked his head around from the corner of the alleyway he was hiding in, only to have a volley of plasma bolts hurled his way. He ducked back before his head was fried. "Best I could see they're on your side, abou' thirty or so meters from yeh! They're in the next alley down!"

"How many?" Scott asked.

"No bleedin' clue!"

Scott looked over at Henrick. The lieutenant's armor had been penetrated, and his chest had a sizzling sear. He was out of the fight.

Scott was in command.

Only days before, the guilt of not knocking on Tacker's door had consumed Scott. He'd sworn to himself that he would never hesitate again. He'd wanted to remember that feeling of personal failure for that reason. And now, he was the one.

There was no hesitation.

"All right everyone, listen up!"

From where he was still repositioning Henrick, John looked Scott's way.

"John and Natasha, lay down some suppression so Mike can get here to the lieutenant! Becan, get on the comm and inform Tacker of our status—tell him I've assumed command! Comm me when that's done."

"You got it, Remmy!" the Irishman replied through the comm.

Scott's focus shifted to Jayden. "Jay, I want you to gain entry to that building right in front of you and get as high as you can! Find a window and get in a good sniping position. As soon as you're set, let me know."

"Yes, sir!"

Enough playing around. Readying his weapon, Scott pressed against the corner nearest to where the Bakma were firing and leaned around to lay suppression of his own.

Within seconds—and with the help of Scott, Natasha, and John—Michael was able to sprint to Henrick's side without getting dropped. Sliding to his knees, he tore out his medical kit and went to work.

So did Scott. "Tasha, what's it looking like by you?"

Across the street and taking cover behind a vehicle, Natasha answered through the comm, "I've got three Bakma clustered on the other side of the building you're next to! There's another firing from behind a couple of cars in the middle of the street. I count four total!"

Becan's voice cut in. "Tacker's notified!"

Scott nodded instinctively, watching Becan reappear by the corner of the original alley they'd come from. In his head, the formation of a plan was in full swing. "Becan and Tasha, *distract*. Don't relent for a second! John and I will work through the building over here and see if we can pop out behind them on the other side. Jay, where are you?"

"Just got in position," the Texan answered.

"Can you confirm four hostiles?"

Jayden answered from the heightened window where he peered through his sniper scope, "Yeah, I can see 'em good. I count four, too."

"Can they see you?" Scott asked through the comm.

"Not right now."

"How many can you take before they're onto you?"

Jayden's eyes narrowed. "Two. The one in the street and one of the three behind the building."

"That'll work. Sit tight and I'll give you the signal once John and I are in position. We'll see if we can find a door and pop out behind them, and we'll hit them from both sides at once."

"Yes, sir!"

Scott looked behind to find John. The soldier was already on his side of the building, standing next to a steel emergency door that led inside. Scott hurried to him, weapon ready. "You get the plan?"

"Straight on through to the other side, catch them from behind," John answered.

"That's the plan. Let's go." Yanking the door open, Scott entered the building with John in tow.

Shifting from one side of her cover vehicle to the other, Natasha fired her weapon liberally, the tips of her red ponytail dancing beneath her helmet where motion had jarred it loose. A streak of white plasma soared past her shoulder, and for a moment, she shrunk back. Gritting her teeth, she rose again, took aim at the Bakma in the center of the street who'd fired at her, and returned a shot of her own.

Her bullet caught the alien in the thigh, and it stumbled to a knee. A split second later, she put one through its head.

Ducking back as the three Bakma in the alley shifted their focus to her, she screamed through the comm, "One Ex down! The one in the street!"

"Atta girl," said Scott as he and John traversed the building, which was some sort of combination office studio and showroom. Ahead, he could see a steel door similar to the one they'd entered through. Their ticket to the Bakmas' alley.

It was time.

"Jay, take who you can get!"

Easing the crosshairs in his scope over the head of one of the Bakma at the edge of the alley, Jayden quickly pulled the trigger. There was a puff of dark red, and the alien collapsed. "One down."

Cracking the bolt-action, he slid the crosshairs over a second target. Another squeeze, another drop.

"Two down! I got one left—he's fallin' back!"

The timing couldn't have been better. Just as Jayden announced the Bakmas' retreat, Scott and John made it to the steel door exiting the alley. Slamming his body into it, Scott burst into the alley just before the Bakma reached his position. The battle-scarred alien flinched and then aimed his weapon at Scott.

John got him first, the soldier firing at the unsuspecting Bakma before the Bakma realized a second human was there. Though the alien got a shot off, it went wildly off course as his body convulsed, and he fell backward. The alien kicked its legs briefly before quick bursts of fire from Scott and John ended its efforts.

Weapon exhaust filled the air. The Bakma lay crumpled and face-up on the concrete. Scott stared at their corpses. Shouldering their assault rifles, he and John approached them.

Scott had never seen Bakma at such close range before. Their cheekbones bulged from their purple, leathery skin. Their eyes, dark and without visible pupils, stared lifelessly skyward. Alien insignias adorned their chest plates in gold coloring, and their plasma rifles lay strewn beside their talon-like claws. Beneath them, puddles of dark red blood oozed. Scott propped his hands against his knees and gazed at them. Finally, after taking in the surreality of it all, he breathed into his comm, "Targets down."

TACKER DUCKED TO avoid plasma fire as he stumbled toward David atop the barricade. "Jurgen!"

David held his fire and looked back. "Yes, sir?"

"We have reinforcements of our own en route. They'll be here in ten minutes! Once they arrive, we're going to press over the mound and into the street. Be ready!" After David nodded, Tacker looked farther down at Henry. "How's he doing?"

David looked at Henry, who was alternating between firing wildly down the barricade and hugging the cover of a giant concrete block. Hesitating before answering, David finally said, "Very good, sir."

"You take care of him," Tacker said, slapping David's chest plate.

"Yes, sir."

Tacker nodded and continued across the barricade.

APPROACHING THE alley where his team had gathered around Henrick, Scott said, "All right guys, check in. How are we doing?" He glanced to the center of the street, where Jayden was the last to approach them, having descended from the building.

"Tha' was veckin' ace," said Becan enthusiastically.

Natasha said, "I think we're all good. What's next?"

What was next was evaluating Henrick. Walking up to Michael, who was still kneeling beside the groaning lieutenant, Scott crouched down. "How's he looking?"

"You want the simple answer or the full rundown?" Michael asked.

"Keep it simple."

Michael rose to his feet. "He's gonna live, but he ain't fightin'. Not anymore today."

"Can we move him?"

"His legs are fine."

That was good enough. "Lieutenant, we're going to get you up, sit tight. This is probably going to hurt."

"Oh, it'll hurt," Michael said.

"Wait, wait, wait," said Henrick through gritted teeth.

Scott grabbed him under one arm while Michael grabbed beneath the other. "No *wait* about it, sir, we've got to get to Cougar Squad." They didn't have the time to send him back to Tacker—and Scott couldn't afford to lose a member of his squad escorting him there, anyway. As Scott and Michael lifted, Henrick screamed in agony. Scott looked at Jayden. "Hey man, come take over for me." The Texan hurried Scott's way, trading places with him to take hold of Henrick.

Scott inspected the building they were next to—the one he'd tried to suggest to Henrick as an alternate way of getting to Cougar. He wondered if, in hindsight, the lieutenant wished he'd listened. It might have been better that he hadn't, at least for the group. Instead of opening fire on them in the street, those four Bakma might have quietly stalked them from behind and killed their whole team. But only one thing mattered now: this building was traversable.

"Yeah, we can definitely cross this," Scott said.

Becan glared at Henrick. "We should've done tha' in the first place."

"For all I knew, the foundation was damaged!" Henrick retorted.

Scott didn't bother with a response. Readying his weapon again, he pulled open a side door and stepped into the building, his team behind him.

Dust hung in the building, but it was passable through and through. The group exercised caution as they trekked from office to office until they emerged clean on the other side. South Wabash came into full view. Weapons fire echoed ahead, and Scott crept up the alley to the edge of the street. The scene was clear now. The pinned soldiers from Cougar Squad were taking cover behind two war-torn cars at the edge of a short structure. From farther down the street, plasma bolts rained in their direction.

"That looks bad," said Natasha in an effort of masterful understatement.

Bad didn't begin to describe it. "We're not going to get to them in the open—that plasma fire is too heavy. Let's take the inside route again and see if we can reach them through this next building. Come on."

The plan was set into motion, and the team traversed from one building to the next. When they reached the alley along the squat structure's edge, Scott searched for a door. He found one, but it was locked. He launched two solid kicks against the doorway, and it burst open.

"Find a room in here that can act as a temporary hospital," he told Michael. "We have to assume they have heavily wounded—they wouldn't still be here if they didn't. Jay, get as high as you can again, find a window, and work on those Bakma. You're on your own, go do your thing."

Jayden acknowledged and weaved up a stairwell. Scott led the rest of the team ahead. The structure was undamaged, though projectile and plasma fire erupted from beyond the walls. Muffled shouts echoed outside. They were close. When Scott stepped into the large room that formed the building's corner, it became clear why the soldiers were still outside.

Only one window offered access to the inside. The corner lacked anything else. Scott pressed against the edge of the window and peered outside. He could see the pinned soldiers. Three wounded were among them, sprawled out behind the cover vehicles. There was no way they'd last there. Plasma flashed toward the window, and Scott ducked back inside.

Three wounded. One window. The vehicles were on the verge of destruction. Scott knelt as the other soldiers watched him. His mind raced. The vehicles. If only the vehicles were closer to the window. Then, they'd have enough cover to ferry the wounded inside.

Maybe they could arrange that, themselves.

Scott leapt to a stand and returned to the window. "Guys!" he announced to the pinned unit. "Sit tight for one minute, we're on our way!" Spinning around to face John, he asked, "Can you hotwire a car?" John was all about fast cars. Maybe he'd picked up an extra thing or two along the way.

"Yeah, I can hotwire a car," John answered.

"Great. Take Becan with you and see if you can find a large vehicle— the bigger the better."

Listening in, Becan said, "I saw a big ol' van across the street on the way here."

A van. Perfect. "That'll work. Go get it. Becan, give him as much cover as you can. Once the van's started, you're going to park it right here in front of the window. We're extending the wall of cars."

"Righ'," Becan said. He and John retreated through the back of the building.

"Hurry!" Scott urged. "We don't have much time!"

Jayden knelt beside a fifth-floor window and leaned against the wall. He was right above the pinned soldiers—perfect position. He snaked his hand toward the window, unlocked it, and slid it upward just enough to give himself an opening to fire. Maneuvering himself away from the window itself to not make himself an easy target, he propped himself against the wall, aimed his rifle, and squinted through the scope. The Bakma suppressors were, as before, clustered in an alleyway farther down the street.

"Timmons to Command," he said through the comm.

Standing beside the window, Scott watched as Becan and John got into position across the street.

"Timmons to Command."

On the other side of the window, Natasha looked at him. "Hey." When Scott looked at her, she said, "You're Command."

"Oh, veck." Scott leaned away from the window to speak through his comm. "Go ahead, Jay."

Jayden continued to peer through his scope. "I'm in position by a window five stories up. I can count five or six Bakma up in an alley down the street—that's where all the fire's comin' from. You want me to start workin' on 'em?"

"Yes, please!"

"Roger." Sliding the crosshairs over a target Bakma, he held his breath and pulled the trigger. The Bakma's head burst, and the alien fell backward. He cracked the bolt action. "One down."

Becan and John bolted across the street. "Keep at 'em, cowboy!" Becan said. "We're goin' to need some time to hotwire!"

"I'm on 'em," Jayden answered. Another shot rang out. "Two down."

The Bakma suppressors held their fire as a third fell. Becan and John skidded to the van doors. They were unlocked. As Becan slid into the passenger seat, John opened the driver's side door and removed the panel beneath the wheel. A few wire twists later, the van's engine roared to life. As John leapt into the driver's seat, Becan shouted, "Go, go, go!"

John slammed the van into reverse and manhandled the wheel toward the wall of cars. Seconds later, it screeched to a stop in front of the window. Becan leapt from the passenger door as John climbed over the center console. The wall of cars was extended. The window was covered.

Time to move. "Come on," he said to Natasha, "let's go!" The two scampered out of the window, took cover behind the van with Becan and John, and dashed to the pinned soldiers behind the wall of cars.

A soldier whose armor was charred with scorch marks awaited them. "Delta Trooper Grammar of Cougar Squad, sir! We have three wounded. Everyone else is dead!"

"What's the condition of the wounded?" Scott asked.

"Well, we've been stuck behind this van, so not really too good!"

Scott looked back to the open window. "Can they be moved through that window?"

"Better than keeping them here, sir!"

Pivoting around, Scott said, "Becan, give us a hand! John and Tasha, come lay some cover fire!"

As Scott, Becan, and Grammar transferred the wounded through the window, John, Natasha, Jayden, and another unidentified soldier held off the Bakma attack. After several minutes of suppression fire and struggle, the transfer was accomplished. Michael wasted no time attending to the wounded inside the building. Becan, John, Natasha, and Jayden continued to engage the Bakma as Scott, Grammar, and the unidentified man slipped inside.

Grammar caught his breath and turned to Scott. "Our team, sir." He motioned toward the only other uninjured man—the one who'd been assisting them. "Delta Trooper Vause, our techie, and the three wounded are Executor Diaz, Lieutenant Bowen, and Gamma Private Parsons. Diaz took command when our captain fell, then Bowen took command when *Diaz* fell. We're all that's left of a team of twenty, sir."

Scott lifted a brow. *Sir?* He shifted his peripherals down to his armor, where dried blood—Henrick's blood—was crusted over his insignia, completely hiding it from view. Grammar had no idea that Scott was an alpha. A moment of decision ticked in Scott's mind, and he answered, "Scott Remington. What were you doing here?"

Through the comm, Becan's voice interrupted. "We could use a bloody hand ou' here!"

Scott hurried to the window. "How many have you guys taken down?"

Laughing, Becan answered, "None!"

"What about you, Jay?"

The Texan's voice crackled through the comm. "I been workin' on a few more I found farther up the road. I killed one and hit another, but there's still more. I think there's still two or three here at the closest alley, but they know I'm here now. S'about five or six more down the road."

Scott turned to Grammar. "The Bakma that had you pinned—were they primarily the ones from that nearest alley over?"

"Yeah, those were the ones."

Scott climbed out of the window and ducked behind the van. He glanced at Grammar. "I guess if you had any grenades left, you'd be using them?"

"Yes, sir. Took a chunk out of the first wave that hit us, but more came pretty fast. We think they used up all theirs, too."

After unfastening a grenade from his belt, Scott placed his finger over the activation button. Through his comm, he said, "Give me three seconds of full cover! Stay on those triggers!"

His suppression team opened fire.

Scott pressed the button, whipped up from behind the van, and flung the small orb toward the alleyway. The soldiers ducked down as soon as he released it. The grenade ricocheted off the wall of the alleyway and bounced out of view. An explosion boomed.

Scott leapt over the hood of the van. "Charge the alley! Let's go!"

"I got 'em pinned down the street," Jayden said through the comm, "go, go, go!"

The charging soldiers reached the alleyway several seconds later. The reek of smoke and open flesh burned their nostrils as they moved into the alley, assault rifles raised to finish off any survivors. Remains were scattered across the ground, and entrails dripped from the brick walls. The ground beneath them turned moist.

"They're movin'!" yelled Jayden through the comm. "The Bakma down the street are movin'!" His sniper rifle exploded through the line.

The aliens were trying to escape. Scott charged into the street, followed by his comrades. The Bakma were in full retreat. "Stop them!" As soon as he and his teammates were in the open, they knelt, raised their weapons, and laid down the triggers. The Bakma toppled over one after the other. Scott leapt to his feet and bolted toward the alleyway whence they'd come, his comrades close behind. They charged around the corner and trained their assault rifles, but there was no need. There were no Bakma left. Their mission was accomplished.

AS REINFORCEMENTS arrived from *Richmond*, the battle on South Michigan turned in EDEN's favor. Several captains—Lilan included—led a full assault against the Bakma foot soldiers. They charged into the Bakma stronghold, where an intense melee began.

David and Henry were in the onslaught and adopted a back-to-back protection system. With David's on-the-spot tactical commands, the two men formed a somewhat effective duo.

Nonetheless, the battle was far from over.

ONCE THE BAKMA corpses were collected, Scott and his team returned to the structure containing Cougar's wounded. Jayden remained on his fifth-floor perch, where he kept watch over South Wabash.

As soon as Scott entered, he approached Michael. "How are they, man?"

"They're all stable," Michael answered. "Diaz, Parsons, Bowen...they're busted up pretty bad, but stable. They should be okay as long as they aren't out here much longer. They'll definitely need more medical treatment than I can give them out here."

Scott turned to Grammar. "Why were you out here?"

Saddling his hands on his hips, Grammar answered, "We were initially sent to disable the southernmost Carrier, but we met heavier resistance than Command expected. We had a cover unit, but they got ambushed before we were even set up to go. The five of us here are all that's left out of a strike force of twenty."

Scott's brow furrowed. "You were sent to *disable* one of the Carriers?"

"Yes, sir. Command wanted salvage, and that was the best way to get it. It also sends a strong message to the Bakma when their big ships don't come back home. Or at least, we hope it does." He half smirked.

A thought materialized in Scott's mind. "How far is the Carrier from here?"

"Not that far. Stay down South Wabash, and take a left on East Balbo. The Carrier's right there past South Michigan, in the middle of Grant Park."

Scott looked away for a moment, still thinking. Six able soldiers. That's what he had. Was that crazy? His gaze returned to Grammar. "Is it still possible to disable it?"

Grammar's jaw sagged, and he cleared his throat. "Uhh...yes, sir. We still have Vause, he's a specialist tech who was trained for this sort of thing."

Becan eyed Scott suspiciously from the corner of the room.

Turning away, Scott stepped out of the room and adjusted his comm to reach Tacker. "Remington to Executor Tacker."

There was a moment of static before Tacker's voice emerged. "Tacker here. You get them out, yet?"

"Yes, sir. Area cleared."

"How's Henrick?"

Scott glanced at the fallen lieutenant, who was sacked out on the floor. Michael must have given him some sort of sedative. "He's okay, sir. He'll make it."

"Outstanding work, private."

Here it went. "Sir, with Command's permission, I'd like to try and complete Cougar's objective. They were ordered to disable the southern Bakma Carrier."

Silence hung before Tacker replied. "Are you joking?"

"No, sir, I think we have a chance. The Bakma here have been isolated and things are quiet. I think we might be able to get close enough to make a real run at this thing."

"How many of you are there?"

"Six able to go."

Tacker's voice sounded floored. "You want to assault a Bakma Carrier with *six* soldiers?"

Was it crazy? No. It was doable. "Yes, sir. It's the last thing they would expect."

"You got *that* right! Give me a minute to talk to the captain."

LILAN WAS IN THE middle of the offensive when Tacker's voice burst through his headset.

"Captain, I have Remington over there by Cougar wanting to make a run at the southern Carrier. Something about disabling it. Do you know anything about that, sir?"

Lilan crouched behind a barricade as around him, orange flashes of assault rifle rounds blazed. "Yeah, Command wanted salvage. That's what Cougar was—wait, Remington wants to do *what*?"

"He wants to assault the Carrier."

"Did he get shot in the head?"

"I have no idea, sir."

Lilan reloaded his weapon and opened fire on the Bakma foot soldiers. "How many men does he have?"

"He says six. I shouldn't even be asking you this."

"He wants to assault the Carrier with *six* men?"

"That's what he says, sir—"

Lilan cut him off. "I'm talkin' to him." Closing the channel, he readjusted to contact Scott. "Remington, this is Lilan. Are you requesting permission to *assault* and *disable* the southern Carrier?"

There was a moment of silence before Scott answered. "Yes, sir. Things are calm on this end. I think we can catch them off guard."

"Do you have any idea what you're asking?"

"Yes, sir. I wouldn't ask if I didn't think we could do it."

Lilan grew quiet. The request was suicide, but there was something unexpected in Scott's tone. It was pure belief. Even in addressing the captain, his voice never wavered. He could have been mistaken for a tried veteran.

EDEN loved salvage. They grew giddy at the mention of it. Six soldiers would never survive a Carrier assault, but they didn't have to for the operation to be successful. They only had to reach the engine room long enough for the technician to disable the drive. Survival was unnecessary—for all of them. But was a captured Carrier worth the lives of six soldiers? Could six soldiers even *reach* the engine room?

"Do you really think you can do this?" Lilan asked.

There was no hesitation from Scott. "Positive, sir."

"Then do it."

"Thank you, sir!"

Lilan gestured with his hands as if Scott was right there before him. "Just get to the engine room! Make that your priority, then do what you can."

"Yes, sir."

"Good luck," Lilan said before he closed the channel. He stared down at the assault rifle in his hands. He'd just given six soldiers permission to kill themselves.

SCOTT RETURNED TO the makeshift hospital. "Listen up, everyone! The original objective for this mission was to disable the southern Carrier." Becan rose from his perch in the corner. "We are going to complete this objective."

Vause's jaw hung loose. Natasha's eyes slowly widened. John blinked and looked at Grammar.

"Becan, Natasha, John, Grammar, Vause, and I are going to infiltrate the Carrier and deactivate its main drive. Mike's going to take care of the wounded here while Jay protects him from above. Jay, just do your thing."

"Yes, sir!" Jayden said.

Scott slammed a fresh magazine into his assault rifle. "Let's have some fun."

7

IT WAS THE COLDEST game Scott ever remembered playing in—a late-season thriller in Michigan Stadium against Wisconsin, a team that had no business competing with them that year. Despite being a two-touchdown favorite, Michigan found itself in a back-and-forth slugfest against a team that, for whatever reason, had decided that this was their game of the year. Though Scott ended up being behind center, it wasn't one of the games he'd started. He'd taken the reins in the second quarter after Michigan's starter was injured. Scott would never forget that moment when his coach said, "You're up, Rem." The rush, the terror, the excitement—it blended like an adrenaline cocktail. He never thought he'd experience a feeling like that again.

He found it on South Wabash Avenue.

As Scott and his five teammates dashed from the cover of one vehicle to the next, steam blowing from their lips as they checked every intersection with tense anticipation, Scott found his mind flashing back to that day he took command of the huddle. A quick three-and-out later, it was the words of his coach that both settled his racing heart and ultimately propelled him and his teammates to victory. *Don't worry about the big play—just move the chains.* Right now, the first-down marker sat squarely in the intersection of South Wabash and East Balbo.

Combat echoed far away in the direction of the barricade, though it was too distant to affect them. As East Balbo awaited just a bit farther ahead, Scott halted his progress and dropped to a knee. He gestured for Grammar to join him while the others kept watch.

"Okay, what can we expect up ahead?" Scott asked.

"A lot of Bakma," Grammar answered.

Becan, who was standing near them, turned their way to eavesdrop.

"Okay, besides a lot of Bakma—"

Grammar cut him off tactfully. "Sir, I don't think you understand.

I'm not talking three, four, five Bakma. I'm talking about the rest of the crew of a Carrier. These things can hold hundreds. Even with most of their warriors in the city, we might be looking at a thirty or forty-strong fortification. There's gonna be a *lot*." Sighing, he looked in the direction of the weapons fire. "Part of the plan was to be supplemented by two other units who were going to serve as a distraction while we made our move. Those units got decimated. That whole open area around the park was supposed to be EDEN's staging area. Couriers took care of that real quick."

Though not commonly seen, Bakma Courier fighters were lightning-fast craft capable of making tremendously damaging strafing runs. With them overhead, it was no mystery why the open area by the park was off-limits. Still, there had to be a way. "Just move the chains," Scott said absently to himself.

Grammar tilted his head. "What?"

Scott looked at the East Balbo intersection before turning back to Grammar. "So step one is getting there in one piece, right?"

"To the Carrier? I mean, yeah, but—"

Cutting out the knees of Grammar's doubt, Scott said, "Then that's what we focus on." Rising to his feet, he set his hands on his hips and took a few steps to gather his thoughts.

Becan approached him from behind. "Wha' yeh thinkin', Remmy?"

He was thinking speed was their ally. Time and distance, the enemy. Grammar was right in that there was no way they would fight through dozens of Bakma. Scott's confidence wasn't grounded in stupidity but in finding unique solutions. Calling audibles and scrambling for the first down when all his receivers were covered. In willing victory through creativity and grit. Finally answering Becan, he said, "I'm thinking we need to close that gap."

"The gap?" Becan asked. "Wha', between tha' intersection an' the Carrier?"

"That's the one." Scott looked ahead. The intersection was just one block away. They might as well get one block closer. Speaking through his comm to the group, he said, "Let's get to East Balbo." The group affirmed and then followed his lead.

THE OFFENSIVE ON South Michigan continued as the arrival of EDEN reinforcements shifted momentum in humanity's favor. The Bakma that remained, though outnumbered, were in full retreat.

David and Henry, out of ammunition, had since returned to the landing zone. Wounded were spread across the ground as the available medical crews hustled between those in critical condition and those more stable.

David stepped through them to reach *Vulture-7*, where Donald, also out of ammunition, waited with Lexie. "How's the rescue team?" he asked.

Unharnessed from his weapon, Donald answered, "They assaultin' a Carrier."

"*What?*"

"Scott found out about that other team's mission. They was supposed to capture one of the Bakma Carriers. Scott got their permission to continue."

Henry stooped to a kneel. "Wait, *Scott's* assaulting a Carrier? What happened to Henrick?"

"He's out," Donald answered. "I guess he got taken down. I don't know if he's dead or what."

David looked at Henry, then back at Donald. "How many people does Scott have with him?"

Donald laughed under his breath and said, "Whoever he left with. So far as I know, that's it."

A look of concern rested on Lexie's face from the open troop bay.

David gripped the back of his neck. "Can they survive that?"

Donald didn't reply. He only feigned a smile and lowered his gaze to the street.

AS EAST BALBO approached, Scott signaled his soldiers to slow their pace. Placing his back against a brick building at the precipice of the intersection, he pulled out a spot mirror and eased it around the corner. Sure enough, he could see the Carrier looming far in the distance—and just as Grammar had predicted, Bakma were fortified all around it. Shaking his head, he slipped the mirror back into place.

Think, think, think. They had a straight shot to the mouth of the Carrier. There *had* to be a way to close that gap. Could they go through the buildings? No—that would take far too long. Was there any chance they could survive a firefight? He knew better than that. Crouching down by the corner, he looked at Grammar. "What are we looking at once we get inside? I mean, is the engine room a straight shot or something?"

This time, Vause—Cougar's nasally technician—answered. "Actually, yes. There's a large main corridor at the end of the hangar. You can probably see it in the mirror, it's almost big enough to drive a car through. The route to the engine room is just an offshoot of that main hall. It's not hard to get to. It's getting to the Carrier that's the conundrum."

Conundrum was one way to put it. Rising to his feet, Scott thought. *Get there. We just have to get there. That's the next set of chains—that's the next first-down marker.* He thought on Vause's words. Once they got through the Carrier's massive hangar, it was just a matter of traversing that main hallway. And that main hallway wasn't exactly hard to find—it was right there at the back of the hangar. They could practically drive right up to it.

Scott blinked. At that thought—at those very words his mind had formed—the synapses in his brain fired and connected.

That main corridor that led to the engine room. Vause said it was almost big enough to drive a car through. But there was no *almost* in Scott's eureka moment—the answer he'd found was absolute. They might not be able to drive *through* the main corridor...

...but they could absolutely drive *to* it.

He shot a look to Grammar. "The van."

"The...the what?"

Becan raised an eyebrow. "The van?"

Nodding, Scott pushed past Grammar and Becan and walked to John. "How good of a driver exactly are you?"

Looking in both directions as if caught off guard by the question, John answered, "Uhh...good? I mean, yeah. I'm vecking good. But what—"

That was all Scott needed to hear. Walking to the middle of the group, he issued the orders. "Donner's going to hotwire another vehicle." Looking past them, his eyes locked onto a delivery van. He pointed. "That one."

"Wait, wait," said Natasha, cutting in, "are you suggesting he *drive* us to the Carrier?"

Scott faced her. "Not *to* the Carrier. *Into* it. Right up to that main corridor that leads to the engine room. We're going to bypass their whole defense force."

Raising a hand, Becan said, "Righ', I see a problem. How exactly is John goin' to drive when he's got plasma burns all over his face from where they shot through the windshield?"

"And how are we going to get *from* the vehicle *to* the main corridor?" Natasha asked. "Just hop out and say, 'Don't mind us, just passing through?'"

Scott looked at them both. "Because he's going to drive the van backward."

Silence. For several seconds, no one on the team breathed a word. It was Grammar who finally did. "Holy veck," he said under his breath. "That could actually work."

Those same synapses that'd fired in Scott's brain were now firing in everyone else's. "An' *we* stay in the back o' the van!" Becan said. "He'll drive us all the way to the corridor, and we literally jus' open the back doors an' jump ou'!"

"It'll plug the corridor's entryway like a cork," Grammar said.

Becan laughed and shook his head. "Tha's bleedin' genius!"

It was nothing if John couldn't do it. Looking at Falcon's resident driver, Scott asked, "Can you do it?" That's all he needed to know.

"Hell yeah, I can do it," John answered without hesitating. "Absolutely."

Scott slapped him hard on the shoulder. "Go get that van."

As John hurried off to hotwire a second vehicle, Natasha walked up to Scott with a look of disbelief. "How in the world did you come up with that?"

Though the indicated praise was nice, Scott wanted to actually pull it off before he massaged his ego. "The only thing you need to focus on right now is what's ahead. It's not done when we get to the corridor. We're literally driving into a hornet's nest." He stepped back so his gaze would include all of them. "Those Bakma are going to be mad, and they're going to be shooting. A lot."

"Yeah, an' we'll be shootin' back," said Becan. "No chance in hell I'm goin' to waste a plan as bonkers as this by gettin' m'self reefed."

In the span of about thirty seconds, Scott's plan had been described as both *genius* and *bonkers*. Scott was well aware of the unorthodox nature of it. No class in the Academy taught "delivery van infiltration." But there was a first time for everything. Checking his E-35, Scott said, "Everybody check your ammo count—make sure you're fully loaded." The soldiers did as commanded. A minute later, John was pulling up to them.

"Anny last words before we die gloriously?" Becan asked as he opened one of the van's back doors.

Natasha hopped in behind him. "I don't know about the whole *die gloriously* thing, but I do know one thing." She looked at Scott as he climbed in himself. "Live or die, this one's gonna make the news."

"On our planet or theirs?" Scott asked, gesturing with a head nod in the direction of the Carrier.

Smirking, Natasha readied her assault rifle.

"All right, team," Scott said as Grammar and Vause closed the van doors with everyone inside. "Let's do this thing." The group responded with a *yes, sir*. Scott looked toward John in the driver's seat. "Let's go, Donner!"

John slammed down the accelerator, and the delivery van rocketed backward into the intersection of South Wabash and East Balbo. The soldiers in the back grabbed the support rails. John spun the wheel, and the van swerved around the corner. He narrowed his gaze in the rearview.

"KU'NESSA TE MACH nass," mumbled a slender Bakma as he leaned against the wall of the Carrier's deployment bay.

A stouter Bakma next to him grunted. "Kanaas. U'tekn no las'tun."

The conversation drew to an abrupt close as the two Bakma and their dozen counterparts turned to the center of the street, where a tall, brightly-colored van was rocketing toward them in reverse. The deployment bay fell silent.

The slender Bakma started, leapt up, and trained his plasma rifle. "Earthae! Earthae!" The Bakma around him scurried for their weapons.

PLASMA SOARED toward the delivery van; the vehicle wavered back and forth as several bolts ripped through its metal frame, streaking past the soldiers who clung to the inner sides of the cargo hold.

John white-knuckled the wheel as the metal ramp loomed nearer. "Hold on!"

Impact. The van slammed into the ramp, the back end buckling off the ground and crashing against the metal floor in an explosion of sparks. Bakma, firing madly only seconds earlier, now dove out of the way to avoid getting run over. All the while, John's eyes stayed fixed on the rearview mirror. The corridor in sight, he whipped his head around and focused through what was left of the van's back window. Rocked with plasma, but still on target. And time to brake.

Foot over the brake, John yelled, "Open the doors!"

Scott and Becan were on it. Shoving with all their might, they managed to open the back doors just as the brakes were slammed. A piercing screech reverberated through the Carrier's deployment bay.

And then came the crash. The van crunched against the metal frame of the corridor, and the soldiers inside were thrown through the air, right through the very back door Scott and Becan had just opened. Hitting the ground hard but tucking into rolls, the five soldiers slid to scampering stops on the Carrier's cold floor.

Whipping his head back around, Scott looked at the van. Just as predicted, it'd plugged the corridor like a cork.

John engaged the parking brake, locked the doors, and dove into the van's cargo hold as plasma bolts crashed through the windshield. A droning siren wailed as he scrambled over debris to rejoin the others.

There was no time to vocalize their next move—within seconds, Bakma appeared in the corridor from inside the ship. Becan and Natasha were already on them, firing their assault rifles just as the aliens appeared.

Behind them, the Bakma in the deployment bay were making their way through the van's interior.

"Sorry, guys," said John to the Bakma as he flicked out a grenade, "it's been a blast." Pressing the activation button, he flung it into the van's cargo hold. The explosion came seconds later, engulfing the van in flames as Bakma screamed in agony. In time with the fire, a series of small, circular holes appeared in the ceiling above the corridor. The next thing the six soldiers knew, they were being pelted from above by the foamy alien equivalent of fire suppression fluid.

Wiping foam from his visor, Scott shouted, "Vause, take point, we'll cover! Let's *move!*"

Fighting to gain traction on the now-slippery Carrier floor, the soldiers skedaddled behind Vause's guidance.

"How far are we?" Scott shouted above the siren.

"That second corridor up ahead, to the left! It's just a little ways down—*veck!*"

Vause's words were cut short as Bakma appeared from the corridor mere yards in front of them. The two forces, human and Bakma, collided before a weapon could be fired.

Sliding in the foam beneath him, Scott avoided getting smashed in the face with the butt of a plasma rifle by the smallest of margins. Grabbing the Bakma's legs, Scott twisted, sending the purple-skinned alien falling to the floor but kicking his booted foot at Scott's head.

The others fared no less chaotically. John was being slammed from wall to wall as he held onto a Bakma's plasma rifle to avoid it being used against them. Natasha was being hurled back down the corridor by a massive specimen, the redhead's helmeted head banging against the floor as she tried to stop herself from sliding. Becan, on the intercept, was literally scaling the giant alien's back.

Rat-tat-tat-tat-tat!

Grammar, who'd put just enough distance between himself and the aliens to make his weapon effective, riddled the Bakma that Scott was engaging with bullets. Caught in the alien's blood spray, Scott wiped his visor again to see clearly. The quarterback in him kicked in as he read through his progressions.

The Bakma fighting John—Grammar and Vause are on it. They'll be fine. Becan. His Bakma's off balance. Becan's reaching for his weapon. That one's finished. His eyes focused on Natasha—and the pair of emerging aliens behind her. *Valer's in trouble. Move.*

Dashing through the fray, Scott pulled up his assault rifle and fired past Natasha, whose eyes widened before she dropped to the floor to avoid getting shot. One of the Bakma behind her fell, but another was left. Plasma bolts seared down the hallway through the brawl but, by a minor miracle, hit no one. In the next second, Scott was there. As Natasha battled for traction on the slippery floor, Scott raised his E-35 and fired. The Bakma leapt aside to avoid the shots, its back hitting the wall as it aimed its plasma rifle to retaliate.

Natasha got him first. With her pistol raised from a kneeling position, she fired several shots at the alien's head. Her aim was pure, and the Bakma was dropped.

All weapons fire—all sounds of combat—ceased. Looking back, Scott watched as Becan, John, Grammar, and Vause checked one another out. They were all in one piece. Scott reached down to grab Natasha's hand. She clutched it hard, and he yanked her up, the tips of her foam-drenched hair dancing beneath her helmet. "You all right?" he asked, clearing her visor for her.

Spitting foam out of her mouth, she wiped her lips and exhaled a breath of laughter. "You know how to party, Remington."

Above them, the sprays of foam ceased. The holes closed back up in the ceiling. The fire must have been out—one less thing to contend with. But they weren't done yet.

Shouts in Bakmanese echoed from the hallway just in front of him and Natasha—from the same direction as the two Bakma that'd appeared to attack her. More were coming.

Turning to Vause, Scott asked, "You said it's not far from here, right?"

"A veritable hop, skip, and jump," the technician answered.

"Then let's get hopping." Moving back to the group, Scott hurried behind them toward the left-hand turn that led to the engine room.

Natasha stopped them.

"Hey!" she called out, prompting the men to pause and look at her. Heaving in exhaustion, she said, "Someone's gotta hold this hallway."

She wasn't wrong. Who knew what awaited them in the engine room? They needed to make sure their six was clear. Turning to the left-hand turn Vause had indicated, Scott said, "I want three people on that intersection."

Grammar was a delta—the most experienced of this mostly-alpha team. "Grammar, Valer, McCrae—you guys got it?"

"Yes, sir," Grammar answered without hesitation.

Becan held out a hand for Natasha to slap; she did, clasping it with a *pop.* "Let's do it, girlie," he said.

Turning to John and Vause, Scott looked at the latter. "Lead the way— we'll have you covered." As the three men turned down the corridor that led to the engine room, Grammar, Becan, and Natasha took position around the corner.

Within seconds, all three were firing.

Scott and John were running full speed to keep up with Vause, whose feet had caught up with his adrenaline level. That otherworldly siren wailed on—weapons fire echoed behind them where Grammar and company were locking it down.

"That's the door!" Vause pointed to a metal door that sat cattycorner to the corridor.

A Bakma soldier emerged down the hall. As Vause hunched down, Scott and John opened fire. Their shots ran true, and the alien was dropped.

Hurrying to the door, Vause pulled out a *handyman,* an all-purpose hacking tool used by combat technicians. Scott knew very little about the devices—only that they were as indispensable to combat techs as medical kits were to medics.

Pulling out several cords with attached dongles, Vause inserted them into various slots next to the door mechanism's interface. "Door's opening!" he called out. Within seconds, the door slid open.

Flitting past him, Scott and John took to the engine room with weapons ready. The room was circular in design, with a slowly turning metal platform at its center. Consoles littered the walls; indecipherable Bakmanese script was posted everywhere.

Behind the circular platform, a Bakma shouted. As Vause readied his handyman to hack into the ship's drive, Scott and John each took a direction around the platform. Plasma bolts soared John's way, and the soldier shrunk back to avoid getting pummeled.

But Scott was in the clear.

Charging around the platform with the alien's attention on John, Scott aimed his E-35 and pelted the Bakma's backside. The alien's plasma rifle flew from its gnarled talons as it collapsed. The room was clear.

A commotion arose from the engine room entrance. Hurrying back around the circular platform, Scott and John reconvened just in time to see Grammar, Becan, and Natasha sprint in like their proverbial tails were on fire. Behind them, white plasma streaked down the corridor.

"We've got company!" Becan yelled, taking a position at the corner of the room's cattycorner entrance. Grammar was beside him while Natasha slammed a fresh magazine into her weapon. When Scott looked at her, she flashed him a half-frown.

"Yeah, we didn't hold the hall," she said.

Scott whipped around to Vause. "Can we seal this door shut?"

"Ahhhhh," was all the technician could muster, his hands working furiously on his handyman.

"Is that a no?"

"I'm working on this—I can't stop!" he said. "I need sixty seconds!"

Sixty seconds. Blowing out a breath, Scott joined his comrades at the corner of the door. "Sixty seconds, guys! Let's get him cover."

The battle that ensued was utter chaos. Bakma warriors had appeared from both sides of the hallway outside the engine room, determined to converge on the door Scott and company were protecting. The only advantage the humans had was that the Bakma had to be mindful of a crossfire, lest they terminate one another. It was a vulnerability Scott and his teammates didn't have—and they took full advantage of it, firing liberally in both directions of the hallway, burning through ammunition as the Bakma continued to slowly progress.

Scott ducked back to reload—Becan took his place. "It's sixty seconds!" Scott shouted at Vause, having no real idea if it'd indeed been a minute or not. At any moment, those converging Bakma would get close enough to make their charge. At that point, there'd be nothing Scott and his team could do to stop them.

A plasma bolt streaked mere inches past Natasha—she gasped and stumbled back. Having exhausted his E-35 rounds, John opened fire with his handgun to buy her time to get to cover. Another plasma bolt exploded against Becan's rifle. The Irishman yelped as its twisted remains skidded down the hall. Shaking his hands like they were on fire, he ducked out of the fight as Grammar took his place.

Click-click-click-click-click-click!

"Veck!" Throwing down his depleted E-35, Scott pulled out his handgun as Natasha rejoined the fight next to him. The redhead held down the trigger of her weapon—the rounds barely pushed the Bakma back at all.

They were about to be overrun.

"Drive disabled!" Vause shouted from inside the engine room.

"Shut this *vecking* door!" Natasha screamed at him.

The technician practically leapt to the door's control panel. Fingers flying on the surface of his handyman, he frantically reattached the various dongles to the panel. "Getting back in the system!" he said shakily.

John pulled out of the fight, handgun pointed at the ground. "I'm out!"

"I'm out!" said Scott seconds later.

Grammar and Natasha took to each side of the door behind them, unloading what few rounds remained in their assault rifles. Becan, relegated to his handgun, prepared to relieve one of them if they pulled back.

Vause shouted, "Door's sealing, get in!"

He didn't have to tell anyone twice. Grammar and Natasha dove into the engine room as Vause inputted the command to shut the door. In the exact second that the Bakma appeared outside the door, it slid shut.

"Sealed and locked!" said Vause triumphantly.

As Becan and John helped up the heaving Natasha and Grammar, Scott asked Vause, "Is it possible for them to figure out how to open it?"

Vause stared at him. "Uhh…"

That answered that. Turning away from the technician, Scott queued up Captain Lilan on the comm.

LILAN WAS BARKING commands to a throng of EDEN soldiers as Scott's distorted voice cut through the static.

"—activated the drive!"

Scott's identifier appeared in his visor's HUD, and Lilan lowered his head to hear better. "Please repeat!"

"This is Remington! We have deactivated the drive!"

Signaling for another officer to take command of the offensive, Lilan marched away from the cacophony of weapons fire. "Private, did I understand you as saying you have *deactivated* the drive on the Bakma Carrier?"

"Yes, sir! Wings are clipped!"

Lilan laughed loudly. "How in the hell did… what's your status—"

Scott nearly cut him off. "We are in *urgent* need of assistance! We're locked inside the engine room with Bakma pressing to get in."

"Roger that—how many wounded do you have?"

"None, sir!"

Lilan didn't hesitate. "I'll dispatch a unit to get you out of there right now. Sit tight for a little while longer!"

"Yes, sir." The comm channel closed.

Snatching the officer who'd taken command of the offensive, Lilan said, "Listen, we have a strike team inside the southern Carrier—they're pinned inside the engine room. Assemble a team and get them the hell out of there! I'll be working on some air support and additional help."

The officer nodded. "Right away, sir."

DAVID PACED IN front of *Vulture-7.* The rest of Falcon Squad stood silently alongside him as they awaited an update.

"They did it!"

They jumped at the sound of Tacker's voice. Turning to the approaching, jubilant executor, they listened with keen ears.

"They did it!" Tacker said again as he trotted toward them. "They grounded the Carrier!"

"Are they okay?" asked David.

Tacker stopped beside him. "They're fine—every single one of them! We've got several units en route to them now."

David thrust a fist into the air. "Hell yes!" The other men around him beamed.

"With six soldiers, they disabled a Bakma Carrier," Tacker said. "That's unheard of." He eyed the barricade. "Look, I've got a few other things to take care of, but I wanted to let you guys know the latest. I'll keep you posted if I hear anything else!"

"Yes, sir!" David said.

As Tacker left, Donald shook his head and smiled. "They's all right. I knew they's all right."

SCOTT AND HIS teammates knelt beside the walls. The few who still had ammunition sat with their weapons trained on the engine room door, as if at any moment it might open and the Bakma might pour in. On the other side of the door, shouting in their alien tongue, the Bakma tried desperately to break through Vause's hack job.

Almost fifteen minutes passed before anything changed. Footsteps were heard, then the Bakma began shouting at each other in a frenzied manner. Weapons fire—both plasma and projectile—erupted. The battle was short-lived, as a familiar word soon spilled from the Bakma defenders. *Grrashna.* The Bakmanese word for self-surrender.

A veritable plethora of footsteps grew nearer, followed by the sounds of weapons clunking together, followed by human voices. A minute later, someone knocked on the door.

"Everyone okay in there?"

Scott signaled Vause to open the door. When it opened, there were no Bakma on the other side—only the relieved expressions of EDEN soldiers. At long last, Scott exhaled in relief.

The soldier who'd knocked from the outside smiled. "I can't believe you guys are actually in here." Placing his hands on his hips, he shook his head in wonder. "There's two vehicles outside waiting to take you all back to the LZ. How'd you guys *do* this?"

All Scott could do was laugh disarmingly. He wasn't sure how else to respond. More soldiers filed into the engine room, and the six-man team stepped out.

As far as Scott could see, there were no Bakma left in the Carrier. EDEN sweeper teams were in the corridors, along with numerous other soldiers, but no one else. As soon as they emerged from the Carrier, the location of the Bakma forces became clear. They were lined up along the street, their wrinkled hands clasped together as EDEN soldiers lorded over them. Scott knew without needing to be told where their next stop would be. Alien Confinement. Each EDEN base had a facility dedicated to it. *Richmond* was no exception. There, they would be poked, prodded, and interrogated for whatever information they could provide. On a normal day, Scott would have found all that fascinating. But at the moment, he didn't much care where the Bakma would go or what would happen to them. He was just happy to be alive.

As promised, a pair of vehicles awaited the six soldiers. The ride back to the landing zone revealed the battle's aftermath. Bloodied soldiers walked the streets as Bakma survivors were herded together. It was all truly over.

When they arrived back at the barricade, Lilan and two other captains were there to meet them. The vehicles stopped, and the six soldiers leapt from them and snapped off salutes.

Lilan was the first to speak through the smile plastered across his face. "Fellas—and lady—this is Captain White of Hawk Squad and Captain Douglas of Gryphon." The two captains saluted the soldiers.

White surveyed the soldiers keenly before his gaze stopped on Scott. He raised an eyebrow. "Remington?"

Lifting his chin, Scott answered, "Yes, sir."

White extended his hand to shake Scott's. "Excellent job, soldier. They'll be talking about this one for a long time."

From Scott's side, Becan, Natasha, and Donner watched him.

"Thank you, sir," Scott answered.

White stepped back, turned to Lilan, and patted him on the shoulder. "Keep provin' them wrong, captain."

Lilan chuckled. "That's the plan." He watched White and Douglas walk away before refocusing on the soldiers. "You turned some heads tonight."

The soldiers regarded him in silence. "Go catch a ride back with Captain White and Hawk. The rest of Falcon's already left for base."

The four Falcons nodded, exchanged handshakes with Grammar and Vause, then hurried to catch up with Captain White.

Grammar waited for them to disappear before clearing his throat. "Permission to say something, captain?"

Lilan glanced at him. "Go ahead."

"I don't know if Remington is your executor or lieutenant or what, but he's got to be the ballsiest human being I've ever fought with."

Lilan cocked his head strangely. "What do you mean, 'executor, lieutenant, or what?'"

"Remington, sir," Grammar answered. "I don't know his rank, I just wanted to tell you, sir—he's awesome."

"Wait, wait," said Lilan, looking back in the direction Scott had left. Pointing that way, he looked back at Grammar. "You didn't know *his* rank?"

Mouth hanging open, Grammar fell silent. A look of trepidation came over him. "I apologize, sir, I just didn't catch it during the rescue." Looking sidelong at Vause, he widened his eyes as if silently asking for help. Vause shrugged, his gaze echoing confusion.

Several seconds later, it was Lilan whose confusion faded away. "Holy veck," he said. Laughing under his breath, the old captain shook his head. "Well, ain't that something?" Looking at the two bewildered soldiers from Cougar Squad, Lilan cracked the slyest of smirks. "Congratulations, boys. You just got duped by a rookie. Scott Remington is an alpha. This was his very first mission."

Grammar and Vause's jaws dropped.

Turning away from them, Lilan walked away, lost in his newly formed thoughts—and once more, he found himself laughing. Scott had snuck into command. Whether on purpose or by accident, he'd worn the guise of an officer and snuck into command. And two veteran soldiers from a specialized task force had bought it.

What Scott had exercised was the opposite of military ethics. What he'd done was reckless, dishonest. It was completely out of line for an EDEN soldier.

Lilan loved it.

*   *   *

WHEN SCOTT, BECAN, Natasha, and John stepped out of the transport and into *Richmond*'s hangar, the rest of Falcon Squad awaited them.

The moment David caught sight of Scott, the older soldier slammed into him with a back-slapping fist hug. "That's how you *do* it!"

Scott laughed as he fought to maintain balance. "I guess it is!"

"Do you have any idea what you guys just did?" As David asked the question, Becan, Natasha, and John stepped closer to listen. "You did something that should've been impossible."

Behind David, the rest of Falcon moved in on the four new arrivals like they were returning heroes. Among them was Executor Tacker. "Remington!" From every corner of the hangar, a palpable energy was brewing.

Scott spun to face him, firing off a fast salute. "Sir!"

Laughing, Tacker said, "That was unbelievable! How in the world you pulled that off is beyond me."

"Thank you, sir."

Tacker looked at all four of the returnees. "Wherever you want to go, that's fine with me. *The Black Cherry*, the beach, I don't care! You guys earned it." He was grinning with every word—a look far removed from the disapproval he'd shown them when he'd made them run Mud Lake. "I've got to get the captain up to speed on some things, but I had to stop and find you guys when I heard you were landing."

When he *heard* they were landing? Was their return that widely anticipated?

"Pull some more stunts like that and you'll have my job," Tacker said, slapping Scott on the shoulder before departing.

Seconds after the executor left, Shekeia punched Scott on the shoulder. "I am so *jealous!*" Despite her words, she was laughing. She turned to Natasha, pushing her playfully. "What happened to your roomie, huh? You forgot about her while y'all were off makin' history?"

"Making *history*?" Natasha asked.

"Um, yeah! They're already talking about it on the news, how a six-man team captured a Bakma Carrier. You guys just gained celebrity status!"

Reaching out to touch Shekeia on the arm, Becan asked, "Wha' do yeh mean talkin' abou' it on the news? Yeh mean they're talkin' abou' *us*?"

"They're talking about the Carrier, but they're gonna know y'all's names soon enough. Everyone *here* does! They're calling y'all the *Six Shooters*—you and those two guys from Cougar."

"Where are Jay an' Mike?" Becan asked.

Shekeia gestured with a head nod to the far side of the hangar. "They're inside getting debriefed. You guys are up next, I'm sure."

Suddenly, a voice from the far side of the crowd emerged. "That's them! They're right here!"

Scott had a bad feeling they were the "them" in question, and the following seconds confirmed it. The crowd that had slowly been gathering around them parted—most of Falcon included. Before Scott realized it, he and his cohorts faced a tidal wave of exuberant onlookers. And seconds later... champagne.

The sprays came from all around them—like this was something that'd been planned. Before Scott could react, he, Becan, Natasha, John, and innocent bystander Shekeia were collectively christened with the frothy liquid. A jubilant, raucous roar erupted from the crowd.

"*Hey!*" Shekeia yelled, sputtering as she lowered her head and shielded her eyes. "I ain't even a part of this!"

Wiping his soaked hair back and squinting, Scott was caught somewhere between excitement and total bewilderment. He looked through the falling champagne toward his comrades. Drenched from head to toe, Becan and Natasha were taking it in thoroughly. With wet hair hanging over their eyes, the pair thrust their fists in the air and shouted along with the crowd. John, on the other hand, was nowhere to be seen, leaving Scott to surmise that he must have found a way to slip through the crowd amid the celebration. Lucky him.

"I blame you for this, future husband."

Still squinting, Scott turned to Shekeia's voice, only to find her staring at him, sopping wet with her eyes half closed. Shaking her braids, she pushed them back over her head—the first gesture that made Scott genuinely laugh. "Hey, get this one!" he said, pointing at her. "This one, right here!"

"Really?" Before Shekeia could say anything else, the remaining christeners directed their bottles over the technician's head. Without a single contextual clue, the crowd around her cheered. "Mm," she said, closing her eyes and embracing it like the rest of them—not like she had a choice. "Okay."

"I mean, it's a good look," Scott said with a smirk as the bottles were emptied.

Pushing her wet braids back again, she ran her hand down her face and said, "You owe me dinner."

Despite the jovial atmosphere around them, there was still work to be done as it pertained to Chicago—namely, a debriefing. Almost as soon as the champagne showers stopped, Scott, Becan, Natasha, and John were escorted by EDEN officers from the hangar to a debriefing room, where the saturated alphas were drilled on their actions in the city.

For as lively as the hangar had been mere minutes before, the debriefing was as emotionless and matter-of-fact an affair as Scott had ever experienced, considering the circumstances. Nothing was said about the fact that the four Falcons reeked of champagne, nor was any commentary offered when Scott and company relayed the events of Chicago that led them to capture the Carrier. Everything was cut and dry—a complete, hour-long recap of one event after another. When the debrief concluded, they were simply told that someone would be in touch with them shortly and that they shouldn't speak to anyone about what had transpired.

They wouldn't need to if the revelry in the hangar was any indication.

Not long after the four were dismissed, exhaustion kicked in in full. Seeming to possess just enough energy to take showers—and little else—the four soon succumbed to fatigue and retired to their quarters. Sleep became a well-deserved ally.

Their comms never beeped.

8

IT WAS 1300 HOURS when Lilan knocked on General Hutchin's door. Outside, the pounding of rainfall reverberated like a war drum; all of Virginia was in the midst of torrential downpouring. Humidity festered in the base. The mustiness was more than apparent in Hutchin's office despite the portable fan that whirred haplessly in the corner.

"Sir," Lilan said as he stepped inside. Hutchin was poring over a stack of memos.

"Hi, Brent, have a seat. Sleep all right?"

"Well enough, I suppose. I never get much."

Hutchin's eyes left the papers as he leaned back in his chair. "I read over the reports from last night, yours several times. Very interesting stuff, to say the least. I'm sure you can surmise why that is."

"Yes, sir," answered Lilan as he sat down, the creaking of the wooden chair drowned out by the storm.

Leaning forward, Hutchin placed his forearms on the desk and entwined his fingers together. "So let's talk about the elephant. Because it's a big elephant."

"That big elephant did big things," Lilan said.

"I don't typically get promotion recommendations in after-mission reports. Imagine my surprise when your summary of events included an entire section dedicated to the subject. Namely, concerning Remington."

Shifting in his chair, Lilan said, "You're a rich man right now because of Remington."

"A delta, Brent? Really?"

"Frankly, he deserves it."

The general shook his head. "That'd be a three-rank promotion. That's borderline absurd."

Lilan heaved his chest, saying, "Sir, with all due respect, the line of absurdity was crossed when I was given a squad full of rookies."

The men fell quiet. The fan continued to whir as the rain tattered above. Hutchin looked at the report on his desk again. "Jurgen, gamma. McCrae, gamma. Valer, gamma. Donner, gamma. Timmons, beta. Carter, beta. Is there anyone you *don't* want to promote?"

"All of that's reasonable," Lilan said, pointing at the papers.

"I beg to differ." Hutchin exhaled and propped on his elbows. "You've been a captain since EDEN began. You know these requests are ridiculous."

Now, it was Lilan who leaned forward. "Do you have any idea what those soldiers did? What *Remington* did? Do you know how many Bakma were on that ship, sir?"

"Forty-four."

"*Forty-four*," Lilan said. "Eighteen killed, twenty-six captured. Do you understand the odds six soldiers have against forty-four Bakma?"

"I will admit, that's fairly impressive."

Lilan nodded in agreement. "It's impressive for *anyone* to beat those odds. But we aren't talking about anyone here. Four of those six soldiers were rookies on their first mission. Remington was on his first mission. The last combat he saw was in a *Philadelphia* simulator.

"Consider that for a moment, general. A rookie *led* a team that *shut down* a Bakma Carrier with a crew of forty-four. And to make it that much better, they did it without a single casualty. This was originally assigned to a crew of *twenty* from Cougar."

Hutchin folded his arms across his chest in contemplation.

"When I first heard that, I was astounded," continued Lilan. "I knew there were three possibilities. The Bakma could have been completely incompetent. They've never been that before. It could have been a fluke of astronomical proportions. They happen. They're inevitable. But the *third* possibility is that Remington out-led the original task force." He leaned back in his chair. "I thought about that when I got back to base. Remington's decision was voluntary. Nobody told him to do it. I listened over his audio transmissions, he was adamant about it. Tacker and I weren't exactly reassuring when we spoke to him. Remington *knew* what he was asking. He knew the odds, and he repeatedly asked for it. He knew he could do it."

"Or he thought he knew," Hutchin said.

"Which would make it a fluke," Lilan answered. He pulled a small disk from his uniform and tossed it on the desk.

Hutchin reached for it. "What's this?"

"That's his audio log. I listened to it from start to finish. He doesn't act like a rookie. Not once did his voice waver. When Henrick fell, he didn't wait for someone to tell him to take over. He took over immediately. He *wanted* it.

"His command style is better than some captains I've worked with. He's decisive, and he's creative. If I was listening to this for the first time without knowing who this was, I'd swear this was a veteran officer."

Hutchin turned the disk over in his palm. "Apparently, some soldiers did."

"Nobody questioned his authority. When a delta confuses an alpha with a bona fide CO, you know something's going on. He had charisma. They *wanted* to follow him. That's not something you can teach."

Hutchin chuckled. "I did enjoy the part about the van. That's as original an idea as I've ever heard. All right, Brent, I'll admit, you've got some valid arguments for this kid."

"There's one more request I have for him."

Hutchin raised a brow.

"I'd like to nominate him for a Golden Lion."

The room quieted. Hutchin stared at Lilan and then lowered his gaze again to the disk. "You realize that the Lion medals are meant for commanding officers?"

"He was the commanding officer. The fact that he was an alpha is irrelevant. The Golden Lion calls for courage, wisdom, and fortitude in a position of leadership against overwhelming odds. Everything it asks for, he gave. His actions define what the Golden Lion is about, maybe better than anyone who's earned it."

"You realize that no rookie has ever received a Golden Lion? Or any Lion medal. Hell, Faerber didn't get one until he was an epsilon, and his first was a bronze."

"I'm aware of that, sir."

"That would make Remington the first man in EDEN history to earn a Golden Lion on his first mission. Nobody else has even come close."

"Nobody else could have led that operation."

Hutchin looked away, his gaze drifting toward the side of the room as if it were a refuge for his thoughts. At long last, he looked at Lilan again. "I'm not going to let you bump Remington to delta. Not this fast. I'll accept gamma, but that's it for right now. I want to make *sure* this kid is what you say he is before he starts scaling the chain of command. I realize, though, that if you're right about him, holding him back will only hurt *us*. Young leaders are hard to come by."

Lilan nodded. "I want to lead him personally in our next assignment, to see how he behaves first-hand. I want to see if he can follow orders as well as he gives them."

"That sounds acceptable."

"And the others?"

Hutchin looked at the report. "Why Jurgen? He wasn't on the rescue team."

"The other soldiers already look up to him. He served with the NYPD for nineteen years, I think he could serve well as a role model."

"I'll let you move McCrae, Timmons, Donner, Valer, and Carter to beta. As for Jurgen…not yet. I realize his experience is valuable, but I still want to see a bit more from him. That's my final decision."

"And the Golden Lion?"

Hutchin leaned back. "I'll think about it. I want to make sure I'm not putting someone in the history books without a good reason. I'll give this disk a listen and talk it over with EDEN Command. Been a long time since they've had a poster boy—or at least, one younger than Klaus Faerber. I'll make his case as you did."

"Understood, sir."

"Is that all you have for me?"

The captain nodded. "Yes, sir."

"All right, then. You're free to go, thank you for the report."

Lilan rose, thanked the general, and stepped out of the room.

*   *   *

SCOTT'S COMM PULSED at 1330. It took several seconds for its repetitive reverberations to register in his mind, at which point his eyes shot open in a dazed frenzy. He bolted upright as David started in the bunk above. *What's going on?* Scott's mind panicked. *Uniforms! Five minutes! Find Tacker!* Then it clicked. His comm wasn't signaling a tone out. This was a personalized ring—the one he'd set for Nicole.

"What in the?" David asked from above.

"Nicole," Scott answered. "It's ringing for Nicole." David flopped back down on the upper bunk. Scott's heart settled, and he fumbled for the comm. Seconds later, he was holding it toward him as he answered the call. Nicole's widened eyes were staring at him. "Hey, babe," said Scott, his morning-deep voice rumbling from his stomach. "What's going on?" Looking at the clock on the comm's display, he saw the time. Unbelievable. He must have been out like a corpse.

She gaped at him. "I just got back from class, turned on the television, and saw that *Richmond* got called into Chicago. They said the city was a war zone. Then I checked and saw that you never called…"

He winced. Of course.

Angling her head, she asked, "Were you *sleeping*?"

"Yeah." He laughed under his breath. "I'm sorry, I should have called last night. I was caught up in everything."

"Caught up in everything? Do you mean Chicago?"

"Yeah." God, how was he going to explain this?

She watched him expectantly, clearly awaiting his elaboration. "So you were there?" she asked after a short span of silence.

David chuckled from above. "Have fun with *this* one."

Was he there? He was more "there" than almost anyone else in the city. "Yes, I was there." He ran a hand through his hair. "Don't worry though, I'm fine. I didn't get hurt or anything." *I just led a strike team into a Bakma Carrier.*

Her screen shook as she repositioned it against something and tucked her legs in. "Was it as bad as they're saying it was?"

"It was…pretty bad. I mean, not like *really* bad, but…" He didn't even know how to begin. "We got called in as backup. The first wave from EDEN got hammered."

"Were there a lot of Bakma?"

"Yeah, there was a pretty decent amount." There were more Bakma than rounds to drop them. But that wasn't what she needed to hear. What she inevitably *would* hear, however, was much more complicated. "So about Chicago…there's something I should probably tell you. Did you hear anything about a Carrier being captured?"

"Uh, yeah," she said a tad sarcastically. "It's only the lead story on every single news channel."

Is it really? Trying to stave off his surprise at that statement, he cleared his throat. "Did they say anything about, you know…who captured it?"

"You mean the *Six Shooters*? Yeah, that's the lead-in."

Holy smokes, they're even calling us the Six Shooters. "Heh."

That utterance, accompanied by his briefly looking down and rubbing the back of his neck, was all it took for her to lean forward and stare. "Oh, you've got to be kidding me."

Sheepishly, he looked up and raised his hand.

"*You're* one of the *Six Shooters*?"

From above, David murmured a single, short, "Mm." Whether his intent or not, Scott took it as a harbinger of something bad.

Nicole blinked. Reaching forward and grabbing the phone, she drew it closer to her face. "Wha..." Her mouth hung open—like she was having trouble computing her thoughts. At long last, she shook her head as if snapping herself out of it. "*How* were you one of the *Six Shooters*? I thought you said you were backup?"

"Well, we *were* backup. Initially. Until we, umm...did the thing. That we did."

Nicole looked stunned. Utterly floored. Then—in the most striking of gestures—the expression on her face shifted. The look of shock fell into one of realization. She covered her mouth with her hand. Her wheels were turning. "Scott."

...uh oh.

Those dark, angular eyes. They were looking right through him. "One of the channels mentioned an alpha private leading that mission."

Her words hung like the blade of a guillotine. Her tone minced nothing. It was both question and accusation. And it wasn't pleased—as if it already knew.

There was nothing else Scott could say. "Babe, that was me."

"Oh, my God," she said with abject flatness. A second later, she asked, "And is it true that you volunteered to do it?"

Vecking media knows everything. The utter futility of the officers' imploring them to say nothing about the mission to anyone. What naivety. "Yeah," he said with resignation. "Yeah, that's true, too."

The seconds that passed next were like torture, only worsened by the fact that David was lying in the bunk above listening to all of this unfold—and staying deathly quiet in the process.

"Scott, what are you doing?" Nicole asked.

He bit back the urge to answer, *Exactly what I came here to do.* But this situation needed to be diffused, not doused with kerosine. "Nikki, before you get upset—"

"Oh, I'm upset."

"I know. But before you get *more* upset, just listen—"

"Do you have any idea," she said, "what it feels like to be in my shoes right now?"

Scott sighed and looked down.

"Do you know how many nights I lay in bed, wide awake, praying for you to be safe? And the very first thing you do is volunteer for a *suicide mission?*"

"This was *not* a suicide mission."

Nicole rolled her eyes.

"Please don't do that," he said.

"Volunteering to assault a Bakma Carrier on your very first mission is *insane,* Scott! It's absolutely insane. Who even *approves* that?"

Gesturing with his free hand, Scott said, "This was nothing like you're imagining it. I asked permission to do it because I saw an opportunity to actually pull it off. I saw an opening, and I took it. It's what I've always done, with everything." It was how he became her boyfriend and eventually fiancé.

"What if the ship would have taken off into space the moment you boarded it?"

"I...actually never thought of that until you just said it." *Veck, that's terrifying.*

She glared into the camera. "That's the thing, isn't it? You don't think, you just do, without a single thought as to what it does to anyone else, let alone *me.* I'm just left to emotionally deal with it."

"Scott," said David quietly from above, "I think you need to get off the phone."

"What?" he asked David absently, placing his hand over the comm's microphone and looking up.

David said, "End this fight before someone says something they can't take back."

"We're not fighting," said Scott.

"If *that's* not fighting, what the hell is it?"

"An intense moment of fellowship."

Nicole's voice drew him back to the comm. "Talk to *me,* Scott."

"I mean, what do you want me to say?" he answered, setting his gaze on her again. "I did what I felt led to do."

"Ooh, no," she said, "don't feed me that 'I was following God's will' garbage because that's the *same* thing you said about us. Nothing about this has worked in *any* way that is good for us. You leave school out of vecking *nowhere* when everything is going great for you, you tell me you'll be stationed in Detroit, now you're in *Virginia,* so yeah, pardon me if I'm a little skeptical of the *God's Good Little Soldier* routine."

Scott bent forward and rubbed his forehead. "Nikki..."

"Please explain how it is that everything God tells you to do pulls you farther and farther away from *me*?"

And that was the chasm between them—the gulf they had not yet found a way to bridge. He was following a calling she didn't believe in. She claimed she believed in it. Or at least on the heels of "intense moments of fellowship" such as these. Yet this felt different. This felt...significant. It felt that after a single act that everyone else dubbed *heroic*, the gulf between him and the one person whose opinion mattered had grown deeper. And so, he answered her question the only way he knew how. "I don't know."

She stared back with vehemence. Nicole was always bright, yellow sunshine—until she wasn't. And when she wasn't, no one rained harder. She was downpouring now. As if in tune with his thoughts, a low, deep thunder rolled outside.

"Actually," David said, maneuvering to the edge of the bunk and hopping down to the floor, "I'm gonna check out for a bit—take a walk, leave you two alone."

Scott wasn't going to argue. The only thing that could make this conversation feel worse was having someone else in the room to witness it in full. "Thanks, man," Scott said to him.

"Thank you, David," said Nicole from the screen.

Poking his head in the camera shot briefly, David offered her an appeasing smile and a casual salute before he stepped away.

Scott waited until the door to the room was closed, and he and Nicole were left in silence. Turning back to her on the screen, he said, "I believe in this, Nikki. I believe in this with all my heart. What happened in Chicago, at least to me, only confirmed it."

"But do you believe in us?" she asked. Her voice wasn't raised. She really wanted to know.

What hurt was that she didn't know already.

"Yes," he answered with firmness.

Nicole wiped away something beneath one of her eyes. If it was a tear, he hadn't noticed she'd been shedding them. "Scott," she said softly, "I do, too. I just don't feel what you're doing. Not at *all*. I feel like you're running off on your own. Like you're chasing something I don't see. But I want you to see me."

"Babe...I see you."

"Can I tell you something?" she asked. And now, he could see them. Those shimmering lights over her eyes. That saline she was fighting to hold back. "My greatest fear is that I lose you." And right then, with those words, she lost the battle. Lowering her head, the tips of her dark strands dangling down, Nicole covered her eyes with a hand and trembled.

It pierced Scott's soul, but his frustration was directed elsewhere. *How could You put me here? I'm trying my best to follow You, but it's killing her in the process. Why did You call me to this place?*

"Scott, I'm trying to trust," she said, sniffling and looking up. "I am trying *so* hard. I feel like this fear that I feel *constantly* is my trust failing. Like I'm trying to muster up this mustard seed of faith in whatever God is doing with this and I just fail, over and over." She swallowed. "Whatever you felt when you signed up for EDEN, I want to feel it. I've never prayed so badly to feel something. But all I feel is the fear that I'm going to be left behind to pick up the pieces of what we once had." Before he could reply, she held up her hand. "I should be so proud right now. I should be so proud of you, and..."

"...and you're not."

"No, I am. I am proud of you—my God, Scott, you're the lead story on the news. But my pride's not bigger than my fear of what you'll do next." She looked down. "And that's where I'm failing."

How he wanted to hold her. To step through that screen and take her in his arms. This was a knife, right through his rib cage and into his heart.

"I need you to promise me something," she said.

"Absolutely." A knot formed in his stomach when the words left his lips. Promises were not to be taken lightly. In the realm of the believer, it was better to never promise at all than to make one that couldn't be kept. But the question was asked, and the word was given. There was no taking that back now.

Those glimmering eyes stayed on him. Those dark, alluring eyes draped in love and mystery. And in this moment, desperation and fear. "Promise you'll never leave me alone."

An impossibility—and she knew it as well as he did. Closing his eyes, he looked down.

"Don't do that," she said when his eyes left the screen. When he looked up again, she continued. "I'm not talking about death. Neither of us knows what tomorrow will bring. I could die tomorrow walking to class. I'm talking about...on this hero's quest that you've set out on. I don't want you to forget that I'm here."

This was a promise he could make. Looking her straight in the eyes, he said, "Nicole. You are the love of my life. You are my soulmate. No part of me wants to experience this without you. No part of me wants to be on this journey without you. I don't care about being a lead story. I'm still me—a man who is madly in love with you. Not with a career. Not with a calling. With *you*." How he wanted to reach out and stroke her cheek. To brush those dark strands away and kiss her. "If you need to hear a promise, then here it is. I will never forget that you're there. Never."

Silence fell until she sucked in a breath and looked down. With eyes closed, she spoke quietly. "There's something I want to tell you. Coming from me, with my struggles, and my fear, and my lack of trust, I hope it means for you to hear what it means for me to say."

Squinting curiously, he waited for her to go on.

She looked up at him. "I believe you're destined for something great."

Whatever resonations she hoped he'd feel, he felt them. From her, those were words not to be taken lightly. They revealed so much—about him, about her. They were words of assurance wrapped in a blanket of vulnerability. But after the conversation they'd just had, he'd needed to hear them. He'd needed to hear them so that he, too, would believe. He loved her so much for that. Angling his head a bit timidly, he asked, "Can we just pray together for a minute?"

"Yeah," she said softly. "I would really like that."

And so pray, they did. For one minute, then five, then ten. Taking turns, asking for wisdom and guidance. Asking for Nicole to have courage. Praying that Scott would stay humble. Quoting the verses they knew so well, first to God, then when the prayer was over, to each other. Reminding each other why they were there. Why they were *truly* there. To be light unto the world.

And then, at long last and with that smile that had no rival, Nicole said to him, "Okay, hero...how in the *world* did you capture a Bakma Carrier?"

He was all too happy to elucidate.

As the conversation went on, so too did the change in her demeanor. Vulnerabilities gave way to fascinations—and to questions about taking command, issuing orders to soldiers ranked higher than him, and turning a delivery van into a weapon of destruction. The questions anyone would ask about such a bold, borderline lunatic endeavor as the one Scott and his teammates had undertaken.

The more Scott told her, the more he saw her pride in him shine through the darkness that had consumed her. That look of wonder in her eyes was so fantastic to see. All the recognition in the world couldn't hold a candle to it. At one point, she told him, "I can't believe I'm marrying you." It was a starburst in his spirits.

Eventually, a knock came at the door—not David, but their neighbors in 421, Becan and Jayden. When they realized he was talking to her, they were all too eager to meet the woman he'd gushed about since he'd arrived at *Richmond*. Thankfully, by that time, she bore no evidence of the bitter conversation she and Scott had had earlier, and she was happy to meet the two members of Scott's team that he'd talked about the most. Jayden, as would be expected, was a charming, shy gentleman, taking off his cowboy hat when he appeared in the camera and addressing her as ma'am—which Nicole absolutely adored. And, as would be expected, Becan was his usual comical, unpredictable, borderline reputation-demolishing self. When he asked Nicole if Scott told her about the champagne shower he gave Shekeia, Scott snatched the comm back and kicked them out of his room—leaving her to flatly ask when they were alone again, "Who's Shekeia?" Her narrowed eyes grew narrower with every word he offered of his explanation. But she was just giving him a hard time. He *hoped* she was giving him a hard time.

He was pretty sure there was a slim chance she was giving him a hard time.

By the time the conversation had ended, there was no trace of the tension and anger that had been there when she'd first called. They were smiling. They were laughing. They were being Scott and Nicole—the way they'd always been, the way he always wanted them to be.

Eventually, the time came for the conversation to close—almost just in time for another knock at the door, this time from David. Shortly after Scott hung up the call, he was able to relay to David how he'd pulled his talk with Nicole up from a fiery nosedive to a moment of love and bonding through adversity. How their "intense moment of fellowship" had become a part of their testimony—their story of overcoming hardships to make their relationship work. David responded with a simple statement.

"Nice work, compadre. That's how it's done."

That may have been how it was done, but Scott hoped he'd never have to do it again.

The next order of business for the two men was grabbing breakfast—or lunch, depending on how one viewed waking up at one o'clock in the afternoon. As they were on their way back to Room 419, they each received a message prompt on their comms, the text indicating there was to be a unit meeting for Falcon Squad in the hangar at 1600. With some time to spare until then, they sought out the company of Becan and Jayden.

In the time between then and the scheduled meeting, the four neighbors engaged in spirited storytelling, mainly from the aftermath of Chicago. David excused himself from the conversation to call Sharon, a call that lasted well over an hour. A solemn yet reassured David returned to them. Jayden spoke of a call he had placed earlier to his parents and brother, all of whom met the news with skepticism and then pride. The Texan was in contented spirits. Becan had no one to call, though he listened to the others with quiet satisfaction. When 1600 arrived, the four men abandoned Room 419 and made their way to the hangar with the rest of the team.

The chairs were exactly as they had been on the first day Scott arrived. Also present—oddly, Scott thought—were photographers and media outlets, all lined up in the back of the hangar. That was certainly a change from day one. Lilan and Tacker were already standing front and center. As soon as everyone from Falcon was present, the captain cleared his throat. The soldiers stood at attention, and Lilan smiled. "At ease," he said. It was a warmer tone than when he'd first met them. It was a more assured one. "Don't worry, I'm not here to scare you today. That day has come and gone…and this day is much better." Scott smiled. So Lilan did have a heart beating in there, somewhere.

"First and foremost, let's state the obvious," the captain said. "Lieutenant Henrick is in recovery and will be for some time, hence his absence. Whether or not he returns to us, time will tell. For the time being, we'll roll without a lieutenant. After what took place yesterday, I don't think that'll be a problem. It'll also please you all to know that every single soldier rescued from Cougar Platoon is going to survive. That's a testament to you all, and that's the reason you're here.

"What transpired yesterday may go down in the annals of EDEN history as one of the most daring captures ever. I'd like to start by recognizing everyone who took part in it—and by rewarding them with the first promotions in this new incarnation of Falcon."

Scott looked to the side, where he saw everyone in the row grinning. The lone exception was Zigler, who looked borderline disappointed, perhaps predicting he wouldn't be among those getting a bump. To each their own.

"Promotions are meant to recognize skill, bravery, and leadership, and these soldiers have shown that to the fullest degree," Lilan said. "They are Michael Carter, John Donner, Becan McCrae, Jayden Timmons, and Natasha Valer. Congratulations to you all—you are now beta privates. You'll receive your patches tomorrow morning, and your armors' insignias will be adjusted accordingly. Now stand up so you can be properly recognized by your peers." Despite the round of applause that erupted as the soldiers stood, the five recognized soldiers wore perplexed expressions. They looked at Scott.

Scott, however, was contented, and he clapped his hands in celebration. He knew better than to think he'd been left out. There was something for him. There had to be. Was it arrogant to feel that way? No. A team wouldn't receive a promotion, and the leader of that team nothing. That just wasn't how things worked. The applause simmered down, and the new betas sat back down.

Lilan smiled. "Somebody is missing, aren't they?" An array of smiles stretched across Falcon Squad—Lilan and Tacker included. "Every now and then, somebody does something so impressive that people can't help but take notice. Last night, one of our comrades did just that, and a *lot* of people noticed. Taking the burden of leadership on his shoulders, he led one of the most impressive capture operations that EDEN has ever seen.

"Allow me to put what he did into perspective. A strike team of over twenty specialists from Cougar Squad was assigned the task of capturing a fully functional Bakma Carrier—a feat that has never been done. These experienced soldiers and their commanding officers were decimated in the attempt and were forced to abandon the mission. When Scott Remington arrived on the scene, only two of them were still in fighting condition." Several of Scott's teammates slapped him on the back. "Remington rounded them up, and of his own accord, requested permission to continue the operation. He, with only *five* other soldiers, assaulted and captured the Carrier. They did it without a single casualty. Thanks to his actions, EDEN has captured not only a Carrier but over twenty-five live Bakma." The captain smiled as he looked at Scott. "It is my honor to promote Scott Remington to gamma private."

Even Scott was surprised. It was more than just special recognition. It was a two-rank jump. That, he had not expected. As he rose, applause broke out throughout the squad. Gamma private. One rank beneath delta trooper, and two ranks beneath epsilon—officer training. He tried and failed to restrain an all-out grin and, after several nods of acknowledgment, turned to sit back in his chair. Lilan cut him off before he could.

"Don't sit yet, private." Scott halted his descent and stared at the captain, puzzled. How could there be more?

"I put in a special request to General Hutchin earlier today, and he promptly forwarded it to EDEN Command. It took only one hour for Command to get back to us." From Lilan's right, Tacker smiled broadly and handed the captain a small wooden box. Lilan continued. "EDEN has a series of awards specifically designed for leaders who have gone above and beyond the call of duty. It's not an award that is handed down very often. It's an award that specifically calls for heroism, wisdom, and fortitude against overwhelming odds." Several hushed gasps crossed the room.

Scott shivered. Only one medal stood for that. A Lion medal. There was no way…not for him. A Lion medal was more than just an award. It was a symbol laced heavily with status. Captains received Lion medals. And even that was a rarity.

Lilan drew a breath, allowed a slight grin to crack, and puffed his chest. " Scott Remington, congratulations on being the youngest soldier in EDEN history to earn a Golden Lion."

An audible silence swept through the hangar.

No. That was not possible. Scott must have heard wrong. Before anyone could utter a reaction, Lilan resumed.

"You are the first soldier to ever receive a Lion on his first mission, and you are the first to earn one as an alpha private. Congratulations, Remington. You just made history." Lilan extended the wooden box as from the back of the hangar, camera flashes illuminated the hangar space.

The applause that exploded was loud and triumphant. Amid hoots and whistles, Scott found himself stepping, almost floating, to Lilan and the medal. A Golden Lion. It was the most prestigious—and beautiful—medal of honor EDEN could offer. The medallion's surface sparkled gold, and the proud pose of a lion's head sat confident in its center, prepared with dauntless ambition for anything that might challenge it. A Golden Lion. EDEN's designation of a true warrior hero. As Scott took the medallion in his hands, his pupils dilated. He was in awe.

Lilan chuckled. "If you think *that's* something, wait till you see your armor."

Scott exchanged salutes with Lilan and Tacker, closed the wooden box, and returned to his seat. *Wait till you see your armor.* What did that mean? It wasn't until Scott sat down that Lilan cleared his throat a final time.

"You all did it," he said. "This unit had something to prove, and you have proved it beyond even my expectations. I have *no* doubts now that whenever *Richmond* needs something done, we will no longer be considered a backup option." He paused. "You have the rest of today and all of tomorrow off. You all deserve it. And with that, Falcon Squad, you're dismissed."

Though the call of dismissal was given, the hangar hovered with activity. Congratulations were given to all those who were promoted, and jovial celebration hung in the air. Lilan and Tacker departed as the rest of the unit was permitted to revel in its success—all with cameras rolling behind them.

For Scott, the success was beyond his comprehension. With a Golden Lion, he was more than an ordinary soldier. He was, well…a Golden Lion.

He celebrated with the others for a short while, though as time passed, he determined himself to do something he'd failed to do in the immediate aftermath of Chicago.

Leaving the hangar, Scott went to Room 419 and called Nicole to tell her about the promotion and medal. She, of all people, deserved to hear it first. Nicole was overjoyed, and the two shared a wonderful conversation of excitement and thankfulness. It was a far cry from their first conversation that day. That was just fine with Scott.

As it turned out, that was fine with her, too.

9

MANY CHALLENGES had presented themselves to Scott over the past thirty-six hours. That initial charge up the barricade on South Michigan, where the sight of combat—real combat—had left him breathless. The overcoming of Bakma forces that had pinned down Cougar Squad and left them with nowhere to run. That final stand outside the engine room in the Bakma Carrier, where time seemed to stand still as they waited for Vause to seal the door. Each situation had brought him to the brink of destruction.

None of them were as stressful as the media press conference. Plopping on a chair outside the media room, Scott leaned his head back, closed his eyes, and blew out a breath of exhaustion.

"You did good, private," said the officer who'd escorted him to the presser, which had been called in light of his heroics in Chicago. The media—and apparently, the world—was thoroughly captivated by the acts of the *Six Shooters*, even though the only name anyone knew was Scott Remington, team leader and Golden Lion recipient. EDEN jumped at the chance to make Scott the flavor of the moment, satisfying numerous media requests for an interview with Scott in a single press conference. With all of sixty minutes of prep time, Scott was woken from bed, dressed, and escorted to *Richmond*'s media room to be sacrificed at the altar of publicity.

How does it feel to be the new Golden Lion?

That was the first question he'd been asked, as if his receiving the award had somehow disqualified all others who'd won it previously. Though he didn't appreciate the question's wording, he showed no sign of it, answering that he was humbled to receive the award and crediting his teammates for coming through for him. In his own words, "If they hadn't done their part, I wouldn't be standing here right now."

What was going through your mind as you assaulted the Carrier?

That one, he'd answered without reservation. "I was praying to God that it would work." Though the answer did warrant a few good-natured chuckles from the attendees, it offered him a moment to touch on his faith—something he always felt an obligation to do when given any platform. This was by far the most prominent platform he'd ever been given. Nothing he'd done as a quarterback even came close.

Are you single?

He could practically see Nicole's eyes narrowing when that question arose, and the first thought in his mind was, "Really?" But the attendees laughed, and so did he, simply to avoid coming across as a prude. "I'm actually engaged to the most amazing girl in the world," he said, taking a moment to give Nicole a shout-out—and praying to God that it was the last question of that nature he'd have thrown at him.

Thankfully, it was, as he found himself being grilled about the various aspects of the mission itself, from the use of the van, to the emotions he felt as he was taking command, to his experiences at *Philadelphia* Academy. But one topic, more than any other, continued to find its way to him.

Are you the next Klaus Faerber?

Or, at the very least, he was asked numerous questions related to that. Had he ever met Klaus Faerber? Was he a fan of Klaus Faerber? Did he see himself as a man cut from the same mold as Klaus Faerber?

To even be mentioned in the same vein as the captain of Vector Squad was, for Scott, too much. Though he took his time and tried to answer each question thoughtfully, in his mind, he continually said, "Knock it off with the Faerber comparisons." Klaus was the most decorated and famous soldier in all of EDEN. In no way, shape, or form was Scott comparable.

But that, at least in his mind, cut to the heart of what was most problematic about all of this. It was becoming abundantly clear to Scott that he was being framed as a poster boy. Part of the catchiness of the term *Six Shooters* was that it insinuated that there were *six* shooters. So why wasn't Becan up there with him? Why wasn't Natasha or John? Why was no one talking about Vause and Grammar, who were technically part of said *Six Shooters* but whose squad was only mentioned as the one needing rescue? All of this felt all about Scott. That didn't sit well with him. Though he tried to insert the names of the other team members as often as possible, only so many of those opportunities were afforded. They mostly wanted to know if he was the next big thing.

He reminded himself time and time again throughout the press conference that this was the media, and this was just what they did. He wouldn't blame them for that. He also wouldn't blame EDEN for taking full advantage of what he'd done for their promotional purposes. God knew they needed as many recruits as they could get. Scott just hoped that, at some point, he'd stop being the story and he could get on with what he went there to do: make a difference on the battlefield.

Reaching to his belt, Scott pulled up his comm and entered a text message for David.

SCOTT
It's over.

Half a minute later, a response came.

DAVID
Hanging in 424, come on over.

That sounded just fine with him. Rising from the chair he'd collapsed in, Scott clipped his comm back to his belt, slid his hands in his pockets, and made his way toward the barracks.

Room 424 belonged to Michael and Lexie, the official odd couple of Falcon Squad. After discovering they'd be sharing a room with someone of the opposite gender and consequently finding out there was nothing EDEN planned to do about it, the two had no choice but to make things work. Though Scott had spent ample time with his teammates on Falcon in the week he'd been at *Richmond*, Lexie was probably the comrade he knew the least. The Australian pilot seemed more of a wallflower when compared to the decidedly extraverted Natasha and Shekeia. Scott had never actually been in her and Michael's room, so a part of him was curious as to how they'd separated the space for privacy's sake.

As he walked through the hallways, Scott's eyes wandered Richmond's various nooks and crannies. Though there was still a level of newness to the place, it felt more like home with each passing day—or at least, each passing day he *wasn't* in the middle of combat. There were subtle things he'd begun to notice about the place—little touches that gave the otherwise militaristic base warmth. For one, each hallway was named after a county in Virginia, complete with framed street signs on the wall

of each intersection. Scott and his friends lived on Accomack, just past
the intersection of Accomack and Warren. He'd never heard of either
before moving into the base, but he appreciated the touch of familiarity
that something as simple as street signs could bring. It made him think
of the streets on which he'd lived and grown up. It conjured up nostalgic,
slightly sad feelings of days gone by. Good days, never to be experienced
again. And some painful ones.

*I wonder if anyone back at Michigan heard the news. Or back home in
Lincoln. What will they think when they do?*

There was something to be said for anonymity, a measure of which
Scott feared he was at risk of losing. It all boiled down to whether or not
this would propel him to some sort of star status or if it would simply be
his fifteen minutes of fame. He hoped it was the latter, not only for his
own sake but for that of his teammates. He didn't want any of them to
think that he viewed himself as better than the team. They didn't deserve
to feel that way.

As Scott approached Room 424, he saw that it was open. Poking his
head around the corner, he smiled when he saw his teammates inside.
Michael and Lexie were there, as were David, Henry, and Donald.

Grin stretching, David faced Scott and sang gratuitously, "There he
is, Mister America!" The five soldiers in the room clapped and laughed.

"Man, c'mon," Scott said, feeling himself tinge red a bit as he slid his
hands into his pockets and slunk inside.

"Look at him, man," said Donald, erupting in a laugh as he pointed
at Scott. "Man's blushing!"

Scott chuckled. "This isn't blushing, just pure humiliation." As he
stepped inside, Scott glanced about the place. A folding privacy screen
had been placed in the corner of the room opposite the bunk beds and
next to a dresser. Atop the dresser sat a hair dryer and makeup mirror.
He gestured toward it. "So that's how you guys make it work, huh?"

With her legs crossed on the lower bunk, Lexie leaned back on propped
hands and smiled. "My roomie was kind enough to have his parents mail
us one overnight. It's heaps better than turning around with your eyes
closed."

"*So,*" David said, "how did it go?"

"Well, we'll find out," Scott said as he leaned back against the wall.
Richmond's public information officer had informed Scott before the
meeting that the press conference wouldn't be aired live. The media would

be permitted to air selected segments from it later that evening. "I think it went all right, though. I mean, I answered every question."

Henry shook his head in awe. "I just can't believe it, man. God, I wish I'd have been able to go on that mission."

"Hey," David said, slapping Henry on the chest, "you were right there where you needed to be, making a difference on the front. You might not get a set of snazzy armor, but I saw what you were doing. It was great."

How warm David's answer made Scott feel.

"*Speaking* of snazzy armor, when are we going to see this bold new look of yours?" Lexie asked.

Shrugging, Scott answered, "I don't know. Maybe next time we go out? I went to look for it in the ship and it's not even there, so maybe it's being worked on or something. I'm kind of in uncharted waters."

The pilot went on. "So we're dying to know—what was it like going after the Carrier?" When she posed the question, all the others in the room leaned forward with interest. The lone exception was Michael, who just sat with a content smile.

Scott had to remind himself that this was a teammate and not a reporter asking the question. There was no need to be careful with his words—so he didn't. "Man, it was *awesome*." As soon as he said the word, their smiles grew wider. "It was such an adrenaline rush." He pointed at Michael. "I mean, you were there."

Laughing, Michael shook his head. "Yeah, we were nice and warm back in that makeshift hospital you had us set up." He looked at Henry. "No offense man, but I didn't want *any* part of that crazy idea he had."

"You know what I meant," Henry said. "I mean, the guy's vecking famous now."

"If that press conference is the last time anyone ever hears my name, I'll be good with it," Scott said. "My fiancée sure wasn't impressed yesterday! She brought up something I never even thought about—what if that ship had taken off with us in it?"

Donald's eyes opened wide, and he chuckled. "Dude."

"I know, right? If that had crossed my mind during the mission, there's no way I'd have kept on with it." A text prompt chirped from Scott's comm on his belt. He looked at it, where he saw Nicole's name on the display. "Speaking of my fiancée..." She was probably messaging him to see how the press conference went.

As the others chatted, Scott pulled up Nicole's message. The moment he saw it, his eyes widened. It was a video—a recording of her television screen, as taken from her phone camera. And right there, front and center on the news, was a clip of Scott and his teammates returning to *Richmond*...and getting doused with champagne. He groaned as he watched himself direct his christeners' bottles over Shekeia's head. Beneath the video was a text message.

NICOLE
Shekeia, I presume?

"What's up, everything all right?" David asked, raising an eyebrow.

All Scott could muster was, "Uhh," as he angled away from them and began tapping a response.

SCOTT
I was caught up in the moment. And yes...

NICOLE
She's cute! You two might have potential.

SCOTT
Thanks, but I'm already spoken for!

NICOLE
Sure about that?

"Man," Scott said with a nervous laugh. When he looked up from the comm and saw his teammates watching him, he said sheepishly, "Someone took a video of us getting back to base."

David looked at him confusedly for a moment before his eyes opened wide. "Ooh, wait. Do you mean...?"

"Yep." Unbelievable. "Yep, that's what I mean."

Henry angled his head at David. "What's going on?"

"It appears," said David, "that the future Mrs. Remington has observed a certain celebratory event." When they looked at him quizzically, he said, "Some knuckleheads broke out champagne bottles in the hangar. Let's just say, Scott and Shekeia had a little moment that got caught on video."

"We did not have a moment," Scott said.

Looking at the others, David smirked. "They had a moment."

SCOTT
It looks bad, I know. Almost as bad as
that car wash you did.

NICOLE
THAT WAS FOR A CHURCH!

SCOTT
You got hosed down pretty good if I recall.

He smirked to himself. Glancing up, he said to his observers, "It's all good, guys." As conversation resumed amongst the others, he returned to the text exchange.

NICOLE
EVERYONE GOT HOSED DOWN!

NICOLE
Stop trying to get out of trouble.

SCOTT
I'm not in trouble, because my future wife
is an amazing and understanding woman
with a great sense of humor.

NICOLE
She sounds like an amazing gal.

SCOTT
She sure is!

NICOLE
...so did you enjoy it?

SCOTT
Enjoy what?

NICOLE
Christening your new BFF?

SCOTT
Yes, very much so.

SCOTT
Highlight of my day.

SCOTT
We're going to do it again sometime.

NICOLE
Mm-hmm.

NICOLE
Who even had champagne there?

SCOTT
No idea. Didn't even know it was allowed
on base. Maybe it was there for special
occasions.

NICOLE
Well, the two of you are beautiful! I'm
really happy for you both.

Chuckling, Scott shook his head.

SCOTT
Thanks! We're excited about the future.

Breathing easier, Scott glanced up at his teammates, focusing momentarily on their conversation. Henry had asked them while Scott was typing how adrenaline worked. For someone who'd worked as a talk-seller, it probably wasn't something he was accustomed to. He'd *definitely* felt it in Chicago.

Scott looked back down to the comm.

SCOTT
Do you want to talk later?

NICOLE
Can't. Nursing final coming up. Must study. Must pass.

SCOTT
You're gonna rock it.

NICOLE
I hope so.

NICOLE
On that note, time to go! Have fun with Shekeia. I can't wait to meet her AT OUR WEDDING.

NICOLE
I love you I GUESS.

Scott rolled his eyes.

SCOTT
Love you too, babe. Hit the books!

Attaching the comm back to his belt, Scott said, "Sorry, guys, I'm good now."

"No trouble on the home front, I hope?" asked David.

"Nah. She's just ribbing me a bit. What are you guys talking about?"

Smiling, David gestured to Henry. "Hank here was asking us about fight or flight—specifically, which one we thought we leaned toward."

"Oh man," Scott said. "Got a bunch of fighters in here?"

David shook his head. "No, actually—we like to survive."

Arching a curious brow, Scott asked, "What, no one in here leans toward fight?"

From the other side of the room, Michael pointed at Scott and smirked. "I know *you* do! I saw you chase after those Bakma down the street before you tore off for the Carrier. You didn't even hesitate." He laughed. "That's a special kind of crazy."

That was probably how Scott would have described it. Sliding his hands into his pockets and leaning back against the wall, Scott said, "Yeah, I totally lean toward fight. I'm kind of surprised you guys all say you're the opposite. Seems like an odd profession to be in for that."

"Well, I mean, flight isn't *cowardice*," said David. "It's just survival instinct. And sometimes to do your job, you have to go against it. You can't tell me if some necrilid was staring you down, you'd go charging at it."

He most certainly wouldn't. "Yeah, I can't argue with you, there."

Angling his head at Scott, Henry asked, "So how do I make mine go from flight to fight?"

"How do you *make* it?"

"Yeah. I'm not going to lie, I was terrified out there. There were times when I wanted to pull the trigger, but I was just frozen."

David raised his hand. "But I *will* say, he persevered and ended up doing great."

Considering Henry's question, Scott answered, "Fight or flight is an instinct. I think you probably either lean one way or the other."

"Come on, man," said Henry, "I'm sure you must be able to train yourself out of it."

"You're saying 'out of it' like flight is a bad thing."

Spreading his arms widely, Henry said, "Well, yeah! I want to do something like you did. I want to go charge an alien stronghold, or lead some rescue team."

"None of which requires a fight response," said Scott. "Henry, man, you shouldn't be trying to emulate what anybody else does. You gotta be you, dude. I don't think anyone here would tell you that the secret to success is being like them."

Michael smirked smugly. "Zig would."

"Man, leave that dude alone," said Donald, Zigler's roommate, good-naturedly.

Scott would absolutely chime in on that one. "Zig came within about a half inch of losing his face out there, so I would *not* try to emulate him."

Grinning, Donald said, "That dude talks to his mama every night, man. Y'all just think he tough."

At that, David chuckled. "We don't, actually."

"That dude, man. He's a kid, just tryin' to act all bowed up. He figurin' things out, give him time."

"He really talks to his mum every night?" asked Lexie, amusedly.

The demolitionist nodded. "He all sweet when he think I ain't listenin'. He didn't know I was in the room one time and he had her on speaker. She asked him if he was making new friends and he was like, 'yeah, mom.'"

"Aww!" Lexie said, a grin stretching. "That's so sweet. And a little bit sad, because he really isn't."

"She already sent him a care package," Donald said. "Snacks and stuff, and a little handwritten note. I saw it on his desk."

Eyes narrowing mischievously, Lexie asked, "Did you read it?"

"Naw. I read the first sentence, then I stopped. Only other thing I looked at was the bottom, that's how I knew it was her. Said, 'I love you, son.'"

Grin still plastered, Lexie looked at the others. "That's bloody adorable."

Not wanting to deviate too far from the point of the conversation, Scott looked at Henry again. "But like I was saying, man, don't put pressure on yourself to try and be like someone else. That's not what gets you success."

Henry's eyes grew distant as they broke away from Scott's, staring off as if the soldier was in heavy thought. At long last, he said, "I just don't want to have come all this way for nothing, you know? Or to just...fail."

"You're being too hard on yourself," said Michael. "We had one mission, that's it. You can't look at what Scott did and try to stack up to that—that was a unique situation that may never happen again."

"Exactly," Scott said. "That was such a perfect storm of weird scenarios, and for all we know, we just got lucky. Don't think that you need to do something crazy like that to make a difference."

Adding to it, David said, "You're making a difference just by being here."

"I don't even know if I killed a single Bakma," Henry said.

"You did," said David, laughing warmly afterward. "I'm not sure you were aiming for him, but I definitely saw you kill one."

Henry half-frowned. "Awesome, I accidentally did something."

"Don't aim to *do* something," said Scott. "Aim to *be* something. And in that, you've already succeeded."

After a deep sigh, Henry said, "I just want to be respected for the first time in my life. I want people to look at me and say, 'That guy did awesome.'"

"They will," David said. "Stick around long enough, and trust me, they will. This first round was Scott's turn. Yours is coming up."

This time, it was Scott with the look of mild disapproval. "For the record, this was not *my* turn. The reason they're calling us the *Six Shooters* is because there were *six* shooters. But," he said, his focus returning to Henry, "he's right in that you'll get your time to shine. Every time we get called out, it'll get easier. Just focus on learning and doing your best. Before you know it, it'll be like instinct."

On his belt, Scott's comm chirped. Another message. Glancing at it, he saw not Nicole's name on the display but Mark's—his little brother. He lifted the comm to read it.

MARK
Hey is the press conference on anywhere?

Sliding his fingers over the screen, Scott went to type back a message but stopped himself short. *No, don't just text a response—give your brother a call.* Looking back to the group, Scott said, "That's my little bro, I need to give him a call." He offered the group a parting wave. "I might swing back in after if you guys are still hanging around."

"Sounds good, man," said Michael.

David waved. "Later, champ."

Turning from them, Scott made his way back into the hall.

Though every sibling relationship was special in its own right, Scott felt he and Mark had a truly unique bond. Mark was barely more than a kid when their parents died. In many ways, Scott had stepped in to fill the void his parents had left. It was a fast track to maturity, most of which Scott felt he'd done decently enough. Ever patient, Mark seemed to understand, even at that young age, what Scott was going through as the new man of their proverbial, two-person house. Scott knew that Mark looked up to him tremendously. He also knew that Mark would make fun of every part of Scott's press conference once it aired.

What were brothers for?

Looking down the hall as he approached his room, Scott paused when he saw someone standing in front of it. Natasha. Her hand was up as if poised to knock, though she watched the door stilly—as if hesitating to commit to knocking.

That all changed, of course, when she looked down the hall and saw him.

Flinching in a genuinely flustered way, Natasha lowered her hand quickly and faced him. Her cheeks tinged red in embarrassment, and she offered a weak smile as he approached. "Busted," she said sheepishly.

Scott looked funnily at her. "Busted?"

"Yeah," she said flatly, averting her eyes from him in a way that was as un-Natasha-like as he'd ever seen. The embarrassed smile, though, remained.

"What's up?" Scott asked.

Crossing her arms and tightening her body, she looked down and answered, "I just wanted to talk for a bit." Biting her lip, she seemed to chew on it as her eyes grew distant—almost as if she was taking in and registering the words she'd just spoken. She remained that way for several seconds before she breathed a sigh of resignation. "Yeah, that's not true."

What in the world was going on?

Natasha lifted her eyes to meet him. Her eyebrows parted; her lower jaw tensed. "I actually wanted to apologize...which is not something I really do much." She looked away nervously. "Clearly."

"Apologize for what?" Instinctively crossing his arms to match hers, he angled his head to be fully attuned.

Several seconds passed before she spoke again. There was no play in her voice. None of the provocative flirtatiousness that'd defined her in Scott's mind. Quite the contrary, her tone was pensive to the point of sounding introspective. "My mom called me this morning. Actually," she laughed softly, "she was made to, by the little girl who lives next door. My mom was outside, and the girl and her friends were playing in the yard and saw her, and I guess word kind of got out about what happened..."

Scott's eyes narrowed intently as she continued.

" ...she and her friends wanted to talk to me. They wanted to talk to *me*. They told my mom they'd never talked to a hero before." There was heavy emotion in her eyes. They weren't quite on the verge of tears, but maybe...just maybe, her heart was thinking about it. When she spoke again, it was with determination to finish. "I'm sorry that I gave you a hard time like I did. And also if anything I did made you uncomfortable. I think for me, it was just messing around, but...it feels kind of bad now—it's kind of weird. But I won't do it again. Not to you."

At that moment, Scott realized what was happening to her. It was the same thing that'd happened to him after his parents died. The same thing that happened when he realized he'd be raising his little brother.

When he realized things were bigger than him.

"When I met you that first day," she said, "I thought you were just some idiot jock." Her gaze held steadfast. "Going on that mission with you is the proudest moment of my life."

Scott fell silent as her words lingered—as their intent lingered. As the seismic shift in her perspective reverberated right before his eyes. What could he say to all that?

Faintly, perhaps self-depreciatingly, she smiled. "That's about as good as I get with the mushy stuff. At least, when I actually mean it," she added with a wink. Lifting her chin, she said, "Enjoy your day, Scott. I'll see you later, I'm sure."

"Thank you, Tasha. What you said means a lot." It truly did.

Stepping past him, Natasha walked down the hall toward her and Shekeia's room. Scott watched her for a moment before opening the door and entering Room 419.

The proudest moment of her life. Wow.

As Scott wrapped his mind around Natasha's words, he slipped off his boots and set them by his bedside. Sitting on the lower bunk, he leaned forward in thought.

God, I still haven't fully wrapped my mind around what You did with us. I wanted confirmation that I made the right choice coming here, and You gave it to me beyond anything I could've imagined. I give You all the glory for it.

Running his hand through his hair, he sat upright and looked around his room—at the Scripture on his nightstand, at David's family photos, at the cracked mirror atop the sink in the corner. At the Golden Lion medallion perched in its ceremonial box. When Scott found out he was being garrisoned at *Richmond*, Nicole said to him, "God is putting you in the place you need to be." That she had the faith to impart with him such wisdom when she herself was struggling was incredible. He felt like he was seeing the fruit of that faith now. How sweet it tasted on what were once such parched lips.

Thank You for this. Thank You for all of this. I know this is exactly where I need to be.

He had told himself—and his teammates—that he needed to call Mark. And he would. But for now, in this moment of solace and reflection, he wanted to keep his priorities in check. He wanted to be a seeker, not only when he struggled but when things were going well. It was hard to imagine things being much better than this. Reaching over to his nightstand, he grabbed his black, leather-back Scripture and opened it to read.

The next few days found Falcon Squad slowly returning to the pace of routine. Though their days of rest were used appropriately, when it was time for regularly scheduled business to return, Falcon was happy to get back to work with combat drills, workout sessions, and discussions of hypothetical mission scenarios.

The media frenzy over Scott, though fervent, was indeed short-lived. Soon enough, more substantial news of the world reclaimed the public spotlight. While the *Battle of Chicago*, as it came to be called, remained in prime coverage, the *Six Shooters* fell back into quiet anonymity. That was well enough with Scott and his friends. Their initiation into EDEN had been a resounding success.

They were eager to find out where they'd be taken next.

10

SCOTT AND DAVID raced into the hangar. Their comms had sounded only minutes before, prompting the two men—and the rest of their Falcon Squad counterparts—to don their uniforms and report to *Vulture-7*. Even before any of them had set foot in the hallways, something about this call resounded as different. There were no other soldiers in the hallways. There was no bustling of squads or technicians in the hangar space. Falcon was completely alone. Ahead of them, *Vulture-7* sat perched in its concrete cage, the hue of the reddening evening sky casting a reflective glow over its nose.

Lilan and Tacker stood at the ramp of the Vulture, waiting as the soldiers made their way closer. The only other person in the unit ahead of them was Lexie, who was already inside the transport and prepping it for flight—indicating that perhaps she'd been called before the rest.

Glancing behind him, Scott saw the same uncertain looks on his teammates' faces. He understood that uncertainty. This was a total contrast to the chaos of Chicago. This felt…

…he wasn't sure.

"Hey," whispered David next to him, "where's Becan and Natasha?"

Scott inspected the group again. Sure enough, the two soldiers were missing. "I have no idea."

Lilan cleared his throat. "All right, team, over here." His voice was calm. Patient. Nothing about his tone indicated any sense of urgency. Slowly, the captain's gaze narrowed coldly. "Where are McCrae and Valer?"

Before anyone could reply, hastened footsteps emerged from the entrance to the hangar. Becan and Natasha tore inside, heaving heavily as they drew to stops by the rest of their comrades. Scott looked at the breathless pair oddly. Becan met his gaze briefly before he looked back at the captain. "Sorry, captain," he said, Natasha following suit immediately after.

Lilan nodded dismissively. "It's okay." He looked sidelong at Tacker and offered the executor a nod. Tacker returned it in kind, then left the group to enter the transport alone. Lilan looked back at the soldiers. "We have an unusual assignment tonight. It's not the first time this has happened, but it's still pretty rare. I'll explain once we get airborne. Get inside and get geared up."

The soldiers climbed aboard the transport and held onto the support bars as they awaited liftoff to somewhere. What a difference, Scott thought. Before they departed for Chicago, the hangar had been flooded with activity. Rushing footsteps, loud shouting, the roar of engines. Now, it was just…them.

Lexie taxied *Vulture-7* onto the runway and, after a minute, lifted off the ground. Once the course steadied and the transport assumed its forward glide, the soldiers stood to open their lockers and don their armor. The recently promoted soldiers were quick to notice their updated chrome badges. For Scott, however, there was a bit more.

He had been tipped about the armor of the Golden Lion, and now he understood what was meant. A strikingly distinct feature of his armor separated it from everyone else's—a polished golden collar molded around the neck of his chest plate. It was boldly simple. It was fitting for the most prestigious honor in the organization. As he fit into it, several of his comrades offered comments of praise.

Nonetheless, a cloud of tension hovered in the troop bay. None of the soldiers knew where they were going or why. The elaboration began as soon as Lilan saw that everyone was geared up.

"Ladies and gentlemen…this evening, you will be partaking in your first necrilid hunt."

And right then, in two words, Scott felt his stomach bottom out. A *necrilid hunt*. Looking at David and then the others, Scott saw they all bore similar expressions. Their faces collectively paled.

"Three necrilids were spotted thirty minutes ago on the outskirts of a town called Harlan in Kentucky," said Lilan. "There were no alien spacecraft in the vicinity, so we're pretty sure this wasn't a drop-off. About two weeks ago, a Ceratopian Cruiser was shot down in the Appalachians, close to where this town is. Our best assumption is that these necrilids were on board the craft and somehow escaped from the scene unnoticed. They probably worked their way through the mountains until they showed up in Harlan. This doesn't happen often, but it isn't unprecedented.

"The necrilids were first spotted approaching a high school and were then seen crawling inside through a hole in the roof—probably one they made. It's a rural area, and everyone has been ordered to remain in their homes. Fortunately, school ended a few hours ago. There were some people in the parking lot who saw the necrilids, but they've since left the scene. The local police are there now keeping an eye on the building in case the critters leave, but we doubt they're going to do that. When necrilids settle down somewhere, it's usually for a while. The school is dark, it's got a lot of corridors, and it's probably going to be pretty warm. If any of them are female, they're probably looking for a place to breed."

Scott's skin prickled at Lilan's words. Somewhere, in some dark corner of that vacant school, alien predators were perhaps breeding. Like a page out of a nightmare.

"Necrilids have an extremely fast gestation period. Eggs can be laid and hatched in a matter of days—that's faster than anything on Earth. It's very easy to miss an egg or two when you're sweeping an area, so infestation is a very real threat. Our orders are simple: hunt these necrilids down and kill them. Once they're dead, a sweeper team will come in to look for any eggs that may have been laid. In most cases, we'd be given a digital floor plan ahead of time to upload into our HUDS. Naturally, these necrilids picked a school that doesn't have that. That means that when we get there, we're going to be on our own to navigate the school."

For a moment, Lilan hesitated. All of the soldiers' eyes were trained on him. Finally, he made his closing statement. "I know none of you have faced a necrilid in combat before. I don't know what they taught you in the Academy, but let me assure you…the reality is much worse. There's a reason nobody wants these missions.

"You're about to fight something that's going to scare the living hell out of you. The last things a lot of soldiers see on hunts like this are fangs and claws. I'm going to brief you as best I can in the short time we have before we land.

"The average necrilid is roughly the same size as an average human. When crawling on all fours, they can lower their profile to about two feet. If they stand on their back legs, they can hit six. They're designed for the dark, and in an unlit room, especially one with a lot of clutter, they *will* find you before you find them. You won't sneak up on one. The one thing you *can* look for is the eyes. They glow yellow like a cat's if they hit any kind of reflection. But that's about it.

"They're quick, and they can move very quietly. Their claws can completely retract, so don't think you'll be able to hear them skittering around. If you hear claws, they're trying to lure you. Use caution. Necrilids can climb walls and ceilings as easily as they can move on the ground, so don't just look ahead. Look everywhere.

"They make a wide range of noises. They breathe loudly, they hiss, they bark, they shriek. Some have even been reported to try and mimic human sounds. They communicate. They coordinate. They have an odor like a wet dog, but if you're close enough to smell it and you still haven't found it, that's not a good thing.

"If you find a necrilid, don't try to outperform it. You won't. Distract it. Go at it from two sides, throw a shoe, veck, do something. Outthink it. Always remember, it is hunting you. Any questions?"

Quiet hung in the troop bay. The soldiers exchanged silent, somber looks. None dared to make a sound.

"All right, then," said Lilan, "get your minds right and get ready. We'll be there before you know it."

IT WAS ALREADY dark outside when *Vulture-7*'s landing lights hit the school. The aircraft set down in front of the school, near the parking lot, on a small patch of grass. Lilan gestured to Lexie, who promptly shut off the transport's exterior lights.

"We're going to break into two teams," Lilan said. "I'll be taking Remington, Valer, and Donner with me—radio sign, Falcon-1. Falcon-2 will be headed by Jurgen and'll have McCrae, Mathis, and Zigler. Once we start to get a lay of the land inside, we'll break into two directions as a pair of four-man teams." His gaze settled onto Jurgen. "Provided Private Jurgen doesn't mind my leaning on his experience in this instance."

David shook his head. "Not at all, sir."

Behind the group, Tacker spoke for the first time. "I'll be remaining in the transport to provide cover fire should one of these things try to get out. Timmons will back me up. Also remaining behind will be Carter and Bell—though hopefully, we don't need either of you." Briefly, he looked to the cockpit. "And of course, Ms. Robinson, for obvious reasons. Our radio sign is Falcon Base."

It didn't take long for the obvious omission to make herself known as Shekeia began to look about with less-than-subtle confusion.

Lilan caught it. "I didn't forget you, Rhodes. So here's your situation."

Uh oh, Scott thought.

"There is presently no power to this school. It went out shortly after the necrilids were spotted going in. That means they probably messed something up while they were digging around. Supposedly, this school has its own auxiliary power supply, but for whatever reason, it didn't kick on."

Slowly, Scott's eyes widened. *Oh, veck, he's not gonna...*

"It will be your job," Lilan said, "to find whatever server room you need to find to try and reroute power to the right place. We'll help you get there, but once you're there, you're on your own. Though you'll be operating solo once you've reached the server room, you'll be identified on radio as Falcon-3."

Scott looked at Shekeia, whose eyes were as wide as plates. Though she seemed to try and hide it, Scott swore he saw her swallow. "Yes, sir," she said.

The captain nodded. "One more thing. I want some weapons diversity out there, so Jurgen, Zigler, and Donner take shotguns. Everyone else, stick with E-35s." The three men nodded and switched out their weapons. "Okay, team. Stay on radio at all times, and move quietly. Follow my lead for now." Lilan motioned toward the rear door, prompting Lexie to lower it. After several seconds of mechanical whining, the ramp thudded against the fresh ground.

There was a heavy odor in the air—one that was impossible to pin down. It was thick. It was brooding. It was fear. Scott felt the sweat emanating from his fingertips as his hands clasped firmly against his assault rifle. This was totally different from Chicago. In Chicago, the enemy was right there in front of him. It fired at him with rifles and grenades. Scott could fight it fearlessly. Here, the enemy lurked in the shadows. And it wanted to eat him.

The soldiers crept from the Vulture toward the large double doors at the school's entrance. Behind them, Tacker and Jayden took position inside the ramp, the weapons training on various points of the school— windows, perhaps, just in case one of them would snag a lucky kill. If only such luck would materialize.

"All right, Rhodes, you're up first," Lilan said as he approached the door. "Without auxiliary power, off-campus security couldn't send the signal for the doors to unlock. That means it's on you."

"Yes, sir," Shekeia said, slipping past the others and taking out her handyman. Scott watched as she set up the device's various plugs and dongles into a panel next to the door. It was impossible not to compare her to Vause. Vause didn't tremble nearly this much. Seconds later, however, a satisfied chirp emanated from the panel. "Door's unlocked," she said, clearing the way for Lilan.

Lilan took hold of one of the door panels and gently pulled it. It eased open without a sound. A ray of moonlight cut through the darkness beyond the doors. Everything else inside was pitch black. "Eyes peeled and weapons ready," Lilan said quietly, his voice tinny in their headset speakers.

Scott swallowed as Lilan took his first step inside. Into darkness. Scott's heart felt as if it would burst in his chest. His palms sweated more fluidly. He took a step forward. Despite his conversation with Henry about fight or flight, there was no fight within him right now. Everything in him told him to turn away. To run. Yet he found himself moving forward.

Were the others feeling this same fear? He looked over at David, who appeared stoic. In control—or at least, good at faking it. Zigler? Zigler was afraid. He *looked* afraid. Becan...Becan wiped damp hands on his armor as if the cold metallic surface might dry them. Everyone was afraid. Everyone but Lilan.

Scott closed his eyes and hesitated. He had trained for this. He knew the fear wasn't real—it was a manifestation of his mind. He had *trained* for this, just like he'd trained for Chicago, and look how well that had turned out. His comrades were there with him. He was a Golden Lion. It was time to show it.

Scott's eyes opened. He centered his focus. He wasn't going to die. Stepping forward again, right behind Lilan, he entered the school.

It felt like a tomb. Aside from the faint sounds of the soldiers breathing, there was complete silence. An unusual warmth hung in the air despite the relative coolness outside. It was a thick warmth. A musty warmth. It felt stagnant. As the last of the soldiers filed inside, the double doors eased shut. They were in total darkness. Scott reached up to his visor and switched on his TCV.

The immediate area was spacious—a commons area and office. Benches and lockers lined the walls. There were two pairs of hallways: one on the right and one on the left. A pair of double doors and an open cafeteria sat at the far end of the commons. There was no sound. No spark of electronics, no skitter of necrilids. Total silence.

"Since power here's momentarily dead, there's no reason to turn off your TCVs," said Lilan. "Don't use your helmet light unless you don't have a choice. Necrilids can already find you easily enough without them." He knelt on the floor and stared ahead at the commons. "Looks like we have two basic wings, here—left and right. Let's label everything."

Scott looked back at the others. David and John had knelt on the ground. The others remained standing. Scott's attention shifted to Lilan as the captain pointed to the nearest pair of hallways on the right.

"The first hall on the right is *Alpha*. The one right after it is *Bravo*." He looked the other direction. "Likewise, the first hall on the left is *Echo*, and the one after it is *Foxtrot*." Everyone listened in silence. Lilan pointed at Alpha hall. "Jurgen, move your team down Alpha. Looks like it runs parallel to Bravo, so hopefully, they connect farther down. If not, well... you'll figure it out.

"We'll check out that cafeteria up ahead and whatever those double doors are way down there. I'll call the double doors *Golf*. After we check that out, we'll hit Echo and Foxtrot."

"Yes, sir," David whispered.

Tacker's voice emerged in their headsets. "Falcon Base to Falcon-1."

Canting his head, Lilan said, "Falcon-1."

"I have a law enforcement rep with me out here. He says the server room is in the very back of the office."

Lilan pointed to the office on the far side of the hall just before Echo. "Office," he said quietly, off-comm. Replying to Tacker, he said, "We have it, thank you Base."

"Base clear.'

"Falcon-1 clear." Lilan turned to look at those behind him, eventually finding Shekeia. "There you go, Rhodes. She's all yours."

Exhaling a wavering breath, Shekeia said, "Yes, sir."

"Do whatever magic you need to do to try and get us some lights—or whatever else you can conjure up."

"Yes, sir."

The captain seemed to hesitate. "Do you need one of us to stay with you, or can you handle that and staying alive by yourself?"

Shekeia nodded. "I can handle it, sir. I'll just uhh...lock the door behind me."

"Yeah," Lilan said blithely before surveying the commons and saying with cement-thick sarcasm, "that oughta stop them."

The technician's shoulders sunk.

"All right, the rest of you," Lilan said, "let's split up and get moving. This place ain't going to explore itself."

DAVID GATHERED HIS crew and crept toward Alpha's entrance. After clearing his throat softly, he whispered into his comm, "All right, team, here's the plan. Hank, you stay with me. Becan, Zig, keep an eye on the rear. We're going to move slow." The others whispered affirmations.

Two parallel corridors intersected Alpha farther down. The vibrant hues of the soldiers' TCVs frighteningly lit them. David paused. "We have two intersecting corridors up ahead, one right after the other. They may both connect to Bravo." The group slowed as they approached the first of the two intersections.

David and Henry's weapons were trained ahead as Becan and Zigler sidestepped from behind. As Becan stopped behind David, he peered back into the commons they'd just left. Everything was silent and still. He stared at the false colors of the TCVs for several seconds before drifting his hand to his visor. His finger floated over the TCV switch, and he clicked it off. All color faded. The world was thrust into blackness. He lowered his stare to the ground. Not even his boots were visible. Becan swallowed and reached back up to flick his visor back on. A massive spotlight burst from his helmet and rayed into the commons.

"Veck!"

Everyone on David's team jumped and slammed against the wall. The stares darted to Becan, who frantically groped his helmet. The spotlight went out, and the halls were again enveloped by darkness.

"What in the hell was *that*?" Zigler spat out.

Becan's heart pounded. "I hit the wrong veckin' switch!"

"You hit the wrong *switch*?"

"I'm bloody nervous, all righ'?"

Scott's voice emerged over the comm. "Everything okay? We saw a light."

David shut his eyes and caught his breath. "Yeah, Becan hit the wrong switch."

"What?"

"He..." David shot a dark look at the Irishman. "What were you doing?"

Becan bent forward and tried to steady his own breathing. "I turned off me TCV jus' to see the darkness, then I went to turn it back on an' I hit the wrong button. I'm a bloody eejit. It won't happen again."

From beside him, Zigler snarled, "What possessed you to do *that*?"

"Enough," David said. "We're moving on." He turned back to the first intersection in Alpha hallway. "Everyone stay right here behind me. I'm going to look around the corner and see if this connects to Bravo." He hesitated. "I guess we'd better label these, too. We'll call this first inter-secting hallway *Romeo* and the one after it *Juliet*." He pressed against the left wall and inched toward Romeo. Once again, there was a total absence of sound.

He pressed against the corner of Alpha and kept a constant eye on the right side of Romeo. Through his TCV, he could see that various doors lined Romeo as far as vision allowed. There were no signs of life. He drew another breath and pressed against the wall again. He inched his head toward the corner just enough to allow his peripheral vision to peek around it. He then poked his head around it entirely, and the hallway appeared. Romeo was long, and it did appear to connect to Bravo. It ran past Bravo, where it ended with a right-hand turn. A U-turn into Juliet. He glanced behind him, where he saw the same pattern. The two ends of Romeo mirrored each other.

"Okay," David said, "it looks like Romeo does run down to Bravo. I see a turn at both ends...it must loop around to Juliet on both sides." His gaze lingered on the Bravo intersection. "We have to check out this end before we move toward Bravo. Henry and Zig, you guys are going to come with me to do that. Becan, I want you to wait here in this intersec-tion while we do so."

"Like hell!" Becan whispered emphatically.

"Becan, we need to check all of the rooms, but we can't let anything slip by. You'll be in constant view of us at all times."

"Bloody grand. So yeh can see me get eaten alive first-hand, class."

"We're only meters away. If you see anything, just let us know, we're right there."

"Yeh think?" Becan scoffed. "Don't be long."

BACK IN THE school's center, Lilan and Natasha explored the cafeteria while Scott and John stayed in the commons. Thus far, only the soldiers' bootsteps had broken the silence.

"Cafeteria looks clear," Lilan said through the comm.

"Commons too, sir," said Scott in reply. It almost began to feel safe where they were, which in itself—and quite ironically—terrified him. Even though the necrilid predators were somewhere in the school, Scott couldn't envision them bounding across the room. It seemed too fright-ening a possibility to be real.

As an added benefit to being where he was, Scott had been able to watch Shekeia gain entry to the office. As nerve-racking as this was for them, he couldn't imagine how Shekeia felt. All he knew was that he'd watch that office exterior like a hawk for as long as possible.

Lilan addressed them again. "Valer and I are going to check out the kitchen. You two sit tight up there, we won't be long."

"Take as looong as you like," John murmured off-comm.

Next to him, Scott huffed a single breath of unamused laughter. "Yeah, you're telling me." After a moment's pause, he looked at John. "If you had a choice between this or charging another—"

"The Carrier," said John immediately. "I'm taking the Carrier."

"Yeah," Scott said, looking ahead again. "I'm taking it, too."

SHEKEIA'S FACE WAS beading with sweat. Upon gaining entry to the office, she'd begun to make her way toward the back, as directed, only to discover that the back was considerably farther *back* than she could have imagined. After crossing the office lobby, she trekked down a hallway containing numerous individual offices and—to her abject horror—another short hallway with a door that led to some other part of the building not connected to the commons. Everywhere she looked, she saw a potential necrilid entry point. And every step she took, she wanted to turn and run away. Yet onward she went.

She did eventually find the server room, which was literally the farthest room from the office lobby. It was long—almost shotgun style, with a single door for entry. But the worst part of all was the terminal itself. It was at the far end of the room, its display screen facing the server room door...meaning Shekeia's back would face the door while she worked on it. She cursed herself inwardly for saying she'd go at it alone, though she dared not utter a sound.

Her efforts to close herself inside the server room had been in vain, as she not only discovered that the door possessed no lock but that its latch didn't engage properly. Every time she released the door after closing it, it would slowly ease back open. Leaving it little more than halfway shut, she removed her handyman, angled herself by the terminal so she could see the door in her peripherals, and went to work trying to access the school server.

BECAN'S HEART POUNDED as he crouched in the middle of the intersection of Alpha and Romeo. Though he kept vigilant watch over all four directions, for some reason, some unidentifiable force lured him toward the far end of Romeo, past the Bravo intersection. Something drew him there—something unnatural. Every moment his eyes left it felt like a mistake. Something about it was not right.

It took several minutes for David, Henry, and Zigler to finish inspecting the near side of Romeo. It indeed U-turned into Juliet, as it appeared to do on both ends. The soldiers peered through classroom windows as they inspected, though there were no signs of necrilid presence. Midway through the near side of Juliet, David spoke quietly to Becan again. "Becan, we're coming back to you down Juliet. Move yourself to the second intersection so we can see you."

Silence hung on the line. Becan's voice murmured through. "Righ', I'd like to stay here. Yis guys can see down tha' hall fine, but I want to keep an eye ou' on tha' corner way up ahead."

David paused. "The other end of Romeo?"

Once more, silence. As David awaited Becan's response, Henry and Zigler drew to his side and watched him. "Yeah," Becan answered. "I think somethin' is down there."

The three men froze. They exchanged widened expressions, and David focused on the comm. "Did you see something?"

Becan hesitated. "I didn't..."

No further elaboration came. "What makes you think something is down there?" David asked.

"It's..." Becan's words trailed off. His attention was completely fixated on the far end of Romeo. The hairs on his neck and arms tingled, and he engaged the zoom on his visor. "...it's jus' a feelin'."

David raised a brow. "A *feeling*?" He turned to Henry and Zigler. "Okay. Becan...stay there, then. We're going to finish here then meet up with you again."

Becan's response was quick. "All righ'. Hurry, I'm brickin' it over here."

David reaffirmed his grip on his shotgun. "Let's get this wing finished. I'll take the doors on the left, you two take the doors on the right. Look through the glass, make sure nothing is there, then move on to the next one." Henry and Zigler nodded, and they continued the search.

LILAN AND HIS team stood outside the double doors of Golf. "I'll go in first," Lilan said, "Valer and Remington follow right behind. Donner, hang back and watch the commons." The captain squared his E-35 against his shoulder and pressed against the door. It opened without noise.

It was an auditorium. There were three seating sections, all angled downward to a stage. Lilan gave a brief look up to the ceiling and grimaced.

It was a labyrinth of spotlights, cables, and helicopter wire. "Okay," he said, "let's move in here. I'll take the center aisle, Remington take right, Valer take left. Sweep the floor and meet on the stage."

Scott and Natasha affirmed, and they stepped ahead.

DAVID PAUSED TO speak to Becan as he, Henry, and Zigler reappeared in the intersection of Alpha and Juliet. "Still feel like something is—"

"Down there," Becan said, interrupting. "Yeah. I do."

David scrutinized the Irishman. His gaze was fixated down Romeo in a trancelike state. His attention never wavered to look at David or the others. Refocusing down Juliet himself, David said, "These corridors run parallel. We'll move in pairs. Henry, stay with me—we'll move down Juliet. Becan and Zig, you two move down Romeo. Step carefully."

LILAN WAS HALFWAY through the auditorium, eyes peeled in every direction, when Shekeia's voice came over the comm. "Falcon-3 to Falcon-1."

"Falcon-1."

SHEKEIA STARED DOWN at the display on her handyman. Numerous wires were connected from the device to the school's network terminal, which was only powered up by a feed from the handyman. As she peered down at the lines of data and code, she said through the comm, "This whole system's busted. Whatever damage is done, it must be extensive."

"Can you elaborate?" Lilan asked.

Reaching her hand under her visor, she wiped the sweat from her brow. "I'm not even getting any DMARC signals from any available rerouting path. Either the signal's dead at the source, or—"

"What the hell is a DMARC?"

"Demarcation point. It's…" Pressing her lips together, she half shook her head. "It's the point between the provider and the customer, the school being the customer and the provider—"

Lilan said, "Let's just stick with busted."

After sighing off-comm, Shekeia said, "Yes, sir. It's busted."

"Do your best to un-bust it. No need for explanations."

She nodded her head. "Un-busting."

THE AIR HUNG WITH an intangible weight. With every step David took, it grew heavier. The temperature was still warm and humid, and sweat drops had formed on everyone's foreheads. There was still no sound beyond their footsteps. The two pairs of soldiers were almost at the adjacent intersections of Bravo when Henry suddenly stopped.

David halted to face him. Henry's expression was locked in a dead stare. "Everyone hold up for a bit," David said.

Becan and Zigler froze in Romeo.

David followed Henry's gaze toward the corner of Juliet, though nothing seemed out of place. His attention returned to Henry. "What is it?"

"Do you smell that?" Henry asked.

"UN-BUST IT," muttered Shekeia off-comm. "Just un-bust it, Rhodes. What's the matter, it's busted? Un-bust it." She removed several inputs from their place in the terminal and slid them into different plugs. After seeing zero readings again on her handyman, she pulled the inputs and reinserted them. "Busted means vecking busted. Like I'm gonna be busted if..."

Glancing behind her at the door to the server room, Shekeia's body went rigid. Hands frozen on the handyman and its inputs, she stared through her visor with wide, locked eyes. The door. The door that she'd left halfway shut.

It was now fully open.

DAVID SHIFTED HIS gaze back down Juliet. He drew in a breath through his nostrils. The air was still musty, as it had been since they first set foot in the school. He cocked his head slightly. "I don't smell anything new. Either of you smell anything over there?"

Becan and Zigler eyed one another; they hardly dared to breathe. "We don't," Becan answered. "Nothin' here."

Quick to defend himself, Henry said, "I smell something. I have a good sense of smell."

"Does it smell like a wet dog?" asked Becan, his senses pricking again.

Henry shook his head from the other hallway. "No, it's..." His expression contorted. "I don't know. I've never smelled anything like this. It's almost...sweet? But not good at all. It's different, it's strong."

Hesitating, David offered a half-nod. "All right, let's keep walking. Everyone, stop if you smell *anything*." The foursome resumed their steady track in the direction of Bravo hallway. Moments later, all four abruptly stopped.

Zigler's voice emerged first. "I smell it."

"I do, too," Becan said.

David inhaled deeply, and the odor came to him. It was not pleasant at all. It was the exact opposite. It was like rancid nectar. It was like nothing else. He recognized it immediately. "It's flesh."

Everyone froze. The hair on their arms stood on end. "Are yeh kiddin' me?" Becan asked in a hushed whisper.

David stepped forward, and the odor intensified. His expression hardened. "Yes," he said as he chapped his mouth. "That's human flesh."

HER HANDYMAN abandoned, Shekeia slowly rose to her feet with her E-35 pointed at the doorway. Her dark eyes shot in every direction of the server room. Amid the walls and racks of network machinery, she saw nothing. Only a wide open door that led to the rest of the office wing.

Her breaths made her whole head tremble. She gripped the assault rifle with wet, clammy hands. Holding the weapon steady as best she could, she stayed motionless by the console—a console that was now a long afterthought.

HENRY'S VOICE wavered for the first time. "I thought nobody was supposed to be in here."

Becan swallowed hard but did not utter a word.

LILAN'S TEAM WAS halfway through the auditorium when David's voice emerged through the comm. "Captain?"

Lilan raised an open hand. Scott and Natasha halted. "What is it?" Lilan asked.

Silence spanned several seconds. "Sir, someone in the school died over here. We can smell it."

Goose bumps erupted across Scott's skin. Someone *died*? Wasn't the school supposed to be empty? If someone was dead, something killed them. That was an obvious truth. He almost wished he didn't know what that something was.

Lilan's voice remained steady. "Do you see anything?"

"No, sir," David answered. "We can only smell it."

Lilan nodded and resumed his slow pace across the auditorium. "Proceed to it. Be careful. Something's probably close."

Something was probably close. *It* was probably close. Scott closed his eyes and prayed.

WITH EVERY STEP Shekeia made toward the server room door, her boots felt heavier and heavier. Her dark eyes were peeled in every direction—surrounded by dead machinery, there was a total absence of noise. Yet closer to the door, she drew.

Just as she came to its precipice, she placed her hand against the door. Gently, she eased it back shut—right to the halfway point where it'd been before. Just to see if it would open fully on its own. Fingers shaking, and with the door in place, she withdrew her hand and waited.

The door never moved.

DAVID REGRIPPED HIS shotgun. "You heard him. Continue forward and stay alert."

After several more steps, all four men were in view of one another in the two intersections of Bravo. The commons area was visible in the distance, though their attention focused on the ends of Romeo and Juliet. The odor grew worse.

Only moments after he passed the intersection, Becan drew to a halt. Zigler froze and stared at him. "What?" Zigler asked.

"There's blood on the wall," answered Becan.

David inched closer to the corner of Juliet. "How much?"

Becan zoomed in his visor. The dark red smears streaked across the walls in long dashes, then dropped to the floor, where they trailed around the corner. "A lot," he answered. "Yeh migh' see some where yeh are. It looks like somethin' was dragged."

Henry's breathing grew heavier.

David inspected the wall ahead. He concentrated his vision and identified speckled crimson against the wall and floor. It would have been impossible to notice had he not known to look for it. "I see it now," he said.

Becan and Zigler remained fixated on the stains. The Irishman could make out a bloodied handprint along the bottom of the righthand wall. It smeared along the pale white paint until it disappeared around the corner. "I'm movin' to it," he said.

POKING HER HEAD out of the server room door, Shekeia looked in all directions. Nothing was visible down any hallway—not the one with the individual offices or the one that branched off to somewhere else in the building. Standing perfectly still, she attuned her ears to the silence. She strained to hear anything.

"CAREFUL, EVERYONE," said David. Though their noses were almost entirely adjusted to the odor, new inhalations occasionally freshened it.

Becan took his final step to the corner. Silence hung in all directions. The smell was as intense as ever. With every second that passed, his stomach grew more and more nauseated. He closed his eyes. He regripped his assault rifle. He counted to three. As soon as he opened his eyes and rounded the edge, he gagged over the comm.

David tore around the other corner. His eyes captured Becan, who had doubled back and covered his mouth. David's attention shifted to the floor, where he saw the cause of the Irishman's disgust. The remains were not even identifiable.

Swallowing, Becan lifted his gaze to David. "Is tha'…?"

"Yeah," David answered.

"God…"

"What is it?" Henry asked.

RETREATING BACKWARD into the server room, Shekeia again set the door back halfway shut. Her face was shiny with sweat behind her visor, her braids damp in her helmet. After she had back-stepped nearly all the way back to the terminal, she slowly angled herself around to face it. The door stayed in her peripherals as she reached down to reclaim her handyman.

DAVID AND BECAN pivoted their heads upward. Directly above the remains, a hole was torn through the ceiling panels. Claw marks were visible from where it was slashed open.

"What is it?" Henry asked again.

Becan closed his eyes and whispered as David spoke into the comm. "Captain, we've got something."

Lilan's voice emerged a second later. "What do you have?"

"Human remains and a hole in the ceiling."

"Can you reach it?"

David and Becan eyed each other. "Possibly, sir," David answered.

"Find a way up," Lilan said. "Chances are, it leads to the nest. Whoever goes first, be *extremely* careful. Don't start searching until at least two people are up."

"Yes, sir," David answered, closing the comm channel. He stared at the hole, then lowered his gaze to Becan. "You're lighter than me."

Becan's jaw dropped. "Now wait one bleedin' minute!"

"Shh!" Zigler warned.

David sighed. "I can probably lift you up enough for you to climb through."

"Well tha's just grand, isn't it?"

"Okay?" David asked.

"Why do I have to go through the bloody hole first?"

"Because there's no way you can lift me up."

"Put Henry in the hole first."

"Hell no," Henry answered.

David's eyes narrowed. "Becan, you're going up first. Someone will be right behind you."

"Who?"

"Zig. He's small, too."

Zigler muttered under his breath.

Becan shot David a look of disapproval and then shook his head acceptingly. "If I go up there an' somethin' bites me head off, I hope to God my body falls on yeh."

David lowered himself to the ground and entwined his fingers together. Becan hesitated, then set his foot into place. He slung his rifle over his shoulder and peered up as he braced for David's lift.

David's muscles tightened, and he raised Becan just enough for him to grab the edge of the hole. He waited until Becan had a firm grip on it and began to pull himself up before he stepped away and took up his shotgun again. Ceiling timbers crinkled in the previously undisturbed silence as flecks of construction material drifted to the floor.

AT LONG LAST, Shekeia picked up something from the demarcation point—it was faint but existed on a branching network pathway that led out of the school. The moving lines of code from the handyman reflected on the surface of her visor. As she traced the pathway, she tapped several points on the screen.

Until the server room door moved.

Eyes widening, Shekeia inhaled, then held her breath. Turning her head, she stared at the door directly. It glided open, inch by inch, with nary a sound nor a force to be seen. After setting her handyman down, she grabbed her E-35 and aimed it at the open hallway. Frozen, she listened. She listened until, very faintly, something prompted her to narrow her eyes in concentration.

Creaking. The subtle groaning of wood, like a house aching in the wind. Like rafters settling in the ceiling. Like...

...like rafters in the ceiling.

Shekeia's eyes drifted upward. Reaching up, she slowly pulled off her helmet so her hearing wouldn't be impaired. Wiping her braids back, she listened again. She listened for that creaking, that groaning. That shifting of wood under pressure. For several seconds, she heard nothing. And then…

Creeeeak.

Above the door. Literally right above the doorframe, from in the attic space itself, exhibiting downward pressure on the door and easing it open.

It was in the ceiling.

Reaching up for her comm, Shekeia remembered that she'd removed her helmet. She was in the process of sliding it back down over her braids when another sound made her stop cold.

The rafters compressed loudly—the ceiling tiles bent. There was a great exertion of force as if something had leapt clear off the ground in the ceiling above. It tore away from her from within the ceiling itself.

Toward Alpha and Bravo.

BECAN SCANNED every direction as he pulled himself into place on a rafter. The ceiling space could be easily traversed via a catwalk of supports. It was warm, and beads of sweat dripped from his brow. He glanced up. The roof of the building was ten feet above him. Everything else was a series of pipes, rafters, and units. He slipped his assault rifle from his shoulder and gripped it. Without a look down, he gave David a thumbs up.

Zigler had watched Becan's climb from beyond the corner. He had yet to see the remains on the floor and fought the urge to duck around the corner and look. The sound of Becan situating himself was disturbing enough.

At that very moment, a sensation tingled across Zigler's arms. Every hair on the back of his neck stood on end. He held his breath as he froze. Silence prevailed all around him. Only the odor of flesh hung in the air. Yet still, his senses screamed. His breath released. His eyes widened.

Something was behind him.

He spun around and propped his shotgun against his shoulder, pointing it at the intersection of Romeo and Bravo.

It was empty.

Zigler whispered into the comm, "I think something was just here."

Becan froze on the ceiling rafter.

"What do you mean?" asked David.

"I think something was just in the intersection."

At that exact moment, Shekeia's breathless voice emerged through the comm. "Necrilid on the move."

David looked around him. "On the move? What do you mean?" The technician's voice was almost rattling. "It was in the ceiling, above the server room. It took off toward the commons."

"You guys smell that?" Henry asked.

David backed against the wall. "Are you saying you *saw* something?"

"Yes. No, I mean—veck, it was in the *vecking* ceiling," Shekeia said. "It's heading your way."

Above, still crouched by the edge of the hole, Becan scanned around him. He saw nothing. "Veckin' bollocks." He looked down at David. "I want to get down."

Holding an open palm to silence the Irishman, David stepped to the corner to look at Zigler. "Zig, did *you* see something?"

"I didn't see it, but I sure as hell felt it," Zigler answered.

"Something stinks over here..." said Henry again.

"Guys," Becan said firmly, "Shekeia said somethin's moving, an' Henry says somethin' stinks. I would really like to get down from this *veckin'* hole."

David looked up at Becan, then returned his focus to Zigler. "It was by the intersection?" Zigler nodded. Silence fell around them, and David stepped back in Henry's direction. "Okay...Henry, work your way—"

He was cut off. From just beyond the intersection, in the visually blocked space between Romeo and Juliet, something shrieked—a horrible, banshee shrill that cut through the silence, its reverberations echoing through the halls. It lasted a mere second, then it stopped.

Everyone in Falcon-2 went rigid. For almost ten seconds, no one spoke. In the ceiling, Becan cupped his hands over his mouth. The next sound they heard was Lilan's voice through the comm.

"Anyone over there hear that?"

David swallowed hard for the first time. "Yes, sir."

"Find it and kill it. Remember what I said. Distract."

IN THE SERVER room, Shekeia closed her eyes and whispered a prayer.

DAVID WIPED HIS hand across his face and then wiped it on his armor. It streaked across the silver metal. He offered Lilan an instinctive nod, then whispered to his team through the comm. "It's right there, in the hallway between the intersections." Henry began to shake. "Henry, I want you to work your way slowly toward it. Zig and I are going to mirror you on this end."

Henry didn't reply. He only trembled in the corridor.

"Henry? You read me?"

"Y-yes, sir…"

"All right," David said. He took a deep breath and exhaled. "Move."

Henry was the closest to the corner, meters from where the creature had shrieked. The odor was exactly as Lilan claimed—like a wet dog. His fingers curled around his E-35, and he crept closer.

A rasping breath sputtered from around the corner, followed by a flapping grunt. The creature was making noise. Henry inched forward, his body pressed close against the far wall, his head goose-necked just enough to give him an angled view of the intersection between Romeo and Juliet.

He froze.

On the floor, thrusting out from the corner just enough to be visible, were two of the necrilid's toes. Its claws tapped twice on the linoleum, then slid back out of view. Henry drew a short, sharp breath, swallowed, and stuttered into the comm. "I'm…I'm in position."

David inched ahead. "We're almost there…hold for a few more seconds…"

Becan's voice cut through the comm. "Throw a veckin' shoe."

David drifted up a foot and began to fiddle with his bootstraps.

Becan breathed again. "Throw a veckin' shoe."

"I'm throwing a vecking shoe! They're not slip-ons—give me a second."

Becan listened to the transmissions from his crouched position on the rafter at the hole's edge, his assault rifle firm in his grip. David's voice came again. "Boot's untied. Few more seconds."

A few more seconds. Every second seemed an eternity. Becan waited for the sound of weapons fire, for some alien scream to pierce the silent tomb. He waited for any sound at all.

Thud.

He started. It was a sound, but not the one he expected to hear. More alarmingly, it was not the sound he expected to *feel*. It jolted beneath his feet as if a loaded sack had dropped from the rafters behind him. His first inclination was to pivot around and look, but he froze before the impulse took over.

He already knew what it was.

The next two seconds were a blur. Becan whirled around. A strong force slammed into his chest. He pulled the trigger of his assault rifle.

Something screamed. The next sensation to come over Becan was gravity as he fell from the ceiling. Everything faded to black.

Zigler leapt against the wall and spun around at the sound of Becan falling. He registered David behind him, also against the wall. Then Becan sprawled out on the floor. Then the sound of contortions in the ceiling. In the split second it took Zigler to realize what'd just happened, it was too late. He whipped his head back to the intersection of Romeo and Bravo. The necrilid was already in mid-leap. The last thing Zigler felt were claws in his throat.

David turned toward Zigler. As Zigler crumpled to the ground, the necrilid bounded straight from his body toward David. David was struck in the chest, and his shotgun flew from his grasp. He landed flat on his back. The creature was atop him.

The necrilid was as horrible as Lilan had described. Its dark gray body was grotesquely emaciated, and its flattened head formed a sinister frame for the rows of razor-trimmed teeth within its oversized mouth. Its yellow eyes gleamed in the True-Color Vision, and it let loose a soulless wail.

David closed his eyes and braced for death.

Rat-tat-tat-tat-tat-tat!

It was Henry. He stood in the intersection of Bravo and Romeo, the barrel of his assault rifle flashing. The necrilid atop David stuttered, leapt off him, and bounded from wall to wall toward Henry. Henry backpedaled and continued to fire. David scrambled back to his feet.

It took a moment for Becan to realize he wasn't dead. Everything was black, and he shot a hand up to his visor. His TCV—it was broken. He reached around the floor. His assault rifle was gone. Above, the ceiling tiles thumped and slid as the necrilid reoriented itself.

Panic struck Becan; he leapt to his feet. Bolting to the nearest classroom door, he felt frantically in the darkness until he found the handle. He flung the door open just as the necrilid landed on the floor behind him. Becan darted inside, whirled around, and kicked the door shut. He fiddled with his helmet until he found his helmet light; he hurriedly clicked it on. The beam cut through the darkness, and the Irishman turned to the door. Through the door's glass window, the necrilid's yellow eyes gleamed at him.

David flinched as Henry's shots ricocheted off the walls. "Henry!"

David screamed as he reclaimed his shotgun. The necrilid was bounding after Henry, growing closer with every leap. "Get down!"

LILAN'S TEAM HAD just finished their sweep of the auditorium and was halfway down Echo hall when they heard weapons fire erupt across the school. Before they could react, another sound emerged from their end—another shriek, just like the one near Falcon-2. Lilan turned to face it. "You two go assist team two," he said, "I've got this one."

Scott blinked. *He's got this one? By himself?* "Sir—"

Lilan erupted. "Go help team two while there *is* a team two—*now!*"

Turning to Scott with urgency, Natasha said, "Scott."

Nothing else needed to be said. Readying his assault rifle, Scott turned and flat-tracked for the commons, Natasha and John right behind him.

"GET DOWN!" DAVID shouted again as he dropped to a knee and raised his shotgun. "Henry, get *down!*"

Henry stumbled backward as the necrilid bounced from wall to wall toward him. His assault rifle fell from his grasp.

David gritted his teeth and pulled the trigger of his shotgun. *Boom!* The necrilid screamed. David pumped the weapon and pulled again. *Boom!* Henry toppled backward. A third pump and another flash of orange. *Boom!* The necrilid's back exploded, and it collapsed forward. It scraped desperately toward the now-fallen Henry.

Becan deadlocked his gape with the glare of the necrilid in the window. Its fangs curved with saliva; the Irishman stared straight into its soulless, yellow orbs. As if under hypnosis, he couldn't move a muscle.

The creature's head snapped around. It rumbled a low growl, and in the next instant, it was gone. Panic overtook Becan as he snapped out of his terror.

It was going after David.

Flinging the door open, Becan bolted into the hallway. His helmet light illuminated the back of the creature as it tore toward David from behind. *"Dave!"* Becan screamed as he reached for his sidearm, *"Mind your house!"*

David whirled around, but the necrilid was already in mid-lurch. David dove into Bravo hallway. The creature swiped at his shoulder in mid-flight; David's shotgun was knocked from his hands. The necrilid skidded past him down the intersection and then spun to face him. David stutter-stepped backward, ripped the handgun out from his belt, and raised it to try and aim. Before he could fire a shot, the necrilid began leaping from wall to wall toward him. Firing off haphazard shots, David managed to hit only the wall. The necrilid was too fast. From around the intersection, Henry let loose a blood-curdling scream.

LILAN STRODE TO the bend as the echo of weapons fire sounded far behind him. There was no stealth or urgency in his steps, and his boots clopped solidly against the linoleum floor. In a single fluid motion, he slung his assault rifle down from his shoulder, engaged the safety, and underhanded it toward the bend. He reached down, unholstered his sidearm, and aimed it forward.

The assault rifle bounced past the corner, and the necrilid lurched from around the corner to chase it. As soon as the creature registered that it was pursuing a mere object, it skidded to a halt and jerked its head at Lilan. It released an angry shriek, but it was too late. Lilan pulled the trigger, and a procession of bullets flew straight into the necrilid's head. A gurgle of blood spat from the creature's mouth, and it toppled onto the floor. Lilan stepped beyond it, bent down, and retrieved his assault rifle.

BECAN STORMED FULL-SPEED toward the intersection. He watched the necrilid as it chased David around the corner, though the tortured scream of Henry captured his primary focus. He could see the first necrilid squatting above Henry, its claws rising and falling with murderous ferocity. Becan raised his handgun, aimed it at the creature, and fired into its back. The necrilid screamed, then collapsed to the side.

"Man down!" Becan shouted with urgency.

A second later, he heard Michael over the comm. "On my way!"

David stumbled backward as the second necrilid pounced toward him. Every attempt to aim was futile—the monster was a dark blur. Before David's mind could even register his level of failure, the creature leapt onto his chest. David was thrown onto his back.

For a second time, a necrilid was poised atop him with its claws in the air, and for a second time, weapons fire saved his life. Bullets tore through the necrilid's body, and it whirled its head around to find Becan firing at it from behind.

The necrilid howled. David lifted his sidearm, placed it straight at the necrilid's head, and pulled the trigger. The creature's head erupted, and it lurched up and backward, where it toppled to the floor. David squirmed away and skittered back along the ground. He gasped to catch his breath, then looked up to find Becan. The Irishman was nowhere to be seen. David immediately knew why.

Henry.

By the time David arrived on the scene, Becan was already there. The Irishman was frantic to the point of delirium. "Yeh goin' to be all righ'," he stuttered. "Just sit tigh' for a minute!"

But David knew better. Henry was a wreck. The lower portion of his body was mauled beyond any semblance of form or function. His chest heaved up and down; he struggled for breath. His eyes bore straight to the ceiling with frozen terror as his teeth rattled together.

Scott, Natasha, and John arrived a moment later. When Scott saw Henry, he whirled around, a wave of vomit spewing from his throat. The others stared at Henry in shock.

David fell to Henry's side. Henry's glazed eyes found him, and David held the soldier's bloodied hand.

Becan continued to stutter. "Yeh goin' to be all righ'!"

As David clutched Henry's hand, Henry continued to stare hollowly at him. The fallen soldier couldn't speak—the only sounds that came from him were gurgled gasps—but he could look. David's eyes moistened as Henry's blurred gaze locked onto his, and he felt the soldier squeeze his hand.

Then it was over.

The hand went limp, and the muscles behind Henry's clenched expression grew soft. He was dead.

David's eyes slid shut as he clutched the lifeless fist. There had not even been any final words. The last sounds Henry ever made were screams of torment. David didn't know what to say.

"Good work, men."

The soldiers swung their heads around to where Lilan stood in the intersection. His voice was completely neutral.

"McCrae, Remington—take Zigler and Mathis back to the ship. Everyone else, help me round up the necrilids' corpses. Nothing stays behind."

The soldiers stared as Lilan turned to walk away, though the captain paused to glance down at Zigler's body.

"If you want to take a minute over there," he said, "that's fine. Just be sure you take one over here, too."

Lilan never said another word. He simply walked away.

A second later, almost in the exact second that Michael and Donald rounded the corner into the intersection, the emergency lights in the school flickered, then came on. Shekeia's voice came over the comm. "Auxiliary power restored."

Scott crouched on the floor between Henry and Zigler's bodies. Lowering his head, he said to her through the comm, "Thanks, Shekeia."

"I came as fast as I could," said Michael, the medic's voice trembling at the two fallen soldiers. "I came as fast as I could!"

Placing his hand on Michael's shoulder, David said simply, "It wouldn't have mattered."

The gathering of soldiers gave Henry and Zigler their moments of silence, and then they did as told, rounding up the necrilid corpses and placing the bodies of their fallen friends into the Vulture. It took just over an hour for the EDEN sweeper team to arrive at the scene. As soon as the sweepers arrived, the Falcons wasted no further time on the premises. *Vulture-7* lifted off the ground, swung its nose east, and returned home to *Richmond*.

Not one person spoke on the whole ride home.

11

SCOTT STOOD BENEATH the tattering spray of a showerhead, palms braced against the tile wall as his hair hung from his lowered head, streams of water trailing from them down to the floor. As steam rose around him, he remained quiet and motionless, eyes closed in an embracement of solitude. In a commitment to it. He gently wiped his hair back with one hand, only to have it slide forward and down once more as his palm returned to the wall.

This was his second shower in less than eight hours. The first, taken after Falcon Squad's return to base, debriefing, and dismissal, was a cleansing of necessity—a washing away of the grime, sweat, and guilt of that bloodbath back in the high school. But this second shower—this morning shower—he just needed for him. He just wanted to stand under it.

Scott's last look at David Zigler and Henry Mathis would forever be imprinted in his mind. He didn't need a passage of time to understand that. Some things were just too horrific to forget. But he tried to forget—even right then, in the morning after. He tried to remember the conversations he'd had with them, the laughter they'd shared, the conversations during downtime. He tried to remember who they were, for those were much better thoughts than what'd become of them. He feared it was in vain.

The fragility of life was not something often considered in the day-to-day—even in the midst of an alien war, even from someone who'd lost his parents when he was a teenager. Henry and Zigler were the first two people Scott knew personally who'd been killed by extraterrestrials. And to go the way they went…it was hard to shake that sense of dread and helplessness from his core.

Scott had sent Nicole a text before bed—a short message stating that he'd been on a mission, that two of his comrades had been killed, but that he was okay. He promised to fill her in the next day after he'd had a chance to get some rest. That next day was now, and for the life of him, he just couldn't bring himself to ring her on the comm. He didn't want to have to explain everything—not yet.

Before taking a shower, Scott had visited Donald's room to see if he was okay. Zigler had been his roommate, and though the spiky-haired soldier had rubbed most of his teammates the wrong way, Donald at least had been close to him. Upon entering, Scott discovered that Donald wasn't there—but Scott did see something that he wouldn't soon forget. It was a letter, sitting atop the nightstand, in Donald's large, scrawly handwriting. Not a prier by nature, Scott would have paid the letter no mind had his eyes not happened upon its first words.

Dear Mrs. Zigler.

Against his nobler nature, Scott found himself drawn in by those words enough to read what came next—and what came next crushed him. Donald had written Zigler's mother a letter. In simple but heartfelt words, the demolitionist told her how good of a friend Zigler was, how much his teammates had liked him, and how he'd died quickly. So little of it was true—but truth was not what Donald was aiming for. As evidenced by the tear stains on the ink, the letter was intended to comfort. To give a grieving mother something to cling to. The thought of her cherishing that letter and reading it over and over amidst sadness and pride was enough to bring Scott to tears himself. He left Donald's room with reddened eyes, never having discovered where the demolitionist went.

Turning off the showerhead, Scott stood still as the spray was rendered to droplets. Slowly wiping his hair back again, his hands came to rest on the top of his scalp. For a moment, he just stood there.

This is what I signed up for. This is the reality. These won't be the first friends I lose.

How contrasting this was to the aftermath of Chicago. How useless that golden collar seemed now. It hadn't helped him reach his friends in time to save them. During that whole mission in the high school, Scott hadn't pulled the trigger once.

Reaching up, Scott yanked down his towel from the shower curtain bar. He needed to call Nicole. He knew he did. But right now, all he wanted was to sit with his comrades. All he wanted was to grieve and reconcile with them. To remember Henry and Zigler with them. It was the only thing that felt right. Drying himself off, Scott donned his uniform again and stepped into the hall.

*   *   *

AT THE SAME TIME

IT WAS 0730 HOURS when General Hutchin's door opened, and Captain Lilan stepped inside. Hutchin was hunched over a letter when Lilan entered. "Have a seat, captain. Thank you for coming in on such short notice." Lilan sat. "Sir."

"Good job last night. The deaths were unfortunate, but that's to be expected."

"Yes, sir, thank you."

Hutchin exhaled. "No use beating around the bush. I didn't call you in to talk about last night. I have something else for you." Lilan remained silent. "You know as well as I do that good soldiers are hard to come by these days. I will admit, I had my doubts as to whether or not you could adequately break in these soldiers, and I must confess that you've done a superb job. Better than most would've."

Lilan's expression narrowed. The muscles in his arms tensed.

"We as a base are fortunate to have received such promising talent. I'm sure you've recognized this already. But not all of our international cousins have been so lucky..."

"No," Lilan growled, "you are *not* about to tell me—"

"We got a request from *Novosibirsk* for soldiers yesterday."

"If you do this to me, so help me *God*—"

"We're transferring one of your sections. The one with Jurgen, McCrae, Remington, and Timmons."

Lilan's face flushed red.

"Quite frankly, you've done such a good job breaking in the new soldiers that we're going to make that your new role, at least for the time being. You'll still run missions, but they'll be mostly low-risk operations for new arrivals on base until we have a chance to place them in more experienced units. *Richmond* may actually be the new hub for rookies fresh out of *Philadelphia*."

"I vecking *knew* it."

"Tone, captain, watch your tone. It's hard to come by officers who have not only experience but patience like yours. You'll be training the future of EDEN."

Lilan inched forward in his chair. "It was all a lie to keep me motivated, *wasn't* it? All that talk of restoring Falcon and all that crap."

"Brent, you know that's not true."

"I've seen this happen before. Use us old-timers until you get enough new blood to put us on the bench. I *knew* this was coming when you gave me a squad full of rookies!"

"Brent…"

"What about Tacker? You want to move him, too? I'm just holding him back, right?"

Hutchin's tone rose. "Captain…"

"In fact, why not transfer me to *Philadelphia*? Put me in front of a classroom giving lectures on the history of EDEN!"

Hutchin pounded his fist on the desktop. "Silence! One more word, *captain*, and you'll find yourself looking for another career." Lilan opened his mouth, but Hutchin interrupted. "I *will not* tolerate disrespect, not from you, nor anybody else. You are to inform Executor Tacker of the situation and have *him* relay the message to the unit. Is that understood?"

Lilan broke eye contact. "Dregg."

Silence descended upon the room. Hutchin's eyes widened. "*What* did you just say?"

Lilan glared across the table. The room was quiet. "I said nothing. Sir."

Hutchin's face remained red. "That is what I *thought* you said."

"Thoor is going to ruin those four men."

"You're dismissed."

Lilan snapped to a salute. Hutchin saluted back, and Lilan swung around to storm out of the room. He didn't bother to close the door behind him.

*   *   *

"SO MUCH FOR bein' the first to go," said Becan. He, Scott, and Jayden sat across from one another in Room 421. They had been there for almost thirty minutes, as it neared 0900.

Scott was stoic. "I still can't believe how fast it happened. Two days ago everything was great. One mission, and bang. Blink of an eye."

"It should've been me bleedin' ou' on the floor," Becan said. "If I had paid attention—"

"Don't think like that."

"I'm bloody serious. I should have been payin' attention."

Jayden glanced at Becan. "It happens, man."

"Won't happen again, I cross m'heart."

Scott turned to Jayden. "Be glad you weren't inside that school."

"I wish I was."

"Yeh don't," Becan said. "Not in tha' hellhole."

"It was like living a nightmare," Scott said. "I didn't even see anything firsthand, and it was still the most terrifying experience of my life."

"How's Dave holdin' up?" Becan asked.

Scott nodded his head. "He's doing all right. He took it hard because of Henry. He liked Henry." He pitied Henry. That was the truth of the matter. David had seen him for what he was: a man with no business being in EDEN.

"I think we all liked him," Becan said. "He was tryin' to do his part. Tryin' to not be ordinary."

Scott smiled half-heartedly. "I think that was his problem. He was here for the wrong reason."

The room fell silent. Jayden slid down against the floor. Becan's legs fidgeted. "How do yeh think they went?"

Scott raised his head. "What do you mean?"

"I mean, do yeh think they were…yeh know, met by someone? Or did it all jus' fade to black? Did their conscious mind jus' shut off, an' now it's jus' over?"

Jayden glanced at the Irishman. "You mean how did they die?"

"Yeah."

Scott gazed down. How does one meet death? What *was* death? They were questions that had haunted mankind for as long as it'd existed. Scott knew his fate—at least, according to his belief system. An afterlife was there for him in Paradise. God was there. But what about Henry and Zigler? Were they met by an angel…or something worse? Zigler always carried an attitude. Angry, coercive, bitter. Who waited for him on the other side? It couldn't have been God. There was no reflection of God in his life. God fueled goodness.

He shook his head. No. What was he thinking? How could he even speculate that on the morning after Zigler's death? *You're a fool for that, Scott. Shame on you.* For a moment, he hated himself.

"…Remmy?"

Scott looked across to Becan. "Huh?"

"Yeh got this blank look on your face."

"Oh," Scott said. "Sorry, just…thought of something, that's all."

Becan fell quiet. "So how do yeh think they died?"

Forgive me, God. Please forgive me for that. Scott's gaze fell. "I hope in peace. It's no one's right to say. We can only hope that they found peace."

"Yeh believe in Heaven, righ'?"

"Yes."

"Do yeh think they made it?"

It didn't matter what he thought. It only mattered what they thought, Henry and Zigler. It only mattered what they believed. "I don't know."

Becan gazed at his feet. "...I hope I make it."

The Irishman's statement pained Scott inwardly. Salvation had nothing to do with hope. It had to do with faith. Belief in God, acceptance of sacrifice and divine mercy. Undeserved grace. Such were the tenets of his faith—but not everyone shared that faith. In fact, it seemed fewer people had faith at all than ever before. But when aliens came sweeping down from the skies, that had to be expected. Truth be told, the invasion raised questions Scott himself wasn't sure how to answer—not to himself, let alone to anyone else. But such was the living experience. Invading aliens didn't rattle his beliefs as it had for so many others. It simply told him there was more to existence than he ever imagined.

There was a knock at the door before Scott could think about it further. "Probably Dave," Becan said.

Scott nodded as Jayden rose to answer it. David, Scott thought. The unit needed someone like him, especially in times like this. David knew about death; he knew about the loss of comrades. Henry's death had hit him hard, that much Scott knew...but he also knew David would pull through. It was funny how much faith Scott had in him. A month ago, the name David Jurgen meant nothing to Scott. Now, it was synonymous with experience and wisdom.

Jayden snapped to attention. Scott and Becan angled their heads to the door. It wasn't David. It was Executor Tacker. They leapt to their feet and saluted crisply.

"At ease," Tacker said. He stepped past Jayden into the room and sat in an unclaimed chair.

Scott's posture relaxed, though not wholly. It was impossible to be completely at ease around superiors, even those as amiable as Tacker. But why was Tacker's countenance so...informal wasn't the word. Blank. He just walked in and sat down. And said nothing.

Something was wrong.

Tacker stared at the floor and rubbed his neck. Silence hung in the air. Becan and Jayden stood side by side as Scott watched from the far wall. Before they could open their mouths to inquire, Tacker took a deep breath and spoke. "You're all being transferred. So is Jurgen."

Scott's jaw dropped; Tacker resumed.

"Don't ask me why, and don't ask me what I think about it. You leave for *Novosibirsk* today at 1020 in *Vulture-15*. That's already close, so get your goodbyes in and get your things packed."

Tacker pushed to his feet. "That's all." Scott's brow furrowed as the executor left through the door and disappeared into the hallway. His footsteps echoed away seconds later.

The room stood in silence. There was no conversation. There was no argument. There wasn't enough time for it.

The rest of the morning was a blur. After seeking out David, Scott and the four men said goodbye to their Falcon teammates. After that, Scott and David called Nicole and Sharon. The calls were almost too brief to be fully registered. Several emotions—shock, panic, and disbelief—emanated from the two women. Even from the two men. But there was no time for that now. There was no time to try to understand. As soon as they hung up, they packed what few belongings they had into their duffle bags. Soon, Room 419 was as barren as the day they had arrived.

Scott and David stored their bags in the assigned transport—*Vulture-15*—then visited *Vulture-7* one last time. They leaned against its hull as conversation ensued.

Neither knew specifics about *Novosibirsk*, though both knew *of* it. It was regarded as one of the worst environments for EDEN soldiers on the planet. It was larger than *Richmond*, classified as a Class-4 facility, and one of the organization's oldest.

Novosibirsk was home to the Nightmen—a defunct sect of the Russian military. The Nightmen had been disbanded and outlawed for its brutality when the New Era began, though *Novosibirsk* became the landing spot for many of its former members. The general of *Novosibirsk*—Ignatius van Thoor—was a former Nightman captain. When Thoor inherited command of *Novosibirsk*, every ex-Nightman who had served under him flocked there to reunite. Thoor was regarded as one of the most brutally effective leaders in the world. His men were proud to serve under him and terrified to stand against him.

It was 0950 when Jayden arrived; his brown cowboy hat gave him away immediately. He joined Scott and David in conversation as soon as his belongings were stored.

Jayden was more talkative than usual as he explained how the news of the move made him miss his hometown of Blue Creek. When he'd called his parents to tell them, they hadn't believed him.

As they leaned against *Vulture-7*'s hull, they stared at the endless blue sky over the distant treetops. As their gazes became lost, all conversation ceased. A moment of tranquility before everything they knew changed.

Becan didn't arrive until 1010—ten minutes before departure. His uniform and hair were unkempt as usual, and his wrinkled duffle bag slung sloppily over one shoulder. He tossed it into the transport and joined his comrades. In the short time they propped themselves against *Vulture-7*, he spoke next to nothing. Even under the circumstances, it was an odd quiet from the Irishman. No reason was given as to why, nor was one requested. Silence was not to be argued.

Nobody was there to send them off when they climbed into the transport. No captain, no executor, no teammates—only the technicians and pilots as they walked about the hangar doing their routine checks. Scott, David, Becan, and Jayden strapped themselves into the transport's matted chairs and gazed out of the cold portholes of its hull. The running lights were lit, and *Vulture-15* taxied onto the runway. As it rolled forward, Scott peered out the window for one last look at the place that'd been his home, even if only for the briefest of times.

Clearance was given for takeoff, and the craft ascended. Scott hadn't slept much over the course of last night, and fatigue was setting in hard. As they rocketed forward, he closed his eyes. He fell asleep right away, and David and Jayden were soon to follow.

Only Becan remained awake for the first half of the journey. He gazed out the window as the clouds glided past, his eyes lingering absently on the sky. He never once turned his head to see if the others were asleep. He only stared at the horizon, eyes distant and thoughtful, as he watched and waited for *Novosibirsk*.

PART II

12

CARL PAULING, PRESIDENT of EDEN, nodded to the slender man across from him. "Proceed with your report, Judge Kentwood," he said as he motioned for the man to rise. The other eleven judges watched Kentwood closely as he stood.

Kentwood covered his mouth with his fist and cleared his throat. "My fellow judges, we have a problem."

A murmur spread through the Council. Pauling's gaze spanned the prominent, black, circular table and the twelve men and women who sat around it—the twelve judges of EDEN. There were no others present in the conference room. There were no others allowed. Behind Pauling, a wall-sized display screen showed a gently rotating Earth.

Kentwood continued. "We're all aware of the increased Bakma activity in North Asia, particularly Siberia and Northern China. Our outpost at the North Pole has been assaulted several times in recent weeks. Though none of the attacks have been heavy, there has been significant damage to the facility's structure, at least enough to force us to allocate our resources there more heavily." Kentwood was eloquent in his presentation. He had always been that way. "It was feared for some time that the Bakma have been targeting the North Pole to clear it completely from EDEN influence and possibly establish an outpost there. An outpost on Earth would be valuable; the two poles represent prime locations for such." He regarded the other judges thoughtfully. "We were half right."

He reached beneath the table to retrieve a manila folder. He opened its pale cover and produced a thin stack of papers, which he handed to the judge on his left. "What I am passing out to you now is a satellite image of Northern Siberia." The stack of papers began to circulate.

"You'll note the red dot just above the Arctic Circle. Its approximate coordinates are 125 degrees, 14 minutes east longitude, and 67 degrees,

25 minutes north latitude. Seven hours ago, *Novosibirsk* radar picked up the signal, marked by that dot, out of nowhere. It was a stationary signal, extraterrestrial in origin. A team was sent to investigate and discovered a crashed Bakma Noboat. There was no indication of a fight between it and another vessel, and they concluded that it must have crashed there accidentally, materializing in the process. No crew members were found alive."

The last paper reached the judge to his right. "When the dispatchers investigated further, they discovered that the Noboat was filled with supplies...food, water, platforms, mountable sensors. We think...we *think* that they already have a base established." The silence was broken with a wave of whispers. The room grew quiet again. "We believe they're using Noboats for cargo ships. By doing that, they could construct an outpost right under our noses, provided they built it underground where it wouldn't be easily detected. We're fortunate that this particular one crashed, or we'd still be completely in the dark about this."

Judge Jason Rath, a slender, dark-haired man, shifted in his chair and spoke. "Siberia would be an ideal location for an outpost," he said, his Canadian accent thick.

"Exactly," Kentwood said. "It's remote, and EDEN has no reason to go there on its own accord. It's not populated, so there's no one there for us to protect."

"How sure is Intelligence that there is indeed a Bakma outpost there?"

"Fairly confident," Kentwood answered. "It fits in place with the recent assaults on the North Pole. We thought they were trying to clear a way for a potential base, but it's clear now that they were more likely trying to destroy the facility with the greatest chance of detecting them."

"What about *Novosibirsk*?"

"*Novosibirsk* would have probably been their second target, or possibly *Nagoya*. *Novosibirsk*'s closer, but *Nagoya* is a larger threat."

"That's debatable," another judge murmured.

"How do we locate this facility?" Rath asked. "If it's underground, it won't exactly be a flashing beacon."

"We're going to have to start heavily scouting," Kentwood answered. "I would like to start an active reconnaissance campaign in Siberia in that area. The primary work would come from units stationed at *Novosibirsk* and *Nagoya*, but we also have *Leningrad* and *Berlin*; they're not much farther away. This is something that we're going to want to consider a priority. The last thing we need is a fully functional alien facility on Earth."

"Agreed," Pauling said. "But let's hypothesize for a moment. Let's say we do find a fully functional alien facility. Who handles it? Do we make this a global coordination?"

Kentwood turned to regard the president. "That all depends on the size of it, sir. It may be no bigger than one of the polar outposts. If that's the case, it may only take several units to isolate it. It will take a much larger effort if it rivals one of our major facilities, which is highly unlikely since we think it's relatively new."

"We're aware of this facility," said Pauling quietly, "and that's been a stroke of good luck. But how do we know this is the only one? If it's this easy for them to set up a base undetected, then who's to say they don't have facilities all across the planet?"

Kentwood nodded. "That's why coming up with a detection system for their invisibility technology is so important. We hope this is the only base they have, but there could very well be more. There could be a Bakma armada surrounding Earth right now that we just don't see."

The president glanced down at his paper for several moments, then placed it face up before him. "Have R&D here allocate more resources to that very thing. Stress the importance of this. It's an issue we can ill afford to neglect. Send a message to Thoor and let him know that *Novosibirsk* may very well be fronting this little campaign. Get in touch with Faerber, too, and inform him that Vector Squad may be needed in the near future."

"Yes, sir," Kentwood answered.

"We have a planet to protect, gentlemen," Pauling said, surveying the judges. "We can't very well protect it if we're fighting an invisible enemy."

Silence lingered in the conference room for several moments before the president concluded. "Everyone is dismissed. Thank you, Darryl."

Kentwood nodded, then left the room along with the other judges. Murmurs accompanied them as they filed out. The room was cleared within a minute, and Carl Pauling was alone. He absorbed the quiet for several seconds before he swiveled around in his chair, slowing to a stop only when the large display screen was in front of him. Earth continued its gentle rotation, and Pauling's eyes fell on the city of Novosibirsk. The city of The Machine.

"Thoor…"

*   *   *

TUESDAY, APRIL 12TH, 0011 NE

2323 HOURS

NOVOSIBIRSK, RUSSIA

SCOTT'S EYES JOLTED open as the Vulture rocked to a landing. Thunder rumbled outside, though the pounding of rain drowned it out as it drummed against the transport's hull. He sat up straight. What was going on? Were they there already? He had woken up from his slumber halfway into the flight and didn't remember drifting back off. Perhaps he was more exhausted than he realized. Aside from the haunting glow of red ceiling lights, the troop bay was dark. He squinted as he returned from the lost depths of sleep.

The pilot emerged from the cockpit. "We're down."

Soft groans came from all around as Scott sat up to see David, Jayden, and Becan stir in their seats—their eyes squinted and glazed as silent yawns escaped their lips. Scott's focus drifted to the rain. It was incessant, murderous. It was a far cry from the warm sun over *Richmond*.

David stood first as he pressed his hands against the wall of the Vulture and arched his back and neck with a series of heavy pops. The others followed suit, and the rear door of the craft lowered with a mechanical whine. They were hit with a blast of icy mist.

"Everyone out!" the pilot said. "This bird's gotta fly!" The clunk of fueling nozzle against metal could be heard from outside as the transport was refueled.

Becan dragged up his bag of clothes and hoisted it over his shoulder. "Wha' time is it?"

The pilot smiled. "Thirty minutes to tomorrow! Welcome to the other side of the world."

Vulture-15 was perched on an open stretch of airstrip amid a storm so deep that it shrouded the very blackness of night itself. The only lights were those of the gargantuan hangar that menaced before them, and even they were only barely visible through the downpour. With no cover between the men and the hangar, they had no choice but to dash from the sanctuary of the transport, through the rain, and toward the structure.

Two silhouettes were poised outside the hangar, assault rifles aimed at the thunder as they stood motionless under the liquid bombardment. Scott, drenched to the skin, scrutinized them as he and his comrades neared. Neither of them were dressed in EDEN armor. Their armor was solid black metal, covering them from head to toe. It made them look huge—like walking tanks. They were obviously guards of some kind, but nothing about them was familiar. Their faces were hidden behind black helmets, and opaque lenses covered their eyes. Their zombified gazes bore ahead without indication of where or what they observed. Uneasiness birthed in the pit of Scott's stomach.

The guards thrust out their palms, and the four transfers drew to a halt. Behind the guards, a larger form came into view. He was dressed in a flat-black uniform, and a black visor hat sat atop his head. His frame was enormous. No patches or insignia were distinguishable on his uniform, but there was no doubt in Scott's mind that he was an officer. He walked like he was *more* than an officer. Behind him, a dark cloak flowed over the ground as if it followed some wicked emperor on his inaugural march.

The officer seemed unconcerned with the downpour as the rain tattered hard against his garments. His gloved hands were clasped behind his back as he patiently strode forward, his eyes shrouded beneath the shadow of the visor.

Jayden removed his cowboy hat from his head and shrank involuntarily as the coldness of the rain hit his face for the first time.

As the officer drew near, Scott could make out the first indication of a symbol on his visor hat. It was a red, upside-down triangle divided by a vertical black line. He had never seen the symbol before.

David tilted his head toward Scott and whispered, "These are Nightmen."

The two guards snapped to attention. Scott and his comrades did the same. The Nightman officer slammed to a halt in front of them.

For the first time, Scott could discern the officer's features. His face bore diminutive scars, none distinguishable enough to stand out on their own, though together they formed an invincible countenance. Traces of brown hair arched above his ears, though the rest remained concealed beneath the visor hat.

His eyes were cold. They bore a kind of hateful arrogance that Scott had never seen before as they shifted from one soldier to the other, and then to the next, and then to the next, as if each stare summed up the men's worth with an unimpressed glance. The voice they heard next was not Russian, but it was unmistakably dominant. Each syllable was enunciated to perfect authority.

"I am Thoor."

Scott's body was captivated by a coldness that had nothing to do with the rain. Thoor. Ignatius van Thoor, former captain of the Nightmen. The general of *Novosibirsk*. It couldn't be. Before any of them could utter a syllable, the man's autocratic drone resumed.

"And you are David Jurgen, Becan McCrae, Scott Remington, and Jayden Timmons."

It was really him. It was General Thoor—the most feared man in all of EDEN, standing right there in front of them.

"Yes, I know you," Thoor said. "I know you well. I know every man and every woman who sets foot on this concrete. I am the first voice you hear when you arrive, and I will be the last voice you hear when you leave if I find you insufficient enough to bear the privilege of being stationed at my facility."

Scott dared not glance at his comrades. His eyes remained frozen ahead in perfect attention.

"I know that Private Timmons scored in the upper eighth percentile as a graduating sniper and that Private McCrae was heralded as one of the more competent fighters in his division. I know that Private Jurgen was a member of the New York Police Department and, after a mediocre run at law enforcement, took his lack of talents to the Academy."

David's eyes flicked downward.

"I know that Private Remington is the youngest soldier to earn a Golden Lion…a young man who has a 'natural talent for leadership,' as his former captain put it." Thoor's glare narrowed. "I know everything that each of you has ever done, and I will know everything you ever do so long as you reside inside the walls of this Machine known as *Novosibirsk*.

"We are not nice here. You will not be catered to, and your opinions will not be tolerated. You are here for one reason—to pull the trigger without mercy. You are here to kill. You are soldiers, not thinkers. The moment you deceive yourself into believing that you have a free will, you will receive an awakening like none you have experienced.

"Those of you destined to remain followers will follow without question. You will obey every order to maximum capacity, putting your lives secondary to completing your objectives. Those of you who are destined to become leaders will learn to lead without sympathy. You will learn to sacrifice your own lives as well as the lives of those around you for the sake of the task at hand without allowing the pitiful shadows of mercy to hinder your judgment. We are not here to protect humanity. We are here to destroy all those who oppose it.

"Whatever leniency you were given before vanishes now. You are here because you are above average for your rank, and you will be expected to execute as if you are above average for your rank. Failure to do so, at any time, for any reason, will result in immediate termination."

Immediate termination. Scott's stomach knotted as he wondered what that meant.

"I will not ask you if there are any questions. If you are asking questions, then you are thinking. If you are thinking, then you are not focusing on the task at hand. If you are not focusing on the task at hand, then you are useless to me and will be extinguished. Your task at hand is and always will be subordination. There is nothing else you need to consider."

Thoor paused, and his haughty gaze narrowed for a final time. It swept from one soldier to the next until it was satisfied, at which point he hammered a conclusive statement.

"That is all."

He swung around, and his saturated cloak sloshed behind him. Without another word, he strode back to *Novosibirsk*.

None of them spoke. The rain continued to pelt down, and the thunder continued to rumble. Not one of them uttered a word. For almost thirty seconds, they stood motionless, their breaths vapors as they huffed in frozen silence. Becan finally broke the silence with a wet sputter.

"God—"

One of the guards cut him off, pointing to a square, looming building just past the hangar. "Report to the billeting office at once." His tone—mechanized behind the veil of his zombified helmet—left no room for argument. They made their way past the hangar to the indicated building with no more outside remarks.

As they entered, they found themselves dripping onto the floor of a dimly lit corridor. The floor was not furnished tile as it was at *Richmond*, but instead flat gray pavement. The walls were a pale green, and they were marred with cracks and chips. The air was stale.

Becan shivered as he closed the outer door. "So where's the bloody billeting office?"

Scott shook his head as water drops ran down his cheeks. "I have no idea." They weren't given anything to go by. They were just turned loose.

So much for not thinking on their own. Next to him, Jayden shook his rain-soaked hat.

Scott inspected the corridor. Several hallways were attached to it, along with various wooden doors. Surely, the billeting office was somewhere nearby. He searched his comrades' faces, where his gaze lingered on David. He hadn't said a thing since Thoor's speech. Since Thoor called his tenure with the NYPD a "mediocre run." Scott frowned but said nothing. He turned back to Becan. "There's got to be a directory here. Let's find it."

It took them only a few minutes to locate a directory down one of the hallways and a minute more to find the billeting office. It was locked, apparently for the night. Aside from themselves, Thoor, and the two guards, they had yet to come across any other signs of life. It was as if the hallways were utterly abandoned.

Scott scanned the hall near the billeting office, finding a terminal embedded in the wall. The EDEN logo blinked on an algae-green display monitor. Scott stepped to the terminal and tapped a finger against it. The logo disappeared, and a list of languages replaced it. Scott selected English, and a screen of user options emerged.

"Here's hoping they're up to date," Scott mumbled as he accessed the personnel directory. An alphabetical list appeared, and he selected R. Once there, it took him only a moment to scroll down and find his last name. They were already in the system. He tapped on his roster entry, and a green screen appeared with his full name, rank, and position. Beneath it, the display indicated that he resided in structure B-1, Room 14.

"Simple enough," Scott said. He returned to the roster and found Jurgen on the alphabetical list. David was in Room 14 as well.

Becan observed from Scott's side. "Roommates again."

Scott nodded. "Wonder if you guys are next door again." Scott navigated the roster until he came to M, where he found McCrae. When Becan's information arose, Scott and Becan raised their eyebrows.

"Mm…"

Jayden stepped over to them. "Where are we?"

"Room 14…" said Becan.

Jayden's expression widened as he craned to the monitor. "What?" David stared at the screen in silence.

"I'm in Room 14," Becan said.

Jayden fidgeted. "What about me?"

"Hang on," Scott said as he backtracked out of Becan's file and found Jayden's.

Room 14.

Jayden's mouth hung open. "We're all in the same room?"

"What are they, quads?" David asked as he squinted at the monitor.

"Must be," Scott said as he inspected the terminal momentarily, then backed out of the personnel files to access the base map. After a brief search, he found B-1. "It's a few buildings behind this one." After a few more taps, he found Room 14.

"That looks like one hell of a big room," said David with some surprise.

Scott laughed under his breath. "Only one way to find out." He took a step away from the terminal and faced his comrades. The four men exchanged looks.

The trek to B-1 was cold and wet, as they were once again forced to dash through the downpour to reach the building. By the time they arrived, they were as drenched as they had been on the airstrip. B-1 was a large building, like the one they had come from, though its hallways were stark gray. As with the building with the billeting office, there were no signs of life anywhere. The men shivered as they trekked to Room 14.

The building was a catacomb. Narrow corridors branched off larger corridors both left and right, and the sheer size of the structure hit them. *Novosibirsk* was more massive than *Richmond* in every way.

The numerical layout was simple, and they could find the door to Room 14 without a directory. It was in the exact center of the building. Only the number "14" graced its pale gray finish.

Becan crossed his arms. "How are we supposed to be gettin' in? We've no bloody key."

Scott gripped the knob, where it turned effortlessly in his hand. The door cracked open, and Scott gave Becan a smug smile. The Irishman said nothing.

A ray of hallway light cut through the darkness of the room. As the ray of light widened, the four men angled their heads to peer into their new home. It took several seconds for their eyes to adjust, but soon, the room's features came into view. It was not the view they expected or wanted to see. Bunks. Rows and rows of bunks. Slumbered breaths reverberated through the room, and Jayden summed up the scene. "Barracks," he whispered. "B-1...barracks number one."

A groggy voice mumbled from the room's dark depths. Scott eased the door shut, then looked at his comrades.

"Aw, man," Jayden said.

Scott almost laughed. If not for the fact that he was cold, wet, and miserable, this would border on humorous. "We're going to have to sneak in and *find* empty bunks. We might end up on the floor tonight."

Becan snorted. "If I were mad, I would!"

"Would you rather sleep out here in the hall?"

Becan's gaze narrowed. "Righ', well how abou' this? I'm knackered an' wrecked as all bloody hell, an' I don't exactly consider barrelin' around in me underrods with a bunch o' torn-off Russian hardchaws suckin' diesel."

"First of all," Scott answered, "I have no idea what you just said. Second, whatever it was, I don't think we can do anything about it."

Becan opened his mouth to reply, but Jayden cut him off. "We're all tired, man. We're all freezin', we're all soakin' wet, but the thing said we're in Room 14, and Room 14 is right here. Personally, I don't care if I get those people mad or not. I'm doggone tired, and they didn't just fly across the world after packin' up everything they own at the drop of a hat. If they have a problem, they can talk to their supervisor, but it ain't my problem. Let's just find some hot showers, get warmed up, and find beds. All right?"

Becan eyed Jayden for a moment and remained silent for just as long before he drew in a breath and gave a single nod. "Yeah. All righ'."

Jayden nodded, and David cleared his throat. "Let's find some showers, then," he said. "Do we all have dry clothes?" The other three men motioned to their duffle bags. "Okay. Let's get warmed up before we catch hypothermia."

They ventured as a group throughout the maze of hallways, though they soon realized there was no shower room to be found. They explored every inch of the building but came across only sporadically placed restrooms. After twenty minutes in search, they settled on a dark corner of the building, where they removed their wet clothes and changed into multiple layers of warmer, dryer outfits. Throughout the entire ordeal, the corridors stayed secluded and silent. Once they were in dry clothes, they returned to Room 14.

Upon entrance to the room, they discovered that, though not spacious, there was sufficient space between the bunks to allow reasonable movement. A brief count by Scott revealed twelve bunks in four rows of three, half of which were occupied. The quest for a place to shower concluded as well, as they discovered three open stalls along the far side of the room, all of which drained through holes in the floor. Only beige curtains sheltered the stalls from the rest of the room.

After a brief search, they found two empty bunks on the far side of the room, one next to the other. They set their bags on the floor, claimed their mattresses, and nestled warmly under their covers. Quickly, they fell asleep.

The Fourteenth of Novosibirsk

Clarke, Nathaniel	Captain	Commanding Officer
Baranov, Ivan	Executor	Executive Officer
Dostoevsky, Yuri	Lieutenant	Tertiary Officer
Novikov, Anatoly	Lieutenant	Tertiary Officer
Axen, Matthew	Delta Trooper	Technician
Navarro, Travis	Delta Trooper	Pilot
Voronova, Svetlana	Delta Trooper	Medic
Lebesheva, Galina	Gamma Private	Medic
Powers, Fox	Gamma Private	Sniper
Carpenter, Kevin	Beta Private	Infantry
Evteev, Boris	Beta Private	Technician
Makarovich, Konstantin	Beta Private	Infantry
Yudina, Varvara	Beta Private	Medic

13

BECAN HAD NEVER felt so tired. He had never felt so out of it. A cold headrush washed across his brain as his eyes squinted and opened. What time was it? He had no idea. He knew it must have been early—the windowless room was still dim. His head rang. He could hear the constant tone assaulting his ears. Russia? Why the hell were they in Russia? It felt like a dream, and for a moment, he wondered if it might have been. No. It was real. Yesterday really did happen, and today, he was halfway across the globe.

He muttered under his breath as he pressed a palm against his forehead. He knew he was out of it. He could feel it in his equilibrium. It felt as if he had just awoken from a merry-go-round. He continued to squint between partially opened eyes. It was painful. God. He felt like a miserable dog. He felt cold. None of them had been given the chance to warm themselves before they snuck into bed, and now it showed. *No bloody showers,* Becan thought. *Don't want to wake up the bloody Russians, do we?* His palm pressed harder into his forehead as he clenched his teeth. *Bollocks. I'm takin' me bloody shower. Drag 'em to hell.*

Still groggy-eyed and disoriented, Becan twisted over to the side of the bed and set his feet on the floor. It was absolutely frigid. He drew in a breath and pushed up. He could still hear the constant tone in his head; it was as if this were a hangover that had nothing to do with alcohol. It was a *sleep*over. He grumbled at the thought of the word as he stumbled forward and to the showers.

Veckin' Russians, he thought. *Veckin' Russians and their stupid veckin' barracks.* One foot in front of the other. One heavy thump forward after the next. His vision was blurry. The tone in his ears still rang. *Veckin' Russians.* He reached forward with reckless abandon and whisked the shower curtain open.

She whipped her shampooed head around as soon as the curtains exposed her. Her eyes shot open as the downpour of water plastered her lathery golden locks to the sides of her face. Becan gasped. She screamed.

"Ahh!" Becan backpedaled and stumbled onto the floor in an eruption of thumps and bangs.

Scott jolted up from his bed as the shower curtain was yanked shut. *What in the world?* Several others had leapt up around him, and he focused on the floor, where Becan was a tangled mess.

"I decided to take a bloody shower," Becan grumbled.

Scott gaped across at the showers, where he heard the hard tatter of water hitting the floor.

Russian words were mumbled out loud from farther back in the room. A woman behind the curtain yelled something back as the showerhead twisted off, and a green towel was jerked down from the shower rack.

What time was it? Everything felt like a blur. Seconds ago, Scott had been off in some distant dream, none of which he could remember now. And now, crashing, yelling, people suddenly rousing all over…it was too early for this. *Was* it too early for this?

"God," Becan said as he staggered to a stand. "Top o' the mornin' to yis."

Scott blinked as a towel-wrapped woman stormed out from behind the shower. She glared through wet blond hair at Becan, and Russian fury poured from her mouth.

Before she could finish her spiel, a male voice farther back in the room cut her off. "Zatknis, Sveta." More Russian ensued.

"English!" someone hollered. "Speak English, you commies!"

The Russian voice groaned. "I said it's time to get up anyway."

The *Richmond* transfers cringed as an overhead light flicked on, and various men and women slid out of their bunks. They approached a long closet that ran along the wall opposite the showers. Scott droned in his morning-deep voice, "What's going on?"

David rubbed his eyes as he sat up. "I think…we just woke up."

Scott pushed a hand through his unkempt hair and regarded David. "Were we *supposed* to wake up?"

"I want to sleep," mumbled Jayden from beneath his covers.

Scott's attention turned to Becan. "What in the world were you doing?"

"Nothin'!" Becan said. "Don't get your knickers in a twist."

"How do you do, gentlemen?"

The rich, new voice came from directly behind them. It was a voice laden with a distinct British dialect. Scott, David, and Becan turned to face it, where they found a bearded black man dressed in an officer's uniform—one so kempt, Scott could only imagine that the man had been awake for some time. After a moment of scrutiny, Scott saw that he was a captain. The captain offered a courteous smile as he trained his eyes on Jayden's bunk, where the Texan was still completely beneath the covers.

"Aah," Becan said as he jerked the covers from atop Jayden. "Get up."

Jayden mumbled something inaudible, then raised his head. When he saw the captain, he briskly sat upright.

"Sorry," the captain said, "it looks like you've all had a rough night. You needn't beetle about, but do get showered and get into uniform as soon as you're able. When you've finished, please join us through *that* door." He pointed to a door along the back wall, where several Russian soldiers were already passing through. The four transfers nodded as the captain excused himself and entered the indicated doorway.

By the time they had woken up, taken showers, and donned their uniforms, they were the only four left in the bunk room. Everyone else had passed through the door. As soon as Scott stepped through it, he realized what it was.

It was a small lounge, complete with a culinary counter and several tables, all of which had a full complement of occupied chairs. The mingled smell of tea and coffee caressed the air as conversation in English and Russian flowed, accompanied by an occasional burst of laughter. Scott immediately noticed there were no other doors in the room—it must have been specifically designed for this unit. Did every unit have their own lounge like this?

They stood in the doorway for several moments before the captain noticed them. He regarded them with a proper smile. "I see you've finally got up and about then? Welcome to the lounge. While you're in here, there's no need for formalities. We wouldn't survive without a casual atmosphere once in a while." Scott nodded, and he and his comrades assumed more at-ease postures. Scott allowed his eyes to scan the soldiers clustered around the tables.

Smiles were few and far between. Most of their expressions were blank, with the captain a rare exception. The only other familiar face belonged to the blond-haired woman from the shower, whose pointed glare narrowed at Becan.

The captain continued. "I'm sorry, you four must be zonked out…I'll go ahead and explain to you why you're here. Just to be certain, you *are* David Jurgen, Becan McCrae, Scott Remington, and Jayden Timmons, correct?"

They nodded.

"Brilliant," the captain said. "As you may or may not be aware, *Novosibirsk* Command are in the process of restocking our base. A few units, ourselves included, have received entirely new sections in addition to the personnel already in place. You're ours. I apologize that your transfer seems to have come in quite an inconvenient manner for you, but you're here, and that's all that matters now."

He motioned his head to the nearest table of soldiers. "I suppose introductions are in order." Introductions. A whole new unit. Scott had just become comfortable with everyone back in Falcon Squad. "At my right is Gamma Private Fox Powers, our only resident sniper until now." Scott glanced toward Fox. He was a tanned, black-haired individual. His expression was stoic yet not uninviting.

"Delta trooper and technician Matthew Axen, otherwise known as Max..." Scott's attention swung to Max. He was a taller American with short, dirty blond hair, complemented by a thick brush of five o'clock shadow. There was something else that stood out about him, though. His eyes. They locked onto Scott with a pointed stare. More than a stare. Almost angered. Before Scott could scrutinize it further, Clarke went on.

"Delta Trooper Travis Navarro, our pilot."

Travis. There was an amiable look to the pilot, who looked like he had Native American in him. He smiled and tipped his head.

"And Beta Private Kevin Carpenter."

Another average-looking, somewhat smaller man.

"At the next table is Executor Ivan Baranov, our second in command..."

There came the change. Baranov was massive. Larger than General Thoor. His dark crew cut was trimmed to perfection; it was utterly militant. There was another distinct feature about him. His uniform...it was different. It was dark, almost free of emblems. Except for a red triangle. A Nightman. Baranov nodded as Clarke continued.

"Leftenant Yuri Dostoevsky."

Leaner but just as militant as Baranov. Maybe more so. His eyes stood out. They were blue, yet they pierced toward the transfers with bridled fury. No...not toward the *transfers*. Toward Scott. Dostoevsky, too, was a Nightman.

"Leftenant Anatoly Novikov, our chief technician." Less stout than the previous two Russian officers. Blond-haired, blue-eyed. Handsome. Another Nightman. The three officers beneath the British captain, all

Nightmen. Scott looked around at the other tables. Everyone else was standard EDEN.

"Beta Private Konstantin Makarovich, otherwise known as Kostya." Scott watched Kostya. He was young. Younger than...was he younger than Jayden? Kostya smiled as he waved.

"And Beta Private Boris Evteev, our final technician." There were three technicians in the unit. That was different from Falcon. This unit was more versatile, perhaps all-purpose. Boris tipped his mop of curly black hair to them as the captain directed them to the final table.

"And at our very last table are the three women you *don't* want to see because if you do, something's gone gammy." He nodded to the first woman. It was the blond-haired woman from before. The one from the shower. "We have Delta Trooper Svetlana Voronova, our chief medic..."

If Scott was being honest, this had to be one of the most beautiful women he'd laid eyes upon—despite the daggers in her deep blue eyes. Her body exuded grace, and her short, pixie-bob hair was slicked back from her interrupted shower.

Moments after Svetlana's name was mentioned, Lieutenant Dostoevsky murmured in her direction. The men around him chuckled.

"Zatknis," she spat back.

The captain went on. "And her medical staff. Gamma Private Galina Lebesheva." Galina seemed the oldest of the three women. She might have been as old as David. Her mahogany hair was short, too—almost butch. Definitely butch. She smiled cordially.

"And Beta Private Varvara Yudina." Varvara also had blond hair, though it was long and darker than Svetlana's. As she smiled, two minuscule dimples emerged from her cheeks. Scott tilted his head. She really smiled. No daggers, no forced politeness. Genuine. He liked her already.

The captain stood abruptly. "And I am Captain Nathan Clarke, your commanding officer. We make up the Fourteenth. When we asked for additional soldiers, I must admit I was slightly concerned when I heard they were sending us men not even a month out of Academy, but when I looked at your records, and what you did in Chicago, I was most impressed." Clarke's focus shifted to Scott. "Congratulations on your promotion to gamma private and for the Golden Lion. I know that's only a medal, but it's never been earned quite like that before. We're going to expect a lot out of you, out of *all* of you. You've all earned excellent marks from your superiors at *Richmond*. Now, I know Remington from the news...who else is who?"

David, Becan, and Jayden briefly introduced themselves. They were met with continued apathy from the tables. Aside from a handful—Clarke, Travis, Varvara, and perhaps one or two others—it was a relatively cold reception.

"Welcome to the Fourteenth," Clarke said. "There are a few things I still need to discuss with you, so I'll tend to that right now. The rest of you may go about your business," he said to the other soldiers. "We won't hold a session this morning."

A sporadic round of acknowledgments murmured forth as the soldiers rose and filed out of the room. Several of them nodded in departure to the four transfers. Most just walked by without acknowledging them. After several moments, the lounge was clear.

Clarke waited before he stepped to the door, closed it, and sighed. "Well, that's that." He smiled half-heartedly and meandered to one of the tables. "Please, have a seat, gentlemen." They joined him as he sat down. "Allow me to explain why you're *really* here." An ill smirk accompanied the words, which were exaggerated in pseudo-suspense. The four looked upon him quizzically, the captain's shift in tone impossible to disregard. "We, and I mean that in the corporate sense—EDEN—are at risk of losing this facility."

After looking briefly at his counterparts, Scott asked warily, "Losing this facility, sir?"

"I'm sure you've identified the party in power here."

The Nightmen. He had to be talking about them. Clarke went on.

"Every day, EDEN's influence wanes as Thoor's grows. I'm not keen on the prospect of the Fourteenth falling solely into Thoor's hands. That's why I put in for additional manpower. That, gentlemen, is why you're here."

David blinked. "So we're here for…politics?" The question was laced with uncertainty, as if David feared it might be crossing a line.

Clarke did not seem offended. "This goes beyond politics, I'm afraid. The Fourteenth are one of EDEN's last bastions of influence, here." His graveness gave way to the faintest of chuckles. "I apologize; I'm sure you're unaccustomed to captains blathering on this way with their subordinates. If nothing else, it should emphasize the desperation we true captains face."

Scott angled his head. "Sir, what do you mean by *true* captains?"

"EDEN captains, private."

"So there are…other kinds?"

Looking down like the cat that ate the canary, Clarke smiled with a sprinkle of smugness. "Oh, the things you gentlemen will learn. You'll know more than enough about the Nightmen in due time. For now, I just want to get you acclimated to the Fourteenth."

After a brief hesitation, David spoke up for a second time. "Sir, if Thoor and the Nightmen are becoming a problem, why doesn't EDEN stop them? I mean, this *is* an EDEN base..."

"Because Thoor is too effective to risk losing," Clarke answered. "And they know he wouldn't readily give up *Novosibirsk* without a fight."

Without a fight? Scott lifted an eyebrow. Was Thoor a madman? "You mean to tell me he'd *fight* EDEN to control *Novosibirsk*?"

"Abso-bloody-lutely. But that will never occur. He stays within EDEN guidelines just enough to keep Command out of his business. They won't risk losing *Novosibirsk* over which uniform he and his men opt to wear."

Scott shot a look toward the lounge door, still closed. If this place was as dangerous as Clarke suggested, what a risk it was to have this conversation.

"How many Nightmen are there, sir?" Becan asked.

Clarke shifted in his chair. "This facility has slightly over ten thousand soldiers...I'd say about three thousand of those are former Nightmen."

"Tha's only a third."

"That third is in command," Clarke answered. "That's how this place is run, with key Nightmen in key positions. Just look at this unit. Ivan, Yuri, and Anatoly—the other three officers. They're loyal to my command, but they're dead loyal to Thoor's. Though my relationship with them is amicable, I know enough not to push, even if I do outrank them. Encouraging an adherence to the chain of command and having a death wish are two quite different things."

As far as Scott knew, most Nightmen were Russian—but not Thoor. His accent had been something different. "Thoor met us on the airstrip when we arrived." When Scott commented, Clarke smirked thinly. "He's not Russian, is he?"

"No, he's not," Clarke answered. "And if you're thinking that most Nightmen are Russian, you're correct. But Thoor himself is Dutch. He was known as the 'Terror of Amsterdam' before he came to *Novosibirsk*. As far as how he became a leader in the Nightman sect, if you knew him well enough, you'd understand. He's a formidable leader. He's heartless, treacherous, merciless, but formidable. He's got the requisite lack of moral compass to be among the great military rulers in human history—if you can stomach being led by a sociopath."

Clarke smiled. "Now, as much as I enjoy the divulging of information, there are a few things that I need to go over with you on the business

front. Morning call is at o600, and we usually start here. Tea and coffee
are always here if you need them. By seven, we're out the door for our
morning routine. We usually run several kilometers in the training center,
though sometimes we swim laps...whatever I decide at the time, really. At
1300 on Mondays, Wednesdays, and Fridays, we meet in the gymnasium
for a group workout in the form of weight lifting, sparring, or something
of the sort. You're free to use the gymnasium as often as you'd like on your
own time, and though I don't demand it, I highly encourage it. There's a
strict base curfew at 2100. Everyone is to be in their unit's room by then,
preferably sleeping, though the lounge is always open for tea or a late-
night chinwag if sleep is elusive.

"And as I'm sure you've discovered," he grinned and glanced to Becan,
"we've got three showers in the bunk room."

Becan folded his arms across his chest and looked down.

"You probably aren't used to showering right next to everyone as they
sleep," Clarke said, "but you'll adjust to such flagrant crudeness. This place
was designed to maximize space—and with all the charm of a gulag. It's
not as bad as you think, so long as you don't mind the constant humidity
and the pleasing fragrance of old soap scum."

We literally just got transferred to Hell, Scott thought.

No one spoke, and Clarke pushed back his chair and stood.

"That's all I wanted to talk about. You gentlemen are free to go about
your business until 1300. I'm going to make my way to the cafeteria for
some breakfast; you're more than welcome to come if you'd like. You
should have privacy here for another half hour or so when people start
returning from breakfast."

Scott rose with the others after Clarke, watching as the captain meandered to the door. This was the strangest military introduction he had
ever been a part of. It was casual to the point of being a borderline breach
in the chain of command—a captain treating subordinates as equals. It
was enough to commit Scott to one last question. "Sir?"

Clarke stopped and turned back to the table.

"Why did you tell us all of this?"

David, Becan, and Jayden looked at Scott, then turned to Clarke. That
very same question lingered on all their expressions.

Clarke scrutinized Scott for a moment before he offered a half-hearted
smile. "It's because you're new here. You haven't been tainted yet. And
I suppose...I want to influence you as much as possible before they do."

Again, silence pervaded the room. They? The Nightmen? Before Scott could think further, Clarke said, "Now, if you'll excuse me, I've got to tuck into some breakfast. Cheerio."

Scott watched him leave the room. No more explanations were offered. The lounge door shut behind Clarke, and the four transfers were alone. They remained in the lounge for another minute, though they said little. They then filed out of the room, retrieved their duffle bags, and set up their bunks for permanent residence.

They finished their acclimation to Room 14 by 0730, at which point they ventured out together in search of the cafeteria. The sun had risen two hours earlier, though no sunlight shone on the ground. The sky was blanketed in pale gray, and the earth was wet from the previous night's storm. The air was frigid. There were few trees on the outskirts of the base, and it seemed to Scott that *Novosibirsk* was in the middle of an epic expanse of nothing—only snow-covered fields.

The cafeteria was bustling when they arrived. Russian soldiers lined up to receive their meals, colorless pale trays in their hands as they anticipated cold servings from uninspired attendants. Nobody looked familiar. From when Scott took his tray to when he received his meal, he saw no one from the Fourteenth in the cafeteria. As expected, all of the conversation he heard was in Russian.

A table caught Scott's eye as they weaved through the cafeteria, searching for a place to sit. It stood out for quite a simple reason: at it sat a black man. He was the only black man besides Clarke that Scott had seen anywhere. Directly across from him sat a giant of a soldier. There were no others with them. Their postures were casual, relaxed. As they talked, their gestures swayed in familiar patterns. From his distance, Scott couldn't make out what they were saying. He didn't need to.

"Americans."

"Mm?"

Scott glanced at Becan. "Americans, over there."

"How can yeh tell?"

Scott offered no explanation. He altered his direction for their table, and his three counterparts followed. The giant and the black man turned to face them as they neared.

"Mind if we sit down?" Scott asked.

The larger man looked surprised, and a broad smile stretched across the black man's face. "USA?"

Scott grinned. He knew it. "USA and looking for more."

"Well, you got two more right here," the black man said as he gestured for them to sit. "Joe Janson. My friend here's William Harbinger."

As Scott sat down, he sized up William. The guy was huge. His hands were like boxing gloves, and his frame was as wide as a door. Harbinger was an appropriate name for him. Scott introduced himself, and David, Becan, and Jayden followed suit.

William flashed a broad grin. "So where y'all from?"

"*Richmond*," David answered. "We got here last night."

William nodded. "We been here 'bout a month. We were both stationed in *Atlanta* for about three days before they shipped us out here. Had one mission in *Atlanta* on our second day, and they got rid of us the day after."

Joe chuckled. "Had enough of us, I guess. What are you guys, infantry?"

Scott nodded. "Infantry and a sniper." He motioned to Jayden, who waved. "What about you?"

"Soldier," Joe answered.

"Scout," said William.

A scout? The pride of the Academy, known for their stealth, acrobatics, and ability to crawl through small spaces? William the harbinger? Scott's eyes narrowed with skepticism.

"Yeah, he's a scout," Joe said. "He's a scout like I'm an Ithini."

"Demolitionist," William confessed with a smirk.

Scott smiled. "That's more like it." He liked them already. Easygoing, conversational, and not equipped with the cold shoulder that seemed standard on Russian personnel. "So what's it like here? You've been here a month—any action?"

"We went out once," William answered, "about two weeks ago, I guess. Bakma Cruiser got shot down about a hundred miles south of here, so they sent our team in after it. That's what got us up to beta. Haven't seen any Ceratopians…not here or in *Atlanta*."

"We haven't either," David said. "We did go on a little necrilid hunt, though."

Joe's expression widened. "Are you serious?"

"Yeah. One of the worst experiences of our lives."

William swallowed a bite of food. "That what got you all to beta?"

"No," David answered. "That was Chicago. For most of us, anyway."

William's attention perked immediately. "Oh man, you were there for Chicago? That made the news everywhere!"

Before anyone else could comment, Joe's eyes shot wide. He stared at Scott and perked upright. "Oh, veck!"

"What?" William asked, looking perplexedly around the group.

"I knew I knew you!" Joe said.

The moment Scott had seen Joe sit upright, he knew he'd been busted. Fame had followed him to Russia.

"Come on, Will, you know!"

William's eyes widened. "Oh, veck!"

"This is the Golden Lion guy!"

"Yeah," William said, "the Golden Lion!"

Scott feigned a smile as he acknowledged with a nod. There it was again. *The* Golden Lion. Was that what he was now? No—he was a soldier, not some movie star or action hero. And certainly not a walking medal. He was a soldier who had done the right thing at the right time, around the right people in the right positions. Nicole didn't think he was a hero when she found out what he did. She thought he was an idiot. "God was watching over me. I had nothing to do with it." He cringed inwardly. What a forced, automatic answer. Did he even mean it?

Joe smiled and shook his head. "Man, if you and God are *that* tight, I want me and you to be good friends." The others laughed.

"Seriously," Scott said, "it was nothing special. Anyone could have done it." Yes, God had been watching over him. But nobody else could have pulled that off like he did. *Anyone* could have done it? That was a lie. He had known what he was doing. He had known it would work.

Yet it didn't save Henry and Zigler the next time they went out.

"What unit are you guys in?" Scott asked.

"The Eighth," William answered. "One of the bigger units here. I mean in physical size, not…size…I mean, we, in the unit, are bigger people than those in other units."

Joe laughed. "Will's a little slow."

"Shut up."

"He's right, though. We're a pretty big group. Got five demos…no mystery what we were made to do."

William gleamed. "Blow junk up."

"How many are in the Eighth?" David asked.

"Eighteen," Joe answered. "Most of 'em ate already. I'd introduce you to some if they were around."

William pointed across the room. "There's Cole right there."

Scott followed William's gesture across the room, where an average-sized man with jet-black hair strode toward their table. He looked scruffy.

214 Dawn of Destiny

A patch of black hair under his chin formed an off-centered goatee. Barely off, but definitely off. To the left. God, that was going to drive Scott crazy. Joe smiled as the man approached. "That's Derrick Cole, one of our infantry. He's American. As southern country as you can get."

David grinned at William. "I don't know—you sound pretty southern."

William shook his head. "No, see...I'm southern. Cole is a hick."

Derrick smiled as he lowered himself into a chair next to Joe. "Hey y'all, how y'all doin'?"

Scott smiled. Will was right. Derrick had the most prolonged drawl he had ever heard. His voice was deep, like a bass. But that goatee...God, how did that happen? Didn't the Eighth have a mirror?

"Cole-C-Cole-Cole-Cooole!" William sang.

Derrick shot him a look. "Shut up, Harbringer."

William's expression dropped. "Hey man, come on, don't do that."

Joe laughed. "They misspelled Big Will's name on his graduate paper from the Academy, put Harbringer instead of Harbinger. Even his name badge was misspelled when they first gave it to him."

William stopped eating. "It's not funny."

Derrick laughed, then lowered his head in silence. Scott smiled. Prayer before eating. It was always nice to see. Suddenly, Scott's smile faded. He had forgotten to pray for his own meal.

Becan glanced at Derrick's tray. It was piled with what appeared to be the *Novosibirsk* equivalent of chili and beans. Or something of the gaseous persuasion. "Hell of a bloody breakfast, eh?"

"Derrick likes anything that makes him fart," said William with a smirk.

"Yer *momma* likes anything that makes her fart."

Joe nodded at Scott and his comrades. "They just came in from *Richmond*."

Derrick swallowed a bite and smiled. "This is definitely a step down from there. What unit y'all in?"

"Fourteenth," David answered.

"Oh, that's what's his face's..."

Joe nodded. "Clarke."

"Yeah, Clarke."

William took a sip of water. "That's one of the general's favorite units. They get a lot of good calls. I dunno if that has anything to do with Clarke, though. Sometimes they get to go on missions that others don't."

"It's because of the Nightmen in it," Joe said.

Derrick nodded. "Y'all got a beastly executor."

William smiled. "Yeah. Baranov's a tank, but word is he's a decent guy, too. Can't say that about many Nightmen."

"What makes the Nightmen so bad?" Scott asked. Brutal, he knew they were that. But every military organization had some level of brutality. William began his explanation with a question. "Do you know what you have to do to become a Nightman?"

"No," Scott answered as he looked around the table. The others, too, wore uninformed expressions.

William shot a quick look at Joe and Derrick.

"You got to tell 'em, now," Joe said. His voice was different now. It was hushed.

William leaned in close to Scott. "You have to kill somebody."

Kill somebody? "Soldiers kill all the time..."

William shook his head. "No, not aliens or anything like that. You have to kill someone here."

"Yeh have to *murder* someone?" Becan asked.

"Shh!" William flagged his hand. "We're not supposed to know that. Although everybody knows it, it's just that nobody talks about it."

"Yeh been here a month an' yeh know it already?" asked Becan. "Tha's not tha' good of a secret..."

"We only know it 'cause someone in our unit told us."

"Was he a Nightman?" David asked.

"Hell no. You ask a Nightman about that, and you're likely to get killed yourself."

Scott shook his head slowly. Did he understand this right? "Let me get this straight...you have to *murder* someone to become a Nightman?"

William nodded. "It's like one of their rites of passage or something. They call it the Murder Rule. The last step."

"But *why*?"

"To sell your soul, I guess. If you'll kill someone in cold blood for them, you'll probably do anything for them. That's what they want."

Propping his elbow on the table and pointing, Scott said, "But wait a minute. Captain Clarke told us there were some three thousand Nightmen on base. How do three thousand murders go unnoticed?"

"Easier than you think, my friend," answered David. "First, I'd assume these people didn't all become Nightmen at once. Those deaths are probably spread out over years, maybe a decade for some of these older guys. And trust me, a lot of crimes don't go reported—even murders. Some people just disappear. Makes me wonder how bad the homeless problem is here in Novosibirsk and the surrounding region, if you know what I mean."

"Then what about the ones who won't do it?" Scott asked. "The Nightman recruits who aren't willing to take an innocent life?"

William shook his head. "To that, I don't know. I don't think I *want* to know."

David leaned forward. "What I don't understand is how EDEN lets them get away with it. They've *got* to know this takes place."

"That's *Novosibirsk*, the exception to the rules. EDEN just looks the other way."

"This place is Thoor's little empire," Joe said. "EDEN doesn't care what he does, long as he does it good."

Derrick fidgeted in his chair. "Guys, let's change the subject."

Joe nodded. "Yeah. Best not to talk about it here. We don't know much more anyhow."

Scott didn't want to change the subject, and by the looks of his friends, neither did they. Even Jayden, silent on the far end, looked engrossed.

William slid his glass of water to the side. "You guys are going to spar today."

Whether he liked it or not, the subject was changing. Scott said nothing, though he had a dozen questions in his mind.

"Are we now?" Becan asked.

"Yeah," William answered. "It's Wednesday, and the Fourteenth always spars on Wednesday."

"How d'yeh know this?"

"Because of Baranov. The guy is a tank. Everyone goes there to watch him."

"Actually, they go to watch whoever he ends up beatin' to death," said Derrick sardonically.

"It's rarely a good fight," William said with a grin. "Except when that other Russian guy in your unit fights him. I don't know his name. Then it's good."

He had to be talking about one of the lieutenants. Unless he was talking about Boris, the technician. Somehow, Scott doubted that.

"Yeah," Derrick said, "that one guy gives him a hell of a fight."

"Hey guys," Joe interrupted, "what time is it?"

William and Derrick looked at their watches. William jumped up. "Oh veck, we got to go."

"What is it?" Scott asked.

"We got a meeting at 0830. It's 0815."

"Veck, man," Derrick said, "I just sat down!" He crammed his mouth full of food.

Scott watched as the three men from the Eighth pushed back from their chairs and picked up their trays.

"It was great talking to you guys," Joe said.

"Yeah, nice meetin' ya," said William in tow.

Scott smiled. "Same here. We'll see you around, right?"

"I'm sure of it."

After exchanging parting gestures, Joe, William, and Derrick stepped away from the table and exited the cafeteria.

Scott, David, Becan, and Jayden remained together for a while as they talked about the conversation with their newfound friends. The Murder Rule was the primary topic. It astounded them that such a rule existed. The entire atmosphere of *Novosibirsk* took on a darker, more sinister persona—as if it hadn't been dark and sinister to begin with. No part of *Novosibirsk* felt more wicked than General Thoor.

Despite their fascination with the lore of *Novosibirsk*, however, there were more immediate concerns for them to deal with—namely, the fact that none of them knew the layout of their new home. As soon as they were finished eating, the four transfers exited the cafeteria to partake in a self-guided tour of *Novosibirsk*.

The contrast between *Novosibirsk* and *Richmond* couldn't have been more striking. Whereas *Richmond* charmed with street signs labeling their hallways, *Novosibirsk* labeled their buildings with chipping Cyrillic alphabet. Everything was some shade of gray—the buildings, the concrete, the sky. It was a world in monochrome. A world of sharp angles and relentless function. *Novosibirsk* and its Nightman inhabitants were often referred to as The Machine. It was easy to understand why. Nothing about this place exuded warmth or humanity.

If there was a positive aspect of the no-nonsense, Constructivist architecture, it was that it made the layout of the base fairly easy to learn and navigate. Though there was no shortage of buildings from one end of the base to the other, the ones that mattered the most to Scott and his comrades were easy to identify. There were four barracks buildings, the first of which housed Room 14. There was a circular running track and a training ground at the far east of the base, not far from the large base cafeteria. North of the cafeteria was the large, square building that contained the billeting office, where they'd first found the terminal that identified them as occupants of Room 14. There were no markings to identify what the building actually was, and when they mustered up the courage to stop and ask someone, they were told simply that it was the "main building." Whatever worked.

Directly east of the main building was the infirmary, and to its west was the hangar and attached garage. It was the hangar itself that housed the most imposing structures on the base in the form of two turret towers at the far corners of the airstrip and a massive tower that looked like a cross between air traffic control and an elevated bunker. That tower, they learned, was *Novosibirsk* Command—the operational heart of The Machine. NovCom. It was an imposing building, easily the tallest on base. It would certainly be the easiest to remember.

Besides those primary buildings, there were many others laid out across the grounds in a grid-like pattern. From supply depots to maintenance shacks, the place was like its own tightly packed city. As a Class-4 base, *Novosibirsk* was among the world's largest in numbers of personnel. All things considered, though, the base's footprint wasn't as massive as that classification would indicate. It was a model example of the utilization of space to meet a desired function. If there was one thing the Soviets had going for them, that was it.

After an hours-long exploration of the base, Scott, David, Becan, and Jayden finally returned to Room 14. Just as Clarke had claimed, they were met by the strange dankness of a room that served as both shower and sleeping area. The captain had told them they'd acclimate. They found that hard to believe. Nonetheless, this was home now—even if it wasn't quite where their hearts were.

With surprisingly few people in the room, it was no surprise whatsoever that none of them made an effort to talk to the four transfers. A slight cultural barrier may have been responsible for that, as everyone present was Russian. Just the same, some sort of warm welcome from their Soviet counterparts would have been nice. Apparently, when Thoor had told them on the airstrip, "we are not nice here," he hadn't been joking. But at least the four transfers had each other—and in each other, they found conversation and common ground. If nothing else, it passed it the time.

According to William, all four of them were destined for a fight later that afternoon—a Fourteenth sparring tradition.

They weren't sure whether to look forward to that or not.

14

WHEN THE FOUR transfers rendezvoused with the Fourteenth in the gym at 1300, they discovered that William had been correct. The unit was gathered around an open area on the floor—a sparring circle. As they approached, Scott tried to associate faces with names. Clarke. He knew Clarke easily. Ivan Baranov was their executor and the one William and Joe had referenced earlier—the tank. He would be hard to forget now. As they neared the circle, Clarke addressed them.

"How goes it, gentlemen? Glad to see you've found us. Today, we're going to partake in some hand-to-hand combat training."

Scott's gaze deviated from Clarke as he identified the others in his mind. Svetlana would forever stand out for Becan having snuck up on her in the shower. Next to Svetlana was Travis Navarro, the Native American pilot. He was the most average-looking individual, yet his identity stuck in Scott's mind. Perhaps because he seemed friendly.

"We dedicate every Wednesday to sparring, as you'll grow accustomed. I'm sure you've all had your share of sparring in Academy and *Richmond*, as well. The same rules apply here. No ropes, ring, or mat—just the floor and some space."

For the life of Scott, he couldn't remember the two lieutenants beneath Clarke and Baranov. One of their names started with a D. D...something. He remembered Varvara Yudina, the youngest medic. She'd flashed a cute smile at them when she'd been introduced. She seemed engaging.

"You won't have a mat beneath you when you find yourself face to face with a Ceratopian," Clarke said, "so you haven't got one here, either. All right, ladies and gentlemen, please prepare yourselves."

As Scott geared up with the rest of the unit, his mind continued to compare the Fourteenth's faces with his memory. He couldn't remember the name of the mahogany-haired medic with the butch haircut. He remembered Boris Evteev, the technician with the black beard. He remembered Fox Powers, the American sniper. And Max, also American. Something about Max had embedded itself in his mind. It was how Max looked at him when he was introduced to the unit. It'd almost looked like anger, but how could that be? He didn't even know Scott. Before he realized it, he was fully equipped in sparring gear, as was everyone else. He joined them in preparatory stretches.

Scott surveyed the room until his gaze caught William Harbinger. The giant demolitionist stood in the distance, where a crowd gathered to observe what the Fourteenth was doing. God, William was enormous. He stood out like a titan.

As soon as everyone was stretched and ready, Clarke began. "We might as well hold a proper initiation since we've newcomers to the unit. Typically, we all just partner up on our own and spar as we wish, though occasionally, I like to do specific bouts, as we'll do today. Here's how we'll run things. I'll have each of our new arrivals, McCrae, Remington, Jurgen, and Timmons, match up against three soldiers. They shall act as a tag team while you," he motioned to the transfers, "remain in the ring alone. They are free to tag as often as they'd like."

Three-on-one? How disgustingly awkward. Scott got that it was a good chance for Clarke to witness them facing adversity, but there had to be more effective ways than this. They hadn't even met everyone yet or talked with anyone other than Clarke. Maybe this would bond them. Somehow, he doubted it.

"I'll just observe today," Clarke said. "I'd like to see how the four of you handle yourselves. Any questions?"

Tension prevailed.

"Very well then. Anyone care to offer themselves out first?"

Scott stared at David, Becan, and Jayden. They all stared back at him, then at each other. None of them said a word. Scott almost laughed. He didn't know who the first fool to volunteer himself would be, but it sure wasn't going to be him.

"Well then, let's observe Remington first if he'll please. I'm curious to see how the Golden Lion composes himself."

Scott's eyes rolled shut. It figured.

"Leftenant Dostoevsky, please give the good gamma private a run, will you?"

Dostoevsky. *That* was the D-name. Yuri Dostoevsky, like the old Russian writer.

Dostoevsky nodded as he stood. "Yes, captain." He scanned the rest of the unit. "Does anyone want to fight Remington?"

There was no hesitation as Max leapt to his feet. "I do."

Max stepped into the circle. What was it with him? That response was a little too eager for Scott's liking.

Dostoevsky smirked in Max's direction. "Anyone else?" No response came, and he motioned to Varvara. "Varya, come."

The cute one with the engaging smile. Scott didn't want to have to fight her.

"Da, lieutenant," Varvara answered as she stood and stepped to the circle.

Scott flinched as David and Becan slapped his back. The support was a good touch, but he knew what they were thinking. They were glad it wasn't them.

Scott stepped to the center of the circle. Dostoevsky spoke again. "Max will go first, I will follow, then Varya. Ready?"

Scott nodded. "Yes, sir." He was as ready as he'd ever be. All EDEN cadets went through sparring drills in *Philadelphia*. This couldn't be much different. Max was tall, athletic. Experienced. He'd be a good fight. Max approached the circle's center, eyes locked onto Scott's. That familiar gleam was there again. Scott recognized it. It wasn't anger. It looked more like...hatred.

"Ready," Max said.

Dostoevsky nodded. "Go. Tag if you need to, Max."

Scott bounced as soon as Dostoevsky spoke. His eyes focused on Max, who lightened on his feet, as well. From beyond the circle, Scott heard Becan's chant.

"Come on, Remmy, take him down..."

Attack first. Take the initiative. Scott danced forward to jab in Max's direction. Experimental jabs. Testing Max's speed. Max was sure to do the same.

Or not. As soon as Scott's test jab reached Max, Max slammed Scott's arm out of the way and cracked his fist against Scott's face. Before Scott could register a reaction, he was hammered with a follow-up hook. His feet buckled. He collapsed backward.

Becan, David, and Jayden cringed from the edge of the circle.

Scott gritted his teeth and stared at Max. That wasn't an attack. That was a message. *All right, Max, you got something to say? I got something for you, too.* His gaze narrowed as he pushed to his feet. That was a bad start. A rushed start. Now, he'd be more tactical. He cocked his arm and prepared for another jab. Another half-speeded pop. A decoy. As soon as Max stepped forward to intercept, just as he had before, Scott withdrew the jab, bent to the side, and slammed his other fist into the side of Max's headgear.

Becan pumped his fist at the edge of the circle.

Before Max could regain footing, Scott sent a left hook straight into his face. Max stumbled and fell onto the floor.

They exchanged glares, and Max slammed himself to a stand. He leered and wiped his lip. "All right..." As soon as Max was upright, he lurched forward and stomped. Scott flinched. Then, the actual attack came. Max rushed toward him, pounding with blow after blow as Scott struggled to counter. When Scott blocked a jab, Max popped him in the side of the head. When Scott parried an uppercut, Max struck him in the ribs. For every attack Scott blocked, Max landed another. So relentless was Max's offensive, Scott never had a second to retaliate.

What was going on? This wasn't an exercise. This was a brawl. No one in training fought like this. Scott was pushed to the edge of the ring as his defenses faltered. The next thing he knew, Max grabbed him around the waist and hurled him back toward the center of the circle.

Scott stumbled to the ground and spun his head around. Then it happened. Something slammed into his face. His lips erupted with blood. His vision blackened. He flopped flat on his back.

It didn't take long for Scott's senses to reemerge—and for him to realize what happened. Max had kicked him in the face. Max had kicked him in the face while he was on the ground. Everything about practice etiquette just flew out the window.

Get up. You have to get up.

Scott staggered to his feet, but Max was on him. He grabbed Scott's head and slung him around and away. Scott's feet tripped up, and he fell at the edge of the ring. Before Max could attack again, Dostoevsky's voice broke the fight.

"Tag."

Max glared at Dostoevsky, then leaned his mouth next to Scott's ear. "Nice work, Golden Lion," he spat under his breath. He shoved Scott's head, then strolled to the circle's edge.

"Get ready, Remington," Dostoevsky said.

Scott couldn't even think straight despite his slow rise from the floor. What just happened? He got his tail torn off, that's what happened. God, his jaw hurt. No time for that. Only time for Dostoevsky. Dostoevsky.

As soon as Scott moved to face the lieutenant, the attack was there. A jab stung him in the face. Scott flew back, and the assault followed. Face. Chest. Ribs. Strike after strike, Dostoevsky pushed Scott to the edge of the ring again. The lieutenant was fast. Faster than Max. Stronger than Max.

He had to do something. *Defend yourself!* Even an effort was better than a total beating. He mustered his pride and surged forward with a fist. Dostoevsky snatched it in mid-flight. His fingers curled around it, and he twisted it. A simple, effortless twist. The pain was electric. It sparked through Scott's body like a thousand volts, and he found himself completely paralyzed, arm outstretched and pathetic like a captive, helpless fool. Dostoevsky's grip tightened, then he swept Scott's feet from under him.

A groan emerged from the crowd of spectators.

Scott clutched his wrist and pushed to his feet. *Defend yourself, you idiot! Fight back!* He struck out again, though his wrist was grabbed again in mid-flight. Dostoevsky twisted it, and Scott flipped flat on his back with a loud thud.

His spine throbbed, but there was no time to register the pain. Dostoevsky kicked him in the face, just as Max had, then stomped on his chest and stomach with vehement force.

Scott's head rolled backward, and he rasped, his breathing uneven. He couldn't move. Everything hurt. Everything felt battered. He knew he was bleeding. He could feel blood oozing from his lips and his eyebrow. His body was bruised. There was no need for anyone to call this fight. It was over by a country mile.

Dostoevsky murmured something to Varvara, and then he stepped past Clarke. "This is a joke."

Clarke frowned.

The next touch Scott felt wasn't a kick to the face or a foot to the stomach. It was a hand that slid gently beneath his head and neck. Varvara. He hadn't wanted to fight her, and now he didn't have to. What had just happened? *How* could it have happened? This had to be a dream—or a nightmare.

She slipped Scott's headgear off him and rolled it to the side. As Scott opened his eyes for the first time since he last fell, she smiled at him. It wasn't quite the cute smile she had given him before. Now, it was a smile of apology. The Fourteenth watched silently as she aided him upright and then to a stand.

A joke. That's what he was now, so said his new lieutenant. He was a joke in front of everybody...his friends, his new unit, even William and everyone who had observed this disgrace of a fight. Scott wanted to disappear. To take refuge in some deep, dark hole. Sheer determination allowed him to carry himself out of the circle, though Varvara remained at his side the entire way. He lowered himself to a seat, and she took one beside him. The apologetic smile remained as she slid a cloth to his lips and dabbed away the blood. Scott's gaze remained downcast to the floor.

Clarke finally spoke up. "I'm very sorry...that was one of the most heartfelt initiations I've seen in my life...." Silent tension hung in the air. Nobody said a word until Clarke resumed—this time, with noticeable hesitation. "Anyone care to go next, please?"

Becan hopped to his feet, slid on his headgear, and trotted into the ring. "I do."

Scott blinked. Looking up, he watched as Becan hopped up and down. By the surprised looks on everyone else's faces, they were wondering the same thing as Scott. Why in the *world* was Becan eager to go through a gauntlet like Scott just had?

Clarke cleared his throat and turned to Lieutenant Novikov. "Very well then. Anatoly, will you please entertain the good beta?"

Lieutenant Novikov—the third Nightman—nodded. "Yes, captain." He rose and motioned to Travis, the pilot, and Boris, the technician. "Come. Either of you want to go first?"

Becan cleared his throat before they could answer. "All."

Novikov shot a look at him. "What?"

"All three of yeh. Same time."

And now, Scott and everyone around him were utterly captivated. Becan wanted to fight all three of them at the same time? Was he insane?

Clarke laughed. "I'm sorry, but you can't be serious."

"Am are, sir," Becan answered.

Clarke and Novikov eyed one another; everyone else stared at Becan in bewilderment. Farther away with the rest of the spectators, William Harbinger leaned forward against a post.

Clarke half-smiled. "Well, if he desires a three-on-one punch-up, by all means, give him one."

Scott watched Becan as he danced about the sparring circle. Travis and

Boris weren't Nightmen, but Novikov was. Becan was up to something. If he wasn't, then he had lost his mind.

Novikov, Travis, and Boris grouped themselves into a semicircle before Becan, who tilted his head to flex his neck muscles. Otherwise, he seemed unprepared. No other stretches, no loosening up. Nothing.

"Are you ready?" Novikov asked.

"Yes, sir," Becan answered, assuming a loose stance. His eyes darted to the edge of the ring, where they found Svetlana. He winked and blew her a kiss.

"Go."

Before Travis or Boris could acknowledge with a *yes, sir,* Becan leapt at Lieutenant Novikov and flung his foot through the air. It collided with Novikov's face. Novikov spun in a circle and dropped to the floor.

Svetlana gasped.

In the split second that followed, Becan lunged at Boris, grabbed him by his headgear, and punched him square in the face. A mist of red exploded from Boris's lips as he stumbled out of the arena.

Jayden's jaw dropped. "Holy *cow.*"

As Novikov stammered to a stand, Travis thrust a fist at Becan from behind. Becan swirled around, snatched it in mid-flight, and balanced against it as he popped three kicks at the pilot's cheek. Travis teetered as a final kick slammed into his chest. He toppled to the ground.

Before Novikov, who had just staggered to his feet, could gather his bearings, Becan dashed at him, spun around, and smashed an elbow into the center of his forehead. Novikov's head cocked backward, and he collapsed. His body went still. He was out cold—with his two partners sprawled out on the floor, neither trying to get up.

The fight was over.

There was no sound. If a pin had fallen, it would have echoed throughout the gym. Scott's swollen lips parted as he stared at the Irishman. Three men against one. The one had won. A point had been made with thundering authority.

Becan's devilish smile curled up at Max, and he mouthed the word, "you." Max made no response.

Clarke could hardly speak. "That…was one of the most impressive things I've seen in my life…"

"Thank yeh, sir," Becan said as he filtered through the audience back to his seat.

Jayden stared at him wide-eyed. "Why the hell didn't you tell me you could do that?"

"Hold your cards close," Becan answered. "Yeh never know when yeh migh' need one."

Clearing his throat, Clarke regained his poise. "Next, please?"

The rest of the fights were lackluster. Scott observed as David and Jayden held their own in their matches, though neither could replicate Becan's three-on-one feat. As for Novikov, he was tended to personally by Svetlana. When that tender aid involved a kiss, Scott knew that she and the lieutenant were more than comrades. Apparently, the rule about officers being involved with the enlisted didn't apply here. Somehow, he wasn't surprised.

Scott couldn't help but wonder how Becan's impassioned beatdown of Novikov might affect them, especially with the chief medic decidedly in Novikov's corner. He hoped, in a place with such dark rites as the Murder Rule, it wouldn't come back to haunt them.

Clarke's small talk concluded the event, and they dismissed for Room 14. Showers came next, and food in the cafeteria after. As before, Scott and his companions found acceptance with William and Joe, though now they were joined by two others—Travis and Fox Powers. Travis, despite his beating, enthusiastically praised Becan for his fighting prowess. Fox exchanged sniper talk with Jayden.

William was more interested in ribbing Scott for his defeat in the ring than in joining any meaningful conversation, but Scott only laughed it off and changed the subject when possible. By the time conversation died down, it was almost 2100. Almost curfew—and time for the Fourteenth to retire to its room. Day one was over.

Night two was only just beginning.

*   *   *

SCOTT LAY WIDE awake. He peered to the bunk bed above, where David slept out of view. It was past midnight, and the Fourteenth was asleep—all except for Scott. He wasn't sure whether to blame it on jet lag or the day's events, but he lay in sleeplessness, hands behind his head as he listened to the steady breathing of those around him. The soreness had begun to set in. The embarrassment had set in much earlier, despite his efforts at bravado.

For the first time since the whirlwind of the transfer, Scott felt the absence of his comrades from Falcon Squad—Captain Lilan and Executor Tacker, Shekeia and Natasha, Michael and Donald, Lexie and John. Henry and Zigler.

He missed all of them. He missed immortality. But more than anything, he missed Nicole.

He had called her earlier that day, but the conversation was painfully short. She didn't have time to talk. She had other things to do. For the first time, he noticed something different about her voice. Something gone that had always been there in the past. Hope. The thought of *Richmond* being too far away from her seemed laughable now. He would have gladly stayed there had he known Russia was the alternative. But now, what did it matter? He was there. There was nothing he could do to change it.

He recalled every detail about the day he had proposed to her. Every little thing. It had been a gorgeous Sunday afternoon. They'd been on a picnic. She always loved them, and he always got dragged along. But this time, it was his idea. She was delighted with his initiative. The sun shone splendidly. She wore a yellow shirt and blue jeans, and he vividly recalled strands of her hair dancing on her forehead in the gentle wind.

He knew back then that if he tried to pull off anything cute, it would sound clichéd, so he just told her. *You were put in my life to be my love. If I tried to tell you what you mean to me, we'd be here all night. I love you. I intend to love you forever, and there's no other girl who can change that. You are my girl. I want to be your man. Nikki...will you marry me?*

He remembered her eyes as they glistened. He remembered her smile lighting up. She replied in five simple words. *What took you so long?* He could still taste the passion in her kiss.

Once again, Scott rolled over in his bed. Sleep was futile. It felt pointless to even try. He reached down to the floor and felt around with his fingers for the cover of his Scripture. His hand curled around it; he propped himself up and slid out of bed. He was well adjusted to the darkness by that point, and he quietly crept to the lounge.

It wasn't until he was only steps away that he noticed an orange glow beneath its door. Was someone else in there, or had the light been forgotten on? He hadn't heard anyone leave their beds all night.

He gripped the knob, turned it, and gently pushed the door. He saw her the moment he stepped inside. Svetlana. She sat at a corner table, her hands clasped together as her golden pixie bob shone down the sides of her face. Her posture tensed as she turned to acknowledge him. Scott froze in the doorway. The atmosphere became awkward.

Scott wasn't sure how he was supposed to greet her. Was it appropriate to say something? Was he supposed to put on a fake smile and pretend she was a friend, even though he had never spoken to her? Physical comeliness aside, he'd determined but one thing about Svetlana thus far: she was cold as ice. At least, that's how she struck him. He wasn't sure if that was his fault or hers.

Scott stood motionless as the orange glow of the countertop lamp bled through the lounge door. Svetlana and him. Two strangers with nothing in common except forced camaraderie. Nothing in common—and nothing to talk about.

He sensed the bunk room behind him. Someone would wake up at any second, and Scott would again find himself the target of someone's wrath. The Golden Lion—pathetic fighter and disturber of a good night's sleep. Him.

"The longer you stand there, the worse this will get," Svetlana said.

Scott's mind snapped back to the present. His eyes flickered at her. "What?"

"Stay or go, I do not care," she answered, "but whatever you do, don't leave that door open for much longer…unless you would like *another* beating."

It took him a moment to realize what she meant. She was being sarcastic. "I'm sorry," he said. "I didn't know if coming in would bother you."

She sat back in her chair. "Of course, it would bother me. But I am not as dangerous as they are." She tilted her head toward the bunk room as the corner of her lips curved up in a smirk. "So please, come in."

"Heh," Scott said, laughing softly. "Sure." Nodding, he stepped inside and eased the door shut. At least the burden of first words was over.

Leaning against the table, she asked him, "So what is so troubling that it keeps the Golden Lion awake at night?"

He stared at her. It sounded so venomous the way she said it. The *Golden Lion*. It was as if the title itself was created for mockery. It hadn't been that way at *Richmond*.

Svetlana angled her head with insinuated calculation. "I'm sorry, does it offend you when I call you that?"

It didn't offend him. It disappointed him. He wasn't a personified medal.

He was Scott James Remington, a soldier doing his best to help the war. He had never asked for anything else, but he'd accepted it when it was given to him. Did that make him deserving of disdain? No, her words didn't offend him. They hurt him. They hurt him because, in his heart of hearts, he wasn't *just* a soldier. He was a human being trying to make a difference. Not just in the war. In the lives of the people around him.

Why am I here, God? Why have You brought me here? I thought You wanted this...was I wrong?

Nicole said it herself. God's will doesn't contradict itself. Why had God sent him to Russia if He wanted him to be with Nicole? What if... what if God hadn't?

What if Scott had sent himself there?

"Remington?"

For a second time, Svetlana's voice freed him from his thoughts. His focus snapped back to her, and once again, he beheld her. But something was different. Her narrowed gaze was missing. Her pointed expression had melted away. She was no longer the woman who'd invited him in with venomous sarcasm. She was someone who realized he was hurting.

"Remington?" she asked again.

Scott shook his head. "I'm sorry." He hated this. He felt emotional, and he knew he looked emotional. That was why he had come to the lounge in the first place. To be alone. He hadn't expected anyone else to be there.

"It is okay," she said. Her voice was different. It was concerned. She motioned to the chair beside her. "Come and sit, please."

"I really don't want to disturb you," he said. "I didn't think anyone else would be in here."

She shook her head. "No, please. You are not disturbing me. It was stupid for me to say earlier that you were. Come and sit, and we will talk, okay?"

Before he moved to the table and slid into the chair, he allowed himself a moment of composure. He hated sympathy. He hated it more than he hated the spite in the words *Golden Lion* when Max and Svetlana said them.

As he sat, she offered her apology. "I am sorry about what I said when you came in."

He waved it off. "It's all right."

"No, it is not. I am sorry."

Scott took his seat in silence. The room still felt awkward, but not because she was his enemy. It felt awkward because he was vulnerable.

"So let me do it again, better this time," Svetlana said, smiling.

Insincerely, he thought. "I am glad for the company tonight. What is it that keeps you awake?"

He knew she wasn't glad. But at least she was trying, even if only for courtesy's sake. "I don't know," he answered. "Not sure if it's jet lag or just thinking."

Her eyes narrowed, and the forced smile remained. "I think we both know it must be something you are thinking."

It was obvious. "Okay, you win there."

"So what is it then?"

What was he supposed to tell her? He was dealing with all sorts of things. Loneliness. Anxiety. Doubt. She wanted the truth? He wasn't sure he was ready for that. "Just some personal things I'm dealing with."

"Mr. Remington," she said as she shied her smile away. "Chief medics hear all kinds of personal things. You may talk to me. I insist."

"Are you really asking me for 'chief medic' reasons?" Scott asked skeptically.

The lounge fell quiet. As Svetlana leaned back to mirror him, she played her fingers on the table. "No. But now you have me curious." She paused. "So I want to know what you are thinking."

"Why are you curious?"

She pursed her lips. "Can not a girl be curious of the Golden Lion?"

"Why does everyone keep calling me that?"

"Is that not what you are?"

It wasn't what he was. Why couldn't anyone understand? "No. It's not. My name is Scott, not Golden Lion."

She laughed lightly. "Mr. Remington, surely—"

"My name is Scott."

After a slightly scolding look, she said, "Very well. *Scott,* surely you do not expect me to ignore that you are holder of the most famous award in EDEN."

"I honestly wish you would," he said. "I don't want to be treated differently because I got some stupid piece of metal."

She crossed one arm and lifted the other contemplatively to her chin. She leaned closer. "You think it is stupid?"

The medal wasn't stupid. The inflated symbolism that came with it was. "It hasn't brought me anything good," he answered. "Everywhere I go, it's all everyone talks about...how I'm a hero, or a celebrity, or some kind of knight. I'm not. I'm just a normal person going through something

I never asked for." He wasn't a hero to Nicole. "Do you know what my fiancée said after Chicago?"

Svetlana edged back. "No…"

"She went crazy. She was terrified, she was furious. She thought I was a fool for risking my life when we've got a future together. Everyone thinks I've been riding on some high horse since Chicago, but I haven't." Chicago was the easiest thing he had done. Everything after that was downhill. "They gave that medal to me, I didn't pick it out for myself. If I had known what I know now, I'd have never accepted it."

Her gaze remained fixed on him as he continued.

"Look where I am right now, Svetlana. I'm in the middle of Russia. My fiancée's in Michigan. People in my unit hate me for literally no reason when all I ever wanted to be was a good teammate." He didn't understand any of it. "What do I have to do to get rid of this?"

The more he thought about it, the more Scott wished he had never assaulted that Carrier. But he couldn't blame himself for it. He had felt— he had *known* he could do it. He had done what any good soldier would have done. He'd finished the job.

His attention returned to her. The expression on her face was a mixture of confusion and intrigue. She brushed loose strands of hair from her cheek and said, "I did not know you felt that way. I assumed…" Her words trailed off.

"You assumed what?"

She sighed. "I do not know what I assumed."

Scott knew. She thought he was a walking ego. She thought he would walk into the unit with guns ablaze as his attitude pulled the trigger. She thought he would act like a man who'd been given a Golden Lion.

"You see," she said, "when the captain heard you were coming, that is all he talked about. We will be getting the Golden Lion, over and over. And not only that, but you have been here for so little time, and you are already gamma private. It took me two years to become delta, as it did for Max. But you did all of these things in one mission." Her eyes sunk. "So it surprises me to hear how much you seem to…hate it."

It was true. He did hate it. Every time someone talked about it or made a comment to him, he wished everything he had done would go away. Or at least not be common knowledge. "I never asked to be a gamma. I never asked for a Golden Lion. I never asked to be transferred here." He had never asked for anything. "It all just happened. I did the best I could, and this is where it got me. I don't know why I was chosen for any of this, and I know it's not fair. But what am I supposed to do? All I can do is do the best that I can."

She stared at him for several seconds before a smile escaped her lips. "I suppose it is, isn't it? I suppose that is all that any of us can do." Her eyes narrowed just a bit—just enough to indicate closer scrutiny. Moments later, her countenance softened. "I am willing to admit to the smallest possibility that I might have been wrong about you."

Scott laughed pathetically. "Thanks. I guess that's something."

"I am feeling quite guilty about the things I thought about you before."

"You don't need to feel guilty."

Eyes widening indicatively, she said, "No, no...I do. I thought *bad* things."

He looked at her with a hint of trepidation. "...how bad are we talking about?"

"I do not think I want to say."

"Come on, you can't tell me you thought 'bad things' and not tell me what those bad things were."

She peered at him, sifting through his countenance. "And have you hold them against me? I do not think so."

Good God. Were they that bad? "I mean, did you want me to *die*?"

Leering, she said, "I did not want you to *die*." When his gaze stayed expectantly on her, she rolled her eyes. "Fine—but I warned you."

"I've been warned."

"During your fight with Max, I thought you looked better with busted lip..."

"And...?"

The rest tumbled out. "And maybe if he hit you hard enough, we could send you back to America on a rolling bed."

"You actually thought that? And you're a *medic*?"

Her expression grew defensive. "That was before this! Now I feel terrible about it."

"You should feel terrible about it!"

"Do you feel better now that you know?"

"What else did you think?"

She *ugh*-ed exaggeratedly. "That was the worst. Let us leave it at that." As the countertop lamp's warm glow illuminated her, she resituated herself in her chair and loosened her once-rigid posture. Her curved smirk turning into a contemplative smile, she locked her blue eyes on his and extended her hand. "Sveta Voronova. It is a pleasure to meet you." When he arched an eyebrow, she said, "A second chance, if you're willing to accept it."

Willing? He'd take every second chance he could get in this nightmare of a place. He extended his hand to take hers. "Scott Remington. The pleasure's all mine." It was among the most delicate handshakes he'd ever accepted. It was ice-cold elegance. But maybe not as cold as he'd originally thought.

Sliding her fingers from his, she folded them atop the table and smiled.

Leaning forward, Scott asked, "I'm sorry, you called yourself...what, again?"

She chuckled softly. "Sveta. Most people here call me that."

"Sveta. I say it right?"

"Perfectly. I would never guess that you were an American capitalist pig."

At that, Scott himself had to laugh. Sighing as he looked off to the side, he said simply, "Okay."

"We all have our nicknames, as do you Americans. Sveta for Svetlana, Galya for Galina, Varya for Varvara—not to be confused with *Vanya,* which is short for Ivan. You will surely hear them all, so now you won't be confused."

If he remembered any one of those, he'd consider it a win.

The edge of her lips curved. "So tell me something about *you.* Something to remember you by other than the Golden Lion."

That was easy. "Well, I was a quarterback in college."

She shook her head. "I don't know what that is."

Figures. "It's a position on a football team. American football." *Is that the only thing I can tell people about myself?*

"American football. Is that the sport where everyone knocks each other down?"

"Well, I mean...yeah, I guess that's one way to put it."

She lifted her chin slightly, angling her dainty, upturned nose in pseudo-condescension. "It seems uncivilized."

"You're not wrong."

"That you play football was a stupid answer. I'm not going to remember it. Tell me something else."

Okay, this girl can dish it—I can handle that. Laughing lowly, he said, "Well, let's see, then..."

"Can you cook?"

Once more, he raised an eyebrow. "Can I *cook?*"

"I like a man who can cook."

"What do you call cooking? I can, you know, toss some food in the microwave."

A look of disapproval came over her. "That is not cooking."

"Can *you* cook?"

For a moment, she stared silently. Almost calculatingly. Then, she answered, "Exceptionally."

"...you can't cook, can you?"

Now, she chuckled. "...I can cook."

"You can't cook—also, nice job with *exceptionally*."

"I studied English in college. I know all about your words and your strange American customs."

"Name one thing you can cook."

"Name one thing *you* can cook."

His hazel gaze stayed fixed on her like a standoff. "On three, we both name the best thing we can cook," he said.

That curve in her lips slid up again. "Okay."

"One—"

"I'll count," she said.

Unbelievable. He shook his head and laughed. "Why do you get to count?"

"Because I outrank you."

If there was a better setup than that, Scott didn't know it. Shrugging his shoulders haphazardly, he said, "Not for long."

That garnered a reaction. Her eyes widened; she cocked her head and leaned back in her chair to match him. "Oh, really?"

He held his arms out. "I mean, I'm the Golden Lion, here."

Svetlana *mmm*-ed the most dangerous *mmm* Scott had heard in his life. "That one, I will make you regret." Her seriousness held for a few seconds before a genuine laugh escaped her.

He laughed, too.

"How about a little competition?" she asked. "Winner cooks the loser a meal."

Immediately, Scott answered, "How about a race?"

"I was thinking more like trivia."

"Yeah, I'm not doing trivia."

"And I am not doing a race," she said.

Propping his elbows on the table, he said, "Well, it appears we're at an impasse."

For several seconds, she held her gaze on him—until, at long last, she said simply, "So we are."

So they were. And so also were they, for the first time, fully attuned to each other during the silence, in that bathing of the orange glow from the lamp on the countertop. At that moment, Scott realized the depths of the blue in Svetlana's eyes. It was like staring into the ocean. Something swelled deep within him—a thumping in his heart he hadn't felt in a very long time. At least, not in this way. Not with this level of newness.

Oh, veck...nope.

Breaking eye contact, Scott looked away and quickly cleared his throat. Svetlana, too, looked away, tucking loose strands of her golden pixie bob behind her ears.

"So, umm," Scott said.

Svetlana nodded at his Scripture. It looked overtly deliberate—like a woman trying to return to the beaten path. "Are you religious?"

He never tried to think of himself as religious. Religion was manmade. As the burn in his heart transitioned to a deep, dull ache, he answered, "Yeah, I guess you could say that. I rather use the word *spiritual*. What about you?"

"I was," she answered after a moment of thought. "I mean, I am, yes, but I suppose I..." She paused. "I feel like I used to be better at it than I am now."

"It's not about how good you are; it's about belief." It was an automatic answer. But it wasn't untrue. And just like that—like a snap of the finger—his priorities realigned.

A different look came over Svetlana as she contemplated his words. A conflicted look, one of vulnerability. And maybe, just maybe, a shade of distrust. "I have never *not* believed in God. But sometimes, it's..."

Scott angled his head. "Sometimes it's what?"

She drew in a breath. "Sometimes it's hard to believe that we can be forgiven for the things we have done."

"Everyone can be forgiven."

"You don't know what I've done."

Deep inside, the tiniest flame ignited in Scott. A flame that, all too often, he kept tucked away. Leaning forward ever so slightly, he looked into her eyes. "Sveta, if you believe—if you've *ever* believed—then you know you're already forgiven." Her eyes narrowed in focus as he spoke. "Don't limit the Creator of everything that exists to the shortfalls of human understanding. You don't have to understand *how* God can forgive you for whatever you've done. You don't even have to understand why He'd forgive you. All you need to know is that He said He would—and that He's a God of His word."

Svetlana watched him with parted lips until, at long last, she looked down—just for a moment. "My journey has not been so easy."

"But it got you here," he said confidently. She looked up at him again. "It got you in this room, at this time of night, talking to someone you've never met before but who's trying to convey to you just how fearfully and wonderfully you're made—and that it's all been for a reason. Maybe my whole purpose—maybe my whole reason for being transferred to this place was because He wanted you to hear that. Because He wanted you to *know* it. And to get back to that place where you trust Him."

At that moment—unexpectedly—Svetlana reached her hand across the table, like a drowning woman searching for someone to pull her out of the water. Out of water she suddenly realized she could no longer tread. Just as unexpectedly, he found himself taking hold of it. And it was right then, when his fingers touched her icy skin, that the knot reformed. Several long seconds passed before he squeezed her hand and let go.

Staring at him as she withdrew her hand, Svetlana pressed her lips together and nodded. "I think I get it now."

"About what?" he asked quietly.

"About you," she said just as softly. "Because in just ten minutes, you touched a part of me that has not been touched in a very long time." Looking down, she tucked her hair behind her ear once more. "I am beginning to think you are a better man than most men, Scott Remington."

He knew better than that. "No, I'm not."

"You have a pure heart."

Lifting his head, he found her ocean-blue eyes once again. "Not always."

The faint gap between Svetlana's lips closed—a reaction to the subtle tightening of her jaw. She dipped her head just a bit.

Ever since the moment Scott had received word that he'd be garrisoned at *Richmond*, his life had been a tour of uncertainty. Uncertainty about his destiny. In his decision-making. At God's plan for his life, at his ability to carry it out. Uncertainty about everything when Tacker informed him of his transfer to *Novosibirsk*. Uncertainty when he stood in the doorway to the lounge, staring at a woman with blue eyes, a golden pixie bob, and a dainty, upturned nose. Uncertainty when he decided to step inside to join her. But that uncertainty was fading.

Clearing his throat a second time, he rapped his fingers quietly on the table. "Anyway, umm. My fiancée and I talk about spiritual things a lot. Her name is Nicole."

The tightness in her jaw gave way. She smiled.

"We read together," he said, gesturing to the Scripture, "try to keep each other accountable."

Svetlana half-frowned. "Tolya is not religious. I don't think he's ever opened Scripture."

"...Tolya?"

"Lieutenant Novikov. Tolya is short for his first name, Anatoly. Yet another nickname you must remember."

Scott nodded. "Yeah, I saw you guys, umm..."

She exhaled a single breath of laughter. "Kiss? You mean after your friend, Becan, busted his lip?"

"Yeah," said Scott remorsefully, "he was just sticking up for me."

"Must be nice to have such loyal friends. As it also must be to have a fiancée like..."

"Nicole."

"Nicole," she said. "She is a lucky woman. I am sure there are many women who would not mind being in her shoes." Svetlana smiled sweetly, before her countenance evened out into something more reflective. "It is not to say that I am not lucky to have Tolya, it is just..."

Scott knew what she was teetering on saying. He met her halfway. "He's a Nightman?"

The look she gave him was one of apology. "They do not have the best reputation, as I am sure you will learn—if you have not already."

He had—but that part, he wouldn't approach. "How'd you guys meet?"

"Here," she said plainly. "And I suppose *because* we were here. Must there always be a reason?" she asked, smiling in the quasi-pitiful way people did when the answer to their own question was not to their liking. She propped her elbows on the table and entwined her hands beneath her chin. "I am sure you and Nicole have a much better story."

"We met in high school. She accidentally kicked me with a soccer ball, so...I threw her in the mud."

Eyes widening, Svetlana borderline chortled. "*What?*"

"I'm telling you," he said. "The stuff of fairy tales."

Laughing, Svetlana shook her head. "Well, she must be quite a *forgiving* woman. I am not sure I would have reacted so well to that. I prefer to stay clean."

Leaning back, Scott said, "I have a theory that it went exactly how she wanted it to. I think she had a crush on me, kicked me with the ball on purpose, and wanted me to get her back to initiate this sort of playful, back-and-forth thing. She *swears* that's not true, but…she wears this smirk when she denies it."

"And so the smirk means it's true?" Svetlana asked, smirking herself.

"That's what *I* think. It's my theory, anyway."

"Well," said Svetlana, leaning back, "if it was all her plan, then good job for her. She got a Golden Lion out of the deal."

"*The.*"

Svetlana raised an eyebrow.

"*The* Golden Lion," Scott said.

Slowly, the edge of her lips curved up. "I can think of another reason she may have kicked you with a ball." The two laughed before she sighed and brushed her hand back through her hair. Looking back at him, she smiled. "I apologize for how I treated you before—and for how I thought of you. I thought you would be someone detrimental to the unit." Genuine warmth resonated from her. "I no longer believe that will be the case. You act like how Golden Lion *should* be."

Considering where they'd started from, he'd take it. "Thank you. I mean it. And thank you for taking the time to hear me out—and to laugh with me, too. That felt…good."

Her smile was broad. "As chief medic, hearing that makes me happy. If anyone in the unit asks me about you, I will tell them to give you a chance, as I did. I will tell them you are not the *dangerous capitalist pig* they all think you are." The two laughed gently before her bright eyes lifted to meet him. "If you will be there for me, I will be there for you. I promise."

That was all he ever wanted—all he knew he needed. Someone he could look out for who would also look out for him. Of all the friends he'd made in EDEN, the serendipitous occasion of earning Svetlana's friendship might have felt the best. Because he won her over. He had earned her respect, not by some so-called heroic deed, but by just being who he was. "I'll be there for you," he said. "I promise."

As a smile broke from Scott's lips, Svetlana matched it—until, at long last, she sat up straight and got serious. "Now, what you need to do is sleep. Medic's orders. You will feel better about everything in the morning."

"I feel better already, to be honest." He offered one more sly smirk. "Which is surprising—I didn't think Russians made for good company."

"Oh," she said with an exaggerated eye roll, "well in that way, I am glad to disappoint." Winking, she added, "We are not so bad as your media makes us out to be. Occasionally, we are even happy."

His smile widened. "Stop the press."

"We smile, we laugh. And I *must* say, if I am *just* being honest..." She leaned closer and whispered, "We make better friends than Americans."

"Now, hold on a minute."

Laughing, she said, "It is true! We will give you what you call 'tough love,' even if you don't want to hear it. And a Russian friend will fight to the end for you."

"And Americans won't, eh?"

She waved him off. "Pff. You are all like babies, with your hurt feelings and your trying to be cool. Russians don't have to try—we just are cool."

"All right, all right. If believing that makes you feel better, I'll just let you have it." Another shared laugh, and the slightest crinkling of her nose. It was adorable—and the perfect way end the conversation. Tiling his head in her direction, he said, "What about you? Medics need sleep, too, right?"

"I will, eventually."

It wasn't until then that he realized he had no idea why she'd been in the lounge alone. It hadn't even crossed his mind to ask. "Why *were* you in here by yourself, anyway?"

Her eyes held steadfast, though she offered no initial response. At long last, she smiled with gentle—if not a tad pointed—dismissiveness. "Another time, perhaps."

Don't force the ball—just kick the field goal and take the points. Lifting his hand to wave in self-awareness, Scott said, "I'll take that as a 'Good night, Remington.'" Laughing as his wave turned into a bona fide shoo, he turned to walk away. "Night, doc."

"Good night, Golden Lion." Though he couldn't see it, her smile widened.

With his Scripture in hand, Scott quietly made his way back through the lounge door.

Purpose. It was always what Scott sought, ever since the first day he put his faith in a God he couldn't see. Whatever purpose that hidden God had crafted him for, he wanted to fulfill. It was a search he could honestly say had taken him to the ends of the Earth.

One of the greatest frustrations of the faithful was attempting to discern whether a conviction was from God or oneself. He'd struggled with that relentlessly since his decision to enlist. He'd known at the time, undoubtedly, that it was a calling from God. But that time had come and gone. His easy path to marital bliss with the woman God had blessed him with had gone. With thousands of miles between them, it was hard to look back objectively and say that he'd interpreted his convictions correctly. But tonight had helped. If not in the tangible sense, it had helped his emotions. And if that got him through another day in the relentless pursuit of purpose, then so be it. He certainly wouldn't feel bad about feeling halfway good.

Scott slid under the covers of his bunk and placed his Scripture under the bed. He laid still for a moment before exhaling and closing his eyes. *Thank You for tonight, God. Thank You for a new friend in Svetlana. I'm sorry that I doubted.*

In the end, it all came down to trust. Not trust in himself, his ability, or even his sense of continual discernment. Trust that in that moment that'd mattered—in that spark of a conviction occurring at just the right time to *be* discerned—he'd made the right call by simply exercising faith and enlisting in EDEN. That faith had now taken him away from everything he knew. Away from all of his comfort. But no one followed God to be comfortable.

Scott didn't know why God had taken him to the city of Novosibirsk, nor did he know how long he'd be there. But he knew it was where he was supposed to be. At least at *this* moment. At least at this time. With the cover of the night came all manner of doubts and confusions. In the morning, everything would feel better. In the morning, he would be all right.

Scott never heard Svetlana leave the lounge. He was asleep before the lamp was turned off.

15

THE SOLDIERS OF the Fourteenth awoke to the presence of Captain Clarke. It was the presence of a man who, according to his pressed uniform and precisely trimmed beard, had been awake for some time. Without a word, his aura of controlled urgency enveloped Room 14. Something was amiss. For Scott, it was a morning of clarity—despite his fatigue from less than a full night's sleep. Judging by the bags beneath Svetlana's eyes, she was right there beside him on the exhaustion front. His conversation with her was still fresh in his mind. He would forever credit her with being there and restoring his faith at a time when he'd desperately needed it. Though he felt far from rejuvenated physically, he was nonetheless ready for whatever Clarke had to convey to them.

Within minutes, the soldiers had donned their uniforms and gathered in the lounge. There was no coffee or tea in brew. There was no casual banter. There was only the stern countenance of a man whose quiet authority ended with a single sentence. "Today, we face a formidable challenge," said Clarke.

That was it. No small talk. No ice breaker. Every soldier stared with total fixation.

"Approximately three hours ago," Clarke said, "a squadron from *Nagoya* intercepted a Bakma cargo vessel detected shortly after it entered Earth's atmosphere. It was far enough along its flight path to allow a calculation of its trajectory. An investigation of that trajectory revealed a fully functional Bakma facility on Planet Earth." Silence captured the lounge. "It will be our responsibility, with the aid of two supplementary units, to isolate and incapacitate this facility."

An alien base assault. On Earth. That was unprecedented.

"It gets worse," Clarke said. "The Bakma constructed this facility between Cherskogo and Verkhoyanskiy, in Northern Siberia." The Russian officers closed their eyes and inhaled. Clarke measured his words. "The coldest place on Earth."

Scott unconsciously rubbed the back of his neck. The coldest place on Earth? How had they gotten there? How had they built it without being noticed?

Clarke continued. "This place holds the record for the all-time lowest temperature in the northern hemisphere. Expect temperatures anywhere from thirty below freezing on down—it will be harsh.

"We've got daylight, so visibility should be good. Though the facility lies underground, what Intelligence hopes to be an above-ground entrance has been sighted on the surface. EDEN Command estimate that the facility is still relatively new and probably small in size, though, as always, we won't know until we arrive." He hesitated. "General Thoor will be overseeing this operation personally."

All eyes shot open. Thoor? Personally overseeing the mission? What did that mean? Still, no one spoke aloud. The only one who came close to breaking the silence was Dostoevsky, who leaned close to Baranov and whispered something.

"As always," Clarke continued, "I shall settle for nothing less than your maximum potential. Come. Let us move to the hangar."

Scott exchanged a look with his *Richmond* comrades. Their expressions echoed the same sentiment. Was Clarke to be taken literally? Was the general of *Novosibirsk* actually going with them?

There was no time to speculate. The soldiers made their way back through the bunk room and into the hallways.

During this trek, Scott saw the Russian officers in their Nightman armor for the first time. The armor was black, much like the armor of the guards who had met them when they first arrived. But it was different. It was leaner. It was more purposeful. Dark curves outlined their frames; only the crimson symbols of the Nightmen stuck out in bold proclamation. On two of the Nightmen—Executor Baranov and Lieutenant Dostoevsky—the armor came with spiked back half-collars, like horns on hell-spawned knights. The contrast between them and EDEN was astounding.

No comments were made about Scott's golden collar. The prestige of the Golden Lion paled next to the dark luster of the Nightmen.

The walk itself was silent. *General Thoor will be overseeing this operation personally.* What did that mean? Surely, the general of *Novosibirsk* would know better than to risk his life on a ground mission. Or would he? As soon as Scott stepped into the hangar, he knew the answer. Thoor stood along the far wall. His stature was unmistakable.

"Yeh got to be pullin' me wire," Becan said.

In minutes, all three units—the Fourteenth, the Twelfth, and the Third—were lined up before the general. The silence was unholy. It was as if the whole hangar stood before an evil deity that would strike them down if they dared to open their mouths on their own accord. From across the hangar, Thoor began his approach. The same visor hat shrouded his eyes, and the same black cloak swirled behind him. The only difference was that now, beneath it all, he wore a full suit of Nightman battle armor.

Thoor stopped in front of the soldiers; his cold glare surveyed them. "You know my expectations."

The hangar's occupants collectively snapped into salutes as a unified *da, general* erupted. Thoor spun around and strode toward the Vultures that waited on the runway.

Scott and Becan exchanged looks of uncertainty. Clarke cleared his throat and spoke. "Our orders shall become more clearly defined as we approach the structure. For now, please board and prepare for ascent."

The soldiers of the Fourteenth boarded their Vulture. It was the first time that Scott had laid eyes on it. It was an older craft with a vast array of scars and dents along its hull. A single word was painted across its dorsal fin in black letters: *Pariah.* Scrawled in paint above the name was the head of a feral dog, its gray fur blotted with disease.

Scott's seat in the *Pariah* was on the opposite side of his old seat in *Vulture-7*—and close to the troop bay door as opposed to the cockpit. Sandwiched between David and Becan, he was at least close to his friends. Poor Jayden was on his own across from them, between Fox and Varvara—not that those two represented the worst of options.

Shortly after the ships were boarded, they ascended. Only when the ride smoothed out did the crew leave their assigned seats to gather in various places and converse.

"Wha' do yeh think abou' this whole business with Thoor?" Becan asked.

Scott was wondering the same thing. "I don't know. I don't understand why he's coming."

"Think we're onto somethin' big, here?"

Jayden nodded toward Baranov, Novikov, and Dostoevsky, all three of whom huddled in quiet discussion. "Those guys ain't stopped talkin' like that since Clarke gave us the mission."

The four fell silent. Scott turned his attention to Svetlana. She, Galina, and Varvara were conversing quietly across the troop bay. She'd know what was going on—better than any of them could speculate, anyway. His eyes lingered on her for a moment until she made contact. She nodded at him indicatively, then returned to her conversation.

"Wha's all tha' abou'?" asked Becan suspiciously.

"Just getting her attention," Scott answered.

"Righ'…didn't know yis was all buddy-buddy."

"I talked to her for a bit last night. She's not as bad as you think."

Svetlana left the two other medics and knelt beside them. "What is it?"

"What's the deal with Thoor?" Scott asked. "Is he actually *fighting* with us?"

Her eyes flitted between Scott and the other three, all of whom were listening intently. "Maybe. I don't know. It is how he is. He does this occasionally—goes on a mission with his soldiers. He is the only general I know who does such a thing."

"What if he gets killed?" David asked.

She stared at him in silence. "He will never get killed."

Scott arched an eyebrow. *Never?* It was a pretty bold statement, even if hyperbolically so.

Becan cleared his throat. "I have a question."

Svetlana turned to Becan. Her eyes narrowed. "Yes?"

"If you were my pilot, would yeh take me for a ride?"

Scott closed his eyes and slammed his head against the wall. David stifled a chortle.

Svetlana's eyes narrowed in irritation and disgust. "Not in your best of dreams."

"Then how would I go on anny *missions*?"

She rose, turned away, and stalked back to the other medics.

"Nice work," Scott said. "That was brilliant, thank you."

Becan smirked. "She's charmin', really."

David continued to chuckle.

As the Vultures continued to fly toward Verkhoyanskiy, the EDEN soldiers in the troop bay prepared their gear. They replaced the standard blue and silver armor plates with ones shaded in white and slate, a more appropriate combination for the terrain of Northern Siberia.

Amid the hustle and bustle, Clarke rose to his feet. "We should be receiving more specific orders at any moment. Make sure your internal heaters are in working order."

"Hey Fox," Becan said as he finished checking his weapons, "why do they call this one the *Pariah*?"

"Do you really want to know?"

Becan nodded.

"Are you sure?"

The *Richmond* transfers exchanged wary glances. "Is there a reason you're askin' like tha'?" Becan asked.

Fox chuckled and leaned back in his seat. "When it got called out on its first mission, it wouldn't start. It was with the Sixth, then. They sent it to *Atlanta* to get repaired. When *Atlanta* turned it on, it fired up with no problem. They sent it back. Second mission, wouldn't start again. Sent it to *Atlanta* again, it worked, and again they sent it back. Couldn't find a problem with it.

"Third mission, starts up fine. Ceratopian mission. The Sixth cleans out a small Cruiser, packs up some salvage and a couple of corpses to bring back to base. About halfway home, *Novosibirsk* loses contact with it. It's still on radar, it's still coming home...there's just no communication. Comes in for a landing, touches down right on the strip where it's supposed to. Still no contact with the crew.

"They opened her up, and it was a mess. Blood everywhere, mangled bodies. Not a person alive, not even the pilot. In the middle of the troop bay, in the middle of the bodies, was the corpse of a necrilid. It killed them mid-flight before it died. They had thought it was dead before they loaded it."

The soldiers stared, momentarily speechless.

"But...how did it...?" Becan stuttered.

"Autopilot," Fox answered. "Thing flew itself home with a dead crew."

The hair on Scott's arms tingled. All four of the *Richmond* transfers swapped dreadful looks.

"So they started calling it that," Fox said. "The *Pariah*. The ship nobody wanted. Thing went through more than a few units. They all swore it was cursed, and it just got passed right on down the line. Now it's with us."

Nobody said a word. Their gazes drifted off Fox and around the inner hull of the craft.

Fox smirked and resumed his gear-up. "Welcome aboard."

Clarke spoke from the front of the troop bay. "Attention, everyone—we've got our orders." He stepped over to a display on the wall, where a satellite map of Verkhoyanskiy appeared. "The entrance to the facility rests directly between two small ridges in a valley of sorts. The structure is not particularly large, perhaps slightly larger than an industrial lift." Clasping his hands behind his back, he faced his soldiers. "We will be landing hard and fast to minimize their response time. Executor Baranov will lead an assault team down the lift after Captain Kulik and members of the Twelfth clear the way. Joining him on that team will be Leftenants Dostoevsky and Novikov, along with Axen, Lebesheva, Jurgen, and Carpenter."

Scott looked at each soldier whose names were listed. Yuri Dostoevsky—the fierce-looking Nightman. Anatoly—Tolya—Novikov, a combat technician and Svetlana's boyfriend. He glanced briefly at Svetlana, whose concerned eyes were already on Novikov. Max Axen, unfortunately, would be etched in Scott's memory forever. Galina Lebesheva, the butch-haired, older medic, and Kevin Carpenter, a young American soldier. Rounding it all out was David.

"Axen," Clarke said, "it will be your job to operate the lift once it's isolated."

Max nodded. "Yes, sir."

The captain continued. "Remaining on the surface around the lift's perimeter will be myself, Voronova, Makarovich, Remington, and McCrae, both to defend the surface if Noboats materialize and to act as reserve forces should the assault team require them." He looked at Galina and Svetlana. "Galina, any wounded you can't handle, send up to Sveta."

"Da, captain," Galina answered.

Clarke turned his gaze to Jayden and Fox. "Once our teams have been dropped off by the lift, the two of you will be dropped off on the westernmost ridge. Powers, I want you watching our backs. Timmons will serve as *your* backup." He looked at Jayden. "You're not to engage unless ordered."

A somewhat dejected Jayden answered, "Yessir."

Straightening his posture, Clarke said, "Evteev and Yudina will remain in the *Pariah* with Navarro."

Boris the technician, Varvara the medic, and Travis the pilot. Scott's mental efforts to remember first and last names continued.

"Forces from the Twelfth and the Third will assist in all aspects of this operation. General Thoor will be overseeing the entire operation inside the Third's Vulture. The assault team leader on the ground will be Captain Kulik. Are there any questions?"

No hands raised.

"Very well, then. Everyone, prepare yourselves for descent."

Snow. As far as the eye could see, Scott saw snow as he looked out the porthole across from him. It was as far removed from *Richmond* as it could possibly be. "How cold do you think it is down there?" he asked, eyes still on the window.

"Looks like a bleedin' ice box," answered Becan.

David shook his head. "I'd love to recant some story about how I went to school this way, but I don't have one."

As the transport descended lower, Baranov grabbed the support rail above his seat. Descent thrusters kicked in, and the nose of the transport pitched up. The shift lasted mere moments before the *Pariah* leveled off again, coming to a hovering stop just off the ground.

Scott watched Baranov clamp on his helmet. Unlike the four armored guards who'd met Scott and his friends when they'd arrived, the helmets belonging to Baranov and his Nightman ilk had no visible lenses for viewing. They were featureless, black helmets comprised of metal strips laced one atop the other—like the helmet of some dark Medieval knight. When Baranov spoke, his voice was amplified through some sort of speaker system. "My team, get ready!" He looked in the cockpit's direction. "Lower the door."

"I guess this is our cue," said David gravely.

"You guys be careful," Jayden said from across them.

David offered the Texan a half-smile. "Just like Chicago."

Scott smirked. This was *nothing* like Chicago. In Chicago, they had been on the defense. This was the opposite. Scott's eyes swept across the troop bay until they rested on Svetlana, whose hands encircled Lieutenant Novikov's waist. She leaned her forehead to rest against his shoulder. She whispered something, and her eyes closed. Novikov slid his hands around the small of her back as he held her against his body.

"Imagine you and Nicole getting ready to disembark together in this frozen hellhole," David whispered.

"No thanks," Scott answered. "In this moment, I like Nicole exactly where she is."

"Back door's comin' down!" Travis yelled. "Put on your mittens."

As soon as the first crack appeared at the top of the rear door, the temperature in the *Pariah* plummeted—the cold blew in like an arctic hurricane. The soldiers shrank back despite the internal heaters in their armor. Icy wind whipped through the air.

"Good *God*, that's cold!" Jayden said, his teeth chattering.

"Why can't they build a base in Bermuda?" Fox grumbled.

Scott stared out the bay door as the initial blast of iciness died away. Whiteness. It stretched out ahead as far as he could see. Pure, smooth, pristine whiteness. Not a single tree anywhere—only the occasional gray rock that jutted up from the ground. It might have been beautiful if not for the reality of why they were there.

Closing his eyes, Scott lowered his head in prayer. *Father, I don't know why we're here or what You have planned, but protect us. Protect us from whatever is out here to harm us. Give us the strength to...harm it instead...* Choose us over them. As cut and dry as this scenario seemed, what justified asking God to grant one party victory over another? What if the Bakma, the Ceratopians, and the Ithini were all on some holy war ordained by the very God Scott was praying to? Who was to say that the conquering of Earth wasn't for the greater good of the galaxy? The more he tried to rationalize his thoughts in those precious seconds, the less comfortable he felt one way or the other. *I know that I don't understand, Father. Just give me the wisdom and clarity to see Your will and the strength and courage to follow it. I will not be afraid, for Your Hand protects me. So be it.*

"Gotta quench the imagination, huh?"

Opening his eyes, Scott turned to the unexpected voice. Max.

"No god's gonna save you out here, Goldilocks," Max said, raising his assault rifle to disembark. "Just cold, hard metal."

Jaw tightening, Scott readied his own weapon. He didn't bother to respond.

Baranov approached the precipice of the ramp. "All teams, let's go!" He jumped down seconds later, his massive boots crunching in the snow beneath. One by one, the strike team soldiers followed him.

The alien structure was barely twenty yards away. Low to the ground, the squat, square building looked like a small hangar. Forging through the snow, the soldiers kept their weapons aimed.

Not lost on Scott was that it was Baranov and not Clarke who was taking command on the ground. Perhaps this was the established way the

Fourteenth worked on ground missions—or perhaps Clarke had given Baranov the instruction to lead. Just the same, Scott couldn't help but feel that part of it was because, at *Novosibirsk*, EDEN played second fiddle to the Nightmen—whether they outranked them or not.

The first signs of resistance appeared as a large double door slid open on the structure. Four Bakma emerged, their plasma rifles raised and ready to fire. The strike teams fired first, and the aliens were felled before they could muster a defensive. Behind the alien bodies, the double doors slid shut again.

As Scott took a defensive position along with Clarke's team, he glanced down at the bloodstained snow. He knew this was only the beginning of the bloodshed. Above, Vindicator fighters streaked into a low orbit.

A tall, slender officer slipped past Scott toward Baranov. "Executor Baranov?"

Baranov nodded.

"I am Captain Kulik. Our orders are to storm this compound and isolate it. We take as many captives as possible and keep the facility intact. If we cannot do this, our orders will be to destroy the facility by demolition. Our technicians have high explosives. They will set the charge and explode the facility remotely if need be.

"Your technicians will now open the door to the facility, and we will send a strike team down the shaft into the complex's core to set up a stronghold. Our technicians will go down second, followed by supplements from the Fourteenth. Is all of this understood?"

"Da, captain."

"Good," Kulik said. "Open the door."

Baranov turned around. "Max!"

Max moved quickly to the same metal double doors that the Bakma had emerged from and removed his handyman from his belt. After inputting several commands into the hacking kit, he pulled a corded suction device from it, placed it against the doors, then pressed a small button. The suction device clicked and whirred. The doors slid halfway open. A small circular lift was inside—far smaller than the total size of the structure.

"That's as good as it gets," Max said.

"That is all we need," Kulik said. Six soldiers from the Twelfth slid through the metal doorway. Kulik turned to Baranov. "We will need your technician to operate the lift."

Baranov looked at Max. "Go with them."

"Naturally, sir," Max said. He slid through the doorway into the lift.

"Goin' down, fellas?" He used the same suction device, and the metal doors slid shut. Behind it, the lift rumbled. Max's voice emerged through the comm. "We're on our way down."

Kevin slung his assault rifle over his shoulder and said to Scott and David, "Nothing to do but hurry up and wait, eh?"

"Yeah, something like that," Scott said.

Baranov fidgeted as he placed a hand on his helmet mic. "Progress?"

"Still going down," Max answered. "Hell of a deep hole. We've traveled some thirty meters or so, so we've got to be getting close—wait, we're slowing."

Looking around him, Scott paused when he caught sight of Svetlana and Galina. The two medics were prepping their medical kits, just in case they'd have to use them.

"We're down," Max said. "Opening the door."

Metal clunked through the comm, and then the channel went silent. Baranov placed his hand against one of the doors. The silence broke. Weapons fire erupted. Shouts flooded the comm. The noise lasted almost ten seconds before it faded, and a Russian voice emerged.

"Area secure, bringing the lift back up. One casualty on his way."

"Max?" Baranov asked, the Nightman sounding concerned.

"It's not me," Max answered.

From beside Baranov, Kulik said, "Bring the injured up, and we will send down our technicians." Kulik signaled to his team of techs, who positioned themselves beside the structure's doors. The lift reached ground level within a minute, and the doors slid open. Max was the first to emerge, followed by the wounded man. His shoulder was gored straight through the armor, and his teeth clenched firm.

Svetlana and Galina tended to him immediately, the former scanning the soldier with her medical scanner while the latter extended a stretcher.

The same Russian voice from before spoke through the comm. "We will need more help down here. There are many more hostiles." Weapons fire rattled in the background.

Kulik whirled around to face Max. "How many can fit in the lift?"

"I wouldn't send any more than what we just had, about seven. Maybe eight," Max said.

Kulik turned his attention to Clarke. "Have you established a base assault team?"

For the first time, the Fourteenth's captain spoke. "I have. Executor Baranov will be leading a team of six."

"Are they all ready to leave now?"

"They are." Clarke's focus shifted to the Fourteenth at large. "Everyone on the executor's team, get ready to descend!"

"Should be fun," David said to Scott as he and his counterparts slipped through the elevator doors with Max. Galina, who'd been assisting Svetlana, left the chief medic's side to make her way into the lift.

"Be careful!" Scott said to David.

David laughed out loud. "Come on, man, it's me!"

"That's what I'm worried about!"

Kulik knelt beside Svetlana and the injured soldier. "How is he?"

"He is stable but cannot stay here," Svetlana answered. "We must get him to a transport."

Kulik nodded. "Please escort him to our Vulture." As Svetlana acknowledged, Kulik turned back to the structure. "Status?" he asked the soldiers who had already descended.

A Russian voice crackled through the comm. "We are under heavy fire, captain!"

"There is a team dispatched," Kulik answered. "They should arrive soon."

Nearby, Svetlana called out to Clarke. "Captain! I will help escort their injured soldier to his transport, then I will return."

Clarke looked at the wounded soldier and then in Becan's direction. "McCrae! Go with her."

Svetlana and Becan made eye contact briefly before the Irishman shouldered his weapon and hurried to Svetlana's side. With her medical kit, she and Becan assisted the wounded soldier away from the structure.

AS THE LIFT lowered Baranov's team to the sublevel, the crackle of weapons fire intensified. "Prepare to engage," the executor said. David, Max, and Kevin pressed themselves against the lift walls while the three Nightmen—Baranov, Novikov, and Dostoevsky—stood front and center. All weapons were aimed at the elevator door.

Max gripped the lift controls. "Get ready." Next to him, Galina hunkered down. The lift slowed, then clunked to a halt. "Open in three... two...one!" yelled Max.

The Nightmen wasted no time. All three burst through the door the moment it was open, the muzzles of their assault rifles flashing in the direction of the plasma fire ahead of them. A fog of weapons exhaust covered the hall.

David and Kevin exited right behind them. The instant David emerged, he knew that despite the Nightmen's bravado, they were collectively in trouble. The circular lift had dropped into a circular room with a diameter not much larger than the lift itself. A corridor led straight forward, and glancing at the left and right indicated two more on each side of the lift. Ambush points surrounded them. Throughout the interior, a blaring, ethereal klaxon sounded.

Plasma streaked toward the lift as within, Max and Galina pressed against the wall to avoid getting scorched alive.

At the front of the human offensive were Baranov and Dostoevsky—the executor firing relentlessly at the fortified aliens as Dostoevsky slid, dodged, and took precision shots. Behind both men was Novikov. "Where is the initial strike team?" he shouted over the drumming of weapons fire.

"Over here!"

The voice came from the corridor farthest left. Novikov spun to face it, seeing a small gathering of soldiers exchanging heavy fire with Bakma defenders. Shooting a look back to the elevator, Novikov yelled, "Max, take the lift up and get the demolitions team! Jurgen and Carpenter, hold the lift."

An injured soldier, screaming as his comrades carried him, was laid down on the floor of the lift. The soldier's thigh was a mangled mess. As Galina knelt to treat him, the soldiers' comrades returned to the fray.

David gestured to a pair of hallways and told Kevin, "You watch that hall, I'll watch this one!"

"You got it, man!" answered the younger soldier.

"Hey, Sveta," said Max through the comm as he watched Galina work, "we're coming up with one injured!"

Through the static, Svetlana's voice emerged. "I am taking an injured soldier to Kulik's Vulture! Can Galya do it?"

Galina replied through the channel, "Da—I have him."

The lift door slid shut, and they began their ascent.

Baranov and Dostoevsky pressed forward against the barrage of plasma fire being hurled their way. The underground structure was far more extensive than its size on the surface would have suggested, with corridors that branched off in every direction and rooms lining every hallway in sight. None of it slowed the two Nightmen down.

A Bakma charged around a corner right by Baranov. Reaching out with his palm, the executor grabbed the alien's face in his massive hand.

Thrusting up, then forward and down, he pile-drove the alien onto the metal floor below.

Over the comm, Novikov's voice emerged. "Executor, I am at the location designated for the high explosives. We will have it isolated soon!" A plasma bolt struck Baranov in the shoulder, blowing his black shoulder guard clean off. Unshaken, the executor aimed his assault rifle and fired, downing his alien assailant. "Clear the area and wait for Kulik's technicians," he answered Novikov. "Yuri and I will continue our forward push."

"Da, executor!"

On the surface, the lift's double doors opened. Scott watched as Galina and Max carried out an injured soldier and placed him on the ground, and then Galina began working on him.

"Demolitions team, let's go!" Max yelled, gesturing emphatically for them to enter the lift.

Pointing to Scott and Konstantin, Clarke said, "Makarovich and Remington, go down with them to provide extra support!"

Clarke's orders were interrupted by Captain Kulik. "Negative. Captain Gavich of the Third will provide any reinforcements. The rest of your soldiers will remain on the surface."

"With all due respect," said Clarke, "I'm not going to wait patiently while Gavich ponders his options! If you have issue with that, I'll gladly discuss it when this is over." Once more, he looked at Scott and Konstantin. "Go with them!"

Scott certainly wouldn't argue with that, and he rushed toward the lift with Konstantin.

"Executor," Clarke said through the comm, "I'm sending Makarovich and Remington down with the demolitions team. Make sure they—"

He was cut off mid-sentence as the sky erupted with a tremendous explosion. The soldiers threw back their heads to witness it. Behind the Third, the fiery remnants of a Vindicator plummeted to the earth.

THE COMMS EXPLODED with pilot chatter.

"Noboats! We have Noboats! Two—three materializing!"

A squadron of Vindicators streaked past; three more Bakma Noboats appeared behind them. Within seconds, a second Vindicator was set ablaze with plasma fire.

ON THE GROUND below, Kulik swung toward the soldiers as two of the Noboats rotated for a descent. "Behind the structure! Take cover behind the structure!"

Baranov's voice broke through the comm noise. "What is going on up there?"

"Half a dozen Noboats have just materialized!" Clarke answered. "Bakma ground forces incoming!"

The descending Noboats touched down—seconds later, Bakma soldiers poured out from them.

THE SCATTERED VINDICATOR fighters reoriented over the structure. Their pilots' voices flooded the airwaves.

"Pull back and close in. We have four descenders and two strafers."

"Copy that, wing commander."

"Red Flight, are you in position for a run?"

"Negative, Green Flight, we're split two-one."

"Red, run the gauntlet on the ground. We'll take the strafers."

"Affirmative, Green Flight, regrouping."

"TRAVIS," CLARKE SCREAMED into the comm, "get ready for an extraction!" The pilot acknowledged, and then Clarke addressed his two snipers. "Powers and Timmons, make a dent!"

JAYDEN WAS ALREADY aiming his sniper rifle as both he and Fox fired at the charging crowd of aliens.

INSIDE THE STRUCTURE, David roared as a plasma bolt struck his left arm and knocked him backward. "What did they just say?" he asked, jumping back into position by the corridor.

Kevin, who himself had taken a grazing plasma bolt to the leg, reloaded his assault rifle and resumed firing. "Six Noboats just materialized!"

David inspected his shoulder. His armor was sizzled, and charred flesh reeked underneath. He gritted his teeth and returned to the defense effort.

"Any orders?" asked Novikov through the comm as the underground fight continued. "Is anyone up there?"

The comm channel crackled. A solitary voice resonated over the airwaves. "This is Thoor. Prepare the facility for detonation."

Novikov looked at the soldier near him before returning his attention to the comm. "Da, general!" Shifting comm frequencies, he queued up Max. "Max, is the demolition team down?"

"They're about to be! Hang tight. We'll be with you in a second."

IN SYNCH WITH the Bakma ground assault, a pair of airborne Noboats began strafing attack runs on the area around the structure. Bodies flew through the air as the soldiers around the structure scrambled to stay behind cover.

Farther away, the regrouped Vindicators looped around for a counterattack.

"Staying here is a losing proposition, gentlemen!" Clarke said as plasma fire from the Bakma on the ground reached them.

Kulik spoke through the comm a moment later. "This is Captain Kulik requesting an evacuation!"

Thoor responded. "Request granted. All Vultures, rendezvous with the ground team for immediate extraction."

Getting on his comm, Clarke queued up Svetlana. "Sveta, have you and McCrae reached the Twelfth's Vulture yet?"

SVETLANA HAD JUST transferred the wounded soldier into the Twelfth's custody. With bloodstained hands, she adjusted her comm to reply. "Da, captain!"

"He's abou' to tell us not to go back," Becan said to her, his eyes transfixed on the battle by the structure.

"Don't attempt to come back to us! That's far too long a hike—you'll never make it." Clarke said. "Catch a ride with the Twelfth back to *Novosibirsk*."

She acknowledged, then closed the channel and looked at Becan. "If they need us…"

"Then we're goin'. I don't care wha' he jus' said."

Her eyes stayed steadfast on him, and she nodded her head. Readying her pistol, she came to the Irishman's side to watch the battle unfold.

IT ONLY TOOK a minute for Max and the demolitions team to reach Novikov's position. As the soldiers around Novikov kept the Bakma at bay, he pointed to a cleared storage chamber. "Set the explosives in here!" As the demolitions team acknowledged and rushed into the room, Novikov asked them, "How long will it take?"

"Only a few minutes, lieutenant!" one answered.

Max growled as he reloaded his assault rifle. "Tolya, I don't know if we have a few minutes."

Novikov whipped his head back in the technicians' direction. "Work *quickly!* Time is what we do not have!"

DUCKING BACK AROUND a corner, Baranov slammed a fresh magazine into his assault rifle and then spoke through his comm. "Carpenter and Jurgen, can you hold the lift by yourselves?"

DAVID WAS IN the middle of an exchange with a pair of encroaching Bakma when Baranov's call came through. Leaning low around the corner of the branching corridor, he fired a volley before ducking back again to let Kevin take over. "If we gotta hold it, we'll hold it, sir!"

"Lieutenant Dostoevsky and I have reached an alien stronghold," Baranov said. "We will isolate as many Bakma as possible before we return."

"Yes, sir!" David replied. Next to him, Kevin dropped one of the two aliens that were attacking. "Atta boy, Kev!"

OUTSIDE AND ABOVE, the Vindicators began their attack runs. As they did, two more Noboats materialized north of the valley. Pilot chatter erupted again.

"Two bandits, inbound!"

"What is that, eight?"

"We have two more Noboats inbound, I repeat, we have two more Noboats inbound to our position!"

"Red Flight, we're breaking off the ground assault and engaging the new bandits."

"Copy that, Green, we've engaged the strafer."

"Ground team, we can't help you down there. You're on your own with the evac!"

BEHIND THE STRUCTURE, Konstantin yelped as a plasma bolt skimmed his shoulder armor. He fumbled his gun and dropped it in the snow.

Scott leapt for the weapon, pulling it back behind the structure before looking at Konstantin. "You all right, man?"

The young soldier winced. "Yes. Not hurt too bad—just burns!"

"The *Pariah* is coming," Clarke shouted. "We must hold this ground for the team below!"

ONE EYE CLOSED, Jayden eased his crosshairs over one of the Bakma approaching the structure. A squeeze of the finger and a red puff of blood later, the alien was felled.

BELOW THE SURFACE, the chief technician over the demolitions team sprung around to face Novikov. "Explosives set, lieutenant! We can detonate from outside—all we need to do now is get out of here!"

Novikov was on the comm immediately. "Structure ready for detonation!"

"About time we can get the hell out of here!" Max said.

Thoor's voice resonated through the comm. "What is your overall situation?"

"Explosives are set, general," Novikov answered. "We have a clear path to the lift and are good to exit the structure!"

"Very good. You will remain with the explosives to ensure their detonation. The rest of your team may leave."

CLARKE'S TEAM FROZE behind the surface structure. Scott and Konstantin lowered their weapons and stared at each other.

IN THE TWELFTH's still-grounded Vulture, Svetlana gasped and covered her mouth. Next to her, Becan's eyes shot open wide.

UNDERGROUND BY THE lift, David and Kevin halted their firing. Just a short ways away, Baranov and Dostoevsky did the same.

Max spun to face Novikov. Silence struck amid the weapons fire. The comm channel went quiet.

At the corner of the T-junction, Novikov's mouth sunk open, and he stammered into his headset. "I am—I am sorry, general, could you repeat your last order?"

"You are to remain with the explosives to ensure their detonation. The rest of your team may leave."

SCOTT'S JAW DROPPED as the surface battle raged. The rest of the team may leave? Did...did he just hear that right?

Over the Fourteenth's private channel, Travis's voice crackled. "What the hell? Did I just hear what I thought I heard?"

SVETLANA DROPPED to her knees on the floor of the Vulture. Her hand shot to her chest. "Nyet..." she breathed as her eyes widened in panic. "Nyet!" She clutched her helmet mic. "Tolya, *ne slushay! Ne slushay!*"

"DO YOU UNDERSTAND your orders, Anatoly Novikov?" Thoor asked.

Below, Novikov fell silent as both voices—Thoor's and Svetlana's—cut through the comm channels.

Max faced him head-on. "Tolya, don't tell me you're actually thinking about doing this..."

Thoor spoke again. "I will ask only once more. Do you understand your orders?" Silence brooded over the channel. "You know the price of insubordination..."

Novikov's face froze. His eyes trailed to the floor, and he swallowed. Before Max could say another word, Thoor got his answer.

"Yes, general," Novikov said. "I understand."

"NYET!" SVETLANA screamed. Rushing out of the transport as the Twelfth watched, she collapsed onto her knees in the snow. "Tolya, *nyet!*"

Becan stared at the scene in floored silence. Pulling off his helmet, he stuck his fingers into his hair.

MAX ERUPTED. "LIKE hell, you understand those orders!"

Novikov closed his eyes and murmured through the comm. "Sveta, *ya dolzhen.*" He turned to Max. "I have to. I have orders, and I must follow them. It is not my decision."

"Lieutenant!" David yelled through the comm. "Are you seriously going to listen to that?"

Svetlana screamed. "Nyet, Tolya! *Nyet!*"

"If I do not stay, the mission could fail," Novikov answered. "The explosives must go off!"

"Can you hold this hall by yourself?" David asked Kevin.

"Yeah. Where are you going?"

David backed toward the left hallway. "To insert common sense!"

"How in the *hell* are Bakma going to disarm human explosives?" Max asked, slamming his fist sideways against the wall.

Novikov shot back, "The same way humans can unlock Bakma doors!"

"If the bombs don't go off, *so what*? We come back and attack the base again. It's not like this is the battle for the fate of the universe!" Through the channel, Svetlana continued to wail. "Tolya, nyet!" David rounded the corner nearest to Novikov and Max. He shouted as soon as he saw the lieutenant, all formalities tossed to the wayside. "How can you hear that voice pleading with you and still stay?"

"If I do not stay…!" Novikov began. He cut himself off. Removing his helmet, his glare first fixated on David, and then it blazed at Max. "*You know,*" he said off-comm. "You know what will happen."

Max opened his mouth to reply, then bit back the words. The men fell in silence.

"*What?*" David said. "What's going on here?"

"This is not like the rest of EDEN," Novikov answered. "Orders must be followed. This is not my decision."

"*Why* does this order have to be followed?" asked David in frustration. "What the hell could be worse? They'll kill you when you get back to base? Well, *great,* add an extra hour to your life, but give it a vecking *chance!*"

All the while, Svetlana's voice pleaded. "Tolya, *nyet!*"

Gravely, Novikov looked at David. "…there is much worse."

David stared back, his dumbstruck stare holding as weapons fire continued around them. Then, slowly, his expression changed. The realization had dawned. He took a sharp breath. "No…you have got to be kidding me…"

Novikov pointed at Max as his stare held on David. "Ask him. Ask him what will happen."

Max turned to David and said solemnly, "If Tolya doesn't listen, he's not the one Thoor will kill. She'll be."

David stared at the two, stunned.

"This is how it must be," Novikov said. "I do not do this for me. I do this for her! You know this now. I have no choice."

David tore off his helmet. "No! How can he get away with that? How could *anyone* get away with that?"

"It's the truth!" Max answered, interjecting again. "You don't like it, it doesn't matter! This isn't EDEN you're dealing with. You might have thought that when you got here, but you were wrong."

Novikov said to David, "You hear? There is not even time to think about it."

"It's the truth," said Max.

Before David could respond, Novikov asked Max, "Can you lock me in the chamber with the explosive?"

"Yeah…" Max muttered. He retrieved the suction device from his belt and moved to the detonation chamber. "You can close the door from inside. It'll lock when you do."

Novikov nodded and lowered his assault rifle to the ground. His eyes lingered on his fellow technician. "Max…I have to ask you to…"

"I'll watch her. I promise."

"Thank you. You were always my favorite capitalist pig." He feigned a smile.

Max offered a failed smirk. "Whatever, communist."

David listened silently as the lieutenant said, "Now, get out of here before we *all* die."

Max adjusted his comm. "Attention everyone underground—if you value your life, get to the lift. We're going back up."

CLARKE WAS SILENT on the surface as Max's words broke through the airwaves. None of his team had spoken since Thoor's order. Before they could, an explosion shook the ground in front of the structure. The Bakma were on the attack.

"There's no time to think about it," Clarke said. "Get ready to get them out of the lift!"

SVETLANA LAY CRUMPLED on the ground at the ridge, her pleas reduced to desperate, choking sobs. Becan knelt beside her, his hand falling against her back.

SCOTT DUCKED BEHIND the structure as a plasma bolt soared past his head. The Bakma were closer, and with every shot he fired, the intensity of their oppression grew heavier. Not only was EDEN outnumbered, they were out-positioned. This was not going to last.

When a scream rang out, he shrank behind the structure to avoid fire. Konstantin. Scott surveyed the immediate area where he caught sight of the soldier. His thigh had been struck dead on by a plasma bolt.

"Hold on!" Scott said as he darted from the structure and through the mass of soldiers toward the young Russian soldier. He knew as soon as he saw the wound that it was severe.

Konstantin winced and clutched his leg. The once-white snow beneath him was stained with blood.

Scott scanned for Galina, but she was overtaken by other wounded. He grabbed the injured soldier's armpits. "Hang on—I'll get you to cover!" Max's voice emerged from the comm. "We're coming up, and we've got wounded!"

Scott growled under his breath. Everything was happening too fast. The Noboats. Novikov and Svetlana. Konstantin. The lift. He didn't know what to focus on first. As soon as Konstantin was behind the structure, Scott scanned the area to find his teammates. Be it the freneticism of the situation or his own frantic state, he couldn't find any of them.

"We're approaching the top," Max said. "We'd *better* have cover!"

Scott abandoned Konstantin for the front of the structure, where the lift exited. Konstantin was safe where he was—what mattered now was securing Max's team. The doors were going to open in the direction of the oncoming Bakma. When Scott arrived on the scene, Captain Kulik and several others were already in mid-battle. The mechanical clunks of the lift resonated in the background.

"Assist the wounded first!" Kulik said. "Draw the fire away!"

Before Scott could fire a shot, the doors to the structure slid open. Soldiers crammed the lift.

The wounded were ferried from the lift first as EDEN defenders held off the Bakma. "How many are in there?" Kulik asked.

"Everyone!" Max answered.

"I didn't think the lift could *fit* everyone."

"Necessity is the mother of compromise!"

THE ENGINES ON the Twelfth's Vulture roared as the transport waited to lift off. Thus far, the sky above them was too volatile for the Twelfth to launch. As it stood, only the Third's Vulture was en route to rescue the Twelfth's injured.

Placing his hands against Svetlana's back, Becan said, "Yeh got to get up, girlie. Come on, let's get ou' o' here."

The Russian medic was a wreck, her face tear-streaked and her whole body shaking.

Gently, Becan eased her up to her feet. "Let's get on board." He placed his hand on her shoulder as they entered the transport, though the chaos of the bustling soldiers within soon separated them. Looking back, Becan waved her onward. "Come on—righ' with me!" The Irishman looked ahead again as more soldiers got between them.

Svetlana followed, her face devoid of expression—shocked numb.

Then, she stopped. Turning around, the blond medic stared down at the structure, at the battle taking place there. She lifted her hand to sweep her hair back. Slowly—and unnoticed by anyone—she took a step back into the snow.

SCOTT WAS IN the middle of the transfer of wounded from the lift when a scorching blast slammed into his left shoulder. His feet left the ground, and he landed flat on his back. For a moment, his vision flashed white. There was silence. Then, like a washing wave, there was pain and the reek of burnt skin. He'd been shot. As suddenly as his vision had disappeared, it returned to him. He found himself staring at the overcast sky above. He was alive…and he could hear his armor sizzling. Teeth clenched, he peered at his shoulder. His shoulder guard was torn entirely open. It burned like fire.

Before he could muster the endurance to stand, a pair of hands grabbed him and yanked him to his feet. They were David's.

"You all right, compadre?"

Scott winced as he regained his balance. His assault rifle lay sprawled in the snow. "Yeah." He lied. "Veck!"

David hurried him to the secure side of the structure. "If it makes you feel any better, the rest of us are shot to hell, too."

It took a few moments for Scott to register David's presence. David was okay. Shot, but okay. But what about…? "Did Novikov actually stay down there?"

David's expression shifted. "I'll tell you about it later. There's nothing we can do."

Before Scott could reply, Travis's voice cut through the comm chatter. "We're landing—get everyone in quick! This place is getting ugly fast!"

Scott and David turned their faces skyward, where the *Pariah* and the Third's Vulture began their descents.

The rush to the transports was frenzied chaos. Konstantin was the first of the Fourteenth to be assisted into the *Pariah*, followed by the also-injured Kevin. Varvara was quick to give them attention.

Baranov and Max were the last two in, as the executor carried Max against his shoulder. Max's armor smoked, and dots of blood were on his face. Inside the *Pariah*, Clarke stared at them. "What happened?"

"He got shot while assisting the wounded," Baranov answered.

Max gave the okay sign. "I'm all right, I'm not dying. I was almost behind the structure when some lucky dregg caught me at the last second."

"Do we have people missing?" asked Baranov, looking around.

"Voronova and McCrae are riding back with the Twelfth," Clarke answered. "They're waiting for the sky above them to clear. We've still got to pick up Powers and Timmons."

As the soldiers strapped themselves in, plasma bolts slammed into the *Pariah*'s hull. "Is anyone back there critical?" Travis asked.

"No, let's *go!*" Max clenched his teeth.

"I'm keeping the back door open till we pick up Fox and Jayden!" Travis said. "Don't fall out!"

Baranov glared. "Do not *make* us fall out!"

THE SCENE INSIDE the Twelfth's Vulture was chaos. Becan was jostled to and fro as soldiers strapped themselves in. Some were injured. Some had only just returned to the transport from the structure, the evacuation order coming while they had already been between the ship and the structure. Everything, in every direction, was frantic and loud.

There was no order to the process of strapping in. Soldiers just took whatever seat was nearest. Becan was no exception. Slamming down his harness as the call to lift off was made, he blew a nervous breath and looked out of the porthole window across from him. Then, he looked for Svetlana. And that was when he froze.

The medic was nowhere to be seen.

His brow arching, he extended his neck to get a full view of everyone. "Sveta!" he called out, only to repeat the word when he got no response. Lifting the harness again and with his head whipping in every direction, he desperately sought Svetlana out. He saw only unfamiliar faces.

TRAVIS'S FOCUS NARROWED on the ridge as he centered the *Pariah*'s nose. They were midway between the two snipers and the Bakma outpost.

In the troop bay, the soldiers peered down at the bloodstained snow. Bodies were strewn across the ground, none of which had been recovered before the mass retreat. They would return for bodies later—after the Bakma were gone.

Kevin was the first to catch sight of the straggler. Despite the many figures that trekked through the snow—almost all Bakma—this one stood out. It was a lone EDEN soldier sprinting across the battlefield. "There's someone down there," he said, pointing.

The others followed Kevin's stare. David raised a brow. "Where do they think they're going? They're running straight for the outpost..."

Before another comment could be made, Kevin's jaw dropped. "Oh my God!"

Becan's frantic voice over the comm gave away the revelation. "Does annyone on the ship see Svetlana? She's gone!"

From his seat at the very front, Clarke lurched forward. "What the bloody hell? Is that *her*?"

Scott leapt to his feet. Svetlana! What was she doing? No...he knew what she was doing. She was doing exactly what he'd be doing.

Max propped himself up. "Oh my God. She's going back for Tolya!"

Galina and Varvara gasped; Baranov sprinted to the back of the *Pariah*. "We just passed over her! She's running back to the outpost. She's running straight for the Bakma!"

Yelling in the comm, Clarke said, "We have her, McCrae! She's running back to the outpost!"

"*She's wha'?*"

Plasma bolts streaked in Svetlana's direction. Grabbing onto a support rail, Scott watched her in horror from the open bay door. "She's not gonna make it..." His friend. The one that he'd earned. She was going to die.

Cupping a hand over his mouth, Baranov shouted from the doorway. "Sveta!" Just as he called her name, a plasma bolt clipped her in the leg. She toppled forward into the snow. Baranov ran his hand through his hair. "She's going to be gunned down!"

"I told Tolya I'd watch her!" Max said, panicking.

Scott's heart pounded as he lurched toward the doorway. She would die any second. "She's not gonna make it!" His legs tensed. His eyes judged the ground.

As soon as Scott bent his knees, David looked at him and shouted, "Scott, don't even think—"

It was too late. Scott leapt from the open door of the *Pariah* and free-fell to the snow.

Max froze as Scott disappeared.

David sprinted to the door. "What are you *doing*?" Before he could say another word, Baranov's hand intercepted his chest and held him in place.

"Wait," Baranov said. "Let him go..."

Far below, Scott hit the snow and tumbled into a ball.

AIRBORNE IN *VULTURE-3*, distant but not oblivious, General Thoor's eyes narrowed on the newly snowbound soldier. The soldier's golden collar shone atop the snow.

THE STING THAT surged through Scott's arm as he landed hard reminded him that he was wounded. He bit back the pain and scrambled to his feet. It wasn't hard to find Svetlana—she was the only other human on the ground. The nearest Bakma trained his weapon on her. Scott lifted his assault rifle and fired first. He missed.

"Sveta, stay down!"

The Bakma shifted his aim to Scott, as did several others. Diving into the snow as they opened fire, Scott propped himself to a knee and pulled the trigger. One Bakma fell.

He was outnumbered. He knew it. He counted five Bakma close enough to Svetlana and himself to engage actively, and he was too far away to make a difference. He would never make it to her in time.

Suddenly, one of the Bakma jolted back and dropped. Before Scott could react, a second Bakma did the same. Jayden's unmistakable Texas drawl slurred over the comm.

"Git 'er, man. I got you covered."

There was no hesitation. Scott leapt to his feet and chased full speed after Svetlana. With Fox and Jayden's suppression, he immediately caught up to her.

"Sveta, stay down!" He grabbed her from behind and tackled her into the snow. She was very much awake, though her armor was charred deep. Her eyes were half-crazed. "Are you hurt bad?"

She shoved him back and spat a torrent of Russian his way, then twisted to escape his grip.

He grabbed her a second time. The pain in his arm surged again. "*Stay down!*"

Before he could utter another word, gunfire erupted behind him. He looked back. It was the *Pariah*. Its nose-mounted chain gun blazed orange, unleashing a flurry of rounds into the Bakma below.

Svetlana screamed as she attempted to wrench herself free. Scott slammed her to the ground and wrestled himself atop her. "Svetlana, stop it!"

"We're coming down on your position," Travis said over the comm. "Look up."

Engines roared above them as the *Pariah* descended. Baranov and

David knelt by the bay door, their arms outstretched to retrieve Svetlana and Scott.

Svetlana continued to struggle; Scott held her firm. "Don't make me knock you out!"

"Lift her up!" David yelled from above.

Scott grabbed her from behind and hoisted her into the air. She kicked and screamed, but Baranov and David snatched her before she could writhe away.

Scott was next. He moaned as his burned shoulder flexed its muscles, but with the help of the others, he was pulled inside.

"Hold on," Travis said from the cockpit. "We're picking Fox and Jayden up on the ridge!" As the bay door rose, Scott collapsed to the floor.

"What the hell were you *thinking*?" David asked.

Scott didn't respond. He didn't know what to say.

It took only another minute for the *Pariah* to arrive at the ridge, where the two snipers were retrieved. Once they were on board, the transport set its course for *Novosibirsk*. The outpost and the Noboats were left behind; there were too few Vindicators to counter them. Instead, the fighters looped back and escorted the transports home.

Almost half of the soldiers in the Fourteenth bore some sort of injury. Of the initial ground team, only Baranov and Dostoevsky returned unscathed, the former of whose armor was severely charred. Konstantin sat numbed on the floor with a cauterized hole in his thigh and Scott's entire shoulder and arm cramped. David cautiously cradled his arm, and Kevin scrutinized the small gash in his leg.

Max's chest wound was the most serious. Galina monitored it constantly and made it clear that serious medical attention would be needed as soon as they landed. As she watched over him, Varvara kept watch over Svetlana, who remained huddled in the corner. Though her armor was charred and twisted, she was not seriously hurt.

A somber quiet permeated the transport as it cut through the Siberian sky. It was a quiet indicative of many emotions—fear, anger, sadness, and bewilderment. Even the Nightmen among them, Baranov and Dostoevsky, remained silent and still. The only sound in the rear bay, aside from the hum of the *Pariah*, was Svetlana's choked breathing as she cried. Her crumpled and weak body shivered as Varvara sat beside her, her arm supportive around Svetlana's shoulder. There was little more that could be done. This was something no one had prepared for.

Everyone heard the click. It was impossible not to. It was a static noise, a subtle crackle, and it caused every one of the soldiers to lift their heads and turn their attention to the wall. To the speaker.

Someone was on the channel.

None of them could have prepared for the voice they heard next.

"Sveta?"

Nobody made a sound. The soldiers all riveted their eyes on Svetlana. She trembled as the voice repeated itself through the speaker.

"Sveta?"

It was him. Deep within the walls of the Bakma outpost. It was Novikov.

Svetlana leapt to her feet and scrambled to the wall. She shot up her hand to press the button beneath the speaker as tears streamed down her face. "Tolya?"

The voice moaned. "Sveta…"

She swallowed at the sound of her name. Pressing her forehead against the speaker, she held one hand firm on the button while the other braced against the wall. Her body trembled, and she broke down.

Scott watched as she lost her composure. He watched as her body surrendered against the cold of the *Pariah*'s hull. The cursed ship. Around him, other eyes began to glisten. Behind the lifeless frame of the speaker mount, Novikov's rasping breaths heard her. His voice wavered, and he began to whisper.

Svetlana choked sobs as she leaned against the wall. "Nyet, Tolya… nyet…" The words barely escaped her lips.

Novikov whispered back inaudibly as Svetlana whimpered and closed her eyes. She couldn't make a sound. Her lips parted in a frozen gasp. Her hand sunk down the surface of the wall.

Her sobbing was interrupted as Thoor's voice cut through the speaker. "Are all units cleared of the facility?"

"Twelfth clear."

"Third clear."

Travis covered his mouth with his fist as moisture trailed down his cheeks. He lifted his gaze to the sky. In the seat beside him, Boris wiped his eyes and turned to face him. Neither man spoke.

"Fourteenth, are you clear of the facility?"

Svetlana trembled as she attempted to stand. She pressed her face against the speaker and said softly through the waver in her voice, "Ya tebya lyublyu."

Novikov smiled. Everyone could hear it. "Ya budu vsegda lyubit' tebya, Svetlana."

"Fourteenth, you will respond."

Closing his eyes, Travis leaned back against the seat cushion and raised his hand to rub his face. He reached out and placed his finger on the comm button. Beside him, Boris looked away.

Travis's finger lingered for several seconds before he gave the button a weak press. The channel was open. "Fourteenth clear."

"Detonate."

"Ya budu vsegda lyubit' tebya," Novikov said.

Static. The signal was gone.

Svetlana collapsed against the wall. The tear-stained faces of the Fourteenth followed her movements. Nothing else came from the speaker. Nothing else came from anyone. Svetlana froze in mid-sob, and she slid to the floor.

Only Baranov moved, rising to his feet and stepping behind her. He knelt on the floor and embraced her with a reddened stare. She crumbled into his arms.

There were no congratulations when they arrived at *Novosibirsk*. There were no handshakes. The *Pariah* was docked, and the Fourteenth retired in silence. No one needed to speak. The empty bunk in Room 14 said enough for all of them.

16

EVERYONE IN THE conference room focused on Judge Kentwood as he adjusted his bifocals and cleared his throat. "Detonation occurred at 0814 hours on Thursday, April 14th, Novosibirsk time. Scouts confirmed the detonation with a visual check just before 1100. There were no hostages taken, and as far as we can tell, no survivors. The access lift caved during the explosion, so it's only right to assume that any Bakma who might have survived below ground will perish. As far as we're concerned, this chapter is closed."

The room was quiet as Kentwood lowered himself into his chair. Pauling leaned forward. "Thank you, Darryl. I assume a full report will be ready within the next few days?"

Kentwood nodded. "Yes, sir. We'll have a unit investigate the site on hand—hopefully, we'll get deep enough down there to get some kind of salvage. Unfortunately, considering the facility was destroyed internally, we aren't sure how probable that is."

Pauling nodded. "Our priority was to incapacitate the base, and that was done. Salvage was secondary."

Before he could comment further, another judge spoke up. It was Richard Lena, one of the younger judges in the Council. "I think it should be noted that General Thoor was once again present during this operation."

"Yes," Kentwood said. "I was going to mention that, as well. It's only a matter of time until he gets himself killed. Perhaps we should consider a reprimand of some sort. We *have* mentioned this to him before."

The room became quiet. Pauling's expression was momentarily distant. Then he turned to Kentwood. "No. That would only spark retaliation."

Kentwood sighed. "With all due respect, sir, *we* control EDEN, not General Thoor."

"Thoor is too valuable to lose," Pauling said adamantly. "If he feels he's losing his authority in *Novosibirsk*, he may pull himself and everyone at that facility away from us."

Lena interrupted. "The backlash from such retaliation would be overwhelming, sir. Does he truly think that those soldiers would choose to side with him if given a choice between EDEN and Novosibirsk?"

"Yes. He does," said Pauling. "And he'd be right. Remember, Mr. Lena, *Novosibirsk* is run more by the Nightmen than by us."

"Which is something *else* that needs to be addressed," Lena said. "It's high time we let the general know that *Novosibirsk* is an EDEN facility, contrary to popular belief."

Several of the judges closed their eyes. "Thoor is a unique situation," Pauling answered. "This is a case where it's in the best interest of both EDEN and Thoor if he is allowed to do as he wishes, provided he doesn't get out of control. We've had this discussion before."

"I second that."

The vote of confidence came from Judge Rath, who sat several seats left of the president. "Thoor is too valuable to lose. The minute he feels we're threatening his authority, he'll pull himself and every Nightman away."

Lena sighed. "I still feel it would be best to at least send a message asking him to consider *not* doing that in the future. We don't have generals coming out of the woodwork. Regardless of how we feel about him, he'd be a very hard one to replace if he got himself killed."

"The hardest," Kentwood agreed.

"Noted," Pauling answered. "Mr. Lena, I'll have you tend to that notice. I do advise you, however, to be careful in how you choose your words."

Lena nodded, and Pauling looked at his watch. "I'm sorry to have to call this meeting to an end early, but I have an important call concerning the new base in Sydney. Before we leave, are there any further comments? Questions?"

Silence presided over the table until Kentwood cleared his throat. The rest of the Council turned to face him. "Yes, sir…"

"Very well, Darryl. Go ahead."

"As you know, sir, I've been doing a lot of work with Intelligence lately." He reached down to the tabletop, producing a single sheet of paper. "There are some…"

The sentence trailed off, and his eyes lingered on the document in his hand. The rest of the room watched in silence.

"…there are a few things I've found that concern me. I'm not sure if this is the appropriate time to discuss this, but I've come across some interesting findings. I don't have a full report ready, but given time, I should be able to produce one. I was wondering if I could be allowed full access to the Intelligence Department. Supervised, of course."

Several of the judges raised their eyebrows.

"I don't want to report anything that I can't prove or at least back up to some degree," Kentwood said. "Given a few weeks, I should be able to have a full report of what I'm talking about on your desk."

Pauling looked thoughtfully for a moment, then said, "I don't have an issue with that. I'll notify Kang tomorrow."

"Thank you, sir," Kentwood said.

"Is there anything else?" No one else spoke. "Very well, then. We'll reconvene tomorrow at 1500. You're dismissed."

The members of the Council rose and filed out of the room as Kentwood gathered his papers. Before he could step out, Judge Rath approached him. "What exactly did you find that's so intriguing?" Rath asked. "Is it something we should be aware of?"

Kentwood smiled and offered a half laugh. "It's probably nothing. It could just be errors in documentation, for all I know. I'd rather not get into details until I've looked into it further. No use spreading news that may not be news at all."

Rath cocked his head. "So it's nothing we should be worrying about then?"

"No, not yet, anyway. It's probably nothing, just me looking at things too critically."

"Nothing wrong with that."

"No," Kentwood smiled, "I guess not."

"All right. Well, good luck with the report. I look forward to hearing about it."

Kentwood bowed his head in dismissal. He departed from the room, and Rath followed several steps behind.

Rath slowed to a stop just outside the conference room. As soon as Kentwood disappeared ahead of him, Rath scanned the hall until his gaze came to rest on the eyes of another judge—Malcolm Blake—who stood at the far end of the hallway. The two locked eyes for several seconds before the brown-skinned Blake nodded in acknowledgment and disappeared around the corner.

Rath remained in front of the conference room doors, where his gaze sunk to the floor. Several moments passed before he, too, turned to walk away. The meeting area was left empty, and the doors to the conference room closed in silence.

*   *   *

2032 HOURS

NOVOSIBIRSK, RUSSIA

JAYDEN STARED AT the bottom of the bunk above him. "That's twice in a row now," he mumbled. Over twelve hours had passed since the strike on the Bakma outpost, and the unit was divided. Scott, David, Kevin, Konstantin, Max, and Svetlana were injured enough to require medical housing. The others remained unharmed in Room 14. While most of those in the medical bay were expected to be released within the week, Max and Konstantin were in for considerably longer recoveries.

Becan, in his own bunk next to Jayden, said to the Texan, "Mmm?"

"Twice they left me out," Jayden repeated.

Silence fell around them. "Righ'."

"I'm serious. The necrilid hunt and this one. The only mission I got to be a part of was Chicago." Jayden's hand reached down to drag his cowboy hat from the floor. He lifted it to his chest.

"Yeh didn't want to be at the necrilid hunt," Becan said. "An' wha' are yeh talkin' abou'? Yeh saved Remmy's life. Saved Svetlana's, too. Yeh think they could've lived through tha' withou' yeh?"

"Both times, on the necrilid hunt and in Siberia, they told me I had to be the backup."

"Righ'," Becan said as he rubbed his face. Though it was late, none of the soldiers slept. Aside from Becan and Jayden, the only others present were Galina and Varvara, who exchanged quiet conversation on the other side of the room. Curfew seemed not to matter, as none of the other non-injured soldiers were there.

"Scott's the only reason I got to do somethin'," Jayden said. "I feel useless."

"You're not useless," Becan answered. "If yeh were useless, yeh wouldn't be here at all."

Jayden stretched back his neck. "I just want to be a part of the action, that's all. I want to be trusted to do my job. I want to be given responsibility like everyone else is."

Becan hummed as he pursed his lips. "Righ', well yeh need to talk more."

"What?"

"Yeh need to talk more. Remmy talks to everyone. It's not tha' he sucks up, he doesn't, but he jus'...well, he talks. The more yeh talk, the more people get to know yeh. The more they get to know yeh, the more they trust yeh."

"So you're sayin' I don't talk?"

"Yeh don't. All yeh do is say 'yessir' an' snore."

The bunks fell quiet. Jayden slid his cowboy hat to cover his stomach. "I don't snore."

At that point, the door to Room 14 opened, and Executor Baranov stepped inside. Becan and Jayden observed as he offered a subtle nod to Galina and Varvara, then closed the door behind him. The two women replied with sad smiles, and Baranov lumbered toward his bunk. As he sat, the frame of his bed sunk several inches.

"Start talkin'," Becan urged Jayden under his breath.

Jayden cleared his throat. "Hello, executor," he said nervously.

"Gentlemen," Baranov said as he leaned forward to untie his boots. He released a long breath as he stretched his neck to the side, where it popped out loud.

Jayden cleared his throat again. "How are you doing, sir?"

Baranov scrutinized the Texan suspiciously, then unzipped the top half of his uniform. "As good as one could be on a terrible day."

"Are they letting anyone into the infirmary yet, sir?"

"Yes. I am just coming from there now."

"How is everyone? Sir."

"They are all resting now. Max is lucky to be alive, but he will pull through. Kostya is lucky, as well."

Jayden hesitated. "How's Svetlana?"

Baranov shifted on his bunk until he sat sideways across it, at which point he leaned back and propped his hands behind his head. His eyes slid shut. "She is not badly injured. Her armor saved her from that, but...I do not know. I think her heart has died already."

Silence overtook them until Becan addressed Baranov for the first time. "Why did tha' happen this mornin'?"

Baranov sighed. "I cannot give you an answer for that. Some things happen sometimes that do not seem as if they are right." Becan listened intently. "There are many things that the general does that many people do not agree with, such as what you have seen today. I know I do not like it. I do not think I could ever order such a thing as he ordered. But General Thoor is one of the greatest military leaders of our time. If you look at his history and the history of other EDEN generals, you will see that nobody else even compares. He does good work...he just does not do it in a...good way, if I may say that.

"Lieutenant Novikov had no choice today. I cannot tell you why this is true...but Tolya did what needed to be done. We may not like it, but we are not required to like everything. The general knew there was no way the base would be captured, so he knew it had to be destroyed. He had to make sure that it was destroyed the first time, and the only way to do that was to leave someone behind. If the lieutenant would have disobeyed..." His words trailed off. "He did what he had to do."

Jayden spoke up. "What would have happened, sir?"

Baranov hesitated before he answered. "If the base would have needed a second attack, there would have been more loss of life. The general knew this. He did what had to be done for the situation to work the first time, which is why he is such a great leader."

"A great leader?" Becan said skeptically. "Tha' 'great leader' killed one o' his own for no bloody reason. Doesn't tha' upset yeh at all?"

"It does, but what can I do? I have shed my tears already. Tolya was my friend. I have known him for very long time. Nothing I can do will bring him back. What has been done has been done." He hesitated. "I have lost comrades before, and it is not something I enjoy at all, but it is inevitable. There comes a point where death does not surprise one anymore—one comes to expect it. I will probably die here. The two of you will probably die here. It is something that has to be accepted."

Becan scoffed. "Accepted, yeah, but not in the way the lieutenant died today. He should be here now. The bomb went off, there were no problems. He died a needless death." He paused, then added, "An' wha' abou' Svetlana? Wha' is she supposed to do, eh? Do yeh think everythin' you're sayin' now is goin' to make her feel better? She's still goin' to be alone, an' *tomorrow* she'll still be alone. She can't even fall back on the mindset tha' the lieutenant died a hero, 'cos he didn't. He died 'cos some bucket o' snots told him to die."

Baranov sighed. "Today, a Bakma facility was destroyed. That is what was supposed to happen, and that is what happened. The general did what he felt needed to be done to guarantee victory."

"Yeh never answered me question. Wha's Svetlana supposed to do? How is she supposed to take all this?"

"She will grieve," Baranov answered. "That is her right, it is what is to be expected. She will hurt, as we all hurt when we lose someone we love. But she will move on. It will be hard for her, and it will take some time, but she will move on. She is a strong-hearted woman."

"If she had a righ' mind on her, she'd take a rifle an' blow tha' plonker's head off," Becan said.

"That is enough."

"Enough until when? Someone else is told to die?"

"I said that is enough." Baranov's tone became firm. "You are not expected to like everything that goes on here, but you will accept it. That is how things are done. Now, that is the end of this discussion."

"Yessir," Jayden quickly answered. He turned and glared at Becan.

"Wha'?"

"You're gonna get us fired!" Jayden whispered.

"Aw, you gackawacka. Nobody's goin' to get fired."

"Well, you'd better watch how you talk to the executor."

"Blarney. I could take tha' overgrown ape anny day."

"I can hear you, you know," Baranov said. "I am like, two bunks away."

Becan and Jayden shifted their attention to the executor. His eyes were still closed, and his hands still rested behind his head. The rest of the room was silent.

Jayden flopped down on his pillow and turned away from Becan. "You need to talk less."

"Aw, dry up."

*　　*　　*

THE INFIRMARY SAT in quiet desolation. Two entire rows of beds were occupied by those injured in the outpost assault. With the initial bustle of stabilization over, the aides exchanged whispered conversations as they prepared to clock out. The evening had set in.

There was a disinfected stench in the air. Wounds of various degrees, from full burns to clean incisions, poured their peculiar odors into the atmosphere. Despite attempts by the medical staff to dampen them, the smells lingered—a reminder of the mortality that loomed over *Novosibirsk*.

It was past eleven when the last lights were turned off, and the last nurse made her designated nighttime round. For Scott, it couldn't have been more welcomed.

The room had been silent all day, and aside from the occasional cough or grunt, it remained that way. It was fitting that when it came time for Scott and David—comrades from day one—to engage in conversation, their first words were not words at all.

Scott's lips parted, and he released a solitary sigh. The noise disturbed little, but it did garner David's attention. Silence prevailed, and then David finally spoke.

"What are you thinking?"

Scott remained fixated on the ceiling. What was he thinking? It was a question he was used to hearing all the time. Just not in this context. He feigned a smile. "That you just sounded like my fiancée." David made no response, and the smile faded from Scott's lips. "I'm thinking things were a lot better about a month ago."

David's head straightened, and his gaze, too, fell upon the emptiness of the ceiling. "I keep thinking about Sharon."

Scott's stomach twisted into a knot. David continued.

"I keep thinking about the look on her face when that EDEN officer comes knocking on the door and tells her that her husband is dead. I see the boys running to the door to see why mommy is crying, and she asks the man why…" Scott closed his eyes as he listened. "…and he can't give her a reason."

Scott slid his arm across his abdomen. That was every soldier with a family's greatest fear. The fear of death, not for themselves, but for those they would leave behind. For those who would suffer from it. "That's not going to happen," Scott said.

"I have two sons," David said. "They haven't seen me in two months. I want them to see me again."

"They will."

"You keep saying that, but how do you know? What if Thoor asks me to do what he asked Lieutenant Novikov to do? And I have no choice but to listen?"

"He's not going to say that."

David offered no response. Across the room, a soldier's cough disturbed the air. Scott's gaze remained on David until the older man said, "I shouldn't be here."

Scott blinked. This, from David? From Henry back at *Richmond*, yes, he would have expected that, but…David? He was everyone's pillar of strength. If *he* was having doubts...Scott could only stare with bewilderment. "What?"

"I should be home," David said, "being a father. I should be doing something safe. Selling real estate, giving financial advice. Being a vecking talk-seller, anything else. Something that gives them something other than a knock on the door from a total stranger."

Scott frowned. He had never thought about it until then, but when he first met David, David told him that his family was moving to Richmond—to be closer to him. David never brought it up again. The transfer to Russia must have been killing them. And Scott never thought to ask him about it. For a moment, he sickened himself. "Dave, back at *Richmond*, you were helping me through this same thing with Nicole..."

David made eye contact with Scott. "This is different now. Now, we're being *told* to die. Tell me you haven't been thinking about this, too. Look me in the eye and tell me you haven't been thinking the same thing after what just happened."

"Dave, I haven't stopped thinking about it since Chicago, but..."

David said nothing. His stare returned to the ceiling, and he slid his hands behind his head. Scott's eyes remained on him as he lay there. The infirmary was quiet.

He was supposed to say something. But what? Wisdom, realistic expectations...that was David's department. What did Scott have to offer? It didn't take long for him to find it. It was the only thing he knew.

"None of us are promised tomorrow," Scott said. "Not me, not you...not Sharon or Nicole. We live in a world where things happen all of a sudden. But I know things happen for a reason. I'd like to think they happen for an overall good that's just a little too far ahead for us to see." Why was it so effortless to say? Was it all that programmed in his head? "I know that God has a plan for me. I know He has a plan for you. I know He'll never put me, or you, or any of us through something we can't handle."

David was listening intently.

"You know I think about it," Scott said. "I think about it all the time. That same scene you replay in your head? I see it, too, with Nicole. I love her, Dave. I can't *not* be terrified at the thought that I may never see her again. I know it must be ten times as bad for you. I can't even imagine what runs through your head at night when you think about it. But I know that every night I pray and ask God to watch over us, me and Nicole, you and Sharon. Your kids. Every night, I pray for as many people as I can remember their names. Everyone in the unit here, everyone in Falcon back home, everyone. I don't do this to feel self-righteous or to feel good about myself. I do it because sometimes prayer's all we've got. I believe God listens."

David's gaze remained on Scott, but his eyes fell distant. Several seconds passed before he replied. "I wish I had your faith."

"No, you don't," Scott said. "I don't have enough." It was true. All of his talk about spirituality and his reading of Scripture, and when night came, his fears were the same as the most faithless around him, like he was some spiritual hypocrite.

David cleared his throat and looked up. "You hear anything about Svetlana?"

Scott leaned back his head. He didn't want to think about Svetlana. It hurt too much. "No. I don't think she got hurt too bad, just..."

"...yeah, I know," David answered. "I don't think I could take it. I don't know how she's taking it now."

"What makes you think she's taking it? She's across the room, but I still haven't heard her say a thing all day. I know she's not hurt that bad."

"Poor thing."

"She wanted to die with him," Scott said. "Just run down the hill and get mowed down by the Bakma. She was ready to do it. If she'd have made it to him, there's nothing she could have done. Just died with him."

David's head tilted to the side. "Would you have done it for Nicole?"

"In a heartbeat."

David nodded. "Me too." He adjusted his hands behind his head. "You saved her life, you know."

Scott frowned. He did know that. But it didn't make him feel any better about anything that'd transpired.

"Why did you do it?" David asked. "You didn't have to. The transport would have been there in another minute, and she might have been fine."

Scott shook his head. "Might is too big of a risk. I couldn't accept that. She could have been killed."

"You could've, too."

Scott stared at the ceiling. "It just felt like the right thing to do."

David chuckled. "You'll always do the right thing even if it kills you, huh?"

Scott furrowed his brow. Even if it killed him? It had almost killed him. It had nearly killed both of them, he and her. But who else would have done it? Nobody else had tried to save her. They just watched her run. They watched her almost die. Would they have left her body to be picked up later, too? "I hope so," Scott answered. She was worth it. She was worth the jump, she was worth the risk. She was worth it to him. He looked narrowly at David. "You'd better not have just jinxed me with that." Ever so faintly, a smirk appeared on David's face. "What are you going to do if I did? You'll be dead."

"I'll haunt you," Scott said. The two men quietly chuckled. Staring back at the ceiling, Scott released a long sigh. "Man, it feels good to laugh, even if just a little bit."

"Yeah," said David, "not a lot of that since we got here, huh?" After Scott shook his head, David went on. "We'll get there, I guess. To that place again where we can actually do that and not feel...wrong about it."

Scott knew what his friend meant. "Well, we can start anytime you're ready."

"What? Laughing?"

"Yeah—or at least, trying to find a reason to. To laugh, smile, anything but lay here miserable. We've been miserable since we set foot here—not like we haven't had reasons to be." Silence prevailed for a moment before Scott turned his head David's direction. "What do you think Becan and Jay are doing back in Room 14?"

"I don't know," David answered. "Whatever Jayden's doing, I'm sure he's doing it very quietly."

Scott stifled a humored breath. "Poor guy."

"Jayden's great." A moment passed before he looked Scott's way again. "Hey—I didn't think to mention this until now, but I think I figured out something pretty significant about Captain Clarke."

His focus fully attuned, Scott listened intently. "What?"

"Listen to *this*...his first name is Nathan."

Scott looked at David expectantly. When no elaboration came, he raised an eyebrow in confusion. "So...?"

"What's short for Nathan?"

Blinking, Scott said, "Umm."

"Nate."

"Okay?"

David's eyes stayed transfixed on Scott's. "*Nate.*"

Reaching up to scratch his head, Scott stared at David perplexedly. "Wherever you are going with this, I am not following."

"The enchilada guy!" David revealed.

It took Scott a second, but he finally understood—and scoffed fervently. "Oh, come on."

Pointing toward the infirmary door as if Clarke himself was standing in it, David said, "I'm telling you, Captain Clarke's the enchilada guy. Nate's Yummy Enchiladas. That's our new captain."

Scott said, "I'm gonna go out on a limb and say there's a zero-point-zero chance that Captain Clarke is that Nate."

"Well," said David, "there's only one way to find out, right? We have to try his enchiladas. And if they're yummy? Well, I think we all know what that means."

Scott nodded in faux sageness. "Solid quantifier. Subjective yumminess."

A Russian voice from several cots down interrupted the conversation. "Do you two ever stop talking?"

"Yeah, you two quiet it down over there!" David called out.

Scott fought off a laugh. David was forty, but there was still some kid in him.

"Idiots," the man from several cots down murmured.

Looking briefly toward the voice, Scott said to David, "We better be quiet. Some people need to sleep."

"Hey, you said you wanted to laugh," said David, smirking. When Scott shot him a hard, but good-natured glance, David said, "All right, all right, message received. We'll table the enchilada talk until some other time." Scott relaxed as they lay in silence, and the natural sounds of the night resumed. After a time, David whispered, "I'm going to try and get some sleep, but...I have to say this."

"Come on, man, we gotta be quiet."

"No. I mean what I'm going to say."

Scott furrowed his brow and turned to face him.

"You're a good guy," David said solemnly.

Scott turned his head. It wasn't what he'd expected to hear. "What?"

"I mean that. You're a great soldier and all—I mean, you won a Golden Lion on your first mission—but what you did out there for Svetlana...that was something different. Nobody else was willing to do that. I respect you a lot for it." Scott began to speak, but David cut him off. "I know what you're going to say." He smiled. "It's okay. Just accept it."

Silence fell between them. Finally, Scott nodded. "Thanks, man. Really. I appreciate it."

"Keep praying, man. Don't ever stop doing that."

"I won't."

"Good night."

"Night, Dave." Scott rolled onto his back and stared upward. A good man. If that was all he accomplished in life...that was okay. If that was all Nicole thought him to be...that was even better. His eyes slid shut, and the sounds of the night again took their place in the room. The rest of the infirmary was quiet.

Within minutes, they were both asleep.

17

RAIN POUNDED ON the city of Novosibirsk. It had done so for the last several days, as the weather in the city had turned into something strange. Novosibirsk had never been known for its hospitable climate, but now a different kind of thickness loomed in the air. The sky seemed forebodingly overcast, almost to a supernatural degree, and the north winds moaned like a chorus of banshees delivering a chilling farewell. Some soldiers blamed Thoor for the heaviness, while others blamed the Nightmen. Some pinned it on something different—something new. It was as if God Himself was looking down on *Novosibirsk* through His darkened clouds, warning it of wrath that loomed over the horizon. But *Novosibirsk* was not afraid of God, or of banshees, or of anything.

Inside, the men and women of the Fourteenth slept, lulled by the elemental onslaught that waged outside. Even amid the constant pound of rain, none stirred—not until God struck the Earth with His hand, and a violent crack of thunder cut through the steady thrum of rainfall.

Jayden's eyes flew open like loaded weapons cocked and ready to fire. He scanned the rest of the room. As his eyes adjusted, the darkness gave way to faint details. All bunks were still. All soldiers slept. Only he was awake.

His brow furrowed, and his senses perked. Something was off. His ears adjusted as they tuned out the thunderstorm, and they began their silent interrogation of Room 14.

It was an accepted truth that snipers were in a class of their own. There was something distinct about the composure of their senses that few others possessed. It was their innate ability to attune to the world around them while simultaneously isolating and removing selected distractions. It was an ability that allowed them to pick apart their surroundings and examine what they found. Snipers were born for one purpose—to be snipers. Jayden was no exception.

He filtered away the outside noise—the rain and the thunder. Then he removed the breathing of those who slept, followed by the creaks of bedsprings as soldiers turned. Only then did his ears perk, his senses honing in on something tucked away in the silence. There was another noise, one distinct among the sounds of the night. Several noises. Voices.

Someone was in the lounge.

A glance at the lounge door revealed sparse light beneath it. Jayden threw a glance around the room. Becan was in his bunk, as was Boris. Only Fox and Kevin had been released from the infirmary, and both were visible under their respective covers. Galina and Varvara were in plain sight, leaving three unaccounted for: Clarke, Baranov, and Dostoevsky. The officer core.

Jayden slid from the covers of his upper cot and slipped down the ladder of his bunk, where his bare feet touched the floor with a jolt of iciness. The rain still slammed, and the thunder still boomed, though now they were little more than glorified distractions. Cautious to remain silent, he tip-toed across the room until he was beside the lounge door. He crouched to a knee, cocked his head, and placed his ear by the doorframe. Despite their hushed tones, the voices he heard were clear and recognizable.

"Well, we don't technically *need* someone to replace him in that regard," Clarke said, eyeing Dostoevsky, whose face was lit by the small lamp that illuminated the countertop. "But you all know I don't like to leave holes. As Max moves to leftenant, there *will* be a vacancy in the delta corps. We can certainly promote one of the gammas to fill the void—at least if we want to keep things in-house, which I would wholeheartedly prefer."

"Would anyone here honestly consider Travis for delta?" Baranov asked, sighing in something akin to boredom.

"He does what's expected of him," Clarke said.

"But only what's expected of him."

Dostoevsky leaned back. "That's why he's flying a Vulture and not a Vindicator."

"I think we're all in agreement regarding him, then," Clarke said.

"I have always liked Fox," Dostoevsky said. "He's composed, and he has a lot of common sense. Quiet, but...he's a sniper. He is supposed to be quiet."

"I agree," Baranov said.

Dostoevsky played with his fingers. "The only other gammas are Galya and Remington."

"We've already discussed our medical situation," said Clarke. "So let's chew on Fox a bit more."

"Graduated almost two years ago, high scores," said Baranov blithely. "We all know this already, we do not need to discuss it."

Dostoevsky folded his arms. "What I see is consistency. Fox has never done anything spectacular as far as I can remember, but he has always done his tasks well. He'll do the job right the first time. He is still young, yes, but he is dependable. He is a good role model."

"I agree," Baranov said. "Fox is a smart choice. He is a safe one. We do not have to worry about surprises."

Clarke propped his elbows on the table. "The question *now* is how would he be as a leader? Delta teeters on the edge of epsilon, and epsilon is a primer for leftenant. Standing back and taking orders is fine and well, but when it comes time to pick up the reins and take command, will he have the initiative and the ability if we ask it from him?"

Jayden shifted as he listened by the door.

"I believe so," Dostoevsky answered.

Clarke nodded. "As do I."

Clarke and Dostoevsky faced Baranov, who drew in a heavy breath. He hesitated before saying, "I am unsure. You cannot tell how a person will react until they are in a situation that requires it. Fox has never been in that situation before. He is not very vocal, but this is sometimes good." He hesitated again. "I do not know. That is my answer."

Clarke nodded, then paused for a moment. "And then we have Remington, our little gift from *Richmond*. I'm very curious about your thoughts on him, particularly after what occurred earlier in the week."

"I like Remington," Baranov spoke without hesitation. "I had doubts at first, just as we all did, but after what he did...how can you not be impressed? He has courage and initiative."

"Remington is overestimated by everyone," Dostoevsky grumbled.

"And where were you when Sveta was running away?" Baranov asked.

Dostoevsky eyed his counterpart but said nothing.

"The only time he acted was when somebody *had* to act," Baranov said. "He was not waiting for an opportunity to be a hero—he watched Sveta run down the hill like the rest of us. He jumped only when he saw that she would not make it, and then there was no hesitation.

"I have often seen new soldiers foolishly rush into battle to prove themselves. I am even embarrassed for some who try so hard to be noticed. But I did not feel that way about Remington. He did not make me think he was *trying* to be a hero. I was not embarrassed for him. I envied him."

Clarke listened carefully.

"I am a leader," Baranov said. "I am supposed to lead by example. When I watched him running across the snow, I remember thinking to myself…that should be me. We have all known Sveta for a long time, and none of us," he glanced at Dostoevsky, "*none* of us did anything to save her. It took someone who had known her only for a few days to jump out of a ship and run after her alone. My heart hurt after that. When I visited Sveta for the first time, it was hard for me to look her in the eyes. If not for Remington, we would have all just watched her get shot to death."

"And we almost lost two soldiers instead of one," Dostoevsky said.

"Do you *have* a heart?"

Clarke edged between the two. "*Personally,* I've never been fond of soldiers taking matters into their own hands, but at the same time, there is an excellent chance that Svetlana would have died had he not intervened. That's undeniable."

Dostoevsky remained silent as Clarke continued.

"Mr. Remington's knack for heroics, whether intentional or not, is also undeniable. Believe me, I pored over the report filed by his captain at *Richmond* after Chicago. It was an awe-inspiring read. I wouldn't exactly call choosing between him and Fox *difficult*, but it's certainly interesting." Baranov and Dostoevsky stared at Clarke, who smiled and leaned back in his chair. "Do I need to ask you for your verdicts?"

"Fox," Dostoevsky answered.

Baranov shook his head. "I say Remington."

The lounge fell quiet as Clarke scrutinized the tabletop. Rain continued to drum outside. "Remington might have a high ceiling," he said, "but I know what I'm getting with Fox."

Jayden muttered.

"Fox is a good choice. He will do well," said Baranov.

Clarke nodded. "He's one of the most consistent soldiers I've worked with. I think he'll do brilliantly." He looked between the two men, where his gaze held on Dostoevsky.

Dostoevsky's eyes moved away from the table and trained on the crack at the bottom of the lounge door. Clarke opened his mouth, but Dostoevsky snapped a signal of silence. Clarke held his tongue, and he and Baranov stared at the bottom of the door.

Dostoevsky stood and stepped away from the table. Clarke and Baranov watched as he edged to the far wall, then glided to the door's edge. He placed his hand atop the doorknob, gripped his fingers around it, and jolted the door open.

No one.

Dostoevsky padded into the bunk room and scanned it. Every soldier was accounted for beneath the covers of their bunks. He hesitated for several seconds, then his gaze narrowed.

Beneath the covers of his bed, Jayden lay still. The only movement from his body was the subtle breathing that caused his chest to rise and fall. Though the rain pounded outside, he could hear the quiet clump of the lounge door as it was closed. He made no attempt to look. He simply lay there and waited for proper sleep to catch up with him. Almost thirty minutes later, after he heard the three officers leave the lounge and retire to their bunks, it did.

*   *   *

WEDNESDAY, APRIL 20TH, 0011 NE
0618 HOURS

BY THE NEXT morning, the violent thunderstorm that had shaken *Novosibirsk* had evolved into an airy snowfall that blanketed the base—typical Russian weather for that time of year.

The Fourteenth's morning routine came traditionally as soldiers donned their attire and set the coffee and tea to brew. Soon after the initial wakeup, the first breakfast crew ventured out of the living quarters—Becan, Jayden, Fox, and Travis. It was a new custom for them to meet with William and Joe for breakfast. They met in the hallways of the barracks and typically went to the cafeteria together. On this particular day, only William was there to find them.

The days began to lengthen, with sunrise coming at almost a quarter after five. It gave *Novosibirsk* the stark comfort of brightness to greet the base's earliest risers. The frigidity lasted throughout the day.

The snow-covered landscape in that region of Russia was different than in America. Together with the faithfully overcast sky and the coldness of the base itself, the scenery was more bleak than beautiful.

The cafeteria was bustling with activity when the soldiers arrived—the conversation of comrades, the stifled yawns of the recently awakened, and the clang of metal utensils. It took a short while for the five-man entourage to claim their breakfast, at which point they wandered through the room until they discovered an unclaimed table.

Travis adjusted his tray as he sat down. "How long do you guys think everyone will be in the infirmary?"

Becan sipped his tea. "Remmy an' Dave shouldn't be in there too long. They're not as bad off as the others."

"They might be let out today," said Fox. "I know Sveta is supposed to be released tomorrow. As far as Max and Kostya, they might be a while."

Travis offered a sad chuckle. "Strange how that happens. One minute, you're fine. Next minute, you've got bullet holes. That's got to be a scary thing."

"Yeh never been shot?" asked Becan.

"Nope," answered Travis, shaking his head. "Been lucky so far."

"How long yeh been in EDEN, if yeh don't mind me askin'?"

"Four years. All of 'em here, all of 'em with Vultures."

Becan whistled. "I can't see how yeh can stand bein' here so long. I been here a week an' I already miss *Richmond*."

Fox took a sip of tea and nodded. "*Richmond* is one of the nicer facilities. I'd imagine *Novosibirsk* ranks among the worst, comfort-wise. Maybe with *Leningrad*."

"Russians don't exactly put luxury at the top of their list," said Travis, half-frowning. "But hey, it's the military. If we were supposed to be staying at a first-class resort, then we'd have a right to complain."

"Yeah," Becan said, "guess you're righ'."

They were drawn into a lull of silence. As the collective chewing mixed with the conversation around the cafeteria, William shifted in his chair to face Jayden. The Texan's eyes surveyed his plate as he ate quietly. William watched for several seconds before he pointed and spoke. "You're too quiet. You freak me out."

Jayden opened his mouth, but Becan cut him off. "He's a wee bit cheesed off at the moment. See, he never gets to see annythin' cool 'cos he has to sit so far away from everyone in his little sniper stand."

Jayden shook his head and took another bite. Next to him, Fox chuckled.

"He thinks his life's so difficult 'cos he's from Texas, and they don't favor education much over there. Long as yeh can rope a steer an' spit tobacco, you're good to go in their eyes. Tha's why the rest o' the world is such a challenge to them."

Jayden could not stifle a laugh, and he set his fork down. The others grinned.

"So as yis can imagine, bein' inherently distanced from coolness an' withou' anny formal education, me boyo's kind o' had the odds against him from the get-go."

Fox turned to Jayden and smirked. "You don't have it that bad. At least your parents didn't name you Fox."

The others laughed, and cheerful conversation returned in full force. As the group talked, Travis's gaze shifted to the cafeteria door. "Fox, you said Svetlana was supposed to be let out tomorrow?"

Fox nodded. "That's what I heard."

"Well, for the first time in as long as I can remember, you're wrong about something."

Fox looked puzzled, then followed Travis's gaze to the cafeteria's front. The others at the table did the same. There, propped in the archway of the cafeteria door, was Svetlana. Galina and Varvara were at her sides as they inched toward the food line one step at a time. All conversation at the soldiers' table stopped.

Galina and Varvara each held a hand on Svetlana's shoulders. Svetlana's look was non-cognizant; she stared blankly at the floor in front of her. The expression on her face was no expression at all.

They watched silently as Galina and Varvara led her to the line, where they progressed until they reached the counter. There, they took a small portion of food, then left to claim a solitary table in the far corner of the room. Neither Galina nor Varvara carried a tray for themselves.

The three women lowered themselves into their chairs and sat motionless. Svetlana's tray was placed squarely in front of her, though she made no effort to sample anything on it.

Becan watched silently as Galina and Varvara's hands remained on Svetlana's shoulders. They made occasional gestures to the untouched tray of food, none of which prompted a response from her. Becan's gaze fell to the tabletop, where his tray of half-eaten food sat.

Before his comrades could say anything, Becan pushed back in his chair and rose. They watched as he excused himself in silence and began to weave through the cafeteria toward the table with the three women.

Varvara caught sight of him as he neared. She offered him a sad smile as she massaged her hand on Svetlana's shoulder, then leaned into Galina to whisper. A moment later, Galina glanced Becan's way. Her expression mirrored Varvara's, and she slid from her chair to stand. She joined Becan as he drew close, then turned to regard the now-empty chair next to Svetlana. "Please sit," she whispered. "That would be good for her."

Becan hesitated. He looked at Galina, then Svetlana, who made no indication that she was aware of his arrival. Finally, after a slow approach, he lowered into the chair.

Svetlana was a mess. What was once a striking and elegant appearance was now ragged and unkempt, as the golden hair that flowed to her shoulders was now tucked behind her ears in an oily slickness. The blue eyes that once entranced with dangerous allure were now dim, suppressed above dark bags, revealing a woman who had not slept in days.

She stared at her tray despite Becan's presence beside her. Silence surrounded them until Becan rested his hand against her back. "Yeh have to eat." She offered no response nor indicated that she was aware of him. Becan's eyes trailed to her tray, then returned to her. "Please…"

There was nothing. No response, no movement, no lift of the eyes. Svetlana sat beside him, thousands of miles away. Becan closed his eyes, slid his arm around her shoulder, and inched against her. As he hugged her, he leaned in to whisper in her ear. "We're here for yeh, girlie." Her head turned a bit, though that was the extent of her reply. Stillness fell again.

Becan withdrew his arm, pushed away, and stood up. Galina joined him, placing her hand on his shoulder. "Thank you," she mouthed. Varvara offered the same expression from her seat before the two women resumed their attempts to aid her.

Becan stepped away from the table and slid his hands in his pockets. He looked back to the table from which he had come, where his male counterparts watched him. He locked eyes with them for a moment, then back-stepped, turned around, and shuffled out of the cafeteria.

Jayden frowned as Becan exited, then looked at the Irishman's abandoned food tray. "Man, that sucks."

"Yeah," Travis said as he looked at his own plate. "He tried, though. That's the best he could do. I feel for Svetlana. She really is a good person." Fox turned in his chair to face them. "Tolya was a good guy—relatively speaking, of course."

"What do you think's gonna happen with you guys now?" asked William.

"How do you mean?" Fox asked.

"Well, you lost a lieutenant. I mean, someone's gotta replace him, right?" Jayden stared deliberately at the table space in front of him.

"That is true," Fox nodded. "I'm surprised nobody's been moved up yet. Clarke's usually very good with that kind of thing. He's probably just been busy." He reached for the untouched apple on his tray and held it in hand. He raised it in front of his face, inspecting it thoroughly. "But I don't know who'll end up getting promoted when all of this is said and done."

Travis offered a half-smile. "I wonder if I'll get moved up at all."

Jayden looked at the pilot, saying nothing.

Fox smirked. "You've only been here, what, four years? I think pilots have to be in for at least a decade before officer consideration."

"Yeah, that seems about right," Travis said, laughing.

"I wonder about Remington," Fox speculated. "They wouldn't be crazy enough to promote him to lieutenant, but I'm positive they'll need someone to take an extra delta role."

"They certainly ain't gonna bump him based on his fighting skills," William laughed.

Fox chuckled under his breath. "He is an interesting individual, though. Don't forget—he is the Golden Lion. It's not every day someone like that comes around. Some people just have it."

"What's 'it'?" William asked.

Travis offered an absent nod. "I like him."

Fox pointed immediately. "That is 'it.' Why do you like him, Travis?"

"I don't know," Travis shrugged. "He just seems like a really good guy. And I mean, look at what he did on that mission. He saved Sveta's life."

Fox nodded in conclusion. "Travis doesn't know him, but he likes him. And that's what 'it' is. It's a combination of initiative and charisma that not everybody has."

"But he can't fight." William shook his head.

"Well, I'm sure there's a lot he can't do," said Fox. "One thing he can't do is please everyone, as is obvious with Max. But you don't have to please everyone. You just have to please your superiors. If you can do that, there's no limit to how far you can go."

For the first time in the discussion, Jayden sparked to life. "Scott doesn't suck up. He's never sucked up."

"I never said he did."

"And what he did in Chicago was great."

Fox sighed. "I never said it wasn't. What he did in Siberia probably saved Sveta's life, too. I'm simply stating the facts."

"Yeah, well," Jayden said, "Scott's a great leader. I'd rather follow him than anyone else."

"Come on," Fox said. "How can you say that? He's not even in a leadership position."

The Texan sat upright. "Because he's the only person who gives me a chance. I never get to do anything—I'm always told I have to be the backup sniper. It happened on the necrilid hunt back at *Richmond*, and it happened on the mission here. And it's all because I don't go around talkin' to everyone."

All eyes focused on Jayden as he continued.

"I can't help it—I'm not all social like everyone else. I wish I was, but I'm not. Nobody even notices me around here, and I know it's me, but that's just me. That's who I am. But that shouldn't stop me from being given a chance. In Siberia, they needed snipers, but I'm the only one that had to get permission to shoot my rifle. That's not your fault—you're probably a great sniper, but if nobody gives me a chance to do things on my own, how am I supposed to prove anything?"

Jayden was forced to take a breath before he went on. "When Scott was in control in Chicago, he gave me a chance. He told me to get high in the building and hold down the fort, and he put faith in me to do it right. It wasn't like he was there watching me to make sure I didn't screw up. He trusted me. He even said, 'Go do your thing.' I was so proud to be a sniper that day, and I did a good job.

"He gave everyone a chance. He told Becan to take command if he went down, he told Mike to set up a hospital, and he even let John drive the van. Nobody got left out—everyone contributed."

He paused briefly. "That's why I say I'd rather follow him than anyone else, 'cause he gives everybody a chance. And that's why I don't appreciate you sayin' things behind his back, like that he sucks up and stuff. So please don't say stuff like that, 'cause he's a hell of a good guy who tries to get everyone involved."

For several moments, nobody said a word. Jayden's face was flushed red, but he eventually slid back and reassumed his silent persona.

Twenty seconds passed before Fox replied.

"Sorry."

From that point on, the conversation dulled. Though a few words were spoken about those in the infirmary, as well as speculation on the lack of recent alien activity, it all served more as end-of-discussion filler than relevant subject matter. Eventually, the four men stood up from the table, replaced their trays, and filed out of the cafeteria. William bid them farewell and departed to his unit's room. The rest of them journeyed back to Room 14.

When they returned, Clarke awaited them. He, along with Dostoevsky and Baranov, sat beyond the open doors of the lounge at the central table. Kevin and Boris were with them, as was Becan; it became apparent they were just in time for an impromptu meeting.

As soon as those present were settled in the lounge, Clarke shut the door and cleared his throat. "There's a small bit that I'd like to speak with you about this morning while it's just us. I don't mind going on without the medics this morning, as this is a rather touchy subject, and their time is best spent together right now. For us, however, I'd like to conduct some business, and a small bit of personal reflection and wisdom, if you'll see it as such."

He took a beat before he went on. "I know that Leftenant Novikov's death was hard to swallow, for all of us. In no way do I intend, however, to look back upon his life and claim that his death was a wasted one. I know that this has been a cause of tension in the unit in several areas, understandably so. Still, the leftenant died doing what he dedicated his life to doing: protecting Earth. He was given a direct order and followed it to the fullest extent of his capabilities. The general expects no less from every one of you, and I expect no less from every one of you.

"Svetlana has my heartfelt condolences; I've told her that already and left it at that. I've permitted her to request a temporary leave of absence if she desires it. She's yet to respond to me on the matter."

The group was silent as he continued.

"I've been serving in EDEN since its inception. If there is one lesson I have learned and one that I suggest you all learn quickly, it's that no one is given the promise of a tomorrow. We live in a time when attacks come unexpectedly from all directions. We're forced into situations we can't plan for against an enemy with a technological advantage. Deaths are going to happen. I have lost many friends throughout my years serving this organization, as you have all lost friends. While this is something I hope is never treated with apathy, it is something that must be accepted. The only thing we, as soldiers, can do is move on and continue doing our jobs to the utmost capacity. That is precisely what we, the command staff, intend on doing."

At that moment, Clarke glanced at Executor Baranov and nodded. "Executor."

Baranov cleared his throat. "The following changes have been made to the ranking structure of this unit. Delta Trooper Axen will be promoted to lieutenant and tertiary officer. Gamma Private Powers will be promoted to the rank of delta trooper. And last, Beta Private Jurgen will be promoted to gamma. Though Axen and Jurgen are not here, we cannot wait any longer before implementing these changes. They will be notified today of their new roles."

Clarke spoke as soon as Baranov was finished. "These changes are effective immediately. Fox, you're the only one of those three present, so I'll tell you here. I expect from you the excellence that you've always given."

Fox bowed his head. "Yes, sir."

Clarke offered a faint smile. "Very well. Now, everyone, get prepared for our morning session. It has not been overlooked. Today, we'll run several courses, so dress for the cold. Dismissed."

As Clarke, Baranov, and Dostoevsky remained behind in hushed discussion, the soldiers filed out of the lounge to change.

As Becan crouched down to open his duffle bag, he grumbled under his breath. "Tha' was nice an' motivational."

Travis gave Fox a faint smile as he changed into workout clothes. "Congrats, man."

"Thanks," Fox answered, offering a grim smile of his own. "Hate to get it that way, but that's how it goes, I guess."

"Well," Becan said, "I'm glad they moved Dave up a rank. Keepin' him at beta is a waste o' his experience. Who d'yeh think is goin' to tell him?"

Fox knelt to tie his boots. "I'd imagine they'll send a courier or something. Or maybe one of the officers will go tell them today."

"Righ'," the Irishman said. "Hopefully, they'll be back on their feet in a little bit annyway."

It took several minutes for the soldiers to get bundled, at which point they gathered together and made the trek outside. The cold tore at them throughout the workout, though it mattered little. As the procession of laps and exercises carried on, conversation flowed freely among them. There was a sense of forced but necessary return to normality.

By the time the workout was finished, almost two hours later, all of the soldiers present were adequately exhausted. It did not take long for Room 14 to fill with warm steam from the showerheads. It was justifiable compensation for the cold sting of the outside. As soon as the rush of showers was over, each soldier returned to their expenditures of time. The routine of *Novosibirsk* once again set in.

18

THE NURSE SMILED as she placed a finger on Scott's shoulder. "You be careful with that," she said in her Russian accent before she turned her attention to David and teased. "And you...why were you here again?"

David, whose left arm was almost completely healed, allowed a sly grin to creep out. "I just came to get some sleep."

The nurse laughed. "Take care, you two," she said with a gentle wave as she checked off their exit forms.

Scott and David waved in return, then made their way out of the infirmary.

They had spent eight days in the infirmary in total, and it was decided that morning that they were both cleared enough to return to active duty. While David was without hindrance, Scott wore a protective bandage over the burnt area on his shoulder and arm. It was an area that, while limited, was functional. He would have to return to the infirmary in several days for a reexamination. However, the advanced healing gels were expected to do their work well, as modern medicine usually did.

They left the medical wing in lifted spirits. It was impossible not to. After so many days, the odor of the injured became too familiar for comfort. When that happened, they knew they had to get out soon. The medical staff agreed.

The morning was freezing as always, though they welcomed the change. Anything different was better by that point, even if it was the icy chill of Russian air. Nonetheless, they soon longed for the warmth of the inside as they trekked across the grounds.

Room 14 was abandoned, though they didn't mind. The reunion of their nostrils and the stale smell of the room was as wonderful as anticipated. The others didn't need to be there for it to feel like home. The beds were all made, and the scent of old tea hung in the air.

"They must be working out," Scott said as he stepped in through the doorway and made for his bunk.

"Must be," David answered. His course differed as he veered past his bunk and straight to his closet. He flipped through his clothes until he came to his uniform. The gamma patch was embroidered on the front of its chest. "That's a beautiful thing," he said with a smile.

Scott smiled, too. "Welcome to the club." He looked around the vacant room. "You think they're running?"

"Yeah, something like that."

"They'll probably be back in about a half hour then."

"We'll find out soon enough," David said. "Want to get breakfast before they return?"

Scott nodded his head. "Sure. I actually miss the cafeteria's ambience."

David grinned. "Which is a very revealing sign of the times."

They checked over their personal belongings, and then they made their way out of Room 14. As they ventured across the grounds toward the cafeteria, something out of place caught their eyes. Off in the distance, away from the sidewalk but close enough to be seen, stood the form of a massive man. His backside faced *Novosibirsk* as he stared off into the unending snowscape. Scott recognized him immediately.

"Is that Will?"

David's brow furrowed. "I think it is. What's he doing out there in the snow?"

"He's not getting a tan," Scott quipped.

They stepped away from the sidewalk and trudged toward the demolitionist. The snow crunched under their feet with every step. Within seconds, William turned, indicating his awareness of their presence.

"Hey, man. What's up?" said Scott.

William's expression caught Scott entirely off guard. It was hardened. It was devoid of emotion. It was the most un-William-like expression Scott had seen on the man.

"Hey," William rasped.

"You lookin' for Yeti out here?" David asked.

"No." William's cheeks were glossed over with a frozen red, and his hands were shoved in his pockets with little ambition. Several awkward seconds passed before he moved away from them and returned his gaze to the icy landscape.

"What's wrong, man?" Scott asked.

The wind whipped up with a gusty blast, and William said nothing. His stare remained dedicated to the nothingness that stretched out in the distance. It wasn't until David took a half step toward him that he answered. "Joe's dead."

Scott's jaw gaped. Joe's dead? Joe *Janson's* dead? He blinked. "What did you say?"

"He's dead," William answered dully. "You want me to spell it out for you?"

David's expression fell. "I didn't know anybody got called out..."

"Nobody got called out," William said, facing them. "He died in his sleep."

Scott and David stood speechless. Died in his sleep? How could Joe have died in his sleep? Old men in their nineties died in their sleep. The chronically ill died in their sleep. But healthy soldiers? Scott asked the unavoidable, *"How?"*

"He went to bed early, said he had a headache. When we woke up this morning, he was dead." William looked away.

"He died of a *headache*?"

William shot him a glare. "That's what I said, isn't it?"

The conversation lingered in awkwardness as neither Scott nor David spoke a word. William broke the tension. "I want to be alone right now."

David hesitated. "Sure thing, man. Whatever you want."

Scott was quick to affirm. "If there's anything we can do, let us know. Definitely."

"I appreciate it," William answered.

They turned back to the sidewalk and left William on his own. When they were out of earshot, Scott shook his head. "How does that happen? You think he had some kind of a problem?"

David looked at him. "If he did, you think he'd be here?"

Scott's gaze sunk. "They came in together from *Atlanta*."

"I know," David answered soberly. "I know."

They resumed their trek to the cafeteria despite the news from William. Neither had known Joe beyond a handful of short chats, though they nonetheless felt the inevitable emptiness of one less conversationalist at the table. The man had been good company.

They picked at their plates, finding themselves devoid of the desire to eat, at which point they rose from the table and once again journeyed across the grounds, back to the barracks.

The Room 14 they found when they returned differed from the one they'd left. Laughter reverberated through the walls, and when they opened the door to step inside, they realized that the whole of the healthy crew was back from their morning workout. The two new arrivals were welcomed immediately.

"Remmy! Dave!" Becan leapt from the foot of his bunk, skipping across the room to greet them. "It's abou' time they let yis ou'!"

A wide grin spread across Jayden's face. "Hey guys!"

The room bustled as a mist of warm steam rose from the occupied showers and shrouded half the room. Conversation flowed back and forth in Russian and English, as was the custom whenever soldiers returned from the morning session.

David slapped a hand out to Becan. "You guys missed out," he said, hitting the Irishman with a fist hug. "The infirmary is where the party's at."

"I bet it is, but I'm sure it's not as happenin' as the pool," Becan laughed.

Scott grinned. "Is that where you guys have been?"

"All mornin', nice an' warm!"

Scott scanned the room, looking at the rest of the soldiers. Sure enough, their damp hair affirmed it. It made him jealous. Every time he went on a morning workout, it was a bitter-cold jog.

"You should see the pool, man," Jayden said. "It's awesome. I hope we go there all the time."

"Yeh jus' like seein' Varvara in a swimsuit," Becan smirked.

"Man," Jayden said, "she's *hot*." He glanced across the room to the medic.

Scott smirked at Jayden's words. Saying *she's hot* wasn't exactly making a move, but for Jayden, anything was progress.

Travis joined them and slapped David on the arm. "Congrats on the promotion."

"Thanks," David answered.

Scooting past them and whisking a pink towel through her hair, Galina smiled and said, "Welcome back."

Clarke and Baranov emerged from the lounge a moment later. "How goes it, gentlemen?" Clarke asked with a grin. "Glad to see you both back here in one piece! I trust your recovery went well?"

"Yes, sir," they said.

Clarke drew nearer and motioned to the protective bandage wrapped around Scott's shoulder. "How long will you need that?"

"Doctors say just a few days, sir. It's precautionary. I have a checkup on Sunday, and if it looks good by then, I'm good to go without it."

Clarke smiled. "Brilliant! Well, I'll let you go ahead and get reacquainted with your comrades. If you need me or the leftenant, we'll be in our office." He smiled and gestured to the lounge. "It's good to have you two back with us."

As Clarke returned to the lounge, David remarked, "This place has livened up since we were here last."

Becan smirked. "I wonder if tha's indicative o' annythin'."

David stifled a laugh. "Right."

The door to Room 14 opened as Dostoevsky stepped inside. The lieutenant's blue eyes surveyed Scott and David for a moment before he silently made his way to his bunk.

Only Baranov, who'd remained in the bunk room, noticed Dostoevsky's entrance. Approaching Dostoevsky with his hands in his pockets, Baranov asked quietly in Russian, "Where have *you* been?"

Dostoevsky's gaze shifted to Scott as he answered Baranov, "I have been given a task."

"A task?" asked Baranov. "By who?"

His eyes narrowing, Dostoevsky looked at his counterpart. "Who do you think?"

Baranov's eyebrows lifted. He walked away without a word.

At that moment, Scott realized that someone was absent—someone he knew had already been released. Svetlana. She was nowhere to be seen.

"Hey," he said as he leaned toward Travis, "where's Sveta?"

Travis's smile faded. "Svetlana?"

"Yeah."

Travis cast his eyes upon the floor and slid his hands into his pockets. "She's leaving, man."

"She's *leaving*?" asked Scott incredulously.

The pilot nodded. "She told us bye before we left for our workout—she went straight to the hangar right after. She's probably still here—I don't think her flight was leaving right that minute. But yeah…she's leaving EDEN."

Scott's stomach bottomed out. "You've got to be kidding me."

"I wish I were," Travis answered. "Supposedly, she talked to Clarke about it last night—exercised her *personal loss* clause, if I'm not mistaken. She packed her things this morning and told everyone bye."

Becan chimed in. "If yeh could even call it tellin' everyone bye."

"Yeah," Travis nodded. "A few hugs…she really didn't say much of anything. Clarke did all the talking." Galina, who stood within earshot of the conversation, listened quietly.

Scott slumped against the wall. "I can't believe it. I mean…I can believe it, it's just…"

"We know wha' yeh mean. We feel the same way. It wasn't righ' wha' happened, but at the same time, it's never good to see someone leave like tha'. It's a bloody mess."

"Everything's been all gloom and doom around here," said Travis. "It wasn't exactly the best way to start the morning, but what can you do? Who's to say any one of us wouldn't have done the same thing in her shoes?"

No one could say that. Scott knew for sure that he couldn't. But…gone? He couldn't believe it. Not Svetlana. Not the Svetlana he had come to know.

He stopped at that thought. He hadn't even known Svetlana well at all. They'd had only one meaningful conversation; before that, they'd almost been adversaries. She was an acquaintance. She was an acquaintance who had listened to him when he needed someone to listen. What if Galina had been in the lounge that night instead? She would have done the same thing, right?

Scott came out of his reverie. "You said she might still be here?"

Travis nodded. "Yeah. I think she left early more to be alone than to catch a flight. She's probably still in the hangar if you want to catch her. To say goodbye, or whatever." He frowned. "I thought about going, but what would I say? I don't see how anyone could even convince her to stay. I don't know how she would after what happened. I wasn't one of her closest friends, so it'd be awkward. That's kind of how everyone felt, I think."

Galina cleared her throat with a soft cough. She said to Scott, "I was going to stay with her until she left. I had morning workout, so I could not go until now. If you would like to come, you may do that."

Scott stared at her. What would he say to Svetlana if he did see her? One conversation. That was all they'd had. One conversation that had lasted for only a short while. It would be just as awkward for him as it would have been for Travis. His being there would only make Svetlana more uncomfortable. It would be stupid to go.

"Yeah," Scott answered. "I'd like that. If you don't mind."

"Not at all." Galina smiled. "I'm sure she would love to know that you cared. In fact, I can finish this tea on the way over there. Do you want to go now?"

His words deceived his thoughts. He had to see her. He didn't know why—he just had to. "Yes," he answered. "We can go now."

"Let me go get my boots on." Galina stepped away, leaving Scott with his thoughts.

It was right. It was the right thing to do. She was sitting in the hangar right now, by herself, waiting for a transport that was cold and lifeless. Everything around her was cold and lifeless. Someone else had to go, someone aside from just Galina. She had to know that someone else cared.

"Are you ready?" Galina asked as she returned.

"Ready."

As they stepped into the hall, Scott said to David. "Don't forget to tell them about Joe."

David nodded, and Scott and Galina departed. David's gaze lowered briefly before Becan stepped to him and cocked his head.

"Wha' happened to Joe?"

AS SCOTT AND Galina traversed the halls, Galina offered Scott a faint smile. "She will be happy that you're coming. She likes you."

Svetlana liked him. That gave him a warm feeling. When they first arrived at *Novosibirsk*, every reception had been so frosty. But she turned warm. She proved that it could be done. But it was more than that. He felt warm because, despite their short time together, he didn't think of her as simply an acquaintance. She was his friend.

One he was about to lose.

"I like you, too," said Galina with a smile.

"I just tried to be friendly. That was it."

"She noticed. Nobody else here gave her that when they first met her. Not even Tolya."

"I don't understand why not," Scott said. "She's a great person."

Galina paused a moment, then smiled. "Yes. She is."

Though snow no longer fell outside, the stark coldness of the wind still burned through the air. The scent of open oxygen brought the only aspect of life to the grounds of *Novosibirsk*. The land itself was devoid of activity; Galina and Scott found themselves a rare couple in the outdoors.

The walk to the airstrip was bleak, as the whole of *Novosibirsk* seemed on the verge of hibernation. A lull of extraterrestrial activity justified the recent stillness, and no one complained.

Vultures and civilian transports were perched outside the hangar doors as mechanics tended to prepping and fueling. It didn't take Scott and Galina long to find Svetlana. She was the only woman in sight, seated alone on a bench along the far wall of the hangar. Her only company was a duffle bag.

She sat with her head bowed and her hands clasped together. As she lifted her head to see them approaching, her golden pixie bob fell behind her ears. Her blue eyes widened.

When she rose to greet them, Scott saw her body perk up. She gazed from Galina to him and then back to Galina again. As she took her first step toward them, Scott noticed the shimmer of tears beneath her lids. When their paths finally met, Svetlana collided into Galina's embrace just as her arms opened up to accept her.

Svetlana wrapped her arms around Galina's back and pressed her face against her chest. A burst of tears choked out as she gripped the back of Galina's uniform. Galina's expression softened; she placed a hand on Svetlana's shoulder. She was saying something. Scott couldn't understand it, but she was saying something through her tears. The Russian words were repeated over and over.

Galina slid her hand to massage Svetlana's back. "Shhh…it's all right."

"It's going to be okay," Scott said as he touched her shoulder. He didn't know what else to do. "*You're* going to be okay." He looked past Galina to the technicians as they went about their business. He watched them as they traveled back and forth across the hangar. They were utterly oblivious to the scene. Or utterly uncaring.

His attention returned to Svetlana as she lifted her eyes to regard him. "Thank you," she said shakily, "for saving my life." The words were sincere but forced. Scott felt his heart break.

"Let's go sit down, okay?" said Galina.

Svetlana looked up at her. "I am sorry," she said.

Galina smiled. "Sorry for what? You have nothing to be sorry for."

Svetlana stepped away from Galina and wrapped her arms around Scott. He had known that an embrace was coming…he just wasn't sure how he'd feel when it did. It felt good. Strangely so. Something felt right about holding her. They stood together for several moments until Scott pulled away and peered at Svetlana's face, where he reached up to brush away a strand of hair. Svetlana managed a small smile. Though she remained silent, her lips still curved faintly.

They returned to Svetlana's bench, where the two women lowered themselves. Scott knelt on the concrete floor, propping his hand against the bench's frame. Svetlana sat in silence, feet crossed and head bowed. Behind them, the footsteps of technicians tracked across the concrete floor. Svetlana slumped against Galina, and her eyes glazed over.

"Sveta..." Galina said as she angled her body to support her friend, "are you *sure* you want to do this?"

Svetlana was quiet for a moment, then she nodded her head and sniffed. "I cannot stay here," she answered. "I cannot work for *him*."

Galina closed her eyes, and her hopeful expression faded. "I understand." Her hand massaged Svetlana's back.

"I am sorry," Svetlana whispered.

Scott's own gaze sunk as she spoke, and he rested his hand above hers on her knee. There was nothing Galina or he could do. Her decision was made. It was a decision nobody could hold against her. Her spirit was dead. It had been murdered by the lord of The Machine.

Had he been in her shoes, Scott knew he might well have made the same decision. What if Thoor had killed Nicole? What if her life was tossed in the trash like a piece of debris, an unnecessary expense for an unnecessary assignment? Lieutenant Novikov had spoken with Svetlana until the moment of his death. There had been no Bakma voices in the background, no pounding on the door of the room where he hid. The bomb stayed secure. He'd stayed with it for nothing. He'd died for nothing, and there was nothing anyone could do to make it different.

"You Voronova?"

It was a new voice. Scott turned to face an oily technician observing them, wooden clipboard in hand.

Svetlana looked from Galina to Scott. Her transport. Her ticket out of *Novosibirsk*. Her escape. Scott watched as she offered the technician a nod. For a fleeting moment, Scott swore he saw hesitation.

The technician continued. "That bird over there's gonna fly in about five minutes." He pointed to one of the civilian airbuses. "Might wanna go ahead and board right now."

Svetlana rose, sliding her hand from beneath Scott's.

All Scott knew to do was be there and remain calm. "Do you need any help? With bags or anything?"

"No," she paused. "I will be okay."

Galina placed her hand on Svetlana's shoulder, and Svetlana pulled her in for a final hug. Galina whispered something into Svetlana's ear, to which she nodded.

Galina smiled as they separated, then Svetlana turned to face Scott.

"Be safe with yourself," she said as she stepped toward him and embraced him. "There is a beautiful young woman in America waiting for her love to come home."

Scott fought to restrain emotion of his own as he held her close. A week ago, he had known nothing of Svetlana Voronova. Now, the thought of her leaving was crushing him. "You too," he said. "You'd better come back and visit us, all right?"

Svetlana dipped her head, and she peered into his eyes. "Don't let them change you," she whispered. "Please."

It was the second time he had been told that, first from Clarke, now from her. His mind returned to the present as she leaned in, pressed a kiss between his cheek and lips, and then pulled away. She bent down to pick up the strap of her duffle bag.

She backed away from them, then turned toward the airbus. As she walked away, Galina fell back to Scott's side. Svetlana was in the doorway of the airbus when she turned to offer a final wave.

Scott allowed his gaze to linger on her. Despite the wear and tear her emotions had taken on her, she was such a beautiful woman. Her hair shined golden again. The sparkle in her eyes was subdued, but it was still there. Blue like the ocean. Just like he wanted to remember them. He didn't want her to go.

He lifted his hand to bid her farewell, and for a moment, he thought he saw her smile. The door to the airbus slid shut.

She was gone.

The airbus sat for several more minutes before its engines roared to life, and it taxied down the runway. They watched as it rolled forward, picked up speed, and rose from the ground. It rocketed skyward with a thundering roar.

Scott dropped his hands to his sides. "There she goes."

Galina nodded solemnly. "Yes. There she goes."

For almost a minute, they stood by the entranceway to the airstrip and watched the airbus grow smaller and smaller in the distance until it finally disappeared from view. Scott turned back to the hangar. The technicians still hustled back and forth, and the other aircraft still awaited their turns for flight. Everything continued on. It was as if nothing had changed at all.

Perhaps nothing had.

He sighed and glanced at Galina. "What time is it?"

She looked at her watch, and then she shifted her gaze to the airstrip. "8:57."

8:57. A day of routine awaited them. Scott slid his hands into his pockets, and he faced the main building of *Novosibirsk*.

Galina's gaze lingered on the horizon, then she turned to join Scott.

They walked away from the hangar and began their journey back across the grounds to the barracks.

The technicians never noticed they were gone.

19

SCOTT STEPPED INTO the lounge, where he found Captain Clarke leaning against the counter, a cup of steaming tea resting on the marble surface beside him. Scott had been summoned to the room moments earlier, a request that tugged Scott away from the company of his comrades in the bunk room. He didn't mind. Any business Clarke had for him took priority—that was in the job description.

The past week had consisted of a stark routine that was becoming almost alarmingly normal to Scott. Every morning, the unit worked out, and the remainder of each day was spent in personal training. The only new development was the final report on Joe Janson. According to the local coroner, the soldier died of the Silent Fever, an illness that had reportedly reared its head at *Novosibirsk* several times. No further elaborations were offered.

"You wanted to see me, sir?" Scott asked.

Clarke scrutinized him. "Yes, private, I did. Come in, and please close the door."

"Yes, sir," Scott said as he turned to seal the room. It was an odd request, he thought, but not wholly unwarranted. The crew in the bunk room was prone to ruckus.

"Ask the captain if he wants some cereal!" Jayden said as he lifted a bowl of dry oat puffs. The others around him laughed as they reveled in their juvenile banter.

After the door was closed, and Scott again faced Clarke. The captain's face was deadpanned. "How is your shoulder?" he asked.

Scott rotated his shoulder several times and offered an uncertain smile. "It's all right, sir. Feels a little more like normal every day. Not completely there yet, but it's coming."

Clarke nodded. "Good, that's very good." The lounge was silent. Clarke's dark eyes were fixed on Scott, who continued to stand in a semi-attentive pose. Scott knew it wouldn't be a normal conversation the moment the captain resumed.

"Remington…you know that I expect a lot out of you. I hope I've made that clear since your arrival."

There was a moment of hesitation before Scott answered. "Yes, sir…" Clarke continued in a calculated tone. "I'm going to be expecting more, now." As Scott stood, puzzled, Clarke stepped to the countertop, where he retrieved an opened envelope and letter. He appeared all too familiar with its contents. "Effective today, your new rank is epsilon."

Scott blinked. "I'm sorry, sir…*what?*"

"Your new rank is epsilon."

Epsilon? How in the world had he become an epsilon? That rank was designated for officer training, the stepping stone between delta and lieutenant. A quick promotion like after Chicago was understandable considering what he had done, but a leap like this threw red flags everywhere. "Sir, there has to be some sort of a mistake."

Clarke almost cut him off. "It's no mistake. Believe me, I wish it were. In three missions, you've managed to move up four ranks. Some soldiers wait years to reach the delta corps, and you've flown up the chain of command like your daddy's a judge."

A chorus of laughter, unrelated to the lounge, could be heard in the bunk room. "Why'd you do that!" Jayden's voice whined. "I didn't do a *thing*! I didn't even touch yeh!"

But Scott heard none of it. His stare remained locked with Clarke's. The captain obviously wasn't thrilled with Scott being an epsilon, but it was Clarke's unit. If he didn't want Scott there, why had he promoted him? "Sir, I don't think I understand what's going on." It was an understatement.

Clarke folded his arms across his chest. "This wasn't my decision."

"Sir, whose was it?"

Clarke removed the letter from its envelope and jostled it open in his hand. His glare lingered on Scott briefly before it moved down to the letter. "'Advance Remington to the rank of epsilon. Signed, General Ignatius van Thoor.'"

Thoor? General Thoor, demanding his promotion? That didn't make sense at all. What did he have to do with Thoor? Aside from their one meeting on the airstrip, Scott hadn't spoken to the general at all.

Placing the letter blindly on the countertop, Clarke slid his eyes back to Scott. "I discovered it in my letterbox this morning."

Dumbstruck, Scott listened on.

"I'm sorry," Clarke said, "but you've done nothing to show me you deserve this. I see no reason to consider moving you to delta, let alone epsilon. But the general does. I was never asked to understand it." Tension hovered heavily. "Apparently, you've found favor with the general. Not many men can do that." Clarke leaned forward. "Please show me you deserve this."

What could Scott say? He agreed with Clarke one hundred percent. Summoning up as much dignity as he could, he said solemnly, "Yes, sir."

The captain nodded. "That's all I wanted. Thank you."

"Yes, sir."

As Scott stepped back into the bunk room and eased the door shut behind him, his comrades halted their levity to stare in his direction. All of them wore etched-in grins. Dry oat puffs were scattered across the floor as a shirtless Jayden knelt to pick them up.

"Welcome back!" Becan said. He glanced at Jayden. "Show him tha' thing where yeh throw your cereal all over the room again."

Jayden laughed. "Shut up! It was your fault!"

"I didn't touch yeh!"

The group laughed, and Becan returned his attention to Scott. Scott's expression remained solemn. Becan sobered up. "Wha's the matter, Remmy?"

Scott stood silently in the doorway for several moments, then sighed over the inevitable. This one was going to be fun.

*   *   *

"SO THEN HE comes up to us an' says, 'I just got promoted,'" Becan said as William listened from the weight machine.

William huffed. "Man." He pushed the massive set of weights up from his chest. "Some people are born lucky."

"Righ'," Becan said. He watched in awe as the demolitionist lifted. "God, how much is tha'?"

"Four hundred," William grunted. He held the bar up momentarily, then steadily lowered it.

"But annyway, isn't tha' bloody grand? Someone up there must really like the lad."

William sat up and reached for his bottle of water. "Yeah, well, he saved that blond chick's life, didn't he?"

"Yeah."

"Then I don't really have a problem with it. I mean…I'm a beta, and I've only been on one real mission. Well, only one that I've been any big part of, anyway. I got no problem with Scott. He's always been cool to me."

Becan lifted his hands in defense. "No, no, don't get me wrong now, I don't have anny problems with it at all. Hell, after Chicago, I'd just abou' rather follow him than annyone else."

"Well, there ya go. Good deal all the way around."

"Yeah."

William ran a towel over his face. "I've been meanin' to ask you something. Where the hell'd you learn to fight like you did that day?"

"I'm sorry?"

"Like you did in that practice fight way back when you first got here. Where'd you learn that junk?"

Becan fell silent as William stood up and moved to another machine. "Oh, I guess I've just been in a few scuffles here an' there. Yeh pick up new stuff every time."

"You musta been in a hell of a lot of scuffles." William sat in front of some pull-down bars. "No…wait, hell no, you were kickin' and flippin' and junk. I never met nobody in no street fight who kicks and flips. I know you studied martial arts, had to."

"I didn't. I mean, how hard is it to kick, yeh know? Yeh lift your leg an' push."

William laughed. "Harder than you make it look."

"Jus' got lucky, I did. I didn't think I'd win when I went up there."

The demolitionist eyed Becan. "Okay…I don't believe you, but I'll let it go for now." He gripped the bars above his head, grunted, and heaved down the ridiculously massive set of weights.

"God! You're a bloody veckin' ox."

William only laughed.

*   *   *

THE FOLLOWING DAYS passed as normal. Max and Konstantin remained in the infirmary, visited on a daily basis by their comrades from the

Fourteenth. Max stoically accepted the news of his promotion to lieutenant, as well as the promotions of Scott and Fox. On one occasion, Scott
ventured to the infirmary to pay Max a visit, but spans of awkward silence
discouraged him from a second attempt.

Scott remained emotionally detached from the unit for several days.
His unexpected promotion sent a slew of questions his way, none of which
he could answer. Though Nicole was noticeably detached, she still offered
him her support. "God is putting you in the places you need to be," she
said, though it didn't sound as if she believed it. All Scott could do was
hope she was right.

None of the promotions were accepted as graciously as David's. It
seemed a silent indicator of the respect his comrades held for him, and
several times, much to his delight, he was granted the opportunity to lead
the morning workouts. This went over well with the crew, who relished
their chances to be led by the fourteen-year NYPD veteran. Scott did get a
chance to ask David about the status of his family, and he was pleasantly
surprised to find out that Sharon and the kids were handling David's
transfer well. They had cancelled their move to Richmond to remain in
New York, but anxiously awaited an opportunity to reunite with their
father and husband. Scott admired their perseverance.

Becan's skills in hand-to-hand combat sparked a reputation surge
among those who observed the Fourteenth's free-sparring sessions. He
rarely lost, and when he won, he won convincingly. Only Dostoevsky and
Baranov challenged his level. Becan's ability to consume alcohol bought
favor among the Russians, as he became one of the regular late-night
vodka drinkers.

Jayden was quickly learning the social skills of an extrovert, to the
point where he ventured into a flirtatious relationship with Varvara. One
evening, by way of a Becan-proposed dare, he pinched Varvara's side as
she walked past, an action that garnered a shocked, though tantalized
response from her, one that hinted of mutual enjoyment. The distance
between joking and seriousness was unknown, though it did begin a
fresh set of rumors around the coffee machine. When asked about the
relationship, Jayden laughed and refused to comment.

The most noticeable transformation took place in Galina. After the
departure of Svetlana, she scheduled a series of personal examinations
with each of the operatives, for the purpose of getting acclimated with
their individual levels of health. It was executed so professionally that
it garnered praise from all three officers, and the debate on whether to

recruit a new chief medic was promptly forgotten. She socialized more with the men than Svetlana had, as she often joined them in late-night rounds of vodka and poker, though she never drank herself.

On one occasion, she snapped at Baranov for his excessive drinking, and he laughingly mocked her by downing half a bottle of vodka in front of everyone. She did not take offense to the gesture; rather, she calmly informed him that he was denied his alcoholic privileges for the remainder of the week. Baranov treated it as a joke until Clarke informed him that she indeed had the authority to impose such restrictions. Needless to say, Baranov was in a bad mood for the next three days.

Clarke, Baranov, and Dostoevsky grew more anxious with every passing night. When questioned about it by the soldiers of the Fourteenth, they insisted that things in *Novosibirsk* were moving along as scheduled, and there was no cause for concern. The three officers still talked and joked with the unit, though when it came down to business, they spoke among themselves under a veil of secrecy that the older members of the unit had never seen before. There was concern on Scott's part that he was a cause of their apprehensiveness, though a brief discussion with Baranov absolved him of any involvement.

Such were the conditions of the Fourteenth when Saturday, May 7th arrived. Life phased into as much a routine as possible in a unit decimated by circumstance. The weather in Novosibirsk remained frigid, as the rain evolved into snow. Everything was cold. Everything was miserable. Everything was normal.

20

THE ROOM WAS quiet. The soldiers of the Fourteenth had been permitted to enjoy free time so long as they adhered to the nine o'clock curfew, and thus, many were away. Only Scott, Kevin, Boris, and Varvara remained in the bunk room, with Clarke and Baranov behind the closed doors of the lounge. Each soldier was sprawled across his or her bunk; Kevin and Boris exchanged hushed conversation while Varvara flipped through the pages of a fashion magazine.

Scott, like Varvara, kept his mind occupied through the pages of a book, though in his case, it was Scripture. Lately, he had felt alienated from it. Perhaps even alienated from God. His internal frustration—that ever-present, spiritual time bomb—was ticking away. Like a roller coaster, his walk with God was a series of highs and lows. This rut he was in certainly qualified as the latter.

The rest of the room showed signs of casual abandon. Boots were strewn in front of closets, and a concluded chess game sat in strategic disarray in the corner. The organized mess was a welcomed sanctuary for those who chose to spend their time in the room.

Stretching, Scott felt his neck pop. He reached beneath the bunk with his fingers until he found his bookmark, which he slid into his Scripture. He placed the book beneath his bunk.

A hot cup of coffee. That was what he needed. He could already smell its aroma in his mind. It was a walk to the lounge and the press of a button away.

As he sat up, he made eye contact with Varvara. She offered him a smile, which he promptly returned along with the word, "kofey."

Her smile broadened, and she proceeded to speak in a flow of steady Russian.

Scott laughed. He didn't understand any of it. "I'm not that good yet."
She grinned. "I said, you muster to go get some."

Scott chuckled at her slightly flawed English. While English was the
"official" language of EDEN—much as it was the official business language
of the world—Varvara was still very much learning its finer points. This
was no doubt an attribution to her young age. She knew enough to get
by, clearly, but when it came to freely flowing conversation, she still had
a little ways to go. "I *must* go get some?" Scott asked with a smile.

"Yes, sorry! You *must* go get some." She laughed and winked. "I am
not that good yet, too."

It was those kinds of little interactions that reminded Scott that, even
though he was newer to *Novosibirsk*, it didn't mean everyone else there
was more experienced than him. As it turned out, Varvara had graduated
from the same *Philadelphia* class as Scott, David, Becan, and Jayden. It
was possible she'd even crossed paths with Falcon's medic, Michael Carter.

That Varvara had managed to make it through *Philadelphia* without
learning conversational English wasn't necessarily odd. Determined not
to let language become a barrier to a single, centralized training program,
EDEN utilized translation software to ensure that everyone was on the
same page, linguistically speaking. That same software was built into
every EDEN helmet, ensuring that though humanity came in many makes
and models, they could all speak with one voice.

Offering Varvara a smile and parting wave, Scott stepped through
the lounge door.

As soon as he entered, whatever conversation that was taking place
between Captain Clarke and Executor Baranov ceased instantly. Both
officers stared at him as he stood in the doorway. Scott raised a hand in
defense. "Am I interrupting something?"

Clarke shook his head. "No, you may enter." Baranov remained quiet
as Scott slid into the room and shut the door behind him. Clarke motioned
to an empty chair. "Have a seat, epsilon."

Scott offered a polite smile. "Thank you, sir. Just going to get a cup
of coffee first."

Clarke pointed to the counter. "There's a pot brewed. We put it on,
what, half an hour ago?"

"Close to that time," said Baranov.

Scott retrieved a coffee mug from the cabinets, which he promptly began to fill. As the black liquid steamed into the mug, he looked back at the captain. "You're sure I'm not interrupting anything, sir?" Clarke shook his head. "No, not at all." As soon as Scott's coffee was poured, Clarke asked, "How is your training going?"

Scott chuckled under his breath. That had been an unexpected aspect of the epsilon rank—personal sparring lessons from Lieutenant Dostoevsky. The purpose was to train Scott beyond his inferior education, as Dostoevsky put it, from the Academy. The lieutenant made it clear that imperfection was unacceptable, thus personal lessons were born. They were daily and brutal. He had the bruises to prove it.

He slid the coffee pot back into its holder and dropped a spoonful of cream and sugar into the mug. "Painful," he answered. "But helpful. Lieutenant Dostoevsky is a good trainer."

Clarke nodded. "That he is. He says you're picking it up quickly."

"It's hard work," Scott said as he sat down. "But I enjoy it. I've always liked training."

"That's good. Effort will always pay off."

Scott drew the coffee to his lips and took a sip. It tasted every bit as good as he'd expected. A tea kettle—undoubtedly Clarke's—sat beside the coffee pot.

As soon as Scott sat the mug down, Clarke cleared his throat. "Ivan and I were discussing the absence of activity lately. Since the attack in Siberia, there hasn't been a single registered Bakma intrusion anywhere on Earth."

Scott focused his attention on the captain. "What do you think that means, sir?"

"That's what we were discussing. We've got no idea what it means. That's over three weeks, coming on four, with nothing. Not so much as a reconnaissance craft, anywhere. It's as if we've won the war."

Scott smirked. If destroying the outpost had defeated the Bakma once and for all, then EDEN had seriously overestimated its most stringent enemy. "What about the Ceratopians?"

"We're at a bit of a lull right now concerning them as well," Clarke answered, "but that's come to be expected. For some reason or another, their attacks are more sporadic. But we've had two Ceratopian hits this week...one in America and one in India, nothing unusual there. It's the Bakma who've got us baffled."

"What does EDEN Command think?" Scott asked.

"Command are like us—they don't know what to think," answered

Clarke. "I personally believe the Bakma are gearing up for something big. I'm afraid it will only be a matter of time."

Something big? What did that mean? "Big like what, sir?"

"Of that, I'm uncertain. An attack, a full-fledged invasion. I've got no idea. I still don't understand why we're still here in the first place. Their technology is obviously superior, both the Bakma and Ceratopians. They can *get* here…so why toy with us this long? Why not send an entire task force here to wipe out humanity once and for all in a single sweep? Why send ships every now and then?"

Scott didn't have any answers.

"Granted, most of the strikes are tactically placed," said Clarke, "but we've got two separate species, both attacking Earth for reasons that we're still unaware of, and neither bringing anything resembling an armada to the table. Why shove when you can punch?" He leaned back from the table, crossing his leg over his knee. "We're not winning these little skirmishes because we're stronger. If anything, we're just good enough to compete. We're winning because we can match them with numbers and because they allow us to beat them. I know they must have magnificent bombing capabilities, but we've yet to see them bomb anything. They always land and engage in ground warfare."

"The Ceratopians bomb on occasion," said Baranov.

Clarke eyed him. "The Ceratopians, perhaps, but as far as I can recall, we've never had a Bakma bombing."

Scott thought for a moment. "And you think the Bakma are setting up for something bigger?"

"I don't know," Clarke answered. "But I'm afraid that may very well be the case. We've never had such a drop in activity before, at least not after any defining event, such as what happened in Siberia. From that day forward, we've had nothing. That's making a lot of people nervous."

"Whatever plan they had, many think we may have disrupted it when we destroyed their outpost," said Baranov. "What they do next is what we do not know."

Scott looked from one officer to the other. "But this may be nothing, right?"

"It's possible it's nothing," Clarke answered. "But this *is* very odd behavior, even if on a large scale. It's not to the point where it's making headlines yet, but give it another week or so, and it will."

That was the last thing the world needed. The rumor mill was already a driving force in media misinformation. "Have a lot of the soldiers noticed yet?" Scott asked.

"It's starting to draw some attention," Clarke answered. "People notice when no one gets called out for Bakma attacks."

"What about the general? Has he said anything about it?"

Baranov spoke up. "General Thoor knows it. He does not have to speak of it to let others know he is aware. You can look at him and tell that something is not right. He is a smart man."

Clarke nodded. "He's had Vindicators flying to and from Siberia since the attack, checking to see if anything has picked up there. The site hasn't been touched. It's as if the entire Bakma army have decided to leave Earth completely alone."

Scott sat up straight in his chair. Brain strike. "Maybe they can't afford to attack right now." Clarke and Baranov looked closely at the young epsilon. "Aliens have to have money, too, right? Maybe every time they send a ship, it costs their government umpteen billion dollars, or whatever it is for them. That outpost might have been the most expensive thing on their budget, and maybe they don't have the funds to send anything else."

"It's possible," Clarke answered. "Anything is possible."

It was an idea, at least. It was better than nothing. The thought of his own theory at least gave Scott a sense of contribution, which was far more than anything he had felt since his promotion. Whether he was right or not, at least he was trying.

Taking his last sip of tea, Clarke set the cup on the tabletop. "I'm sorry. I think I'm going to catch some zeds early tonight. I've been knackered all day."

Scott looked at the captain as Baranov nodded. "Stress," the executor said.

Clarke smiled ruefully. "May bloody well be it." He stood and walked to the sink, where he deposited his empty cup. "I'm going to my quarters tonight, Ivan. Make sure everyone's in bed by nine."

"Yes, sir," Baranov answered. "Good night, captain."

"Good night, sir."

"Good night Ivan, Remington. I'll see you both tomorrow morning."

Clarke straightened his uniform and stepped out of the lounge and into the bunk room. The door eased shut behind him.

As soon as he was gone, Scott asked Baranov, "His quarters?"

"Yes."

"I thought everyone slept in there."

Baranov shook his head. "That is usually the case, yes. But all officers have their own personal quarters. The captain has his, I have mine, Dostoevsky has his, and so will Max. They are just rarely used by us."

That made no sense at all. If Scott had his way, he'd sleep in his own private room every chance he got. "Why not?"

"It has more to do with the captain. In many units, all officers stay in their quarters...they are like small rooms, but they have beds, desks, and privacy. Clarke prefers for us to stay together as a unit. If it were up to me," he laughed, "I would sleep in my quarters every night. But it is not up to me, and if the captain asks us to stay here, we will stay."

Since his first day at *Novosibirsk*, Scott couldn't remember when any of the officers slept anywhere else. "Why is he going to his quarters tonight?"

"Probably because he is very tired," Baranov answered. "He does hard work, harder than most people realize. He is responsible for this unit, and sometimes, he simply needs to be on his own to sort things out. Tonight is one of those nights, I am sure."

"Must be nice," Scott said. "To have your own room."

"It is."

There was still so much for Scott to learn. Until then, he thought he had seen everything *Novosibirsk* had to offer. Now, he knew otherwise.

It struck him just how much he didn't know, not only about *Novosibirsk* but about everything. For one, aside from their reputation, he knew little about the Nightmen. Every rumor he had heard pinned them as monsters, but then here he was, in the middle of a pleasant conversation with Ivan Baranov, a Nightman himself.

A Nightman. Ivan Baranov was a Nightman. That meant, if the rumor was true, Baranov had murdered someone to become one. That was the Murder Rule.

It was so hard to imagine the man sitting across from him outright murdering another human being. The executor was a brute, but he was an amicable brute. Outside combat, he rarely saw the man in anything but an easygoing demeanor. But William and Joe had heard about the Murder Rule. They'd heard about it from someone who knew. And then they'd told Scott about it. Joe had told him about it. Joe was dead.

It hit him right then. Joe was dead. A chill broke out across Scott's skin. Had the Nightmen found out? Had they discovered that Joe had unveiled their secret, and had they killed him for it?

Wait. No. Joe hadn't told him. It had been William who'd told him, and William was still alive. William was in perfect health. Scott's mind was just running down rabbit trails.

Before Scott could reflect further, the first sounds of life came from the bunk room. A brash laugh erupted, easily recognized as Becan's, and the once quiet room livened with activity.

Baranov smiled. "Time to settle everyone down."

Scott watched as the executor pushed from his chair and stood. "Good luck, sir," Scott said, offering a smile.

Baranov smiled wryly. "I can always just knock them out."

Scott chuckled as Baranov made his way out. He heard the executor shout a stream of Russian words, only to be refuted by an Irish drinking song yelled from Becan at the top of his lungs. Scott chuckled further as the bunk room erupted with laughter. And then, just like that...

...he was alone.

Staring into his mug at what little coffee remained, Scott's mind drifted into reverie. Just as it'd felt so normal at *Richmond*, things at *Novosibirsk* had begun to feel that way, too—not only as it pertained to the Fourteenth, but for the base as a whole. Perhaps it was because of Svetlana's urging in that very same lounge, but he'd paid particularly close attention to the personal interactions of the Russians around him in the week and a half since her departure. He watched them laugh, joke, and occasionally even explode into good-natured boisterousness. He could feel that cold Russian stereotype inside him melting. The Nightmen were still the Nightmen—cold and machinelike by nature. But the Russian people felt far less "Russian" than they had previously. His taking the time to reprogram his western preconceptions was a good thing, and he felt he had Svetlana to thank for it.

It was hard to believe, but he'd been with the Fourteenth for longer than Falcon Squad. Memories of such moments as his mad flight from *The Black Cherry*, celebrating in the hangar with everyone after their return from *The Battle of Chicago*, almost seemed like another life entirely. Just as he'd come to appreciate his camaraderie with his fellow Falcons, he was beginning to appreciate that same feeling with his teammates in the Fourteenth. It'd taken a while, but Room 14 was starting to feel like home. Almost. But not quite.

Because *Nicole* wasn't there.

Sighing, Scott lifted the mug to his lips and took a final drink. How was any of this supposed to work with Nicole? How was she supposed to get on board with his living in Russia? It'd now been weeks of emotional distance. Of short calls and unspoken inner turmoil. This wasn't where Scott had envisioned his calling taking him. It certainly wasn't where she'd envisioned it. His weeks in Russia had accomplished something no other time away from her had. It'd made him question. Her. Them. Everything. Even God.

It wasn't so much that his faith was shaken. It was just that there were so many things he didn't understand—like where all this was heading and how she would fit into it. EDEN wasn't like the militaries of the Old Era. Tours didn't last for four years. It was a job. It was a job as much as it'd been a calling. And as a calling, he'd been all in. And so here he was.

But how he loved her. How he cherished and adored her. Had he known at the time of enlisting that he'd be stationed at a frozen dystopia on the other side of the planet…well, he may have just stayed put at Michigan. But perhaps that's why he hadn't known then. Perhaps that was why he *couldn't* have known. God knew he'd have turned away. And so soldier on, he had to do—believing that all things worked for the good of those whom God had called. No matter what.

No matter what.

Chirp.

Scott raised an eyebrow. Leaning back in his chair, he looked down at his comm attached to his belt. When he unclipped it and raised it to look at the display, he saw it was from Nicole. Before he even opened the message, that aching knot in his stomach began slowly twisting. But open it, he did.

It was a video. She was standing outside—he could recognize it as one of the parks on Michigan's campus. He recognized the gothic architecture of the buildings in the background. Much to his relief, she was beaming from ear to ear—for whatever reason. He tapped the play icon in the center of the thumbnail.

"Scott Remington!" she screamed. "This is your best friend in the universe, Nikki Dupree, with an important announcement!"

He could see shadows moving beyond her, he could hear other girls snickering—and he could tell, quite clearly, that someone else was holding the phone and recording. *What in the world is she doing?*

"I just thought I would send you this message at nine o'clock in the morning to saaay…" She thrust her fists triumphantly into the air. "I passed my nursing final! *Whooo!*" Jumping up and down emphatically, she cheered at the top of her lungs. She winced her eyes as if bracing for something.

And then something came—from the right, then from the left. Frothy, foaming, and completely enveloping. Her mouth opened in shock. Champagne.

"What the?" Scott said out loud, cracking a grin as he looked closer.

As Nicole danced and tried her hardest to cheer, a half dozen girls appeared around her—friends and sorority sisters. Each with a bottle in hand, they doused her with vigor. Bottles were flung up and down; some were poured right over her head. Amid the cackling of her compatriots, Nicole was rendered a sputtering, champagne-soaked mess.

"Oh my God," said Scott, laughing as the last of the bottles was ceremoniously outpoured.

Foamy strands dangling in front of her face, Nicole stepped to the camera, reached out to take it from whoever was filming, and then walked away from the girls to grin into the screen. Haphazardly wiping her dripping hair back, she said, "I can hang with the best of 'em, Scotty McHottie. Don't you forget it!"

Seeing this, how could he?

Wiping her face again, she said, "Firstly, this is freezing cold, and it kinda burns my eyes! Secondly and most importantly, I love you." She peered deeper into the camera; her smile widened. "I love you, Scott. You are worth fighting for."

Scott rubbed his hand down over his mouth. He wanted to tear up.

"I'm sorry I haven't been as supportive as I know you'd have been for me had our roles been reversed. Because you would have supported me, one hundred percent. Please forgive me, and accept this—" she picked up several strands of wet hair and dropped them down over her face, "—as a token of my apology." Pushing them back again, she peered more deeply at him. "I want you to know that I'm all in. On you. On us. On everything."

Wow, God. Just wow.

"Call me when you get this!" she said. "I don't care what time it is!" Another bottle of champagne appeared from the edge of the screen. Seconds later, another spray rained upon her. "I love you!" she sputtered with a laugh as her friends converged to rub their hands through her hair. "I love you, Scott Remington!"

"She loves you, Scott Remington!" her friends repeated jovially.

Seconds later, the video stopped—the final frame one of Nicole closed-eyed, laughing, and utterly drenched. She looked ridiculous.

Laughing and tapping on her name at the top of the screen, Scott placed the call just as she'd told him to. It didn't take her long to answer.

Her face appeared on the screen, the picturesque backdrop of Michigan's campus replaced by the warmth of her poster-adorned room. The moment she saw him, she grinned. Her hair was damp, combed back over her head from what had to be a shower.

Before she could say a word, Scott laughed and shook his head. "You're insane."

"Well, that was *fast*," she said, leering at him in that sly way that always gave him chills.

"You are absolutely, totally insane."

Nicole shook her head playfully, sending her damp strands back and forth before letting them collapse over her face. Staring through them, she said, "Just so you know, I did this for you." Raising a finger, she said, "Check that. I did this for *me*, just in case some Russian Shekeia is hangin' around over there!"

There wasn't.

Pushing the strands back for good this time, she looked at him more seriously. "I meant what I said in the video. I'm so sorry for how I've been."

"Babe, you don't need to say that." Of course, her emotions would waver. His had wavered, too.

"Yes, I do. I don't want you ever to worry that I'm falling out of love with you. I'm still your Nikki. I always will be."

He got it. He did. "I know you are, babe. This has been an…" He didn't even know how to say it. "Unprecedented time for us."

Faintly, one corner of her lips curved up. "I would say that, yes. But we'll get through it together. You, me, and God. That's all we need."

It was so good to hear her say that. It was so good to hear after the doubts that had plagued her. That had plagued *them*. He needed her behind him, backing him. Believing in him and what he was called to do. She was called to it, too.

"You're the love of my life, Scott. You're my soulmate. You're worth all of this."

How hearing those words warmed him. He smiled, then he laughed. Nodding his head at her, he said, "All of *that*? You sure?"

Squinting and closing an eye as if thinking, she finally said, "Yeah. All of this."

"So I have to ask: how does champagne taste?" He'd never had it before.

Lee Stephen   327

She looked up for a second, then returned her gaze to him. "Can I tell you a secret?"

"Sure."

"It wasn't champagne." She laughed. "It was apple cider—I was a good girl! So it tasted pretty great, actually! But it kinda burned my eyes. I hope you enjoyed it because I'm never doing it again!"

Narrowing his eyes, he asked, "Whose idea was that? Bailey?"

"Nope!" she exclaimed proudly. "That was one hundred percent Tricky Nikki."

"Well, color me impressed."

She smirked. "Yeah, it's pretty amazing how fast your friends say *yes* when you ask them to hose you down in public."

"Well, they did quite a good job."

Cackling, Nicole said, "I'd say so! Here," she picked up her phone from where it was propped, "I'll send you some pictures they took."

"You are so incredible," he said solemnly.

Eyes lifting from the screen where she was tapping, she settled them on him. Slowly, her smile grew—and she fell quiet.

"Everything about you is so incredibly beautiful," he said. "I must be…" Biting his lip, he half shook his head. "I must be the most blessed man on Earth to have landed someone like you. You're more than I ever deserved." He continued as she listened on. "*I'm* sorry for not making you as big a part of this as you should have been. I haven't thought of you as much as I should have during this whole process, and that's been such a mistake. You, umm…" He looked down briefly. "You told me that I was worth fighting for. I should be the one saying that to you. That's my fumble." Sighing, he said, "That's more like a pick-six."

Softly, her smile deepened. Nose crinkling, she said, "Good thing quarterbacks have short memories, huh?"

They did. That, they did. "I'm going to be an awesome husband to you, baby."

"I know you will. I have faith in you."

"Don't have 'faith' in me. Watch me prove it to you."

Again, those pearly whites showed—just for a moment. Just enough for him to see how much those words meant to her. For a moment, she held her breath. And then, she smiled. "You mean after all we've been through with this, after I've *finally* mustered up that mustard seed of faith, you're tellin' me not to use it?"

He laughed gently. "Nah, babe, you use it. On God."

Dipping her head a bit, she looked at him with satisfaction. "Okay. I can do that."

The door to the lounge opened behind Scott. Starting a bit, he looked behind him to see Dostoevsky enter. Scott's posture instantly tensed. Angling her head a bit, Nicole watched and listened.

"Lieutenant," Scott said. He pushed back in his chair to stand.

Holding out an open palm, Dostoevsky said, "No need. Please, stay seated."

Whispering from the screen, Nicole asked, "Should I go?"

For a moment, Scott teetered as if at the precipice of a choice. It was a choice quickly made. *I don't have to apologize for talking to my fiancée— and I won't.* Still standing despite Dostoevsky's command to remain at ease, Scott glanced briefly at Nicole before turning to the lieutenant. "I was just talking to my fiancée, sir."

Lifting a hand, Dostoevsky said, "Do not let me stop you."

"Thank you, sir." Only then was there hesitation. None of the Fourteenth's Nightmen were as cold and machine-like as Dostoevsky. He was the last one Scott would expect to extend any measure of friendship. But effort went both ways. "Sir, would you like to meet her?"

On the screen, Nicole's eyebrows lifted. "I just got out of the shower, Scott!" she emphatically whispered. "My hair's wet!"

"Oh," he said, half-stuttering as he glanced back to the screen. *Veck.*

"Sure," Dostoevsky answered, oblivious to Nicole's hushed warning.

Well, this wound's self-inflicted. Scott looked at the display again, where Nicole was desperately pushing back and wiping aside her damp strands to look in any way presentable. Mouthing an *ugh*, Scott heard her whisper, "veck it." Whipping her hair back, she dipped her chin and waited.

Scott rubbed the back of his neck. "Lieutenant, Nicole. Nicole, this is Lieutenant Yuri Dostoevsky."

When Dostoevsky saw her condition, his eyes widened a bit.

"Hi," said Nicole with a wave. "Sorry, I look a little rough at the moment!"

Smiling as pleasantly as Scott figured he could manage, Dostoevsky said, "It is quite all right." Lowering his chin a tad uncomfortably, he said, "I am sure you must be proud of him for all he has accomplished."

"I am," she said.

Offering Nicole a cordial nod, Dostoevsky briefly made eye contact with Scott before looking at her again. "It was a pleasure to meet you. I will leave the two of you to your conversation." Taking a step back, Dostoevsky pivoted for the door.

Nicole's voice stopped him. "You'll be proud of him, too!" Dostoevsky paused and looked back at her. She spoke on. "I'm sorry, it's Lieutenant Dostoevsky, right? Can I say something real quick about my future husband?" A butterfly arose deep inside Scott. He watched as Dostoevsky walked back to the screen.

"I want you to understand the caliber of man you have in my fiancé. I've heard your name before. I know you and a lot of people there were... less than excited to get him on board. I forgive you for that. I know he does, too."

Facing Nicole fully, Dostoevsky stepped closer to the camera. "I understand his value," he said.

Scott, in his wisdom, stayed quiet and listened.

She smiled like someone trying to do so politely. "It's okay if you don't—I get it. It takes a long time to trust. It takes *me* a long time to trust. So when I say that I trust this man with my life—with my whole future—I want you to understand what that means. Scott Remington is the man who showed me that I didn't have to settle. That I could find a man who would make me strive to be a better woman every single day. Because he does.

"You see, lieutenant, Scott's more than what he did in Chicago. He's more than a medal and a golden collar. He's a man of character in a world with far too few of those left. He's a New Era paladin. And if you let him, he will make it his personal mission to bring *you* honor." Pausing, she nodded to emphasize the point. "That's what he does. He lifts up everyone around him. He makes everyone better. So give him that chance. Give him that trust, as I gave him my trust. He'll make you thankful you did.

"I just wanted to tell you that. I think I'm the only person in the world who can fully convey who this man is—this man who just fell into your unit's lap over there. You deserve to know the caliber of human being you have in your unit."

Nicole fell silent. So did the lounge around them. As Nicole awaited Dostoevsky's response—if indeed she would get one—Scott looked upon his soulmate with reverence. Whether her decision to speak on her own accord would result in something good was yet to be determined, but there could be no questioning the courage of that beautiful young woman with those deep-diving, soul-searching eyes. Scott had looked into those eyes more times than he could fathom. They always challenged him, they always spoke truth to him. They were challenging Dostoevsky now. Personally, it was a move Scott wouldn't have made. But he wasn't going to

question it. Far be it for him to diminish what could have been the stir-
ring of God in her heart to speak.

Drawing a long breath through his nostrils, Dostoevsky finally
responded. "Thank you for your words. I do not believe most women
would have said them."

"Thank you for listening to them," she said back solemnly.

Looking at Scott again, Dostoevsky nodded in the same manner he
had when he'd first turned to go. Without a word—and without anyone
else's words to stop him this time—he walked through the lounge door
and returned to the bunk room. The door eased shut quietly in his wake.

Blowing out a breath, Scott widened his eyes and looked at her.

She closed her eyes. "I know."

"Do you, though?"

"I had to. I couldn't help it." Laughing quietly, and perhaps a tad nervously, she wiped her damp strands back over her head. "I was cashing
in that mustard seed."

Of course, she was. "Just had to spend it right away, did you?"

"What else was I gonna use it for?"

"You ever heard of interest?"

Nicole cracked a grin. "Sorry—but kinda not."

"Well," Scott said, "I'm going to *trust* that you spent it wisely."

"Ah, there's my hero." Her eyes locked with his, and both of their smiles
widened. Seconds later, she sighed. "Well, I'm gonna let you go before you
introduce me to anyone else while I'm rocking the wet look over here."

How he hated to hear it. Every one of their conversations ended too
soon. "I love you, Nicole Dupree."

Slowly, her smile widened. It always did when he called her by her
real name instead of *Nikki*. "I love you, Scott Remington," she said back.
A second later, she released a breathy laugh and looked away. "You just
gave me chills."

"Good." Chills, he would take.

"Bye, my love."

"Goodbye, babe. We'll talk again soon." A second of lingering eye
contact remained before she reached forward to tap her side of the display. The screen went dark.

The lounge was quiet.

Leaning back in his chair, Scott exhaled a long, centering breath. He
took the conversation in. *She called out Lieutenant Dostoevsky. I can't*

believe it. On second thought. *No, I can believe it. I can actually completely believe it.*

His comm beeped with a message prompt. Looking down at the display, he saw Nicole's name. Flipping open the conversation, he saw a series of pictures appear on the screen. His hushed laugh was immediate. It was Nicole, in all her apple-cider-soaked glory, as taken by her friends in the park. Flipping from one to the next, he shook his head. *This girl, man.* Seconds later, a text message appeared.

> NICOLE
> They drowned me!

That they had. He tapped out a response.

> SCOTT
> They sure did.

> NICOLE
> The things I do for my future husband…

> SCOTT
> I'm digging that last one. Might be your
> new contact pic.

> NICOLE
> You better not!!

Scott laughed. There was zero chance he was replacing the contact picture he had for her now. It was the same one in the framed photo she'd given him when he'd left for the Academy. That one was there to stay.

> SCOTT
> Thank you for what you said on my behalf,
> babe. You didn't need to do that.

> NICOLE
> Yes, I did.

> NICOLE
> I have faith in you, Scott. I believe in you.

NICOLE
God is putting you in the places you need
to be.

He'd struggled to believe that for so long. He'd questioned his decision-
making, his discernment, his convictions. Doubt had been his constant
adversary. No one could alleviate those feelings like she could.

SCOTT
I love you so much. I cannot wait to marry
you.

NICOLE
Soon…

NICOLE
…right?

NICOLE
…RIGHT?!

Scott laughed and shook his head.

SCOTT
Yes, soon.

NICOLE
Okay. I'm off to dry off now! Enjoy
my hawt pics.

SCOTT
Can't wait to show the guys.

NICOLE
…

SCOTT
Don't worry, you're safe!

NICOLE
I'd better be! Bye, hero.

Typing his final farewell, Scott closed the message window and set his comm on the table. Angling his head to the doorway, he listened as the showers in Room 14's bunk room hissed to life. Sighing deeply, he looked around the lounge. Closing his eyes, he imagined for a moment that Nicole was just a room away from him. Just a few steps and an open doorway. Right there...

...just out of reach.

Such was reality. For now.

By the time Scott returned to the bunk room, almost everyone else had taken their showers, and all chatter had declined into pre-sleep whispering. Baranov ordered the lights out soon after, and the soldiers filed into their beds. With Room 14 enveloped by silence, everyone inside found peaceful slumber.

*   *   *

SUNDAY, MAY 8ᵀᴴ, 0011 NE
0134 HOURS

THAT NIGHT

IT WAS COLD and late. The main airstrip of *Novosibirsk* stretched out in front of the hangar's giant doors, and the fresh scent of arctic stillness hovered in the calm of the night. Aside from the faint dusting of snowfall that drifted onto the ground, the airstrip was a desolate span of frozen emptiness. It was almost pitch black, and if not for the dim illumination of the guard shack and the hollow glow of runway lights, only the moon and the stars would have cast their glow upon the earth.

In that guard shack, the only signs of life outside of *Novosibirsk* were found—two Nightmen outfitted in their black sentry armor, huddled in the warmth of the primitive building. One was complacent, his feet propped on a desk, and his body eased back in a metal chair. He was listening to a radio at low volume—the rebroadcast of a soccer game; there was nothing else to listen to.

The other Nightman was taller and watchful. He stared out the window, his arms folded across his chest and his helmet set aside on the desktop. All was quiet. All was still.

Clunk.

Both Nightmen flinched. The sound was barely audible over the crackle of the radio, but it was there. The Nightman by the window scrutinized the landscape while the other turned off the radio. "Did you just hear that?" the sitting Nightman asked.

For several seconds, both men fell quiet and listened.

There was no more sound. There was nothing at all. The Nightman by the window moved to the edge of the door.

The one behind the desk stood up. "You did hear that, right?"

"Yes." The taller man twisted the knob and eased the guard shack door open. Coldness crept into the room, and he stepped to look out. "Where did it sound like it came from?" he whispered.

The Nightman from behind the desk inched over to the window. "From right outside."

The airstrip was empty. The snow continued its steady downward drift as the dim runway lights illuminated the ground. There was nothing else.

Both Nightmen peered outside until the taller one finally stepped from the doorway to the desk, where he retrieved his assault rifle and slung it over his shoulder. "I'm going out there." Moments later, he slipped out of the door and onto the airstrip.

What little wind there was howled around the corners of the guard shack; aside from that and the sound of the Nightman's footsteps, there was nothing. The air burned with cold, and he winced as the frost bit at his eyes. Nonetheless, he continued forward as his comrade watched through the window.

The airstrip was empty. He swiveled his head in all directions as he marched on. There was nothing. There was nobody. His pace slowed until he drew to a stop halfway down the strip, his attention drawn to the hills that loomed in the distance. Snowflakes floated down around him, barely swayed by the gentle breeze that hung in the night. His gaze narrowed on the hills. He reaffirmed his grip on his assault rifle and strode forward once again.

Clong!

The sound was simultaneous with the force that slammed into his face. His nose and mouth contorted; he stumbled backward and toppled onto the ground.

Back at the guard shack, the other Nightman raised a brow.

The fallen Nightman scrambled to his knees and reared his assault rifle. Then he froze.

There was nothing there.

He propped one hand on the ground and pushed himself up; his other hand hovered over his face. His fingers touched the end of his nose, and he felt wetness. Withdrawing his hand, he focused his jostled gaze on his fingertips. Blood. His nose was busted open.

He shot up a sharp glance, his eyes flitting in every direction. But there was nothing. Only hills loomed in the distance, and only the snowflakes drifted in the air. All was quiet. He was alone.

Then he stopped.

In front of his face, splattered unceremoniously against the surface of the air, was his own blood. He blinked as it dripped down the surface of nothing whatsoever and trickled into invisible indentations and unseen curves. He stared at it for several seconds, and then he took a step back. His gaze widened the moment he did.

None of the snow that fell over the airstrip was reaching the ground. Something was stopping it before it could. Slowly and with realization, the Nightman's eyes widened.

Spinning to face the guard shack, he shouted, *"Noboats!"*

The armada, already on the ground, materialized one ship after the other. Across the airstrip, their ramps began lowering. Before the fleeing Nightman could scream another word, his back was riddled with plasma.

The other Nightman's jaw hung open as he reached out to sound the alarm. He stared in horror as a wave of plasma missiles screamed toward the guard shack.

21

A WAIL REVERBERATED from the walls of Room 14. Its occupants were brutally awakened—half lurching upright from dead sleeps.

Groaning, Travis slammed his head against his pillow. "Come on, seriously? They're doing this tonight?"

From the next bunk over, Fox muttered and wrapped up in his covers.

Boom!

The floor trembled—those soldiers who'd closed their eyes opened them again.

Boom!

Galina gasped and leapt out of her bunk. "This is *real!*"

Shooting a glance at Galina and then to the wall, Scott listened as shouts rang out from the neighboring room. Jolted from its slumber-induced lull, Scott's heart was suddenly pounding.

"Everyone up!" shouted Baranov as he charged for the weapons locker. "This is not a drill!" The room burst to life as the soldiers dove out of bed and scrambled to their closets. Within seconds, Baranov was passing out assault rifles and handguns. Another explosion shook the earth.

"What about the captain?" asked Galina as she shoved her hands through the sleeves of her uniform. "He is in his private quarters!"

Feet from her, Dostoevsky queued up Clarke through his comm. "Dostoevsky to Clarke."

Clarke's voice crackled back almost immediately. "*Yes, I feel it! I'm on my way—everyone, prepare for combat!*"

"Combat against *what?*" Dostoevsky asked.

"I don't yet know, leftenant."

"Is the base under attack?" Scott asked as he slammed a magazine into an E-35.

David loaded a pistol and said back, "Sure feels like it, compadre!"

The entire foundation of *Novosibirsk* shook—as the ceiling lights swayed and flickered, the whole of Room 14 looked up at them.

Approaching Scott and David, Becan said, "This would be abou' the time they tell us to turn on our TCVS if our armor wasn't in the *bloody transport!*"

Once more, the building shook—but this time, with force that could be felt.

"That felt like something just took a chunk out of the building!" said Kevin.

As if on cue, Clarke's voice emerged through the comm again—this time, unit-wide. "Squad, we have a problem!"

"We felt it," Baranov answered.

"A plasma missile just took out one of B-1's outer walls!" said Clarke.

A plasma missile? Wide-eyed, Scott looked at David and Becan with urgency.

The captain continued. "There are Bakma soldiers on the premises! I cannot make it to your position. The officers' wing is completely cut off. We're being forced outside." Clarke's voice competed with what sounded like abject chaos on his side of the channel. Weapons fire, screaming... total mayhem. "Ivan, you're—"

And that was it. No final word. No burst of static. The transmission just died. Across the room, Galina gasped.

"Oh veck, he's *dead!*" said Travis.

Was he? The transmission just died—that didn't mean the *captain* died. Still, this was all kinds of bad. Outside, a veritable stampede of footsteps resounded through the halls. Looking to Baranov, Scott and the rest of the Fourteenth awaited the executor's response.

It did not take long. Readying his E-35, Baranov said, "They are moving in the hall. So must we. Wherever they are going, we will go also—that is where the conflict is."

"But the captain!" said Galina. "Vanya, we must not leave him."

"Whatever is happening, it is happening fast," Baranov said. "We cannot afford to send soldiers to someone who may already be dead." Before Galina could retort, Baranov went on. "I do not like it, either. But we have no choice."

Clarke. All the warnings, all the calls to heed his words about *Novosibirsk* that he'd shared with Scott and his friends upon their arrival. If the captain was a Nightman, would they send someone after him then? Scott didn't know the answer—all he knew was that at that moment, he

felt some of the most gut-wrenching hurt he'd felt since putting on an
EDEN uniform. Yet he could not refute the executor's words. It was clear
this was bigger than one man. There was no way they could afford to send
a team after the captain.

But they could afford to send one man. Before Scott even realized
what he was doing, he looked at Baranov and said, "I'll go after him, sir."

David grabbed him on the shoulder. "Scott, you can't—"

"You know vecking well, I can," Scott said. Cougar in Chicago. Svetlana
in Siberia. Rescues were what he did. He could tell by the look in David's
eyes that his older friend knew it.

So did Baranov. Looking at Scott, he nodded his head a single time.
"Go. Quickly."

He could do quickly.

Gesturing to Varvara, Baranov said, "Go with him, Varya."

"Da, executor," Varvara said, making her way across the room to Scott.
Pistol in hand, she locked eyes with him and nodded.

"Everyone else," Baranov said, "with me!"

Acknowledging, the soldiers of Room 14 made their way into the halls.

However chaotic the hallways had sounded from Room 14, the reality
was worse than Scott could have imagined. Frantic soldiers were running en masse toward the main exit, which was in the opposite direction
of where Scott needed to go. Though he had intended to go after Clarke
alone, Scott was thankful Varvara was with him—not only in the event
that Clarke was injured but because Scott had no idea where the captain's
private quarters actually were.

Using some of the barrack's back hallways, he and Varvara were able
to circumvent most of the freneticism of the barracks' mass exodus. With
everyone in the barracks *leaving* the facility either to fight or escape, it
wasn't long until the pair found themselves the only two traversing the
hallways. Though combat could be heard in the distance, none was in
their immediate area.

"We are almost there," said Varvara as they rounded a final turn on
the back route. As soon as they did, they saw firsthand what Clarke had
been talking about on the comm. The hallway was smoldering far ahead of
them, what once must have been a fire kept at bay by overhead sprinklers.

Taking point now that he knew where he was, Scott raised a fist to
indicate a slower pace. Regripping and raising his assault rifle, he bristled
for a shower and stalked forward.

WHEN BARANOV AND the others emerged outside, *Novosibirsk*'s situation became clear. Far from the barracks—in the direction of the airstrip—plasma fire lit the sky. Orange plumes exploded against the hangars as the sounds of total warfare ripped apart the night. Units and individual soldiers stampeded ahead.

"This is *not* good," Travis said as he reached for his handgun.

Before anyone else could comment, a squad of Bakma emerged west of the barracks. A wave of plasma streaked past; Baranov swiveled around and dropped to a knee. "Bakma!" The rest of the Fourteenth followed suit; the whole squad returned fire.

"Bollocks," Becan said, "they're this far in *already*?"

Fractured chatter burst through Baranov's comm, and he ducked out of the fight. Dostoevsky took his place at the lead.

David fired a shot, and a Bakma fell. Two more alien squads emerged from beyond the cafeteria. Another explosion rocked the hangar. Human screams filled the air.

As Becan trained down his E-35, he swung to Fox. "How many do yeh think there are?"

"I don't know!" Fox answered. "And I don't like not knowing!"

Baranov returned to the unit. "Everyone! I have news on the situation. Over two dozen Noboats have materialized on the airstrip! Four Bakma Carriers have been detected on approach."

"*Four?*" asked Becan incredulously. "This isn't an attack, it's a bleedin' invasion!"

Baranov continued. "We are to dispatch a team to Confinement. Bakma are heading in that direction right now. If they discover captives, they will surely release them." He turned to Dostoevsky. "Yuri, you will lead the defense effort there. Take McCrae. Two other teams are on their way there, but right now, we are the closest."

Dostoevsky motioned to Becan. The two men pulled out of the fight.

"Jurgen," Baranov said to David, "you and Boris make your way to the infirmary. They are attempting an evacuation. Assist as best you can!"

David looked at Boris, and the two men left immediately.

"Everyone else, come with me to the airstrip!"

SCOTT WIPED WATER from his face. Step after cautious step, he stalked ahead with his weapon aimed. Wherever Clarke was, he'd been close to this place. That meant the Bakma Clarke saw were close, too.

Besides the fact that he and Varvara were getting soaked by the sprinklers without their armor, there was another significant detriment to not having it: with the nav suite in Scott's visor HUD, he would have been able to locate the captain immediately. As it stood, he and Varvara could only keep their eyes peeled and their ears tuned for any signs of human activity.

It did not take long to find some. No sooner had they reached the smoldering rubble pile did the sound of nearby weapons fire catch their ears. The actual rubble itself was part of the outside wall of the barracks, which had collapsed and exposed that part of the building to the outside. And it was there—outside of the barracks just on the other side of the rubble—that the battle was taking place. Orange flashes of what looked like pistol fire stood out against a considerably larger onslaught of white plasma. There was no way to determine if one of the soldiers firing was Clarke, but it was clear to Scott that whoever was firing would be overrun if backup didn't arrive. Thankfully for them, backup had.

Taking position inside the building and using the rubble as a shield, Scott quickly took in the scene. The Bakma force consisted of no less than ten warriors, situated outside between Scott and the other human soldiers and using a pair of dumpsters as cover. Scott had a clean shot on them. Looking at Varvara, he said, "Once I start firing, they're going to know we're here. You got my back?"

Varvara nodded and readied her pistol.

There was no time to waste. Rising from behind the rubble, Scott aimed at the cluster of aliens and opened fire. Next to him, Varvara did the same.

Bullets dinged against the metal surface of the dumpsters; several Bakma were struck and fell. Immediately, the cluster of aliens dispersed, some resituating themselves around the dumpsters to try and cover themselves from both Scott and Varvara's attacks, while others dashed for the very rubble pile Scott was covering behind. Scott laid his finger down on the trigger, but waves of plasma forced him back. The goal, however, had been accomplished. The Bakma, disoriented from a new attack from their blind side, faced sudden new vulnerability from the human soldiers they were initially engaging. And those soldiers, on cue, were taking advantage of it.

But it wasn't enough to stop all of them. Half of the cluster of Bakma that'd been covering behind the dumpsters had made the charge for the rubble pile—and it quickly became clear to Scott that every single one of them was going to make it. "Fall back!" he called to Varvara. Slipping and sliding as they abandoned their doomed cover, they tore off down the hallways of the barracks.

BACK ON THE airstrip, Bakma surged toward *Novosibirsk*'s main building and hangar. As EDEN forces moved to intercept them, they were met by a torrent of plasma fire. All around them, in every direction, there was destruction. Grizzly APCs burned in their garages. Vindicator fighters were blasted before they could leave the ground. Charred pieces of armor and flesh lay scattered amid the concrete.

Far in the night sky, the lights of four Bakma Carriers grew large among the stars.

SCOTT WAS FIRING for all he was worth, he and Varvara suddenly finding themselves pursued by the very Bakma they'd gotten the jump on from behind. Their boots skidded and slipped on the wet floor beneath them—plasma bolts streaked past their heads. There were no corners to turn, no intersections to retreat around. There was just a straight hallway lined with doors.

But at least there *were* doors. Tugging Varvara with him, Scott ran to the door nearest them. Twisting the knob violently and shoving it open, he bolted into the room with Varvara hot on his heels.

The room was roughly the size of Room 14 but devoid of bunks. Instead, rows of chairs all pointed at a large display screen on the wall—like some kind of briefing room.

Scott could hear the Bakma behind them. The aliens were drawing nearer with each passing second. As he and Varvara rushed farther into the room, he realized the direness of their situation. The chairs barely qualified as cover. There was nowhere in the room they could hide. As the pair slid behind the furthest row of chairs in the room, they looked at one another with dread. Outnumbered two, perhaps threefold, there was no way Scott and Varvara would win in a shootout. And with nowhere to run...

The Bakma voices grew closer. They were seconds away from entering the room and making short work of whatever resistance Scott and Varvara could throw at them. Scott's mind raced. He looked desperately around the room for anything he could use to their advantage. His breath caught when he found it.

With hurried hands, Scott pulled out his comm.

The first pair of Bakma who entered the room did so with weapons raised and dark eyes searching. Behind them, two more pairs followed suit. With their gnarled talons on the triggers ready to fire, they instead found their collective focus drawn to the large display screen on the wall. To the human female on it with dark, angular eyes.

"Scott Remington!" the female screamed. "This is your best friend in the universe, Nikki Dupree, with an important announcement!"

The Bakma stared at the video with perplexity.

"I just thought I would send you this message at nine o'clock in the morning to saaay...I passed my nursing final! *Whooo!*"

They watched as she jumped up and down—seconds later, spray enveloped her.

Those were the only seconds Scott needed. Rising from where he'd maneuvered behind the aliens, he rose to his feet, aimed his weapon, and opened fire.

Despite the briefness of the aliens' diverted focus, it was mistake enough for Scott to even the odds. Three of the aliens succumbed to his initial burst. From across the room, Varvara's aim found its own target. Sprays of blood joined sprays of apple cider as the two remaining Bakma scrambled for cover. Nicole's words were lost amid a cacophony of weapons fire.

A plasma bolt obliterated several chairs just to Scott's right. He dove, rolled, and came up on a knee to return fire. Though his shots missed their mark, they were enough to grant Varvara a second of repositioning. With an open shot available, the medic took it. Struck in the torso, the Bakma grunted and ducked for cover.

Scott's attention went straight to the other Bakma, who was running across the room toward Varvara. Aiming his assault rifle, he fired off a burst that struck the alien in the neck. Blood splattered the display screen, where Nicole's friends were still christening her. After scrambling to his feet, Scott dashed for the front of the room to get a clear shot at the last alien remaining—the one Varvara had injured. Scott raised his weapon just as the Bakma reached for a plasma grenade. A single shot ended the alien's effort.

Six aliens down.

Varvara rose from her position behind some of the chairs. After looking briefly at Nicole's still-playing video, her gaze returned to Scott. "Good idea," she said, huffing as she wiped damp strands back over her head.

Exhaling a heavy breath himself, Scott nodded a single time, then gestured to the door. "Come on, let's go." Varvara complied, and the two left the conference room to return to the hall.

Left behind in the room, Nicole's uploaded video looped back to the start.

No sooner had Scott and Varvara returned to the hall than they saw a small gang of soldiers emerge through the smoke and sprinklers. Leading the group was Captain Clarke.

"Remington?" Clarke said incredulously as he saw Scott for the first time. "What the devil are you doing here?"

"Saving *you*," said Varvara as she emerged behind Scott.

Scott approached the captain and said, "We heard your comm cut off in mid-sentence, sir. Varya and I came after you while everybody else went to the hangar."

"Well, I'm bloody glad you did," Clarke said. "Those Bakma came at us when we ran outside to see what was happening. We weren't going to last where they pinned us."

Looking over him, Varvara arched an eyebrow. "Are you hurt, captain?"

"No, thank the gods."

Scott, too, looked at him curiously. "Oh. I think we all assumed you got shot."

"What, because of the comm?" Clarke asked. "No, I didn't get shot. The bloody thing just stopped working!"

Blinking, Scott said, "Seriously?" When Clarke held up his comm to show its undamaged state, Scott said, "Wow. That is…some kind of bad luck, sir."

Clarke smirked. "We call that proper jinxed, epsilon—but it got the two of you here, and I'm not sure how much longer we'd have lasted without the help. I'll take it." His voice grew more stern. "You said the rest of the unit had gone to the airstrip?" When Scott nodded, Clarke gestured to his comm. "May I?"

"Absolutely," said Scott, handing his comm to the captain immediately.

As Clarke turned to march back up the hall toward the rubble mound, he spoke into the comm. "Executor Baranov, this is Clarke."

Taking a moment to catch his breath, Scott crouched and lowered his head. He ran a hand through his hair and exhaled. A second later, Varvara crouched beside him and massaged her hand on his back. "You were *awesome* back there," he said as he looked at her.

"You were, too!"

He held his hand out for her to grip. When she did so, he said, "Good team."

Wiping damp strands from her face, she cracked a grin. "Good team."

Static bursts emerged over the comm, followed by the echo of weapons fire. Seconds later, Baranov's voice finally appeared. "Good to hear you, captain!"

"What's our situation?"

Baranov could be heard shouting in Russian, presumably at others nearby. Then he answered, "I have sent Dostoevsky and McCrae to Confinement to secure it. Jurgen and Evteev, I have sent to the infirmary. The rest are with me on the airstrip."

Speaking off comm, Clarke said, "That's a lot of splitting up." Pressing the transmit button, he relayed to Baranov, "Very well. We're on our way to the airstrip now. I'll get a proper sitrep when I arrive at your location."

"Da, captain."

Closing the channel, he said, "Well, we've no time to waste." He indicated to Scott's comm, still in his hand. "Do you mind if I keep this?"

"Not at all, sir." As if the captain had to ask permission. "Does the executor really think aliens might break out of Confinement?" Scott asked, bristling again as they marched through the sprinklers.

Clarke slammed a fresh magazine into his assault rifle. "He wouldn't send people if there wasn't a concern. Personally, I'd rather be in Confinement than where we're about to go."

"Why, sir?"

Pointing toward the airstrip as they emerged outside, Clarke answered, "Because Confinement doesn't look like *that*."

Following Clarke's gaze, Scott saw the flashes of weapons fire, both plasma and projectile. The bursts exploded like fireworks. "I see your point, sir."

With no further commentary, Scott and Varvara followed Clarke toward the hangar.

"RUN FASTER!" DOSTOEVSKY yelled back to Becan as the pair ran toward the Research Center. The Research Center was located, quite appropriately, at the center of *Novosibirsk*. And in the heart of it was Alien Confinement. Despite its relative distance to the airstrip, some Bakma had already reached the building's perimeter, where a stronghold of EDEN soldiers was fighting to keep them at bay.

After propelling himself up the outer stairs of the building, Dostoevsky jerked the door open and waved Becan in. "Inside, go!"

Wincing at the sheer volume of the combat taking place not twenty meters away, Becan asked as he bolted up the stairs, "Are we supposed to hold this place off by *ourselves*?" He watched a pair of EDEN security guards succumb to plasma fire. "*Veck!*"

Dostoevsky didn't bother to answer, the lieutenant's focus purely on speed as he charged through the halls of the Research Center. Sirens pulsed throughout the building as entire teams of scientists elbowed their way to the exit. Far ahead down the central hall were the double doors to Alien Confinement.

Dostoevsky pointed. "Confinement is ahead! Watch for—"

Two Bakma emerged from the opposite end of the hall. Dostoevsky flipped out his handgun and launched four shots—two for each chest. The Bakmas' backs hit the wall, and they slid to the floor.

"...for resistance."

They reached the double doors a moment later. As the doors whisked open, Dostoevsky darted inside. Four scientists were huddled behind a workstation. "Down," Dostoevsky said. The scientists ducked out of view.

Becan followed Dostoevsky into the room, gaping at what he saw there. Four cells ran along the back wall, and three cells were on each side of the room. Transparent impact glass shielded the cells' occupants. Every part of the room was stark white.

Four of the cells were inhabited. In the first was a Ceratopian—the first Becan had ever seen. The massive beast towered in its cell. Its entire body was covered in golden, scale-covered skin. Atop its prehistoric-looking head was a bone-plated frill lined with spikes that crested over its skull and arched up. Twin horns protruded from its forehead as a third, smaller horn jetted from its nose. Two smaller horns jutted out the sides of its cheeks—five horns in total, like a pentaceratops. The Ceratopian's brown, penetrating eyes narrowed, and it bellowed.

"Bloody God..."

In the next cell, two Ithini were pressed against the shielding, their opaque eyes watchful of the new action. Two cells down, there were contained three Bakma warriors. But the cell Becan's eyes shot to was the one in the rightmost corner.

Inside it was a necrilid. Though the creature was motionless, the glass was ravaged with claw marks. "Bollocks," said Becan with dread.

The Ceratopian rammed its horned frill into the glass and growled.

Dostoevsky took position outside the double doors. "Confinement isolated," he said through his comm.

CLARKE HEARD THE transmission as soon as he reached the airstrip. "I copy that, leftenant," he answered as he, Scott, and Varvara took position behind a dismantled Grizzly APC—the same one Baranov and his team were already covering behind.

"Good to hear you, captain," Dostoevsky said.

"It's good to be *alive*, leftenant."

Baranov chimed in on his comm from several feet away. "Yuri, the other teams going to Confinement should get to you soon!"

Scott looked around the edge of the Grizzly as the Noboat fleet came into his view for the first time. The airstrip was an enemy fortress. As EDEN soldiers flooded the area around the hangar, plasma bolts and plasma missiles soared from the invaders. Part of the hangar itself was engulfed in fire. Bodies spilled across the ground. On the other end of the airstrip, behind the Noboats, four gargantuan Bakma Carriers descended with thundering thrust.

Scott stared in stunned amazement. How had this happened? How could a whole fleet appear out of nowhere? Were the invaders really *that* superior? There was no time to think about answers and less time to think about questions. Scott dropped to a knee at the corner of the Grizzly, propped up his assault rifle, and opened fire.

"I'm ready for that sitrep, executor!" Clarke said to Baranov.

Baranov looked at Clarke for a moment, then pointed to the airstrip. "That is it."

Nodding his head as if he'd known that was coming, Clarke said, "Message received." The captain's gaze then swiveled around them—to the battle taking place, to the soldiers he had with him, to the hangar slowly burning. The soldiers around him, their focuses momentarily averted from the carnage, watched as his wheels of mitigation turned. Then, he spoke. "All right, crew, here's the plan. Travis," he said, eyeing the pilot, "get in that hangar and fire up the *Pariah*. Back her out of the rear of the hangar because, at any moment, it's going to come down."

"Aye-aye, sir!" Travis said.

"Powers and Timmons, find height and engage," Clarke said. "See if

you can make any difference in that hellscape on the airfield." Acknowledging, the two snipers took off toward a nearby guard tower. "Everyone
else, it's time to gear up properly! Remington and Yudina, get to the
Pariah, get your armor, then get back here. Executor Baranov and Lebesheva, do the same after they return. Carpenter and I will go last—by
the time we get geared up and back, Travis should have the ship revved
up and ready to reverse."

Scott locked eyes with Varvara—she nodded her head back at him
with purpose.

Slapping Scott on the shoulder, Clarke said, "Get moving, you two—
and grab me a replacement comm, while you're at it!"

Without a word, Scott and Varvara ran behind Travis toward the
Pariah in the hangar.

Across the airfield, the four Bakma Carriers touched down. Setting
his jaw, Clarke said to Kevin beside him, "Things are about to get considerably more difficult."

Kevin surveyed the fiery furnace that was the airstrip—and the human
bodies sprawled across it. Looking at Clarke, he arched an eyebrow. "*This*
isn't difficult?"

Clarke said nothing, and the two men fired their assault rifles at the
alien swarm.

DAVID AND BORIS arrived at the infirmary just as an attack on it began. A
squad of EDEN soldiers held off the Bakma forces that threatened, though
they were outnumbered threefold.

The evacuation of the infirmary was in progress as surgeons and nurses
dodged past David and Boris, wheeling the bedded patients in their care.
Some unattended patients crawled from their beds and hobbled away
from the fight themselves. Explosions boomed behind the building, and
the earth shook.

Grabbing the nearest surgeon, a heavyset man with a patient in a
wheelchair, David asked, "What do you need?"

The surgeon pointed to the patient. "I could use one more person for
this one!" He motioned to the center of the infirmary. "But they need
more help than I do!"

David said to Boris, "I'll help in the infirmary. You help him, then
come back to me."

Boris nodded and took the wheelchair's handles.

David weaved through the mass of nurses and patients until he found two aides. They struggled to lift an unconscious man into a wheelchair. David brushed past them, locked his arms around the man, and lifted him into the chair.

One of the aides said, "Spasibo balshoye!"

"What else can I do?" David asked.

The aide's mouth hung open for a moment. "Here," she enunciated as she pointed to several more bedridden patients. "Help?"

"Absolutely," David answered as he joined her in the effort.

THE GARBLED SOUNDS of Bakmanese echoed down the halls of the Research Center. Dostoevsky readied his position in the hallway. "They're coming," he said to Becan.

Inside Confinement, the Ceratopian bashed its fists against the glass.

Becan took to Dostoevsky's side and propped himself into a ready position as the four scientists brandished handguns and focused on the Research Center's entrance behind them.

The Bakma grew louder down the hallway, their footsteps clopping against the floor. Dostoevsky's glare focused on the corner. "Get ready."

A Bakma attacker burst into view. Dostoevsky fired his pistol, and the alien fell. Two more Bakma leaned their plasma rifles around the corner and fired. Dostoevsky flinched as the shots careened against the walls.

"Reinforcements!" one of the scientists yelled.

Becan looked back, where four EDEN soldiers charged into the Research Center.

The Bakma fired around the corner again. Dostoevsky and Becan ducked in avoidance as the four scientists fled into Confinement to make room for the reinforcements.

"What unit are you in?" Dostoevsky asked the four EDEN soldiers as they arrived and took positions beside him.

"The Twenty-first!" one of them answered.

A plasma bolt whizzed past Dostoevsky's head. He fired off a shot with his pistol and cut the attacker down. "How many more are coming?"

"We are it."

A team of Bakma broke through the Research Center's main entrance. "Behind us!" Becan said. He and Dostoevsky ducked into Confinement to avoid being caught in a plasma bolt crossfire.

"We cannot hold the doorway!" Dostoevsky said as he returned to the door to attempt sporadic suppression fire. "They will press here soon!"

Behind them, the necrilid came to life. Its claws and fangs collided with the glass shield as it lurched forward with primal aggression.

Dostoevsky sunk back into Confinement to reload. A scientist replaced him in the doorway.

"This isn't going so well!" Becan said as he narrowly avoided getting his head fried by a plasma bolt.

Dostoevsky looked at the computer console inside the room. He slid behind it, and his fingers worked the controls. "Hold them off a little longer!"

BARANOV GROWLED AS a plasma bolt seared past his shoulder, its proximity causing his skin to burn briefly. He took cover behind a chunk of debris, gritted his teeth, and reloaded his assault rifle.

Across the airstrip, the Bakma Carriers opened their doors.

Slamming a new magazine into his assault rifle, Kevin called out, "Here they come!"

Bakma poured from the Carriers.

"*Now* it's going to get difficult!" Clarke said.

The Bakma charged forth like hell-sent marauders. Flashes of orange and yellow reflected in their eyes as their alien war cries filled the air. As they stormed the airstrip, the barrels of their plasma rifles burst with fire.

THE HANGAR WAS a blazing inferno. Scott kept his pace only so slow that Varvara and Travis could keep up with him—and not a fraction slower. Fortuitous for the Fourteenth, the *Pariah* was parked toward the back of the hangar—the farthest point from where the fires were breaking out. But that would only matter for so long. The fire was spreading quickly—much more so than Scott felt Clarke was aware. With his gaze on the flames, he was about to call an audible. "Travis…" he said warily.

"Yeah, I see it!" the pilot answered.

"I don't think Clarke's plan is gonna work!"

Pointing to the back entrance to the hangar, Travis said, "There's a manual override you're gonna have to operate to get the back door open! You see that winch?"

Scott looked toward the near edge of the back door. "Yeah, I think so!"

"Input the password 11731 in that console next to it. That'll release the winch for use. Use it to pull open the door!"

He could do that.

"I'll get the ship fired up in the meantime."

From beside them, Varvara asked, "What I to do?"

"Get geared up," Scott answered. "I've got the winch."

The trio split up, Travis and Varvara to the *Pariah* and Scott to the back hangar door. Skidding to a stop, Scott wiped the sweat from his brow and inputted the code—incorrectly. "*Veck!*" Shaking his head, he found the correct numbers the second time. A green light by the winch illuminated, indicating its release. Gripping the handle with both hands, he pulled back the crank.

Instantly, he knew he was in trouble. This was no smoothly operating system. The gears turned like they'd never seen oil. Scott's muscles flexed, and he grimaced. Slowly—*ever* so slowly—the crank turned. Sparing glances between his straining, he looked up at the hangar's back door. The rate at which it was opening was excruciatingly slow.

This was hard. This was beyond hard. This was mind over matter like he'd never exhibited in his life. He could *feel* his muscle fibers tearing with every rotation. Heaving with his teeth clenched, he looked at the door again.

Two feet. Three feet. Four feet. The gap was widening, but at this rate, his body would give out long before the door was opened. He'd have nothing left for the fight that awaited.

Scott flinched as someone ran up from behind him. Hands still on the crank handle, he watched as Varvara slid into a position across from him, still dressed only in her uniform. Raising her eyebrows, she asked, "Need help?"

Did he ever. Nodding, for it was all he could muster, he maneuvered his hands to make room for hers on the handle. Holding his breath, he nodded at her and yanked back on the crank again.

One rotation. Then another. Then another. Varvara's help by no means made it easy, but it felt worlds less insurmountable than when he was going at it alone. Still, he found himself grunting with every turn. Varvara fared no better, heaving, then gasping, then clenching her teeth so hard it looked like they were about to shatter. "*Oh Bozhe moy!*" she cried through her straining. Scott had no idea what it meant, but it sounded about like he felt. Digging down deep, the pair grinded on.

"Come on, baby," Travis said, engaging the *Pariah*'s auxiliary power unit. The small starter turbines began to rotate as a low whine emerged from the engines. "How we looking back there, guys?" he asked himself off-comm as he looked in the transport's side-mounted rearview mirror. Far behind the ship, Scott and Varvara could be seen doing their work.

Twelve feet. Fifteen feet. Eighteen. The sensation in Scott's arms had transcended pain and was now approaching numbness. More drenched by sweat than they had been by water under the sprinklers, the pair had managed to find a rhythm that was working—provided neither of them stopped. By the adrenaline-induced fury in Varvara's eyes, she wasn't going to any time soon. Neither was he.

"Almost there!" he screamed. "We're almost there!" The temperature in the room was skyrocketing as the flames spread more quickly. Soon, the entire hangar would be engulfed. Overcome by emotion, Scott hollered at her, *"Give me all you got!"*

She was. With every turn, the medic screamed louder. Until finally... ...the winch stopped.

Varvara released the handle, practically falling over before managing to stop herself. Both she and Scott stared up at the hangar's back door.

It was fully open.

Scott couldn't contain it. Pumping his fist, he shouted, *"That's right!"* as if he'd just thrown a seventy-yard strike. Varvara looked at him, laughed in pure enervation, then reached out her hand. Scott clasped it hard—but just for a moment. Turning their shared focus to the *Pariah*, they nodded at one another and then took off for it at full speed.

Travis looked back at Scott and Varvara when he heard them run into the ship. "Nice work, guys!" Engaging the transport's reversers, he guided the *Pariah* slowly backward through the rearview.

Grabbing a water bottle from back storage, Scott twisted it violently open and then tilted it straight up. What he didn't down in large gulps, he poured over his head. By her locker, Varvara did the same. Wiping water from her face and smoothing back her hair, she looked at him. Once more, a grin crept out. "Still good team?"

He laughed a single time, exhaustedly. "Still good team."

Scott's focus shifted to getting into his armor. With each clasp of that resplendent mother-of-pearl, he felt his adrenaline burn hotter. Leg guards. Arm guards. Chest plate, complete with golden collar. With every piece that latched into place, he felt more and more complete. More and more invincible. These Bakma had come to *Novosibirsk* looking for a fight. They were about to get one.

Slamming his helmet down over his head, he stared through the visor as its HUD engaged. Though he could feel the *Pariah* moving, it wasn't enough to shake him. After what he and Varvara had just done, nothing was.

After putting on her own helmet, Varvara focused on him. Scott's HUD identified her immediately, with the words "V. Yudina" appearing in the top corner with her heart rate, which looked about like his felt. "You ready to save some lives?" he asked her confidently.

"You ready to kill some?" she shot back.

It wasn't what a righteous man was supposed to want. Every life—young, old, human, alien—was something special. A tailor-made God-gift to the universe. In a perfect world, killing was never supposed to be the goal. But this world wasn't perfect. Slamming a fresh magazine into his E-35, he said, "Yeah, I am."

Slowly, the *Pariah* eased out of the hangar.

THE SITUATION BY the airstrip was growing more dire with every minute. Bakma were charging from the Carriers toward *Novosibirsk*'s main building. What little resistance EDEN had mustered was quickly losing ground.

Jayden and Fox were situated atop a guard tower near Clarke and those with him, where they rained precision fire onto the impending throng. The tower was two stories tall, and the rim around it gave them a measure of cover.

Jayden's eyes narrowed as he pulled the trigger. A Bakma dropped to the ground.

Fox slid his scope over the Carriers, where several canrassis lumbered down the ramps. Atop them, riders manned their mounted plasma cannons. "Canrassis," Fox said as he aimed at one of the riders' heads. He snapped off a shot, and the Bakma toppled to the ground. "I've got these, keep track below."

"I'm on 'em," Jayden answered.

FROM THE COVER of the dismantled Grizzly, Clarke fired with abandon. He and his soldiers unloaded their ammunition on the battlefield, though it made nary a dent. There were too many Bakma. When one fell, two others took its place.

"Captain!"

Turning around, Clarke registered Scott, Travis, and Varvara approaching—all three were armored, and all three carried large, filled-to-the-brim

354   Dawn of Destiny

duffle bags over their shoulders. Ducking behind cover, Clarke looked at Scott's golden-trimmed armor and said, "Now *that's* a sight for sore eyes."

Tossing down his duffle bag, Scott knelt and quickly ripped open the zipper. It was armor. Looking at Clarke, he said, "We got gear for you, the executor, Galina, and Kevin—it's all we could carry." Holding up the spare comm, Scott said, "As requested, sir."

"Bloody *brilliant*," Clarke said, snatching the new comm and returning his commandeered one to Scott. "Everyone, fall back and get in your gear!" Looking at Scott, Travis, and Varvara, he said, "Can the three of you hold down this fort?"

"We can try, sir." Replacing Clarke at the edge of the Grizzly, Scott leaned around to fire into the approaching throng. On the APC's opposite side, Travis and Varvara did the same.

There were so many Bakma. Swiveling his assault rifle from target to target, Scott fired relentlessly. The truth was, it scarcely mattered whether or not any of his shots connected. The Bakma were moving in like a tidal wave. Looking behind him, he watched Clarke, Baranov, Galina, and Kevin throw on their armor. In the face of what was coming, their effort to carry the gear almost seemed fruitless now. Would it even make a difference? Whether it would or not, they had to fight on. Scott's focus returned to the fray, and he reached for a fresh magazine. In the second he did, a loud whiz reached his ears. Behind his visor, his eyes widened.

A plasma missile.

Before he could whip up his head to find the streaking missile, the nose of the Grizzly exploded, violently thrusting him backward. The APC lurched upward, and Scott, Travis, and Varvara scattered as it crashed upside down against the concrete. It was by the grace of God alone that it hadn't landed on top of them.

Just the same, what had just been sound cover was now a smoldering heap. As Scott, Travis, and Varvara found themselves running toward a concrete barricade, Clarke and the others, all of whom had only just donned their armor, found themselves out in the open—and running in opposite directions. While Clarke bolted for Scott's position, Kevin ran toward a forklift in front of the engulfed hangar. As for Baranov and Galina, they ran toward a stack of supply crates just off the airstrip.

Heart pounding, Scott raised his E-35 and opened fire at the Bakma nearest them, desperate to provide Clarke and Kevin—the two closest to him—with some sort of suppressive cover.

It half worked. In the same second that Clarke dove behind the concrete barricade that Scott was behind, a flash of white erupted against Kevin's side while he was still out in the open. Moments later, a second shot impacted the side of his helmet. Kevin's head rocked unnaturally sideways, and the soldier slumped and fell. Wincing his teeth, Scott looked away briefly before forcing himself to look again—as if perhaps Kevin might be miraculously back on his feet after a second glance. But no miracles were in play.

"He's dead," Clarke said as he rose behind the barricade to fire at the Bakma army. "There's nothing we can do."

There were no moments to spare for the fallen. Leaning around the concrete barricade, Scott opened fire on the advancing enemy.

THE INFIRMARY WAS chaos. David was trying his best to assist the aide he'd been following around, though with the constant flow of doctors, nurses, and wounded, it was just as hard to keep up with her as it was to evacuate her patients.

Amid the bustle, David's eyes caught sight of a familiar face. Max. The newly christened lieutenant struggled to wrench free from a nurse as he tried to push himself up from a wheelchair.

"Do not get up!" the nurse said. "You are not in right condition!"

"I are not stay!" Max snapped back in intentionally broken English. "I go to fighting! You go to hell!"

David abandoned the aide and rushed to Max's side. "Lieutenant, what are you doing?"

Max gave him a withering look. "Not being a gutless wonder." He shoved to his feet against the nurse's demands. He swept his hand to David's belt and snatched David's handgun from its holster. "I need armor. And you. We're about to dial up some payback."

David smirked. "Yes, sir." He looked around until his eyes came to rest on a nearby soldier. "He looks about your size."

Max nodded. "Get going toward the entrance. That's where they're feeling the most heat. Don't wait for me—you can go faster by yourself. I'll meet you there soon!" David turned to go as Max snagged the indicated soldier. "Hey, what size are you?"

The soldier hesitated. "But sir, I'm—"

"And I'm a lieutenant, half-wit, now get out of that armor!"

ON THE AIRSTRIP, the canrassis' mounted plasma cannons exploded with white as the bear-sized war beasts tromped ahead. Their spider eyes darted around the battlefield as their Bakma masters directed them onward.

The forces of EDEN wallowed in futility. Squads were split in half. Officers were separated from their soldiers. Pilots who'd been attempting to rescue their aircraft fled from the hangar.

It was an onslaught.

THE BATTLE RAGED in the halls of the Research Center. Becan and the security guards were burning through ammunition as the Bakma pressed closer and closer in the hallways. Dostoevsky remained inside behind the computers, hands flying across the console.

As a plasma bolt struck the wall next to him, Becan recoiled. "Whatever you're doin', lieutenant, yeh better do it quick! We can't hold them back much longer!"

Dostoevsky looked up from the console. "Everyone clear the door, now. Get inside!" Everyone did as ordered, and the doors to Confinement slid shut. Within seconds, Bakma stormed the hall outside.

Becan propped his hands against his knees and heaved in exhaustion. "A lot o' bloody good *this* does! Now we're trapped!"

Dostoevsky remained behind the console, and two of the empty cells whooshed open. He pointed to the scientists. "You four, get in that cell!" They complied and rushed to the nearest one. "Everyone else get in the other!" Dostoevsky worked the controls, and the scientists were sealed behind the glass barrier. Dostoevsky said to Becan and the security guards, "Stay in the open cell! I will remain here behind the controls! I will open the door to Confinement and let the Bakma in. Then, I will release the necrilid."

Becan's eyes almost popped out. "You're goin' to do *what*?"

"That is why you will stay in your cell!" Dostoevsky answered. "Your cell will stay open, but you will be out of the necrilid's path."

One of the guards stepped forward. "Executor, you will be right in front of it."

"Yes," Dostoevsky said, "but the Bakma will be the ones moving. I feel lucky." Becan and the guard looked doubtful. They back-stepped into the open cell, and soon, Dostoevsky was alone by the console. "Is everyone ready?" Inside its cell, the necrilid rasped at the glass. "Opening the doors now!" Dostoevsky's hands flew from one side of the control board to the other.

The main doors to Confinement slid open. Moments later, so did the necrilid's. The Bakma charged inside. Dostoevsky ducked.

It took less than two seconds for the first Bakma to fall. The necrilid leapt from its cell into the Bakma's chest, clamping its jaws around the Bakma's face and shaking its head violently. The necrilid released its first victim and leapt at the next Bakma, pouncing atop him. Its claws dug into the Bakma's chest as the alien warrior screamed.

The aliens scrambled—some into Confinement and some into the hallway. They trained their plasma rifles on the necrilid as Dostoevsky rose from the console.

"Engage!"

Becan and the security guards dashed from their cell into the room. Weapons fire erupted. The fight for Confinement was in full swing.

ATOP THE GUARD tower, Fox and Jayden continued to rain sniper fire. Jayden picked off individual Bakma on the airstrip, while Fox focused on the canrassis and their riders. Six riders and four canrassis had fallen to him thus far.

A burst of white exploded against Fox's trigger hand, and he howled. His sniper rifle flipped from his grasp and flew off the tower's edge. He crumbled to the floor.

Jayden spun around to face him. "Hey man, you all right?"

Fox clenched his teeth and rose to his knees. He clutched his right hand against his stomach.

Jayden drew to his side. "Let me see it."

Fox trembled as he allowed his hand to be viewed. As soon as Jayden saw it, he recoiled backward and twisted his mouth. Fox's right thumb and index finger were blown off. The rest of his hand was a blackened char of blood and bone.

Swallowing hard, Jayden got on his comm. "Medic!"

Clarke's voice crackled through. "What is it, Timmons?"

"Fox is down!"

"Can you move him?"

Jayden paused. "Yes, sir, I can move him!"

Clarke was quick to answer. "I'm sending Remington to assist. Bring him to the ground level!"

"Yes, sir," Jayden answered. "C'mon Fox, we're gettin' you downstairs."

Fox placed his hand on his stomach and trembled to his feet. Jayden balanced him against his body, and they shuffled toward the stairwell.

DAVID WAS EN ROUTE to the infirmary's entrance when he bumped into Boris. The Russian technician was on his way back inside. He spoke before David could open his mouth. "Kostya is dead. He was killed in the explosion on the other side of the medical bay. It was the first place to get hit." Beyond the infirmary, the sound of projectile and plasma grew heavier. The ground vibrated.

David nodded a single time. "Well, let's make sure nobody else dies." Boris agreed.

"I'm going out front," David said. "I think there are enough extra hands here to help now. You keep doing what you're doing."

"Right."

"You be careful back here," David said, shaking Boris's hand.

Before Boris could respond, a third voice interjected.

"Boris! What are you doing here, boy?"

David and Boris looked back to see Max limping toward them in full combat armor. The handgun he'd taken from David was firm in his grasp.

"Didn't you get the memo?" Max asked sarcastically. "Techs are all supposed to die this month."

Boris offered a weak smile. "Bad news for me."

David stepped to Max's side. "Kostya didn't make it."

"Then we'll see him in hell," Max said as he readied his sidearm.

SCOTT WAS READY for Jayden and Fox when they arrived on the ground. "What happened?" Scott asked.

"Look at his hand."

Scott glanced at Fox's hand and shrunk back. "Come on," he said, sliding his arm around Fox's shoulder. "Let's get him to Varya."

THE NECRILID SCREAMED as its plasma-riddled body fell onto Confinement's floor. Bakma entrails lay splattered around it.

The fight raged in every direction. Every time Becan dropped a Bakma, another challenged him from behind. If not for his knack for fighting, he'd have been massacred.

Confinement was utterly overwhelmed.

WHEN SCOTT AND Jayden returned to Clarke's side, the airstrip battle was in full force. Plasma bolts seared past them as explosions rocked the sky.

"Fox is with Varvara!" Scott said. "He's going to be okay."

Clarke flung a grenade toward a cluster of Bakma and ducked back as it detonated. "Good!"

Scott ducked down as a plasma bolt ricocheted off the tower's corner. Everywhere he looked, plasma fire chased him. His body was covered in cuts and scorch marks, and he couldn't remember where any of them had come from.

Behind him, Clarke screamed.

Scott spun around just in time to see the captain collapse to the ground. A hole was torn through the hip of his armor. "Captain!"

Clarke's teeth grinded. *"I'm bloody all right!"*

Before Scott could respond, Clarke grabbed him by the collar. Scott was jerked to the ground. Behind him, a plasma bolt shattered the concrete where he had just stood.

Scott scrambled to his feet as Clarke pulled himself to cover. Jayden fell back to match them.

"Where *is* Varvara?" Clarke said as he tore off his helmet and pressed a hand to his hip.

Scott thrust himself back behind the barricade. His eyes darted between everything around him. Jayden's sniper fire. Clarke's hip. The hole in the concrete. Everything was happening too fast.

"Over there, sir!" Jayden answered. Varvara was still positioned behind the tower, where Fox lay in her care.

"Get her over here!" Clarke said.

Scott snapped into focus and adjusted his comm. "Varvara! We need you behind the barricade!"

"But what about Fox?" she answered.

Clarke slammed his comm to his lips. *"Fox will bloody live, drag yourself over here!"*

DAVID AND MAX reached the infirmary's entrance. EDEN soldiers were clustered around as several dozen Bakma held the open area just beyond them. Dead and wounded were strewn in all directions. The sound of assault rifle fire rattled the air.

Max groaned as he sunk to his knees and lifted his handgun. Over and over, he fired into the throng of aliens.

The battle for the infirmary had begun.

BARANOV FIRED HIS assault rifle relentlessly in the direction of the airstrip. He had lost count of the Bakma he had dropped long ago. An occasional plasma bolt streaked past him, though he remained protected behind the large chunk of debris. A bolt had caught the edge of his hip earlier, but the wound was easily ignored.

He was about to release another burst when his eyes caught someone on the battlefield. It was Galina. She was far ahead of him, in the middle of the fray, where she struggled to drag a wounded soldier to cover. Almost in the same instant that Baranov spied her, a plasma bolt struck her in the shoulder. She toppled to the ground.

Baranov stood up. "Galya!" A second bolt clipped her side, and she tumbled again. As she cried out on the ground, Baranov's eyes narrowed. "Forgive me, Sveta."

He switched his assault rifle to one hand and charged toward the airstrip. As soon as he was open, a wave of plasma tracked him. He stumbled as a bolt caught his thigh, though he maintained his balance. He swung his assault rifle forward and held down the trigger. Two Bakma fell.

Galina struggled to stand, then collapsed from her lack of strength.

"Galya, I am coming!"

Baranov plowed ahead until he reached her. He lowered his free arm to scoop her up and pressed her body against his. Galina mumbled incoherently. He scanned for the nearest cover—a charred Vindicator that sat unused alongside the main hangar. He fired his assault rifle behind him as he charged toward the fighter.

The small of his back burst open; a spray of blood splattered against the side of his neck. He stumbled, but his legs moved on. A second plasma bolt opened his thigh, followed by a third against his shoulder. His teeth clattered together as he crumbled to his knees. The Vindicator was right in front of him. His knees pressed forward as his internal organs ruptured. When the final plasma bolt struck the center of his back, he lurched forward in one last surge.

Safety. They were behind the fighter. Galina was sheltered in his arms, and he toppled onto her. His gaze sunk to her as he coughed a spat of blood. His eyes glossed over, he lowered his head, and he breathed his last.

THE ENTIRE BASE was a war zone. Bakma pressed against the hangar and the surrounding structures. Mounted riders ripped holes through EDEN's defenses. Blood-crazed canrassis tore apart everyone in their paths.

Chaos was in every direction. The hangar was completely ablaze. The infirmary was being rocked with plasma fire. The main building was on the verge of invasion.

Novosibirsk was dying.

CLARKE'S TEAM STRUGGLED against the tidal wave of Bakma forces. Plasma burned their nostrils as the bloody cries of death tortured their ears.

Though his ammunition ran low, Scott launched volleys from behind the barricade. Jayden abandoned the futility of his sniper rifle and claimed a more versatile E-35 from a fallen soldier. Clarke fell under the care of Varvara, whose armor and skin were stained with blood.

Everything shook. Everything flashed. Everything screamed.

Then, amid it all, the crisp static of *Novosibirsk*'s loudspeakers cut through the maelstrom. Layered behind the cacophony, the unnatural quiet of an open mic arose.

Becan focused briefly on the metal wall mount.

Doctors and nurses looked up from their patients.

Clarke's team panned their gazes to the massive speaker towers.

The voice that addressed them was clear and firm.

"Attention all Novosibirsk warriors. This is General Ignatius van Thoor."

Becan's attention snapped back to the fight as a Bakma warrior swung a fist at his face. He ducked to the floor and bashed a kick into the alien's chest.

"Today, the enemy comes to our doorstep. They feast in our halls."

David growled as a burst of plasma whizzed by his face. He reloaded his assault rifle as Max returned fire.

"They dine on our blood."

On the airstrip, the army of Bakma plowed toward the barricades. Scott slammed a new magazine into his assault rifle and flung his last grenade into the fray.

"For years, you have prepared for a day such as this. You have prepared for a day when they bring their battle to us."

"We're not gonna hold them!" David said. As he raced back to find Max, his eyes locked onto silhouettes in the distance. Their shadowed horns gleamed in the darkness.

Their crimson triangles shone with rage.

"That day has finally come."
Scott was about to rise from the barricade to fire when Jayden clapped his hand on his shoulder. Scott stopped and followed Jayden's rearward gaze.
Amassed in their wicked glory, a legion of Nightmen thundered toward the battlefield.
The hair on the back of Scott's neck tingled.

"Fear is for the weak."
Dostoevsky's scowl twisted as he snapped a Bakma's neck.

"Mercy is for the foolish."
The Nightmen charged the strip. The Bakma forces hesitated.

"We will stand as death. We will fight as victors."
Scott regripped his assault rifle and steadied himself.

"And today, we will show the world..."
"Engage!" Clarke said. "Engage with the offensive!"

"...that The Machine has teeth."

SCOTT ROSE FROM the barricade and unleashed assault rifle fire onto the airstrip. Three Bakma fell before he ducked back into cover.
Around the hangar, the dark knights of the Nightman army charged into the Bakma stronghold. The Bakma advance ground to a halt as the Nightmen stormed through their midst.

IN CONFINEMENT, Dostoevsky exploded to life. The Bakma continued to press in, but the lieutenant's close-range prowess matched their surge with renewed vigor.
Down the halls of the Research Center, beyond the doors of Confinement, the shouts of Nightman warriors emerged from the plasma fire.
"They are coming!" Dostoevsky said as he bashed a Bakma's face with the butt of his rifle. "We will have victory soon!"

SCOTT'S TRIGGER FINGER paused as he stared at the battlefield. Nightmen surrounded the hangar. They charged straight into their Bakma attackers with violent aggression. They were outnumbered five to one, but they refused to acknowledge it. And just like that, a dark tide had swelled against what had moments ago been an overwhelming enemy. Where had then come from? Why had it taken them so long to appear? None of it mattered. All that mattered was that, at that moment, this dark, horned cult had appeared out of nowhere like a vapor—and in a single unified advance, had stopped the Bakma dead in their tracks.

All because of him. All because of the god of The Machine. All because of Thoor.

What monster had the general created?

"Remington! Timmons!"

Scott fell back as Clarke called his name.

"Remington," Clarke said, "we have orders." As soon as Jayden joined them, he continued. "NovCom want us to free the airstrip's turret towers."

Turret towers? Scott looked across the airstrip, where the towers came into view. They loomed in the distance...behind the fleet of Noboats. His attention returned to Clarke.

"If we can activate *Novosibirsk*'s turret defense system," Clarke said, "we can rain hell on them from behind and *end* this." He glanced at his wound and moaned, then his eyes sought Scott. "I cannot do this. And the Fourteenth are scattered in every direction." He hesitated. "I don't have it in me to ask you..."

There was no hesitation from Scott. There was no doubt. "I can do it."

"You realize that the Bakma stand between us and the towers. The canrassis, the Noboats, everything. Are you absolutely sure?"

He felt it. Exactly what he'd felt in Chicago when Grammar told him about the failed strike on the Carrier. Exactly what he'd felt when he earned the Golden Lion. "Yes, sir."

Varvara looked at Scott, and Clarke nodded his head. "Show me why you deserve it, Remington."

Scott rose to his feet and scanned the battlefield. Clarke was right. The turret towers were behind everything. *Unlike* Chicago, this wasn't a task that some worn-out old van would complete.

At that moment—at that thought—Scott suddenly went still. No, *Novosibirsk* didn't have some intrepid van to drive into battle. They had something much more powerful. His eyes flashed across the airstrip until he found them. Their nose-mounted chain guns blazed as they plowed through the fray.

Grizzlies.

He and his comrades from the Fourteenth had spent half the battle taking shelter behind one. It was too bad they hadn't received their orders *then*. But they had their orders now—and now was all that mattered.

"Jayden," Scott said, "get ready to ride." His gaze darted to Clarke. "Sir, can you patch me through to one of those Grizzlies?"

The captain nodded. "I can."

"What's going on?" Jayden asked as he knelt beside Scott.

"You're about to see what you missed back in Chicago."

"You're set," Clarke motioned to Scott. "They're on our channel."

Scott cupped his helmet mic. "This is Scott Remington of the Fourteenth! A comrade and I need to be picked up immediately on the southeast corner of the airstrip!"

A voice crackled through a second later. "Negative, Fourteenth, we are not in position to help you. There's another Grizzly much closer to you; we'll direct him there instead."

Scott nodded. "That'll work, thank you!" As the channel closed, Scott beckoned Jayden. "Come on." He motioned to the corner of the strip. Jayden rose to follow.

"Wait!"

Scott turned. The shout came from Varvara. Her gaze was settled on Jayden.

"Be okay..." she said to him.

Jayden's eyes stayed on her for a moment before his lips curved into a grin. "Yes, ma'am."

Beside them, Scott arched an eyebrow.

Jayden turned around and flashed him a smile. "What?"

Scott smirked as Jayden strode past him. "Nothing, stud. Lead the way."

OUTSIDE CONFINEMENT, the *rat-tat-tat* of assault rifles grew closer. As more Bakma fell and human victory became imminent, what few Bakma remained threw down their weapons, dropped to the floor, and raised their hands over their heads. "Grrashna!" they hollered. Bloodstained Nightmen charged into Confinement from the hallway and trained their weapons on the surrendering aliens.

The Research Center was secure.

THE GRIZZLY AWAITED Scott and Jayden at the corner. Scorch marks charred its hull, and its forward chain gun smelled of cinders. The top hatch swung open, and a giant of a man emerged. Harbinger.

"Son of a gun!" William said.

"Will!" Scott grinned. "You ready to make some fireworks, big man?" William bellowed a laugh as Scott and Jayden climbed up to the hatch. "Hell yes, we are, friend!" William ducked down in the Grizzly as Scott and Jayden slid behind him. Plasma slammed against the APC's hull. The Grizzly shuddered.

The entire Eighth was inside. Their faces glistened in the cabin's red glow. Jayden dropped behind Scott and slammed the hatch shut.

"Here's the plan, guys," Scott said. "We're taking one of the turret towers."

"The ones on the other end of the strip?" asked William.

"Those."

Derrick Cole stared at Scott. "They're surrounded by Noboats. At least two deep on every side."

Scott didn't respond. He shifted his eyes to Derrick, and after a moment of pause, smiles emerged on both their faces.

William thrust his fists into the air. *"Battering ram!"*

A cheer bellowed from the Eighth, and the Grizzly pulled away from the corner.

THE BATTLE AT the infirmary began to sway in *Novosibirsk*'s favor. For the first time, human soldiers outnumbered the Bakma. Max stood and signaled his hand. "Move! Move in on 'em!"

The soldiers charged from their barricades, a wave of bullets before them.

The two forces collided, and a flurry of combat erupted. David swung the butt of his assault rifle against a Bakma's face. Bullets ricocheted at his feet. He unloaded a barrage of bullets. It was a free-for-all.

THE GRIZZLY'S RUSSIAN driver announced to Scott, "The Noboats are ahead!" A two-deep row of Noboats stood between the Grizzly and the nearest turret tower. A multitude of Bakma fired at the APC.

Scott knelt in the cabin. "Once we break through the Noboats, Jay and I will leave the Grizzly and take the tower! Cover us, then follow us. No one stays behind!" The Eighth erupted with a *yes, sir!* "Let's do it," Scott said.

As the Grizzly's giant wheels churned forward, the engine roared in mechanical fury. William snagged a support rail. *"Battering ram!* It only works if you yell, *battering ram!"* The men cheered. Scott and Jayden held on.

Their emotion was interrupted as a white streak emerged from the Bakma. The driver turned to face them. "Hold on! Plasma missile!"

The cabin braced. William cackled maniacally, *"We're all gonna die!"* The driver floored the accelerator and spun the wheel right. The plasma missile rammed against the Grizzly's side. It leapt on two wheels. The cabin roared as a hole blew through the hull of the vehicle. Flames blazed up, and the Grizzly skidded sideways as it crashed down to earth.

The Grizzly grabbed concrete and lurched forward. As the soldiers reoriented themselves, they scanned the cabin. Nobody was dead. A defiant cheer arose, and the driver plunged the accelerator down. "Do not shoot what you cannot stop, you purple monkeys!"

Scott stood and wiped the soot from his face. The battlefield was plainly visible through the newly blown hole in the hull. Two of the larger men knelt beside it and propped rocket launchers against their shoulders. Rockets whizzed out as the Grizzly surged ahead.

The Noboats were upon them, and the driver white-knuckled the wheel. "Brace for collision!"

Scott turned to the cockpit window. His eyes bulged. William screamed. *"Battering ram!"*

Impact.

The Grizzly's frame rocked as the forces of tonnage collided. Sparks and metal exploded as the men flew forward. Shouts bellowed; blood spattered everything. The Grizzly bucked as its wheels whined ahead. Its nose crashed to the ground.

They were through.

The pair of Noboats parted, and the Grizzly cruised beyond them. One more pair stood between them and the tower. Moments before impact, someone in the back shouted.

"Hold on!"

The Grizzly slammed into metal again. Grips were jarred loose as soldiers flew in all directions. The massive wheels churned. The engine screamed. The Noboats gave way. There was a burst of traction, and the Grizzly lurched ahead.

"We are through!"

Once more, the APC's accelerator was pressed to the floor as the turret tower ahead of them drew rapidly closer. At long last, and with a violent, sideways screech, the Grizzly stopped right in front of it.

"Tower's here, pop the top!" said Scott.

The top hatch burst open. Plasma bolts soared toward them from the Bakma they'd just bypassed. "Go!" the driver said. "Get out!"

Scott and Jayden scrambled out of the hatch; William followed. Scott bolted to the tower door, flung it open, and charged inside. "C'mon, c'mon!" he shouted to Jayden and William as they ran into the tower. The rest of the Eighth engaged the Bakma behind them. "Will, turret's yours, go! Everyone else, get in!" He waved the rest of the Eight on.

ACROSS THE AIRFIELD, Clarke issued orders to an orphaned squad through his comm. "The northwest end of the airstrip has become a stronghold! We've got to clear a path to it and reclaim some lost territory!" Varvara placed her hands on his chest to keep him still. He shoved them away and struggled to a stand.

"Captain!" she said. "You must not."

"I can walk," Clarke said as he groaned.

Above them, silver streaks tore across the sky. Clarke swung his gaze upward. Vindicators. "That's *Leningrad*!" he said. EDEN soldiers cheered as the fighters strafed the airstrip. The Bakma scattered. "Rally up, everyone! We're taking back our base!"

ATOP THE TURRET tower, William slid into the forty-barreled chain gun's seat. A protective shield sealed around him, and mechanical gears twisted to propel the turret up. The twin barrels discharged, and a wave of orange poured into the Bakma from behind. The eruption from the turret was deafening.

As the rest of the Eighth reached the top of the tower, they formed an offensive perimeter around the turret. A barrage of heavy weapons fire rained down as the Bakma below dashed for cover. Jayden's eyes squinted as he fired midrange shots from his E-35.

CLARKE'S EYES PEELED across the airstrip, where the twin-barreled turrets roared angrily. For the first time, the Bakma fell into disorganized chaos. Clarke stared at the turrets, and a smile slowly crept from his lips. "Brilliant, Remington," he said quietly to himself. "Bloody vecking *brilliant*." He peered skyward as a pair of Vindicators strafed the Noboats.

SCOTT HELD SUPPRESSION fire as the last of the Eighth rushed inside. He attempted to count them as they bolted up the stairwell. Was that everyone? Yes, it was. Engaging the door lock from inside, Scott heaved the door shut.

It stopped within an inch of the frame.

Oh no.

The door swung back open; plasma streamed in. Scott dove for the floor. As he rolled over onto his back, a pair of Bakma rushed into the tower. His legs flexed, and he kicked the metal door before any other Bakma could enter. The door slammed shut, and the security lock engaged. The two Bakma turned to face him.

Scott knew he was in trouble the moment he saw them. Though one looked like a prototypical Bakma warrior, the other was an absolute beast. Tight muscles rippled across its arms and legs. Even the veins in its neck bulged. The Bakma's opaque eyes shrunk to slits as he glared at Scott. In tandem, both aliens fired their weapons.

Scott dove in desperation. Plasma crashed against the wall behind him. Scott rolled, raised his assault rifle, and hit the trigger. Blood misted the air, and the smaller Bakma fell. Scott scrambled to his feet as the larger one aimed.

There was nothing Scott could do to avoid the attack. The Bakma's plasma rifle fired right in front of him. Time slowed as Scott stood petrified.

Nicole. Every fear, every doubt that she'd harbored and then defeated with sheer willpower and faith. It was all about to be for naught. Scott was about to do the one thing that scared her the most: leave her to pick up the pieces.

No!

Scott hoisted his assault rifle in front of his face. The plasma bolt smashed into it. The weapon exploded, and he was thrown backward. The air fizzed as his vision briefly went white. When it returned a half second later, he clenched his teeth and looked at his rifle. It was destroyed—but it saved his life. A scorch mark was etched in his armor, but that was it.

He was alive.

He swiveled his gaze up. The barrel of a plasma rifle hovered point-blank in front of his face. Right between his eyes. Beyond it, the cold, merciless expression of the Bakma awaited him. The alien's dark eyes gleamed as he touched the trigger. "K'kanak t'ae, Earthae."

Click.

The Bakma blinked.

Scott blinked.

The Bakma looked at his weapon.

Scott raised his eyebrows.

The Bakma hesitated, and his mouth dropped open. "Uhh…"

Dive! Scott lunged into the Bakma's chest, and the two fighters tumbled backward. Scott felt himself being thrust upward, and the next thing he knew, he was flying through the air. His back hit the far wall upside down. As he tried to regain his footing, the gnarled talons of an alien fist hooked across his face. His vision blurred, and he stumbled sideways. Next, something pounded against his sternum. He buckled over. Before he could react, a foot crashed into his chest and knocked him backward.

When Scott landed, his mouth hung slack-jawed. His vision was spinning. He could feel blood trickling down to his lips. Above, the Bakma towered over him. A fight against *any* trained Bakma warrior would be a challenge, but against this peak specimen? Everything swung in this Bakma's favor, except for one minor detail.

Scott still had his pistol.

Without hesitation, he reached down, removed it from his belt holster, and trained it on the Bakma towering over him. The alien froze.

Scott staggered to his feet, backing up the whole while to maintain distance. The handgun stayed out. "Do you understand me?"

The Bakma looked puzzled.

"Do you understand me?" Scott repeated.

"Duthek horu Earthae lkaana?"

What was that word? Scott's mind raced as the weapon-checked Bakma stared back at him. *Grrashna!* That was it. The Bakma word for self-surrender.

"Grrashna!" Scott said emphatically. He motioned his handgun to the ground.

The Bakma tilted his head in a way that genuinely made Scott wonder if he'd made an impression on the alien or further bewildered him.

Sighing desperately, Scott said, "Come on, man, just *grrashna*." The Bakma took a single step closer, then stopped. "Stop!" Scott said. "Don't take another step!"

"Ashalaach dasch viluus, Earthae."

"I don't know what that means."

The Bakma took another step.

"*Veck!*" His breaths intensifying, Scott queued up Jayden on the comm as he kept his pistol aimed straight at the Bakma warrior's head. "Come on, Jay." This was the closest Scott had ever been to a living Bakma. He could see every crevice, every wrinkled pit in the alien's leathery, purple skin. He could perceive the hardness of the alien's flared cheekbones, the darkness of its sunken eye sockets, and the dark orbs within them. The ridgeline that ran up the surface of its skull. He could feel its bridled vitriol as it stared straight through him.

"Ashalaach dasch viluus, Earthae," the alien said again. As if he was daring Scott to pull the trigger.

Scott was just about to when Jayden's voice crackled through.

"Hey man, what's up?" the Texan said.

Wasting no time as he took another step backward to keep distance between himself and the Bakma, Scott said, "I've got a prisoner down here!"

Atop the turret tower, Jayden stopped firing. "You got a *what?*"

"Two Bakma slipped through. I don't know if you heard the gunshots or not," Scott answered.

Jayden shook his head. "I didn't even know you were still down there! I can't hear nothin' up here!" Above him, the turret's deafening blasts permeated the air. Jayden covered his helmet's microphone and earpiece with a hand.

"Well, I got a live one! He looks important!"

"How do you know?"

"I don't know—they all look important! This one's just…I don't know. He's different!"

Jayden asked, "How's he different?"

"Veck, I don't know, Jay! He's talking to me!"

"What's he talkin' about?"

Scott snarled. "Zone blitzes! How am I supposed to know?" As the Bakma stepped closer again, Scott took another step back. "Listen, man," he said to the alien, "I would really like to take you prisoner, but if you keep walking toward me, I will blow your brains out. Just say *grrashna* already!"

"Grrash*taku*," the Bakma said.

Blinking, Scott said, "Grrashtaku?" What in the world did that mean?

"Do you need help down there?" Jayden asked.

"I don't know, man," Scott said, "I keep telling this guy to surrender, but he's not getting the—"

The attack was as blazing as it was brazen. Surging forward and at a sharp angle, the Bakma leaned his head out of Scott's line of fire as he swung an open, gnarled palm at Scott's pistol. Though Scott managed to fire off a shot, it ricocheted past the Bakma's head. In the next instant,

Scott's weapon-wielding hand was swatted aside with prejudice. Though Scott's grip stayed true, the Bakma also wrapped his hand around the pistol. A violent brawl for the weapon began.

Bang! Bang!

Two more shots rang out, both dinging against the inner wall of the tower's lower level. Scott strained for all he was worth to rip the pistol free—it was for naught. Wrapping his free arm around Scott's head, the alien reared backward, lifting Scott clean off his feet before swinging him against the nearest wall. Scott's body slammed against it with force—his helmet was jarred free.

And the pistol fell from his grasp.

The Bakma lurched for it, but a swift kick from Scott sent the weapon skidding across the room. Wasting no time in a dash for the pistol, the Bakma whipped his head to Scott, grabbed him by his golden collar, and lifted him off the ground.

Rearing back with a fist, Scott slammed it against the side of the alien's head. Though the Bakma's head moved, it was by shockingly little. Rearing back, the alien crashed the top of his forehead against Scott's face. Blood flew from Scott's lips; his world spun.

Then came the kill maneuver. Wrapping both taloned hands around Scott's throat, the Bakma squeezed hard. Scott's air was instantly cut off. He tried to pry the alien's hands from his neck; the effort was useless. This mauler—this peak specimen—was levels above anything Scott had experienced.

Leaning his face close to Scott's as Scott desperately squirmed, the Bakma said lowly, "Grrashtaku."

It was at that moment, as the loss of Scott's oxygen supply began to turn his vision dark, that the word's meaning came to him. The Bakma's intent was loud and clear. This was not a play on the Bakma word for self-surrender.

This was, "*You* surrender."

Suddenly, the sound of assault rifle fire erupted from the stairwell. The ceiling above Scott and the alien dinged and sparked. The Bakma jumped in startlement—his hands released Scott's throat as he turned the stairwell's direction. Scott, on the other hand, fell gasping to the floor. Then he, too, turned his head to the new arrival.

Jayden.

"Get on the veckin' ground!" Jayden said.

Still lightheaded, Scott crawled away from the Bakma and toward his friend.

"You want me to kill him?" asked Jayden urgently, the Texan's voice shaking. "I'll kill him, man, I'll kill him!"

Inside, Scott was screaming *yes*. But the words couldn't find their way out. The only thing Scott could do was gasp. Crawling faster, Scott reached out and snagged his pistol where it lay next to the stairwell. Heaving as he spun around to aim the weapon at the Bakma, Scott stopped when his eyes found his adversary again.

The Bakma was on his knees, both hands open and raised in front of him. The alien's gaze was fixed on Jayden until he slowly turned his dark orbs to Scott. "Grrashna."

Scott's head lowered, and he exhaled a disgusted—and exhausted—sigh. His voice just starting to return, he said weakly, "Come on, man, really?"

"You want me to kill him?" Jayden asked again.

There was no EDEN-enforced rule about killing an extraterrestrial in the act of surrender, but it was almost universally considered poor form. Though only Jayden would have been there to witness it—and he seemed a willing participant—Scott knew that didn't make it right. Gritting his teeth as he looked up through sweat-soaked strands of tussled hair, he mustered the words, "No. Don't kill him." Wiping his hair back over his head, he stared at the Bakma and said, "You have no idea how close you are to making me a bad person."

"I thought you had him at gunpoint," said Jayden, assault rifle still held on the Bakma.

Shaking his head, Scott said, "I did."

"Dang."

"Yeah," Scott said exhaustedly. "Dang."

NEAR THE HANGARS, Dostoevsky and Becan had rejoined the fight. Close behind them were David and Max. What other EDEN forces remained poured onto the airstrip to join the Nightmen already there. Captains and their squads, amalgamations of broken units, and any others able to fight rallied together in full force.

Clarke swung up his assault rifle as a pair of riderless canrassis tromped down the strip. They chattered shrilly as their spider-eyes passed from one soldier to the next. Bullets pierced through their fur, and their bodies stuttered in mid-gallop.

"Surround and concentrate!" Clarke said. He dropped awkwardly to one knee and opened fire. It took several trigger pulls before the bullets found one of the beasts' heads. The canrassi roared, reared on its hind legs, and toppled over.

The second canrassi shook as bullets peppered it. It fell toward the nearest EDEN soldier, where its jaws—filled with three rows of teeth—snapped at the desperately scrambling man. Bullets poured into the beast's flesh until it finally landed neck-first on the ground. Its dark blue tongue slipped from its mouth, and it fell still.

EDEN soldiers stormed the airstrip. Nightman warriors fortified the hangar space. Vindicators assaulted the Noboats from above. The Bakma were decimated.

It was almost over.

As the last of the Bakma drew within close-combat range, weapons fire from assault rifles rained at them in torrents. The turret held its fire. The Vindicators ceased their strafes. As human forces broke through the barrier of Noboats, the Bakma that remained threw down their weapons and lifted their hands. Full surrender.

The battle was won.

THE TWIN TURRETS whirred to a stop, and William relaxed. The whole of the Eighth withdrew their weapons and either sunk to their knees or sat back.

The scene overlooking the base was sheer devastation. Buildings burned. Bodies littered the ground. Painful screams filled the air. The scope of the damage was surreal. Too vast to be fully comprehended.

CLARKE REMOVED HIS helmet and released it. After it clunked to the ground, he ran his hand over his sweat-drenched head. Cinders popped as the hangar burned; the smell of charred flesh hung over the airstrip.

DAVID AND MAX fell to the ground—one exhausted and the other injured. Both men lay silent. Dostoevsky and Becan were not far, and they soon joined their comrades. They stared at one another as security teams moved all around them.

SCOTT AND JAYDEN'S weapons remained on their Bakma captive until reinforcements arrived. The tower door whisked open, and Nightmen hustled in, recoiling as they saw the Bakma. They readied their assault rifles to fire, then paused. The alien was no threat—at least, not anymore. Scott lowered his handgun and released an utterly bone-weary breath. He looked at the Bakma, whose hard stare met his.

I don't know where you came from, Scott thought as he watched the alien, *but you put up a world-class fight. Luck saved me once; Jayden saved me the other. I give you props.*

Scott watched as the Nightmen converged on the alien, clasped his hands together behind his back, and thrust him forcefully out of the tower. Lowering his head, Scott ran his hands down his face.

"Man, that thing was a beast," said Jayden beside him.

"You're telling me." Scott looked up at him. "Why didn't you shoot him when you came down the stairs?"

Jayden shook his head. "You told me you wanted to keep him. And y'all were like, right next to each other. I didn't want to accidentally shoot you."

"Dude, you're a sniper."

"Yeah, but…man, look. I was just terrified."

Now that, Scott understood. "Well, thanks—again."

"No problem." Jayden's gaze turned to the door. "Where do you think they're taking him?"

"Honestly," Scott said, managing a self-deprecating chuckle, "I couldn't care less. As long as he's far away from me."

Jayden slapped Scott on the shoulder and then meandered out of the tower.

AS CLARKE LIMPED past the hangar, he found Baranov. The executor lay slumped on the ground with holes scorched into his back. His body was wrecked. For several seconds, Clarke simply stared. Then he blinked. Something else was there. Something was underneath him.

It was a body.

Clarke quickened his stumbling pace and knelt beside the executor. He strained to lift Baranov's corpse to see who it was. Galina. She was curled into a ball on the concrete. She was alive.

Her breaths were small, but they were there. Immediately, Clarke called out, "I need a medic!" He drew his focus back to Galina, rolling Baranov over to set her free.

Nearly ten meters away, Dostoevsky watched the scene unfold. Unlike Clarke, whose attention was on Galina, Dostoevsky's was solely on the corpse of Ivan Baranov, who'd been the only remaining Nightman in the unit besides him.

Gaze lowering in contemplation, Dostoevsky quietly turned and walked away.

AS SCOTT AND Jayden returned to the hangar, Scott allowed himself a careful sweep of the airstrip. Debris and bodies were scattered everywhere. It was impossible not to walk through puddles of blood. In the aftermath of the gruesome battle, he took in the totality of what had just transpired. Despite the victory, *Novosibirsk* had been hit hard. Harder than any base had been hit before.

As Scott drew close to where he'd left the Fourteenth, his eyes caught David. His old roommate was bloodstained and bruised, but he was alive. He looked so tired. Everyone did.

Scott knelt on the ground and covered his eyes with his hands. He ran his fingers back through his hair and looked around again. Every soldier was dirty, and most had some degree of injury. Few had made it through unscathed. Scott closed his eyes and thought a prayer. It was the only appropriate one that he knew.

Thank You for keeping me alive.

He opened his eyes and, with great effort, forced himself up. "I tell you what, Jay..." He looked pointedly at the Texan.

Jayden stood meters from him, his arms wrapped around the small of Varvara's back, as the two stood locked in an embrace. Varvara's lips caressed Jayden's mouth as her arms slid around his neck.

Eyes widening, Scott returned his attention to the airstrip. *Go get her, cowboy.* He laughed to himself and returned to his teammates. Minutes later, the whole of the able-bodied Fourteenth was reunited.

All except for one man.

Yuri Dostoevsky was alone in the barracks. Having bypassed an opportunity to be with his comrades, he'd instead sought solitude amid his contemplation. Not two weeks ago, he'd been one of three highly regarded Nightmen in the Fourteenth. Now, he was alone. It was a new reality that would require processing. For him, the company of comrades had never been good for that. He much preferred the solace of his private quarters—even in the aftermath of a base-wide battle.

As he walked along the wet, bloodstained floors of the officers' wing, his mind was lost deeply in thought—deeply in consideration of his role and his purpose. Of what being the Fourteenth's last-standing Nightman meant.

Until a voice caught his ears.

"Call me when you get this! I don't care what time it is!"

Dostoevsky's brow furrowed. Pausing in the hallway, he looked behind him to see if anyone was present. No one was. Yet the girl's voice went on.

"I love you!" she said amid laughter. "I love you, Scott Remington!"

"*She loves you, Scott Remington!*" other voices joined in.

Angling his head suspiciously, Dostoevsky altered his course to walk toward the source—a conference room he'd sat in many times. When he stepped inside, his eyes were drawn to the corpses on the ground. Six Bakma were laid out, their bodies riddled with bullets.

Then he looked at the screen.

"Scott Remington! This is your best friend in the universe, Nikki Dupree, with an important announcement!"

Blood was splattered on the screen. The crimson streaks were right over Nicole's face.

"I just thought I would send you this message at nine o'clock in the morning to saaay…I passed my nursing final! *Whooo!*"

Dostoevsky's gaze remained transfixed—but it was not on the young woman, her emphatic celebrations, or the sprays that engulfed her. His cold, blue eyes were solely on the red. On the answer to the question. On the missing piece.

"I love you, Scott. You are worth fighting for. I'm sorry I haven't been as supportive as I know you'd have been for me had our roles been reversed. Because you would have supported me, one hundred percent. Please forgive me and accept this as a token of my apology. I want you to know that I'm all in. On you. On us. On everything."

On everything.

Turning away from the display, Dostoevsky walked out of the conference room. No longer was the look in his eyes one of deep contemplation. No longer was it the look of a man mourning lost brethren. Instead, it was a look of determination. Of sudden, unexpected awareness.

Nicole was left behind to loop on.

22

EDEN COMMAND

PRESIDENT PAULING STOOD with his back turned to the Council. His arms were folded across his chest, and his stern countenance scrutinized the EDEN logo on the wall monitor. Silence prevailed throughout the conference room. No whispered chatter. No Council addressor. No presentation. Nothing.

Eleven of the twelve judges sat behind him, their quiet stares split between the president's back and the black lifelessness of the round table. No papers waited on its glossy surface. There were only the hollow reflections of the judges.

Judge Rath broke the silence as he looked from the table to the president. As he began to speak, the judges around him edged their eyes in his direction. "Sir, there was nothing anybody could have done—"

"*I'll tell you what could and could not have been done!*" Pauling answered harshly.

Rath sighed and resumed his quiet observance.

"Complacency!" Pauling said. "This organization has grown complacent, and now we see the results!"

"Sir," Rath said, "if I may…"

"What?"

"*Novosibirsk* was defended, sir. The attack was repelled. If anything, this is a testament to our ability to react without warning."

Pauling drew a sharp breath. "This is a testament to the training of the *Nightmen*. The attack never should have happened in the first place."

"And who is to blame for that, sir?" Rath asked. "Who is to blame for inferior technology?"

"We're to blame for not finding a way around it." Pauling's glare targeted Judge Iwamoto, a more petite man and one of two Japanese judges on the Council. "What's the progress of the Noboat Detection System?"

Iwamoto stuttered through a reply. "We…we…are still trying to—"

Pauling slammed his hand against the table. Several judges flinched. "Trying is not acceptable! We've been trying for years. We need to be *doing*! I refuse to believe that with all the scientists and with all the engineers that we have, we still have nothing!" Iwamoto was speechless as Pauling continued. "For two years, you've been trying! That's *not* good enough."

Judge Malcolm Blake cleared his throat. The eyes of the Council turned to the African Englishman. "With all due respect, sir, Mamoru has had his hands full heading R&D." Iwamoto looked at Blake. "And he's done a superb job. Perhaps some delegation would speed up our progress."

"We have more scientists than sand on a beach," Pauling answered. "How much more delegation do you want?"

"But only one judge to oversee it," Blake said. "That's far too much to rest on one man's shoulders. With your permission, sir, I'll assist in the workload. I'll pick up detection and whatever else Mamoru feels I can handle. With two of us overseeing, surely things will come to speed."

Pauling eyed Blake, then diverted his attention to Iwamoto. "Do you object to this?"

"No, sir," Iwamoto answered. "The extra help would be very good." He looked distant for a moment. "Perhaps detection needs a new approach."

Pauling nodded to Blake. "You have detection and whatever else Mamoru gives you."

Blake smiled. "Thank you, sir."

Pauling addressed Iwamoto without looking. "Get together with Malcolm after we close, and get yourselves organized."

"Yes, sir."

"We're protecting a planet, people," Pauling said. "We can't settle for anything less than perfection. It's a miracle we've arrived this far, and we're barely holding on as it is."

A distinct pause fell over the room as Pauling stood before them, severe and overbearing. His features were different—hardened and aged. He allowed his gaze to slide down to the table, where it lingered. Almost ten seconds passed before he lifted it again to regard Judge Rath. "As much as I hate to bring it up again, the mourning period is over. Have you been able to locate any of Kentwood's Intelligence documents?"

Rath frowned and lowered his eyes. "No, sir. I even spoke with Director Kang. He, too, was unaware of any documents. We can only hope that whatever concerns Darryl found, we can find, also."

"And the investigation about his death?"

"There was no foul play," Rath answered. "It was as natural a heart attack as one can have. It just came at a bad time."

"I have yet to hear of one that comes at a good time," Pauling said. Rath nodded. "I've spoken with Benjamin Archer," said Pauling, "your suggestion as a replacement. You were right. He's an intelligent candidate. He's young, but he has promise."

"Thank you, sir," Rath said. "I'm glad he was a worthy recommendation."

Pauling sank into his chair and stared at the opaque table. His older reflection stared back at him. After several moments, he waved his hand in dismissal. "That's all this morning."

Nods of acknowledgment were offered to him as the judges rose from their chairs and filtered out of the room. Their departure was quicker than usual, and the typical cloud of post-meeting chatter was absent. It was only a matter of seconds until Pauling was alone.

"Judge Archer," he said to himself as he pondered the empty seat where Darryl Kentwood used to sit. His eyes remained there for a moment before he pivoted in his chair and turned his back to the conference room, losing his gaze on the EDEN logo in front of the room. "Welcome to the Council."

*   *   *

NOVOSIBIRSK, RUSSIA

THE SUN BROKE over *Novosibirsk*'s horizon at a quarter to five. A gentle breeze, gliding steadfastly out of the north, polished the freshly fallen snow just beyond the base grounds—the base grounds themselves were a mishmash of virgin snow and scorched earth. Of snow hare tracks and frozen puddles of dark blood. Though the fires that had raged hours earlier were now mostly extinguished, the destruction left in their wake would last much longer.

Novosibirsk's gargantuan hangar had been rendered a cindered husk. Holes camouflaged its concrete walls; an entire corner had caved in. Rubble was piled around it, and cleanup crews hustled to clear the way for repair vehicles. Only a handful of aircraft had survived—the *Pariah* among them, thanks solely to the efforts of the Fourteenth to get the transport out of the hangar before it succumbed to a fiery fate.

Few of the Noboats that remained on the airstrip were in well enough condition to be salvaged. The combination of heavy weapons fire from the ground and strafing air attacks by *Leningrad*'s Vindicators mangled all but a handful of the alien vessels. The same could be said for the four Bakma Carriers, which lay in near ruin at the far end of the airstrip. The infirmary, though defended, had taken a heavy beating. An initial damage assessment revealed massive structural damage that rendered the building more hazard than shelter. All recoverable medical supplies were transported to the gymnasium, which was deemed *Novosibirsk*'s temporary hospital until further evaluations of the infirmary could be made. With *Novosibirsk* understaffed medically, crews of surgeons and nurses from *Leningrad* and *London* were being flown in to assist the staff on hand.

The human body count reached over three thousand, only eighty of which were Nightmen. Some units were leaderless, while others were decimated from one end to the other. It had been the most deadly assault against an EDEN facility in the organization's history. Nonetheless, the battle was dubbed a victory. *Novosibirsk*—The Machine—would live on.

The Fourteenth shared in the casualties. Ivan Baranov, Kevin Carpenter, and Konstantin Makarovich were dead. An equal number were wounded. Though other units at the base had suffered more heavily, the Fourteenth's command structure had taken a considerable hit with the loss of Baranov, one of the most respected officers at *Novosibirsk* by both Nightmen and EDEN alike. He would not be easily replaced. But the Fourteenth's losses were not restricted to the dead.

With one of his hands mangled, Fox Power's career with EDEN was finished. The sniper was already slated to be transported to a United States hospital as soon as medical transports arrived. It was a hard blow for the delta trooper, who had only just been promoted to that rank. But it was the way war went. The Fourteenth would move on with Jayden as their resident sniper. What Fox did with the rest of his life was up to him.

Though Max's efforts in assisting the defense of the infirmary were noble, they did no favors to his recovery from prior injuries. He was still expected to recover fully, but that recovery time would be prolonged. Just the same, no one could blame him for his actions, considering the circumstances—not that he would have apologized if they had. If nothing else, it elevated his status somewhat among the four transfers from *Richmond*. A roughneck, Max may have been, but he was a fighter through and through. Personality aside, the gritty technician had to be respected for that.

Galina Lebesheva was provided a special location in the temporary hospital set aside for the injured among *Novosibirsk*'s medical staff. At Captain Clarke's' orders, nothing was said to her of Ivan's sacrifice to save her life. The right time would come for that to be revealed to her. For now, she just needed to rest. Ironically, it would be easier for her to rest than anyone in Room 14.

By the time Scott and his able-bodied comrades had returned to the bunk room, calmed their hearts down, and taken their showers, it was nearing daybreak. Challenging every odd, they slipped under their covers to attempt to find slumber. Scott knew that he had slept during that time, but it was anything but restful. It was more like periodic glimpses of the unconscious world. He was not alone. No soldier in the Fourteenth remained still beneath their covers.

Scott had abandoned all hope of finding rest by late morning. He rose from bed, donned his uniform, and ventured into the hallway. David offered him company, which Scott accepted gratefully. Together, they returned to the battered outside world.

For the first time in daylight, they saw the aftermath of the assault—the hole-riddled airstrip and the demolished hangar. They saw the unsalvageable Vindicators and the overturned Grizzlies. They saw it all without the need to explore. The damage was in every direction.

Though Scott and David talked little, Scott knew that David's questions must have been as deep and uncertain as his own. What happened now? How would they rebuild *Novosibirsk*? How would they fill the holes in the Fourteenth? And then, the darkest question of all: why was humanity still alive?

Clarke had said it the night of the attack. The advantage clearly weighed in favor of the extraterrestrials. This attack only furthered that point. The Bakma could assault *Novosibirsk* without a moment's notice. They could have obliterated it from above, yet they opted for a ground assault that they ultimately lost. When would the Bakma decide that enough was enough? When would they stop offering humanity a way out and go for the jugular? Why hadn't they done so already?

Scott was in the midst of those thoughts when he saw Captain Clarke. The captain stood alongside the covered sidewalk between the barracks and the cafeteria, leaning on crutches as he stared at the tattered base grounds. He looked tired. His shoulders sagged, and his anguished expression couldn't be hidden even from a distance. Scott understood why. The Fourteenth was a decimated unit, and Clarke was the one it fell upon. Turning Clarke's way, Scott approached him, David following in silence.

As Clarke took notice of the two men, he hobbled in their direction. The smile he met them with was a false one, but the attempt was there. "How goes it, gentlemen?" he asked, his voice hoarse and gravelly.

"Sir," Scott and David answered.

In the seconds that followed, no words were spoken. The three men exchanged glances until their gazes abandoned one another to observe the devastation around them. It was Clarke who broke the silence. "I just returned from the gymnasium. Everyone is in stable condition. For now."

Another breeze brushed past them, then disappeared. Scott shifted his gaze to the unblemished snowfields.

"That's good to hear, sir," David answered.

"Yes. Yes, it is." Clarke massaged the back of his neck as he continued. "None of this should have happened. We're too careful to allow this to happen."

Scott angled his head down as he listened.

"Changes need to be made," said Clarke.

Changes. That was all Scott knew. When he joined EDEN, it was a change. When he fought in Chicago, it was a change. When he was brought to *Novosibirsk*…that part was still changing. The thought of change didn't scare him anymore. Change was home. "What are we going to do, sir?"

Clarke's answer was automatic. "We rebuild." He returned his eyes to them. "We count our losses, and we evaluate where we stand. Then we rebuild." Spoken like a captain. All compasses read forward. "Yuri shall assume the role of executor, and when Max recovers, he'll be good to resume his duties." Clarke looked between them before his eyes settled on Scott. "Which leaves us short one leftenant."

Scott knew it was him without Clarke having to say it. God had put him in the place he needed to be. He knew there was a reason.

All compasses read forward.

Clarke cleared his throat and returned his gaze to *Novosibirsk*. "Remember everything you've learned, Remington. Remember the things I've warned you about."

Scott nodded. "Yes, sir."

"There are things none of us yet understand. Look around here, and we're seeing that now. Your beginning is over. What you give now is what is to be expected."

"Yes, sir."

Clarke stared into the distance as Scott stood deep in thought. Everything had led him to where he was now. Everything had carried him to that moment. Amid the losses, Scott's heart mourned. But in anticipation of the future, it beat with eagerness.

"Gentlemen," Clarke said, "more is going to be asked of you than I expected by this point. But I know you both will serve us well." He straightened out his uniform with a free hand. When he saluted, Scott and David were crisp in response. "If either of you need me, I shall be in my quarters. Prepare yourselves, and prepare the rest of the unit, for new focus."

"Yes, sir," they answered in unison.

Clarke lowered his salute. "Cheerio, gentlemen," he said before turning and hobbling away.

Neither Scott nor David spoke as they watched the captain leave. Their gazes lingered on him for a moment, and then they shifted to the pristine snowfields. They were beautiful. They were pure enough to be God's own artwork. Scott took several steps off the sidewalk, where his feet crunched in the snow.

"You know he meant you, right?" David asked.

Scott heard the question. He knew. In a decimated unit, people were destined to rise. And destiny had taken him there. "Yeah," he answered as he looked into the horizon. "I know." The air was fresh as winter. It frosted as it escaped from his mouth and nostrils. He feigned a smile and turned around. "He meant you, too."

David watched Scott for a moment before a smile crept from his lips. "Whatever you say, compadre." Scott chuckled, and David stepped off the sidewalk to his side. "It's beautiful when you take the time to look at it, isn't it?" he asked.

"Yeah, it is."

It was beautiful. The longer he'd stayed in *Novosibirsk*, the more he'd noticed it. He was determined to notice it now more than ever.

David smiled and stepped back. "Now, if you'll excuse me, a woman a couple thousand miles away just heard about an attack on *Novosibirsk*. I think she's gonna want to know if her man is okay. And I don't think she's the only one."

"Go make your call," Scott said, the slightest smile emerging from the corners of his mouth. "I'll be right behind you."

David turned and walked toward the barracks. Scott continued to smile to himself. There was indeed a woman a couple of thousand miles away who needed to hear from her man. And there was a man in the middle of Russia who needed her just as much.

Scott's gaze returned to the snowfields. They were indeed so beautiful.
Like God's own artwork.

At long last, Scott returned to the sidewalk that led to the barracks.
That phone call he needed to make—that voice he needed to hear—could
wait no longer. All this talk of beginnings and destiny didn't just pertain
to him. They were about someone else's, too. Leaving the frozen battlefield of *Novosibirsk* behind him, Scott entered the barracks and took out
his comm to call Nicole.

*   *   *

AT THE SAME TIME

DOSTOEVSKY'S GAZE bore straight ahead. The path before him—cut from
limestone, more dungeon than modern military facility—was not illuminated by ceiling lights but by the flickering of torches. This was the dark
underbelly of *Novosibirsk*—the skeletal remains of what had once been
Fort Zhukov, atop which *Novosibirsk* had been built. It was a place EDEN
didn't know existed. A den of murderers and self-proclaimed villains.
The true lair of the Nightmen.

They called it the Citadel of The Machine.

As Dostoevsky rounded a corner, a trio of Nightmen—all lacking
the distinctive horned collar that adorned Dostoevsky's armor—quickly
stepped out of his way. Ceasing their conversation, they snapped to Nightman salutes, appropriate behavior when in the presence of a superior. The
titles of "lieutenant" and "executor" meant nothing here. Here, ones like
Dostoevsky were called fulcrums.

Dostoevsky marched onward, past the Underbarracks and the Walls
of Mourning, until he reached his destination: the Hall of the Fulcrums.
Deep within its limestone corridors was the Throne Room of Ignatius
van Thoor. Though Nightman sentries guarded it, none would stand in
Dostoevsky's way. He was well known to them.

The large wooden doors to the Throne Room were pushed open as
Dostoevsky approached. The chamber inside was spacious, and though
various archaic tables and stone outcroppings were present, the room's
centerpiece was a set of standalone stone stairs. At the top of them sat the
room's namesake—a dark, carved throne more befitting a pagan deity

than a general. It was all for theatrics. To get a point across when one needed to be made. It worked.

Thoor was not upon his throne at that moment. He was standing at one of the planning tables with his inner circle. It was a circle Dostoevsky was close enough to touch. As he drew near, he caught the Terror's eyes. Thoor stood upright, those around him falling silent as they watched Dostoevsky approach. "Fulcrum Dostoevsky," Thoor said—his tone indicating that this visit was unexpected.

Raising his hand in a Nightman salute, Dostoevsky waited for the general to approach him.

"What is the reason for this visit?" Thoor asked, stepping away from the table to come closer.

The reason? There were so many. The inevitability of man's sinful nature. The reality of the human condition. The dominance of the heart over one's sense of morality and justice. How quickly—how flawlessly—all of those dots could be connected. All it took was the right catalyst. The right sequence of events.

The right trigger.

Looking Thoor in the eyes, Dostoevsky lifted his chin ever so slightly. It was not an act of defiance. It was an acceptance of his role in the inevitable—and the embracing of all that entailed. "I know how it can be done," said Dostoevsky with confidence.

It took Thoor a moment. Just enough time for the shifting of his internal gears from disaster recovery to the subject at hand. But that shift did come—and the words Dostoevsky spoke were well understood.

Slowly, the Terror's eyes widened.

OUTLAW TRIGGER

www.destinysedge.com

DESTINY'S EDGE
SOCIAL MEDIA

THE WORLD BETWEEN WORLDS

A novel by Lee Stephen in
Sandy Petersen's Hyperspace Universe

Arbiter of a planetary dispute between two of the Lernaean Cluster's most disreputable civilizations, interplanetary diplomat and socialite Aurora Ultraviolet finds herself responsible for determining ownership of a critical border world. Will she give the world to the Broodmasters, grotesque, telepathic blobs who force their will upon all they meet? Or will the planet go to the Dacians, hypnotic space gargoyles bent on wiping out the Broodmasters completely? Join Aurora and her two nieces as they traverse the stars in their space yacht, the Illustré, into the heart of a conflict that threatens the very balance of the cluster! Witness their daring journey through the eyes of Velistris, a crystalline Zepzeg who acts as communications specialist and beautician, and Hank-is-Handy, an ogreish Vorck who serves as engineer and security officer! Experience a perilous mission rife with strange creatures, confounding quandaries, and fabulous hair! In a situation with so many perspectives and possibilities, there is but one thing for certain—you will never look at humanity the same way again!

XENONAUTS

CRIMSON
DAGGER

LEE STEPHEN

CRIMSON DAGGER

by Lee Stephen

The year is 1958. The Soviet Union and the United States of America are entrenched in a Cold War. But for Mikhail Kirov, captain in the Soviet Fourth Army, life is relatively idle. After serving honorably in Hungary, Mikhail is stationed to the base of Zossen Wünsdorf, south of Berlin, where he lives in a government-issued house with his wife and six-year-old daughter. Gone are the days of quelling the Hungarian Revolution. The biggest challenge he faces now is teaching his little girl arithmetic. But things are about to change.

An object of unknown origin has been intercepted over the Atlantic by the Americans. Nuclear missiles are launched. The object crashes in Iceland. In a tense moment of necessity, NATO contacts the Kremlin. The Americans need help.

Crimson Dagger serves as a prequel to the video game Xenonauts, by Goldhawk Interactive, a real time strategy game set in the Cold War era. It is a story about cooperation amid extraordinary circumstances as rival superpowers are forced into camaraderie to combat a superior foe. Selected as the leader of this unlikely alliance, Mikhail must set aside he and the Americans' differences as they enter the unknown side-by-side, prompting the question: is the enemy of one's enemy truly their friend?

ABOUT THE AUTHOR

Lee Stephen is a native of Des Allemands, Louisiana, where he lives with his wife, Lindsey, their three sons, Levi, Lawson, and Linden, and their dog, Cocoa-Grace. In addition to writing, Lee has worked in emergency preparedness in St. Charles Parish since 2005.

Made in the USA
Coppell, TX
23 February 2024

29106209R20236